The Alpine Traitor

Ballantine Books
New York

THE
ALPINE
TRAITOR

AN EMMA LORD MYSTERY

MARY DAHEIM

The Alpine Traitor is a work of fiction. Names, characters, places, and incidents are the products of the author's imagination or are used ficitiously. Any resemblance to actual events, locales, or persons, living or dead, is entirely coincidental.

Published in the United States by Ballantine Books, an imprint of The Random House Publishing Group, a division of Random House, Inc., New York.

BALLANTINE and colophon are registered trademarks of Random House, Inc.

LIBRARY OF CONGRESS CATALOGING-IN-PUBLICATION DATA
Daheim, Mary
The Alpine traitor: an Emma Lord mystery/Mary Daheim.
p. cm.
ISBN 978-0-345-46818-5
1. Lord, Emma (Fictitious character)—Fiction. 2. Newspaper publishing—Fiction. 3. Consolidation and merger of corporations—Fiction. 4. Washington (State)—Fiction. 5. Women publishers—Fiction. I. Title.

PS3554.A264A8395 2008
813'.54—dc22   2007032390

Printed in the United States of America on acid-free paper

www.ballantinebooks.com

2 4 6 8 9 7 5 3 1

First Edition

THE ALPINE TRAITOR

ONE

A BEAUTIFUL BLONDE WITH A FIGURE THAT VENUS DE MILO would've envied walked into my office, sat down on the other side of my desk, crossed her long legs, removed her big, expensive sunglasses, and offered an appealing smile. "I need your help," she said. "I'm in big trouble."

"What kind of trouble?" I asked.

She ran her tongue over her full, crimson lips. "It's tricky," she said, her voice dropping a notch. "I don't know where to turn." A lilting laugh broke out somewhere in her skimpy red tee's deep cleavage. "You'll probably think I'm an idiot."

Had I been a macho private eye with a gun under my jacket and a fifth of Scotch in the drawer, I might have told her she was this idiot's delight. But since I'm also female, the come-hither act flopped. Indeed, at that moment, I was a middle-aged mother and newspaper publisher in a small town with egg salad on my lower lip.

I grabbed the paper napkin from the Grocery Basket's deli and wiped my mouth. "Sorry," I apologized, the words covering various flaws, including the egg salad, my lack of a flattering response, and not knowing my visitor's name. "We haven't met."

"Oh!" She laughed in a disarming manner. "I'm Ginger Roth. My husband, Josh, and I just moved to Alpine. I love the setting here, with all the mountains and trees. I'm from Phoenix."

"This is quite a change for you," I remarked, resisting the urge to gobble a couple of potato chips and cursing my staff for abandoning *The Alpine Advocate* office during lunch hour. "How can I help you?"

"Well." This time Ginger's smile was self-deprecating. "A friend of mine asked me to talk to you about your newspaper."

"Okay," I said. "How does that get you in trouble?"

She grew serious. "My friend's getting an M.A. at the University of Arizona in Tucson. She's focusing her thesis on weekly newspapers, so when she found out Josh and I were moving to Alpine, she asked me to talk to the local publisher." Ginger grimaced. "I don't know zip about journalism, so I haven't a clue how to go about it."

"Your friend didn't give you a list of questions or topics?"

Ginger shook her head, the golden, shoulder-length strands glinting in the afternoon light. "She told me to get an introduction first, and see if you'd be willing to cooperate."

I shrugged. "No problem. Find out the specifics, and then we can set up a time to talk about whatever she wants to know. Is she planning to go into the print media when she finishes her degree?"

"I'm not sure," Ginger replied, her green eyes roaming around the low-ceilinged room. "She worked in an art gallery before going to grad school."

"Newspapers are dinosaurs," I pointed out. "Major metropolitan dailies are losing circulation hand over fist. In some ways, small town papers are more viable because they're so localized. I struggle to make ends meet, but owning a newspaper that serves around six thousand readers is better than going out of business in a big city."

"Wow." Ginger didn't sound terribly interested. In fact, she looked bored. "I'll pass that along," she said vaguely, handing me a slip of paper with her cell phone number. "I'd better go. I'll let you know when I've got those questions." She smiled again, not quite so delightfully, and sashayed out of my office, through the newsroom, and, presumably, onto Front Street. I took another bite of my sandwich.

Two minutes later, my House & Home editor, Vida Runkel, tromped into the newsroom and made a beeline to my office cubbyhole.

"Who was that blond girl?" she demanded. "I've never seen her before."

"That's what I was going to ask you," I said. "You're the one who keeps track of newcomers. How'd she slip under your usually efficient radar?"

"She lives in Alpine?" Vida scowled from under the brim of her daisy-covered straw hat. "What's her name?"

"Ginger Roth, husband is Josh." I popped a potato chip into my mouth. "That's all I know except she's got a friend at the University of Arizona who's doing a thesis on newspapers."

"That's it?" Vida was clearly disappointed. "What's wrong with you?"

"I was trying to eat my lunch," I said. "She arrived unannounced."

That was no excuse in Vida's eyes. "You don't know her address or where she or her husband work?"

I tossed the empty chip bag into the wastebasket. "Okay, so I was derelict in my duty. I'll put Curtis on the story."

"Curtis!" Vida spoke our new reporter's name with disdain. "He's been here two weeks. He won't know where to start."

"He has to learn his way around town," I pointed out. "He's not a bad photographer. The photo spread we ran today on the Summer Solstice Festival was quite good, especially Curtis's kiddie parade shots."

"Perhaps," Vida allowed, "though he chose some of the homeliest children in town. Not at all representative of Alpine's youngsters. I'm afraid it's going to take a long time for him to fit in."

I thought back some fourteen years to my first days as editor and publisher of the *Advocate*. "Fitting in," as Vida put it, wasn't easy for newcomers in a small town. It had taken years and years before I felt generally accepted. One of the biggest hurdles for me was the barrage of names and places, which had thrown me for a loop. Unlike in my reporter's job on *The Oregonian* in Portland, I had to do far more than learn my beat. In a small town, a journalist has to recognize at least half the population on sight. Curtis Mayne was a green graduate from the University of Washington in Seattle, where he'd grown up half a mile from the campus.

"Curtis knows as much about Alpine as a pig does about war," Vida declared. "I'll do it. Really, I can't think this Ginger person moved here and I haven't heard about it."

I, too, found that hard to believe. Vida's extensive grapevine usually kept her apprised of every new face, every marital spat, every bounced check, every illness, and everything in between. Her brain was a sponge; her memory, prodigious. And woe to the Alpiner who didn't pass on the latest tidbits.

"I'm off," she announced, abruptly leaving my office in her typical splayfooted manner. I assumed she was going to track down Ginger Roth.

It was a mild Wednesday in late June. The weekly edition of the *Advocate* was on the streets, the front porches, and in the newspaper boxes. My staff—all six of us, including our ad manager, Leo Walsh; our office manager, Ginny Erlandson; and our production chief, Kip MacDuff—took a bit of a breather after the paper came out. Wednesday was catch-up day, with time to think about what we'd do for the next issue. I'd eaten in so I could go through my files to find inspiration for a fresh, pertinent editorial. I'd gotten stale lately, and hadn't even managed to get my usual spate of "Dear Moron" letters of protest. I was in grave danger of boring my readers to death.

"Hey, Emma," Kip said, leaning against the doorjamb a few minutes after Vida's departure. "We've got a problem."

"Oh?" I put aside some articles I'd been perusing about recent state legislation passed during the last session in Olympia. "What?"

Kip is just over thirty, and got his training on the job. He is unflappable and seems able to solve any and all problems that arise in the back shop, which to me, in this high-tech age, might as well be a foreign land with an exotic language I don't understand. I came of age in the era of cold press and shipping the newspaper mock-ups to an out-of-town printer. Now we could use computer programs and publish the paper on-site. It sounded simple, and it was—except for fuddy-duddies like me who didn't understand the process.

"We need to update our software," Kip said. "The problem I'm running into is—"

I held up a hand. "Stop. You know I won't have the vaguest idea what you're talking about. How much to replace whatever's not working?"

"I'm guessing," Kip admitted, "but probably a few hundred dollars. If we go ahead with the new version, we should also buy a—"

I put my fingers in my ears. "Find out what all this new and improved equipment will cost and bring me a number. We're not exactly rolling in money these days."

Kip nodded. I removed my fingers from my ears. He started to walk away but stopped and turned back. "What about the new roof?"

"Oh, crap!" I cried. "I forgot about that."

"You said last March we'd get it done when the rain stopped toward the end of June," Kip reminded me. "You got tired of falling over the buckets under the leaks."

"I know." I sighed. "I'll call Dick Bourgette right away."

Kip, who by now might as well have left a cloud of gloom behind him in my cubbyhole, finally headed to the back shop. I was looking up Bourgette Construction in the local phone directory when Curtis Mayne came into my office.

"Can I have a peek at your county map?" my new reporter asked, for the fifth or sixth time since he'd started his job.

"Sure." I swiveled around in my chair to face the Skykomish and surrounding counties map on the wall. "What are you looking for?"

"The index," he replied with his usual earnest expression.

"That map doesn't have an index," I said. "What do you need to find?"

"There's a guy named Caldwell who sold a wood carving to Mayor Vaughn, and he wants his picture taken with it while it's still in his workshop," Curtis explained. "He told me I'd find it in the index on the map."

I was beginning to think my staffers didn't speak any form of English I could understand. "Did he mean in the phone book?" I waved the directory at him. "By the way, it's Mayor Baugh, not Vaughn. Fuzzy Baugh to be exact."

"Oh. Right." Curtis dismissed the directory. "I've got my own. There's a map in it. Maybe I can find the index on that one."

"Okay." I watched him walk out the door, heading for the desk that had belonged to his predecessor, Scott Chamoud, who had quit at the end of May to move to Seattle with his bride, Tamara. Scott had worked at the *Advocate* for several years. He was an excellent photographer and heartbreakingly handsome, although he often had to be nudged to meet deadlines. I already missed Scott, and after interviewing a half-dozen candidates, I'd decided Curtis Mayne seemed the best of a mediocre lot. At least he could spell, which was more than I could say for two of the applicants. There weren't many trained journalists who were willing to work for low wages on a weekly newspaper in a small, isolated town like Alpine.

While staring at the map and mulling over the situation, I had a sudden idea. "Curtis," I said, getting up and going into the newsroom, "are you sure that this Caldwell didn't tell you he lived in Index?"

Curtis's round boyish face looked puzzled. "What do you mean?"

"Index," I said patiently, "is a small town west of here on Highway 2, less than ten minutes away. You grew up in Seattle. Surely you've heard of it."

He shook his head with its blond buzz cut. "I don't think so. I don't remember seeing it when I drove up here."

"You wouldn't," I said as kindly as possible, "because it's off the highway." I didn't add that there were also at least two road signs bearing the town's name.

He flipped through his directory. "You're right. Winn Caldwell, Index. Thanks."

I wandered back into my office. For a Wednesday, I wasn't finding much time to ruminate. In fact, I couldn't concentrate, either. It took me ten minutes of staring into space to remember that I was going to call Dick Bourgette about the roof. When I finally dialed the number, I got his voice mail. Obviously, he was out on a job and unable to pick up. I left him a message and wondered if I should go over to Stella's Styling Salon for an emergency appointment. My brown hair was shaggy; my brain was arid. If I couldn't improve the inside of my head, maybe I could do something about the outside.

I got as far as the newsroom. Spencer Fleetwood strolled through the door, looking smug, not an unusual expression for Skykomish County's Mr. Radio.

"Emma Lord," he said in his mellow on-air voice. "Off and running to a breaking story?"

"Don't be a smart-ass," I snapped. We both knew that any big news would always be broken by KSKY-AM, while I had to wait for weekly publication. "What do you want?"

Spencer chuckled, another rich sound he could make with his ever-annoying vocal cords. "Are you flirting with me?"

"Jeez." I sat on the edge of Curtis's vacant desk. "Right. I've been pining away for you ever since I first heard you call yourself 'The Voice of Skykomish County.'" I sighed. "Okay, I'm not in a great mood at the moment. My so-called off day has turned sour. What can I do for you, or are you here to do something for me?" The reference was to the co-op ads that the *Advocate* and KSKY sometimes shared.

Spence grimaced. "Well . . ." The usually glib Mr. Radio suddenly seemed unable to find the right words. He reached inside the pocket of his safari shirt and took out a pack of his exotic black cigarettes. "May I?"

I shrugged. My ad manager, Leo Walsh, was a smoker, and after he'd stopped trying to drink himself to death, I didn't have the heart to insist that he quit smoking, too. Vida carped constantly about Leo's bad habit, but without success. I understood Leo's resistance to give up tobacco. I'd quit smoking a dozen times over the past few years.

Spence held out the black package with its gold lettering. I refused. Politely. I watched him light up, inhale, exhale, and move a couple of steps closer to the coffeemaker on the table by Curtis's desk.

"Last March," Spence began, "I applied to the FCC to increase the station's kilowatts. Today I received official approval. We'll be able to broadcast as far west as Monroe and Snohomish, but not on the eastern slope of the Cascades. Reaching the other directions doesn't matter."

"Yes," I said bleakly. The north and south sections of SkyCo's long, narrow county were virtually uninhabited, since they were primarily state and federal forestlands. But that wasn't what upset me. If Spence was expanding his advertising sales beyond the *Advocate*'s readership scope, the paper would miss out on a lot of co-op revenue. "Congratulations." The word practically choked me.

Spence had the grace to look faintly sheepish. "Hey," he said, "I know what you're thinking. But it won't affect you that much. Maybe some of the Snohomish and Monroe businesses will agree to run ads in the *Advocate*."

"Let me go outside and see if pigs are flying over Alpine."

"Look," Spence said with apparent sincerity, "I'm not doing this to hurt your business. I've got a living to make, too, and this is my chance to add a little more black ink to the bottom line. Can you honestly blame me for that?"

"No." I shook my head. "Of course not. This just isn't turning out to be a very good day." I tried to smile but knew the attempt wasn't convincing. "You have to do what's in your best interests. I appreciate the heads-up."

"Thanks." Spence relaxed visibly, took a puff on his cigarette, and smiled. His effort came off as genuine. "How about me treating you to dinner tomorrow night at Le Gourmand?"

As usual, my social calendar was anything but crowded.

"Okay," I agreed, trying to be a good sport and not wanting to miss an opportunity to eat free of charge at the best restaurant in SkyCo.

"I'll pick you up at six," he said, walking over to put out his cigarette in Leo's ashtray. "Maybe the food tomorrow will make today seem not quite so bad."

"Let's hope," I murmured.

Spence left. Three minutes later, after I'd scribbled a note to Leo about KSKY's venture into new advertising turf, my day got even worse. My former ad manager, Ed Bronsky, waddled into the newsroom, out of breath but full of excitement.

"Hey, hey, hey!" Ed exclaimed. "Guess what? We've sold the house!"

"The house," better known around Alpine as Casa de Bronska, was Ed's monument to his inherited wealth. Unfortunately, he'd overspent and made some bad investments in the past year. Ed had been reduced to working the counter at the Burger Barn until he'd acquired a new and resourceful CPA, who'd at least managed to keep the Bronsky family in chips and dips.

"Who's the buyer?" I asked, wondering what kind of sap would pay almost a million bucks to live in an ersatz Mediterranean villa above the railroad tracks in Alpine.

"The name's Platte," Ed replied, checking the coffeemaker area to see if we had any goodies left from the morning bakery run. We didn't, but Ed's mood remained buoyant. "California types. They could never get a house like ours down there for a quarter of the price."

That much was probably true. "A married couple?" I inquired.

Ed nodded. "Young, virtual newlyweds. You'll want to put a story in the paper."

I ignored the suggestion. "Where will you and Shirley and the kids live?"

"We've got our eye on a place," Ed said vaguely. "Not as big as Casa de Bronska, of course, but . . . cozy. The Plattes are arriving next week to finalize the deal and sign the papers. Snorty's already drawing them up."

Snorty Wenzel was Ed's real estate agent, whose office—as far as I could tell—was a '98 Lincoln Continental. I'd met him only once, about six months ago, when he came in to place a one-column-by-three-inch ad in our classified section. I didn't know his real name, but it wasn't hard to figure out why he was called Snorty. He snuffled, sniffled, and snorted constantly, apparently a victim of sinus problems. The sound was annoying, but I suppose clients got used to it as long as he did his job. "I assume the Plattes have seen the house?" I remarked.

"Our house?" Ed saw me nod patiently. "Oh, sure. On the Internet. You know—a virtual tour, as good as walking through in person. Snorty uses every marketing ploy available. He's tops."

"I'm glad for you," I said. "Did you get your asking price?"

"Almost." Ed coughed a couple of times. "You know those Californians. They're slick, and they like to haggle."

I didn't press Ed further. For all I knew, he'd given the place away. "Let me know when the Plattes get here. Vida will want to do a feature on them for her House & Home page."

Ed looked disappointed. "She'll want to interview me, too, won't she?"

No, I thought, *she won't. She does not have fond memories of you avoiding real work while you were an employee of this newspaper, which barely survived your slothful habits.* "Of course," I fibbed. "You'll have to excuse me, Ed. I was just on my way to Stella's Styling Salon."

"Huh? Oh, sure. I'll walk you out."

We went past Ginny Erlandson's desk in the front office. Ginny looked up from her computer when I told her where I was going. She nodded in her usual no-nonsense manner, murmured "Bye," and returned to the monitor. Ginny, whose husband, Rick, worked at the Bank of Alpine, was expecting a baby in October. The couple had two boys, and Ginny was hoping for a girl. She was also hoping for a raise. I couldn't promise either at the moment.

Ed and I parted company at the corner. Stella Magruder's hair salon was in the Clemans Building across Front between Second and Third streets. Luckily for me, she had an opening.

"June slows down after graduation," she explained, beckoning me to follow her to her station after I'd put on the required purple smock. "When it comes to hair, regulars and weddings are what keep me going in the summer. I'd have gone broke if I hadn't started offering facials and waxing and all the other services a few years back."

I noticed that only one other stylist was busy, a young woman named Naomi, who was wrapping permanent rods in an older woman's gray hair. "We've got a new blonde in town," I said as Stella studied my shaggy brown mane in the mirror. "Ginger Roth. Has she been in yet?"

"No," Stella replied. "Natural blond or product?"

"I couldn't tell," I said, "but her skin is fair, despite having moved recently from Arizona. I guess her tan's faded already."

"Sun!" Stella exclaimed. "We know how overrated sun is around here. Every so often I get some idiot who wants me to install a tanning booth. You can't convince tanning freaks that sun, real or artificial, is downright dangerous to the skin." She stopped fiddling with my hair and put her fists on her hips. "Okay. I give up. What can I do for you that you just might be able to maintain on your own if you'd only take the time and trouble?"

"Um . . . much shorter and layered?" I suggested.

"We've tried that. It lasted less than a week before you turned it into a shrub." Stella looked away as a young man entered the salon. "May I help you?" she asked, moving toward the front of the shop.

The dark-haired and rather handsome newcomer was holding what looked like a map. I couldn't catch most of what he said, but Stella was pointing to her right and then straight ahead and again to her right. Map Man nodded and left.

"Lost," she said.

Naomi, a perky and plump gold-foiled girl, giggled. "He's cute. I could've shown him the way to my place."

Stella smirked. "Forget it. He's from out of state. He was trying to find the golf course. I told him it wasn't exactly Pebble Beach and warned him to watch out for bears crossing the fifth fairway to go fishing in Icicle Creek."

We returned to my coiffure dilemma. Stella suggested a shorter cut and a tube of so-called threads that she insisted even I could manage. "Just put the stuff on your palms, rub it around, clap your hands over your head to distribute the product, and then fluff up your hair. We call it styling. God knows what you'll call it."

"Uh-huh," I said, looking at my mirror image, which showed my expression as only slightly more intelligent than your average turnip. Since the directions involved dexterity and coordination, I might as well have taken the twenty bucks Stella charged me for the so-called threads and tossed Andrew Jackson into the Skykomish River.

The rest of the workday petered out in my vain attempt to find editorial inspiration. Vida had managed to track down

Ginger and Josh Roth. According to Ginny's husband, the banker Rick, they'd moved into a condo at Pines Villa. In fact, it was the one that Scott and Tamara Chamoud had vacated when they left for Seattle. Josh worked for a high-tech company based in one of the Seattle suburbs and apparently was able to handle his job from just about anywhere. As far as Rick knew, Ginger was currently unemployed. They hadn't opened an account yet, but Josh had cashed a traveler's check.

"There might be a story in that," I remarked to Vida. "The ability of people to live in some remote yet cheaper area and work for an outfit that's headquartered somewhere else. It sounds like a growing trend."

"And how wise of them to choose Alpine," Vida pointed out proudly. "No commuting miles and miles, finding the smaller towns less nerve-racking, enjoying the outdoors, and getting to know everyone."

And knowing everyone's business, I thought. But I kept my mouth shut. Vida didn't take kindly to criticism of Alpine. "So *that* mystery is solved," I said. "Do you want to write the story, or shall I give it to Curtis?"

"I'll do it," Vida said. "I'm always delighted to welcome newcomers."

I knew she'd volunteer. The Roths were about to be interrogated with all the zeal—if not the pain—of the Spanish Inquisition.

An hour later I arrived home at my little log house nestled among the big second-growth evergreens that marched up Tonga Ridge. I was eating an unimaginative dinner of chicken breast, green beans, and rice when the current man in my life, Rolf Fisher, called from Seattle.

"Are you as bored as I am?" he asked—and yawned to prove his point.

"Kind of," I admitted, putting my plate aside and wandering into the living room. "What's wrong? No hot news coming over the AP wire?"

"Just the usual wars and terrorists and gang-related killings and African famines and big-time CEOs being hauled off to prison." Rolf sighed dramatically. "I'm trying to get assigned to a Third World country—like Alabama. Look, I haven't seen you for over a month. Isn't it time you came to Seattle for a raucous romp?"

"Maybe," I allowed, gazing up at *Sky Autumn*, an original painting by a reclusive local artist named Craig Laurentis. "Do you realize that in the two years we've known each other you've visited me in Alpine only three times?"

"Do you realize I just told you I was bored?" Rolf countered. "Face it, Emma, there's not much to do in your little mountain aerie. I've actually seen toadstools and gophers before."

I took umbrage. "I thought you enjoyed my company," I snapped.

"I adore your company, I adore your conversation, your big brown eyes, your knowledge of the infield fly rule, your clumsy way of walking into walls and bouncing off of them without so much as a flicker of surprise. But," Rolf went on while I drummed my fingernails on the end table by the sofa, "I do not adore only two choices when it comes to restaurants with palatable food, and the sole entertainment is watching the clouds come down over Mount Baldy."

Rolf was right, of course. I turned away from my favorite painting, with its almost palpable sense of rushing river, velvet moss, and glistening boulders. "What did you have in mind if I drive to Seattle?"

"Well . . ." He cleared his throat. I couldn't suppress a smile.

"Besides that, of course, I thought we might go on a cocktail cruise around Elliott Bay Saturday night. I've been invited, and I'm allowed to bring a guest. Naturally, I thought of you."

"Why," I demanded, "didn't you say that in the first place?"

He laughed the deep, dark chortle that I found so fascinating. "I'm bored, remember? I wanted to play a game, if only via the telephone."

That was part of the problem with Rolf. I never knew when he was playing games and when he was serious. Maybe that was the main reason I kept trying not to fall in love with him. It had been so different with my late and much-lamented lover, Tom Cavanaugh. Tom could be frustrating and, as it turned out, so private that he bordered on secretive, but at least he never toyed with my mind—only my emotions.

"Okay," I said, "I'll come down Friday after work."

"Excellent," he said. "How was your day?"

"Oh—kind of stupid. Just one of those days with a lot of niggling little problems. I'll tell you when I see you."

"Nothing serious?" he inquired.

"Not really." I sighed. "It was utterly uneventful."

I had no way of knowing that several of those nonevents were going to turn my world upside down.

TWO

THE DINNER WITH SPENCER FLEETWOOD ON THURSDAY
night had turned out to be a pleasant interlude. When
Spence removed his radio personality mask, he was good company. He read books, mostly nonfiction, had traveled all over
the world, and, though he was not a sports fanatic, at least had
a passing interest in baseball. We never discussed politics, both
having the same philosophy: As representatives of the media in
an area of small population, we kept our views to ourselves,
lest we start pandering to elected officials, overtly or covertly.

Friday morning, Vida had an eleven o'clock appointment
with Ginger Roth at Pines Villa. At eleven-twenty, my House
& Home editor stomped back into the newsroom with a furious expression under the brim of her floppy green hat.

"So inconsiderate!" she ranted. "This younger generation!
Making appointments and not keeping them! I rang the buzzer
on the intercom several times and got no response. I finally
buzzed my addlepated sister-in-law Ella Hinshaw and she let
me in. But Ginger didn't respond to my knock on her door.
How rude! If you want her life story, have Curtis get it. I've no
time for bad manners."

Curtis was sitting at his desk, only a few feet away from where Vida was standing. For some reason, she rarely spoke directly to him but behaved as if he weren't present. Vida didn't like change. Maybe she was pretending that Scott was still working for the *Advocate*.

"Curtis?" I said.

He looked up, blue eyes wary. "Yeah?"

I took Ginger and Josh Roth's address and phone number from Vida. "Ms. Roth was a no-show for—"

Curtis grinned, a rather engaging expression. "I heard. Ms. Roth is a boor, unworthy of calling herself a resident of Alpine." His eyes flicked in Vida's direction, where she was about to sit down at her desk. "Mrs. Runkel," he said, a bit louder, "I'm not deaf, though it's kind of you to be considerate of my handicap. If I had one."

I stiffened, prepared for a burst of reproach from Vida. But after an awkward pause, she gave Curtis one of her cheesy smiles with plenty of teeth showing. "Ah. So you do have some spunk. Good. I've been concerned about that." She stopped smiling, sat down, and immediately picked up the phone.

Curtis studied the scribbled information on the Roths. "Should I try again today?"

"Early afternoon," I suggested. "She may be out shopping this morning. Thanks, Curtis."

Shortly before noon, Dick Bourgette stopped by to give me an estimate on a new roof. I trusted Dick, who'd moved to Alpine several years earlier with his wife and almost-grown family. The Bourgettes had flourished in every way, with their six children marrying, multiplying, and getting involved in various business endeavors of their own. Dick's wife, Mary Jane, was a friend of mine, and the entire clan were regulars at St. Mildred's Catholic Church. Though the Bourgettes had come late to Alpine, it seemed as if they'd always belonged to the town, and in fact, one of their daughters had married a descendant of Carl Clemans, the mill owner and the town's founding father.

"Okay," Dick said, laying a spec sheet on my desk. "If you want only the section over your office replaced, it's going to cost less than five hundred bucks, including labor and materials. But that old tin roof over the rest of the building is shot. The climate's changed. We don't have as much snow like we did in the old days. I suggest you go with slate. It'll withstand anything and last forever."

I blinked a couple of times. "How much?"

Dick scrunched up his round, faintly florid face and tapped his pen on the desk. "Oh—let's say fourteen hundred. That's a fair price, Emma."

"Well . . ." I hesitated, though I knew Dick was scrupulously honest. "Okay. When can you start and how long will it take?"

"Mid-July," Dick replied, putting his pen back in his shirt pocket. "A couple of days. I can do it myself. It's not a big job." He pointed to two of the buckets I kept in my office. "You better hang on to those. It usually rains just before or after the Fourth of July."

I nodded. June in Alpine could be more like March; May was usually sunny and pleasant; February often brought a few days of what the old-timers called "false spring." The venerable adage about the changeable climate was "If you don't like the weather, wait twenty minutes."

Dick gathered up his clipboard and laptop computer. "I hear the Bronskys finally sold their palace."

"So Ed told me," I said. "Thank your lucky stars you weren't here when they built it. You can't imagine what they put their architect and contractor through."

"Oh yes, I can," Dick responded and chuckled. "Mary Jane

and I went to a couple of their soirees—or as Ed pronounced it, '*soy*-rees.' We couldn't believe how much money they wasted on things like those marble floors with inlays of the family's pictures, including their dog, Carhop."

"Ed started going broke before they could add their new dog, Barhop," I remarked. "I hope the buyers have enough money to undo some of Ed and Shirley's atrocious taste."

"I'd like to meet with them as soon as they get settled," Dick said. "I thought I might drop off one of my business cards at the Tall Timber Motel, but that's probably pushing it."

I gave Dick a curious look. "They're here?"

Dick nodded. "At least the husband is. Our daughter Terri talked to him at the diner yesterday. His first name is Dylan. Dylan Platte."

Terri Bourgette was the hostess at the fifties-style diner owned by two of her brothers. "Interesting," I noted. "We seem to be attracting some younger people to Alpine lately. I'm going to run a story about that after we've talked to the new-comers."

"It's a good little town," Dick asserted. "I'm glad we made the move. That traffic in and around Seattle is really horren-dous."

On that note, Dick left. I decided to call the Tall Timber Motel and arrange an appointment with Dylan Platte. He wasn't in, so I left my name and number.

Vida was still fuming. "I hope you have better luck than I did with the Roths," she declared, taking a hard-boiled egg, a container of cottage cheese, and several carrot and celery sticks from a brown paper bag. It was obvious that she was on an-other one of her intermittent diets. I never understood why—she is a big woman with a big frame, and no matter how much or how little she eats, Vida never seems to lose or gain a pound.

She sniffed with contempt. "Common courtesy was left behind in the last century."

I couldn't argue the point. I decided to go over to the Burger Barn and pick up fish and chips for lunch. If I ate in the office and finished the tasks I'd allotted myself for the week, I could leave for Seattle around four. As I walked through the front office, Ginny was on the phone, standing at her place behind the counter and wearing her coat.

"Just a moment," she said into the phone and beckoned to me. "Ms. Lord is still here." Ginny handed me the receiver. "It's somebody named Platte," she whispered.

"Hello, this is Emma Lord," I said into the phone, waving Ginny good-bye. "Thanks for returning my call so promptly."

"Your call?" The male voice sounded puzzled. "When did you call me?"

"About five minutes ago," I said, equally puzzled. "I phoned the Tall Timber Motel after I heard you were in town."

"Then you must know what I'm calling about," he said.

"You're buying the Bronsky house," I replied, moving around the counter and sitting down in Ginny's chair.

"Yes." He paused. "When can we meet?" he finally inquired after at least thirty seconds had passed.

"I'm on my way to lunch," I said. "Can you join me at the Burger Barn?"

"That doesn't work for me," he responded, sounding very formal. "I'd prefer meeting you somewhere less public, perhaps after work tonight. I see you live on Fir Street, off Fourth."

I was beginning to get suspicious. "I'm afraid that's not possible, Mr. Platte. I'm leaving town for the weekend later this afternoon. Can you wait until Monday?"

"No," he replied. "I wouldn't think that'd suit you, either. There's quite a lot to talk and think about."

"Like what?" I was growing impatient as well as wary.

"I thought you knew."

"I haven't a clue."

Dylan made a sound at the other end that was either a snort or a laugh, I couldn't tell which. "I suppose I'd better make the announcement right now, and then we can talk about it tonight."

"I won't be here," I said, figuring he was one of those people who had some weird idea for a story that would make himself look like a hero, adventurer, entrepreneur, or some other kind of self-seeking opportunist. "I told you that."

"I know what you said," Dylan assured me. "But my time here is limited. I have to be back in San Francisco Sunday night. My wife and I won't return to Alpine until the second week of July."

"Your wife is with you?" I asked, wishing he'd get to the point.

"Kelsey couldn't make it. I had to check out the house by myself."

The name "Kelsey" rang a faint bell. I didn't stop to figure out why. "So what's your proposal?" I asked.

"My wife and her brother and I want to buy the *Advocate*."

I was sure that I hadn't heard correctly. "You want to buy *space* in the *Advocate*?"

This time the noise at the other end was definitely a chuckle—a rather snide chuckle, I thought. "Didn't you get Kelsey's e-mail last week?"

Kelsey. I knew that name. It was unusual, but I knew—or knew of—someone named Kelsey. I thought back to the batches and batches of mostly worthless e-mails sent to me every day. "I don't recall anything from someone named Kelsey," I said.

"The subject was 'Acquiring the *Advocate*,'" Dylan said.

I vaguely recalled a heading like that, but all sorts of syndicates and news services and heaven knew what else were sent to me all the time and usually involved some sort of product for sale, including websites and even porn. I deleted them immediately, fearing that there were viruses attached.

"I never read it," I admitted. "I'm not sure what you're talking about. What do you mean by 'acquiring'?"

"I'll explain." Dylan Platte sounded condescending, as if he were talking to the Alpine Idiot. "My wife, Kelsey, and her brother, Graham, inherited their father's newspaper chain when he was killed a few years ago. For a time, they both left the business up to . . ."

I lost track of what Dylan was saying. Kelsey. Graham. Tom Cavanaugh's daughter and son. The stepchildren I'd almost acquired—there was that word again—by marrying Tom. My son, Adam's half brother and half sister. I'd met them only once at Tom's funeral Mass in San Francisco. Adam and my brother, Ben, had gone with me, but we'd skipped the reception that followed because I simply couldn't handle mingling with so many people I didn't know—including Graham and Kelsey. I worried that they might blame me in part for what had happened to their father. I'd been so numb with grief that I'd barely been able to say more than a mumbled hello. They were only a blur in my mind's eye.

In trying to recall what they looked like, I conjured up only the vaguest of impressions—in their twenties, muddling through mismatched mates and equally incompatible careers. I suddenly realized that the Cavanaugh offspring must be thirty-something by now, and apparently had settled down to take life seriously. The searing wound I'd felt when Tom died had never quite healed, and now I felt as if it had been reopened and was bleeding all over again.

I couldn't speak.

". . . Graham has inherited his father's business skills," Dylan was saying. "He understands the predicament of newspapers in general these days, but also knows that some of the solutions lie in mergers and acquisitions. My background is in advertising, Kelsey is the creative type, and Graham's wife, Sophia, is a very fine writer. It's an ideal situation for all of us, not to mention that living in the Bay Area isn't what it used to be. We assume you're getting close to retirement, and we're prepared to make a very tempting offer. So what would be a good time this evening or tomorrow?"

I marshaled my strength to reply. "I'm not interested, and I won't be in town past four o'clock. I've already made plans with a friend who lives in Seattle."

"Oh?" Dylan paused, but only for a moment. "You enjoy the city, I take it?"

"Of course," I said. "I was raised there."

Here came that chuckle again. "So I imagine you'll move back after you sell the paper. Especially," he added a trifle slyly, "if your friend lives there."

I tried to picture Rolf in my mind's eye. I couldn't. All I saw was Tom—smiling, talking, thinking, sleeping, looking into my eyes. I pressed my free hand against my forehead, willing myself to behave like a mature middle-aged human being.

"I'm sorry," I finally said. "I'm not contemplating a sale of the *Advocate* in the near future. I have to go now. Good luck on your move to Alpine."

"Hardball," Dylan murmured. "I understand. You realize, of course, that Kelsey's father intended to buy the *Advocate* before he died."

"*What?*" I was so startled that I shrieked the word.

"He left a letter—a memo, I should say—about his intentions," Dylan explained, as though he was talking about a request Tom might have made to purchase a filing cabinet. "According to Kelsey, he made that fatal trip to Alpine to negotiate with you in person. My father-in-law was interested in getting a foothold for his newspaper chain in western Washington. Since he knew you, he felt that the *Advocate* would make a good starting point. Kelsey and Graham are simply carrying out what Tom Cavanaugh wanted to do."

I glanced up as the front door opened. Mayor Fuzzy Baugh entered and offered me his best election-year smile. I tried to smile back, but my effort was puny. I spoke quietly into the receiver: "I have to hang up. Someone's here to see me. I'll call you back in an hour. What's your number, or should I contact the motel?"

"I'm not at the motel," Dylan replied. "I'll call you." He broke the connection.

I must have looked stricken. For once, the town's longtime leader dropped his hail-voter-well-met expression and stopped smiling. "What's wrong, Emma?" he asked with a trace of his native New Orleans. "Has something . . . happened?"

I didn't consider Fuzzy Baugh a confidant. "Well . . . not really," I said, trying to regroup. "It was just one of those strange phone calls newspapers get once in a while."

Fuzzy leaned on the counter that separated us. "A threat?"

"No." I wasn't sure I could stand up. "Just . . . an unusual request." I kept my unsteady hands in my lap. "What can I do for you?"

"I was looking for that new youngun of yours—Curtis, isn't it?"

I nodded. "He went to lunch."

"Ah." Fuzzy looked at his watch. "My, my. Where does the time go?" He shook his head. The thinning curls were dyed a pumpkin orange, an unfortunate choice for a man in his mid-seventies. "I'm expecting Winn Caldwell—the wood-carving fella—to deliver my porcupine this afternoon. I thought Curtis would want another photo for the paper."

"Oh. Yes." I nodded several times, probably looking like a bobble-head doll.

Fortunately, Fuzzy had reverted to his usual obliviousness. "You'll tell Curtis? Winn's coming around three."

"Yes." I managed to stop nodding. "I'll write him a note. Thanks."

Fuzzy tipped an imaginary hat and strolled out of the front office. I took some deep breaths, scribbled the message for Curtis, and managed to stand up. Back in the newsroom, I leaned on my reporter's desk and tried to collect my wits.

Dylan was lying. Or he'd been deceived by Kelsey and Graham Cavanaugh. Tom had loved me. He'd loved me for years and years, as I had loved him, even though I'd tried to bury that love when he'd abandoned me after I got pregnant with Adam. Tom had faults—I knew them well—but wooing a woman, any woman, to get his hands on a small weekly newspaper wasn't his style. The Cavanaugh offspring were trying to unhinge me. Maybe it was a business tactic, maybe it was a personal motive. After their mother, Sandra, had died from an overdose of one of her many mind- and mood-altering drugs, Kelsey and Graham had found out that there was another woman in their father's life. I'd had contact via the phone with them because Tom had died in Alpine, and arrangements had to be made to send his body back to San Francisco. Tom and I had been about to get married when he was killed. His children must have known what was going on between us. Or did they?

I glanced at my watch. It was twenty past twelve. I'd lost my appetite. I wanted to talk to my brother, but Ben was attending a conference for Catholic families in Baltimore, where he was one of the priests lecturing on prayer and meditation. For all I knew, he was in the middle of a heated discourse over whether or not teenagers should listen to rap music while saying the rosary.

Adam. My son had to find out what was going on with the half siblings he never knew. But he had followed in the footsteps of his uncle Ben and had become a priest. Adam was living in a remote part of Alaska, ministering mainly to the native community of Catholics in his far-flung parish of St. Mary's Igloo. He had been in Alpine for Easter, but I hadn't spoken with him since. Phone conversations were awkward and frustrating, coming through on a radio transmission delay, so our communication was accomplished via frequent e-mails. I considered going into my cubbyhole and sending off a missive describing what had just happened to his poor mother. Then I thought better of it. I didn't have all the facts, and, being a conscientious journalist, I wasn't going to reveal anything until I had more data.

I was still wandering around the newsroom at twelve-thirty, when Leo came through the door. He took one look at me and stopped in his tracks.

"What's wrong?" he asked in the voice that had endured too many cigarettes. "Are you sick?"

"Yes." I did an uncharacteristic thing, rushing to him and throwing myself against his chest. "Oh, Leo! Tom's kids want to buy the *Advocate*!"

"Jesus!" He spoke softly, putting his arms around me in a clumsy gesture. "Hey," he said after a moment or two, "let's go into your office. Or would you rather hit the bar at the Venison Inn?"

I forced myself to stop acting like an emotional twit. "No."

I slowly disengaged myself from his embrace. "I mean, not the bar. My office is fine."

Despite my attempt at stability, I walked so unsteadily that I ricocheted off the doorframe, hit the other side, and almost fell flat on my face.

"Whoa!" Leo cried, grabbing my arm. "Let me get you into your chair." He gently guided me behind the desk. "There. How many of me do you see?"

I tried to smile. "Only one. I'm not very graceful, even at my best."

"True enough," Leo said, moving to one of my visitors' chairs. He took out his cigarettes and offered me one. I didn't skip a beat, grabbing it and letting him light it for me.

"Thanks," I said. "I'm still in shock, so I'll go on pretending I don't know what I'm doing."

Leo chuckled softly. "Tom's kids—the last time I saw them they were in junior high or whatever they called it then in the Bay Area."

"I hardly remember them," I admitted. "They're all grown up and running Tom's newspaper chain."

"Not into the ground, I hope?"

I shrugged. "Have you heard anything about them taking over?"

Leo shook his head. "When I cut my ties with Tom's papers way back when, before you rescued me from the bottom of a barrel of booze, I didn't want to hear how my more sober replacements were doing. Of course Tom kept track of me—he was that kind of guy. But after he died"—Leo didn't look me in the eye—"I never paid attention to what was going on with his empire. I guess I assumed the kids would sell the papers off." He flicked ash into the clamshell I kept on hand for smokers—and for me. "Now I realize that, if they'd sold out, that's the kind of thing I would've heard on the grapevine without asking."

"I'd have heard about it, too," I said. "My answer is no. But this Dylan doesn't seem to understand the meaning of the word."

Leo's weathered face wore a thoughtful expression. "Are you meeting with him?"

"The answer to that is also no." Out of habit, I blew smoke away from Leo. Maybe I was blowing smoke in another way. Maybe I didn't want to admit to any curiosity about the stepchildren I'd almost acquired. "Besides," I went on, "I'm going to Seattle for the weekend. Dylan is leaving before I get back."

"Ah." Leo nodded twice. "The intriguing Mr. Fisher."

"And sometimes aggravating," I said, perhaps to make up for the touch of guilt I felt after having rejected Leo's tentative advances early on in our working relationship. "Anyway, Dylan and Kelsey are buying Ed's house."

Leo burst out laughing. "No! They must be real suckers! That place is a white elephant."

"I know," I said, putting out my cigarette. "I can't understand why they'd consider buying the house before they bought the newspaper. It should be the other way around. Why else move here?"

"Good point," Leo agreed. "I'd like to hear what's been going on with Kelsey and Graham. You want me to talk to this Dylan . . . what's his last name?"

"Platte," I said. "He's staying at the Tall Timber, but he wasn't going to be in this afternoon."

Leo glanced at his watch. "Quarter to one. Maybe I'll wander over there and see if I can track him down."

"Go ahead. Let me know what you find out about the arrogant Mr. Platte."

"You know," he said in a musing voice, "this may be a good thing. Outsiders are never welcome in small towns. You start writing or talking about those Californians barging in on Alpine with their Golden State mentality, and the next thing you see is local support for the paper, with more subscribers and maybe even more ad revenue."

My smile was genuine. "You're a treasure," I declared. "I hadn't thought about that."

He shrugged and stood up, brushing cigarette ash off his well-worn blue sport coat. "Think of me as your in-house opportunist. As for talking to Platte, I can claim my former decadent advertising stint with Tom's papers as an entrée." He cocked his head to one side. "You okay now?"

I nodded. "I was an idiot to get so upset. All I have to do is say no."

Leo grinned. "You already said that."

"So I did. But I also said that Dylan Platte doesn't take no for an answer."

In light of the tragedies that had already been set in motion, maybe I should have said no to Tom Cavanaugh some thirty-odd years ago.

THREE

"THE NERVE!" VIDA SHRIEKED AFTER I TOLD HER ABOUT Dylan Platte's phone call. "What did I say about this younger generation? No manners—and no sense! I hope Leo puts a flea in his ear!"

"He will," I assured her. "Anybody who can talk Alpine's tightfisted merchants into buying ads knows how to make a point."

Vida drummed her fingers on her desk. "I must say that I'm curious about this Cavanaugh bunch. I wish Leo had waited so that I could've gone with him." When I didn't say anything, she shot me a sharp look. "Well? Aren't you?"

I sighed and leaned against Leo's desk. "I suppose I should be. But I never knew them when Tom was alive. Maybe I don't want any reminders of what might have been."

"Perhaps." Vida stared off into space. "I think I'll go over to the Tall Timber Motel."

"Don't," I said. "Let Leo handle this."

Vida's expression was indignant. "I don't intend to interfere. I merely want to observe."

I knew better, of course. But I also knew that I couldn't stop Vida. Before I could say anything, Curtis came into the newsroom. Vida left while I was relaying Mayor Baugh's message about the wood carving.

"Three o'clock, huh?" Curtis said, looking not at his watch but at the screen on his tiny cell phone. "Got it."

I retreated to my cubbyhole, trying hard to put the aggressive buyout effort out of my head. It wasn't easy, but I had more immediate problems to solve, including how I was going to pay for the *Advocate*'s upkeep. On several occasions, Rick Erlandson had advised me to open a line of credit at the bank. I'd hesitated, seeing in my mind's eye a figure that escalated every second. I didn't need a big personal debt. My little log house was paid for with the money from the bungalow Adam and I had shared in Portland when I was working for *The Oregonian*. I'd bought the *Advocate* with an unexpected windfall from an ex-fiancé who had forgotten to remove my name from his Boeing Company life insurance policy after we broke up. My five-year-old Honda Accord was also paid for in full. The cost of living was far cheaper in Alpine than in either Seattle or Portland, but I was hardly getting rich, and inflation creeps into even the most remote of mountain aeries.

Ginny, whose pregnancy was beginning to show under the loose cotton blouse she was wearing, came into my office carrying a small parcel wrapped in brown paper.

"Marlowe Whipp dropped this off just now," she said. "He'd forgotten to deliver it when he brought the mail this morning."

Marlowe wasn't the USPO's most diligent mailman, but he was all we had in most parts of Alpine. I thanked her. "Are you feeling better?"

She nodded. "I think I've put the heaves behind me. With our first two, I stopped being nauseated after three months." There was a slight frown on her plain, serious face. "Do you suppose that means it's another boy?"

I smiled at Ginny. "It probably is—unless it's a girl. I don't believe all those old wives' tales about how you can discern a baby's sex. Only the ultrasound usually tells whether it's a boy or a girl."

"I'm not sure I want to know," Ginny replied. "Rick told me it was my decision. If I find out it's a boy, I'll be . . . disappointed. And if it's a girl, I'll worry that she's not okay."

I recalled how Ginny had moped her way through the previous pregnancies. Never a high-spirited young woman, she had fussed and fretted for what seemed like far longer than the average gestation period. I'd hoped that we could avoid that problem the third time around, but it appeared this wasn't going to be a charm. Ginny was Ginny, and as she was a diligent and decent employee, I was willing to put up with her long face and doleful obsessions.

"What does Doc Dewey say?" I asked, picking up a pair of scissors to cut open the package she'd given me.

Ginny shrugged. "You know Doc. He says it's up to me."

I certainly knew Doc, who'd joined his father's practice long before I arrived in Alpine. Gerald Dewey was a general practitioner, and while he wasn't able to be quite as hands-on as his late father had been, he had a compassionate, practical bedside manner.

"Doc's right," I said. And frowned. "There's no return address on this package. It's postmarked Alpine, though."

"It's not very heavy," Ginny pointed out.

I read the address, which had been printed with a black marker pen:

Emma Lord
507 Front Street
Alpine WA 98289

I uttered a small laugh. "I hope it's not a bomb from some irate reader."

"You never know these days," Ginny said, shaking her head and taking a few backward steps away from my desk.

"Right," I said, aware that the hint of sarcasm was lost on my office manager.

The small tan box inside had no markings. I lifted the lid, removed a bit of tissue paper, and stared at a pearl-and-diamond bracelet. "If it's not fake, it's rather pretty," I said in a puzzled tone as I dangled the bauble from my index finger.

Ginny showed a hint of excitement. "Is it a present?"

"I'm not sure." I put the bracelet on my desk and opened a gift card that lay on the bottom layer of tissue paper.

"Mr. Fisher?" Ginny suggested as I opened the card.

My jaw must have dropped. "What is it?" Ginny asked in a startled voice.

For a moment, I couldn't speak. I reread the handwritten message, recognizing the large, inelegant penmanship. "Here," I said, quickly handing the card to Ginny as if it were on fire.

She frowned. "I don't get it."

I'm aware that pregnant women tend to be self-absorbed—all their intellect and emotions focused on themselves and the child they're carrying—but Ginny's response angered me.

"For God's sake," I snapped. "What do you think it means?" I snatched the card away from her and read the scrawled sentiment aloud. " 'Sandra—Happy St. Valentine's Day, February 14, 1991. You are the only woman I've ever loved. With all my heart, Tom.' "

Ginny let out a little gasp. "Oh!" Her fair skin grew flushed. "*That* Tom!"

I threw the bracelet and the note back into the box. "Yes." I couldn't suppress the barb: "*That* Tom. Not Tom Sawyer, not Tom Hanks, not Tom Seaver."

"Tom Seaver?"

I'd forgotten that Ginny wasn't a baseball fan. "Never mind." I tried to stifle my anger. "You might as well know," I said. "Tom Cavanaugh's children want to buy the *Advocate*."

"No!" Ginny was aghast. But it didn't take long for her usual practical nature to reassert itself. "That's too stupid. It must be a joke." She pointed to the box while I was covering the bracelet and card with the lid. "I still don't get it. What's that got to do with it?"

"Probably part of a war of nerves," I said. "They're serious." I explained that Dylan and Kelsey Platte were buying Ed's house. "This is no joke," I emphasized. "Why would they move here if they didn't think they could take over the paper?"

"Maybe they like small towns?" Ginny suggested. "Every so often we get more people coming to Alpine, especially from California." She looked at me with a hint of dismay. "You wouldn't dream of selling, would you?"

"Of course not." I paused, wondering how ugly the Cavanaugh campaign might get.

"So," Ginny said slowly, "they sent the bracelet and the card to upset you. That's mean. Is this the guy who called just as I was going to lunch?"

I nodded. "He's married to Tom's daughter, Kelsey. If he calls again, tell him I've gone to Madagascar for the weekend."

"Okay," Ginny said. I think she knew I was exaggerating, but judging from her stoic expression I couldn't really tell.

After she left my cubbyhole, I realized I had to tell Kip and

Curtis about the buyout offer. Or the *demand,* I thought, my anger returning. In fact, it occurred to me, I should hold a staff meeting. Having sat through endless talk fests in my reporting career, I had a long-standing hatred of meetings, most of which were worthless opportunities to add huge quantities of hot air to the ozone layer. I couldn't remember when I'd held one of my own. Maybe never. It was a record I didn't want to break.

Vida and Leo returned together a few minutes before two, just about the time I realized I was famished.

"No luck," Leo grumbled. "Platte wasn't at the motel."

"I didn't think he would be," I said. "He told me I couldn't reach him this afternoon."

"His car was there," Vida asserted. "Minnie Harris said she hadn't seen him leave on foot, but she'd been in the back eating lunch."

Minnie and Mel Harris owned two of the three motels in Alpine. Years ago, they had bought the Tall Timber from Alma and Gus Eriks, who wanted to retire. More recently, the Harrises had bought Alpine's oldest motel, which had started as an auto court after World War Two. Mel and Minnie had spent almost a year remodeling and updating what was now known as the Cascade Inn. The third—and newest—was the Alpine Falls Motel, a squalid bunch of built-on-the-cheap units that had opened a couple of years earlier.

By coincidence, my entire staff was on hand a little after three-thirty. Bravely, I asked them to come into the newsroom. When my production manager and my reporter heard me drop the bombshell, Kip was shocked, but Curtis thought it was funny.

"Nothing funny about this," I said, giving him a reproachful look.

I showed them the bracelet and the note I'd received earlier. Vida was outraged—and not just at the scare tactic. "Mean-spirited," she declared, "bordering on harassment. You should take that to the sheriff."

I'd already thought about doing that, but I didn't want to bother Milo Dodge with crank mailings. Certainly I never pestered him with the ordinary crank calls and letters. As long as bodily threats weren't involved, they were routine for editors and publishers.

"So," Curtis put in, fingering his dimpled chin, "this goes back to a guy you were going to marry?"

I shot my new reporter a dark glance. "Yes. You should look through the archives. The whole horrible story is in there. In fact, it made the Seattle papers, even the AP. You *are* a newspaper reader, aren't you, Curtis?"

"Oh, sure," he replied. "I belong to that dying breed."

"Then you probably read about Tom's death," I said in a waspish tone. "It was almost five years ago."

Curtis grimaced. "Gee—I'm not sure I knew how to read that far back. I was only six."

He was sinking in quicksand, and the expression on my face must have warned him. "I went to Europe that summer on a student tour," he explained soberly. "I didn't get back until the end of summer quarter."

With a curt nod, I acknowledged what I assumed was meant as an apology. "The important thing now is that you understand I have absolutely no intention of selling the *Advocate*. These people apparently are playing hardball, but it won't get them anywhere. Your jobs are safe, and I'm entrenched behind my desk. If anyone approaches you about buying the paper, tell them to forget it. Hopefully, we'll soon hear the last of this offer. Meanwhile, have a good weekend. I'm going to Seattle this afternoon, but I'll be back Sunday night. You can always reach me on my cell phone."

My small staff began to disband, except for Vida, who

stood ramrod straight by her desk. "I'm serious, Emma. Whoever sent you that is meaner than cat dirt. Before you leave,
take that ridiculous bracelet and note to Milo."

My watch informed me it was three-fifty-three. "Okay," I
agreed after a pause. "I certainly don't want the damned
things. I'll see Milo as soon as I finish a couple of chores. I'll
start for Seattle right after that."

At ten after four I was walking briskly down Front Street in
mild if cloudy weather. What little snow we'd had the past winter had long since melted on Mount Baldy to the north and
Tonga Ridge on the south. From three blocks away, I couldn't
hear the Skykomish River, but I knew it was running well
below its banks. A freight train whistled in the distance, followed by the clang of bells for the red and white crossing bars
by the bridge leading out of town.

The sheriff was behind the curving mahogany counter,
chatting with Deputy Dwight Gould and the receptionist, Lori
Cobb.

"Don't tell me on a late Friday afternoon you've got a crime
to report," Milo said. "I'm going fishing as soon as I grab a bite
to eat."

"Not exactly," I replied, taking the box and its original
wrappings out of my handbag. There was no need for privacy.
In Alpine everybody knows everybody else's business. Secrets
are almost as scarce as old-growth trees. "Take a look."

Out of habit, Milo examined the brown wrapping paper
without touching it. "No return. Hunh." He used a letter
opener to lift the lid and the tissue paper. Dwight and Lori were
watching. "Bracelet?" the sheriff said.

I nodded.

"Pretty," Lori noted. "Are those real diamonds?"

"Probably," I said.

Milo looked down at me from his six-foot-five advantage. "You've already mauled this, I suppose."

"Yes."

"Then you show me the card."

I was tempted to say he could damned well pick it up himself, but I complied. "You can read, can't you?" I snapped as I held it up for him.

"As long as the words are short," he retorted. Milo grimaced as he tried to decipher the handwriting. "Did a chicken write this? It's not legible."

"It is to me," I said and quoted from unhappy memory. "Tom Cavanaugh, to his lovely, loony wife."

The sheriff shook his head. "So how did you end up with it?"

I sighed wearily before relating the story. Milo seemed mildly surprised; Dwight looked indifferent; Lori appeared intrigued.

"Nasty," she declared. "Not very professional, either."

"I agree," I said.

"So what do you want us to do?" Milo asked. His hazel eyes glinted faintly, as if, like Curtis, he thought this was somehow amusing.

"Nothing at the moment," I said, "but I don't want it anywhere near me. I'm going to Seattle for the weekend."

The glint in Milo's eyes faded. "A hot date with Rolf?"

"A cocktail cruise," I said without expression. My off-and-on romantic relationship with the sheriff had been off for a long time. But I was very fond of him and never wanted to hurt his feelings. He deserved better. In fact, he deserved a lot better than what I could give him.

"I'll put this in the evidence room," he said. "You aren't going to consider selling, are you?"

"Of course not." I made a face. "But their tactics are unsettling. I suppose it's only natural that Tom's children might be a little strange, given their mother's mental and emotional instability."

Milo opened the gate in the counter. "I'll walk you out."

I shot him a puzzled glance. "Okay."

On the sidewalk, he stopped just out of viewing range from his office. "That note—you sure it's Tom's handwriting?"

Every once in a while Milo shows an unexpected sensitivity. "It looks like it," I said glumly. "His penmanship was deplorable but distinctive."

Milo nodded once. "Still, it'd be easy to change a number."

That hadn't occurred to me. I realized what the sheriff was trying to say and smiled wanly. "You mean Tom wrote that before I knew him."

"Maybe." Milo shrugged. "Do you know when he got married?"

"In 1970," I replied. "A year or so before I met him when I was an intern at *The Seattle Times*."

"So," he said, keeping an eye on what might have been an unsecured load on a pickup truck that was moving along Front Street, "changing a 7 to a 9 wouldn't be hard."

"You're right," I said. "Thanks." In another uncharacteristic gesture, I stood on tiptoes and kissed his cheek. "Have a good weekend. Catch some trout."

"I'll try." The sheriff patted my shoulder awkwardly before loping over to his Grand Cherokee. Before crossing the street at the corner, I turned around to see him pulling away from the curb. The weird ga-goo-ga siren that he'd bought online sounded as he drove south on Front Street. Apparently he'd decided to stop the pickup. The driver's weekend was off to a bad start.

Fifteen minutes later I was driving my Honda west on Highway 2 with the windows down, sniffing the evergreen air and catching glimpses of the Skykomish River as it narrowed and tumbled over the rapids near the road. My spirits began to lift as they often did when I could see a slim but lively waterfall cascading over the rocky face of the foothills that lined the route. Moss and lichen, ferns and foliage all spoke to me of the mountain forests. Soothing, no matter what the season.

Traffic was growing heavier, typical for a Friday in June. I eased up on the gas pedal, dropping to forty miles an hour. I'd just passed Sunset Falls and the turnoff to Index when my cell phone rang. I refused to answer on this winding stretch of dangerous road. Another six miles and I'd be able to pull over at Gold Bar. Whoever was calling could wait.

Just beyond the next bridge over the Sky, I slowed even more as a big RV loomed ahead. Maybe I'd wait until Sultan. Having skipped lunch, I was starving, and a hamburger and fries sounded good. It was ten to five. I had plenty of time to get to Seattle before seven—if traffic wasn't tied up too badly in the suburbs. As much as I love the city, its transportation system is a mess.

When I was a child, back in the fifties, my parents were among those who were opposed to any kind of—gasp!—"California-style" freeway. Along with many others, they believed that if a freeway *had* to be built, it should not be anywhere near the city. Later, when wiser heads prevailed and the route was destined to go straight through Seattle itself, Mom and Dad sided with those who thought it should be hidden under plantings of trees and shrubs and flowers and vines. I remember thinking that might be rather pretty. But it was too expensive, and I-5 began to creep through the town, asphalt and concrete bared for all the world to see—except for Freeway Park, which was built on top of it, complete with the requisite flora and even a waterfall.

I was still musing on the past when I drove off the highway at Sultan to the Loggers Inn on Main Street. I was getting out of the car when my cell phone rang again.

"Damn!" I said under my breath, having forgotten that the cursed thing had rung while I was on the road. I got back in the car, dug out the cell, and answered on the fourth ring.

"Where are you?" Milo asked in an irritated tone.

"Sultan," I replied. "In the parking lot of the Loggers Inn."

"Your buyout troubles may be over," he said. "Dylan Platte's dead."

FOUR

I WAS STUNNED. "DEAD?" I REPEATED STUPIDLY. "HOW?"
"How dead? Dead—as in not alive," Milo said, still sounding irked. "He was shot twice in the chest. Minnie Harris found him in his motel room."

I leaned back against the car seat. "He was murdered? Or was it suicide?"

"Let's say suspicious. No weapon at the scene."

"I don't know what to say."

"Well . . ." The sheriff's voice dropped a notch. "That's the problem. You're going to have to say something, because you're the only one who knows much about this guy."

"Oh, good Lord!" I cried. "I'm a person of interest?"

"Yes. Come on, Emma. You know the drill. Get your butt back here ASAP."

It was tempting to lash out at Milo and tell him I thought *he'd* shot Dylan Platte just to screw up my weekend with Rolf Fisher. But the sheriff, who always went by the book, was right. Even if I'd never met the victim, at least I'd spoken with him and knew the details about his next of kin. What was worse, I had a motive for wanting Dylan dead. That thought sent a shiver up my spine.

"Give me an hour to get back to Alpine," I said, hunger pains still gnawing at my stomach.

"You don't need an hour. Didn't I say ASAP? Point your car east and drive. Nobody's going home early tonight." Milo obviously wasn't in an accommodating mood.

"You're a real jackass," I snapped. "I'll see you when I see you." I hung up and immediately dialed Rolf's number at the Associated Press. It was after five, but he might still be in the office near Elliott Bay.

He wasn't. He'd left fifteen minutes earlier, according to the honey-voiced female on the other end of the line. I tried his cell, knowing that he usually walked to his lower Queen Anne Hill condo. I got his voice mail, so I didn't leave a message but called his home phone. This time I got a wrong number. Someone with a heavy Eastern European accent informed me that there was no "R-r-a-a-w-f" at that number. Taking a deep breath, I tried again. Still no answer, just his voice mail.

"I'm sorry," I said earnestly, "*really* sorry, but I got as far as Sultan before the sheriff called me to say that"—did I want to unload the whole story into thin air?— "that there's been an emergency and I have to go back to Alpine. Maybe I can come down tomorrow. Call me."

I had to wait a minute or so to get back on Highway 2. Eastbound traffic was increasing with vehicles from the more heavily populated western side of the state headed over Stevens Pass. It was officially summer, and vacationers were on the move.

Driving thirty-five miles an hour on a narrow two-lane mountain road with sharp curves and slow-moving traffic keeps me alert but still allows my mind to think about other things. As I was passing Gold Bar again, the impact of Dylan Platte's murder began to sink in.

A random killing, maybe. A drug-addled thief who burst in on Dylan to steal the motel's TV or the occupant's wallet? A greedy hooker Dylan had hired to while away the afternoon? A drug deal gone bad? A jealous husband with a case of mistaken identity for his wife's lover?

Milo hadn't mentioned any details. Dylan hadn't been in Alpine long enough—that I knew of—to have made enemies. *Except,* I thought glumly, *me.*

Just before six o'clock, I turned off Highway 2 and crossed the bridge into Alpine. Traffic on Front Street was mercifully sparse. The local commute lasted about fifteen minutes and rarely went on after five-thirty. I was able to park on the diagonal just three spaces down from Milo's Grand Cherokee. As soon as I stepped out of my car, I could smell the grease from the Burger Barn's grill across the street. My stomach was growling as I entered the sheriff's headquarters.

"Don't say it," Milo growled from behind the counter.

"I can't help it," I retorted. "I haven't eaten since this morning."

"I didn't mean that," Milo said. "Your usual gripe about serious crimes happening way ahead of when the paper comes out."

"In other words," I said, dumping my big handbag on top of the sheriff's log, "Spencer Fleetwood has already been here."

"He's in my office, ready to do the live six o'clock news broadcast." Milo looked smug. "Got to go. He's interviewing me." The sheriff turned on his heel and headed for his sanctuary.

Lori was eyeing me with sympathy. "Can I get you some takeout?"

"I can get it myself," I said, snatching up my handbag. "Tell your boss if he wants me, he can find me hiding in a booth at the Burger Barn."

Lori rose partway from her chair. "You'd better not. I think Dodge mentioned that if you got here before six, Mr. Fleetwood would want to interview you, too. You know—after a commercial break."

"Tell him he can find me in . . . Madagascar." I stomped out the door.

I must have been plagued by bad luck, because the first person I saw upon entering the Burger Barn was Ed Bronsky. He was no longer slinging patties behind the service counter but apparently had just arrived as a customer.

"Emma!" he exclaimed, looking up from a long piece of paper that I assumed was a list of his family's take-out orders. "What's this about Platte?"

I'd almost forgotten that Dylan Platte was the prospective buyer for Casa de Bronska. "I just got back in town," I said. "You know as much as I do."

"It's terrible!" Ed's chins quivered in agitation. "Snorty Wenzel called me half an hour ago with the news. What are we going to do?"

"Buy some burgers?" I had long ago stopped being dismayed by Ed's self-absorption.

He didn't appreciate my flippant remark. "I'm serious," he said, lowering his voice. "We'll have to start all over. I can't imagine Mrs. Platte'll want to buy the house now."

"Probably not," I agreed, noting that the Burger Barn was getting busy and the take-out line was growing long. "I gather you never met Dylan Platte?"

Ed shook his head. "Snorty thought he was coming over tonight. I guess Platte had driven by our villa. According to Snorty, he—Platte, I mean—was really excited about it." He uttered a little grunt that might have been a laugh. "Who wouldn't be?"

"In alphabetical order?"

"What?"

"All in good order," I hedged. "I mean, given time, you'll get another buyer."

"Well . . . maybe," Ed conceded after a pause. "Now we probably won't be able to buy that new place we like so much."

"Where is it?" I asked, inching toward an empty stool at the counter.

"Great location," Ed asserted, regaining some of his usual bravado. "Close to the golf course, real quiet, not so much garden maintenance, and a nice cozy feeling." He suddenly noticed the take-out line. "Oh, gee, I'd better get going. Say," he said, digging into the pocket of his forty-eight-inches-at-the-waist summer slacks, "you got a spare twenty? I must've left my wallet on the credenza."

I hesitated, always loath to enable Ed's tightfistedness when it came to necessities such as food but readiness to squander his inheritance on Venetian chandeliers and faux Louis Quatorze chairs with legs that couldn't support half his weight.

"Okay," I finally said, getting out my wallet. "You're sure a twenty is enough?"

"Got a ten to go with it?"

I handed over thirty dollars. "Pay me back Monday," I said in a stern voice.

"Oh, sure, no problemo. See you."

"Yes." I'd see Ed all right, he was unavoidable. He wouldn't have the thirty bucks, of course, but we both knew that.

I'd just sat down at the counter when I felt a tap on my arm.

"Sorry, Ms. Lord," Lori Cobb said with a pained expression on her pale face. "Sheriff Dodge wants to see you. 'Pronto,' as he put it."

I sighed. "The man has a way with words," I muttered. "Would you mind getting me a burger and fries with a Pepsi?" I took out my wallet again and handed Lori two fives and four ones. "That ought to cover it. If there's any left over, I'll have a small salad with blue cheese dressing. Thanks."

I hopped off the stool and made my way outside. When I reached the sheriff's office, Milo and Spencer were chatting behind the counter. Mr. Radio saw me and shook his head in mock reproach.

"You missed your big chance to be a star," he said.

I glared at Spence—and then at Milo. "Gosh, I'll bet you and the sheriff would've been a hard act to follow. Which one of you was Edgar Bergen and which one was Mortimer Snerd?"

Spence turned to Milo. "She's bitter. Ignore her." He patted Milo on the shoulder. "Thanks, big fella. Keep me posted." Mr. Radio collected his equipment and strolled out of the office.

"Male bonding," I remarked, going through the counter's gate. "I hate it. You two better not have mentioned my name on the air."

"We didn't," Milo said. "You know damned well I wouldn't do that this early in a homicide investigation."

"Yeah, right, sure," I grumbled as he led the way into his private office. The room smelled of cigarette smoke. I could imagine Mr. Law Man and Mr. Radio puffing their heads off while they got buddy-buddy over the microphone.

"Ever consider airing this place out?" I asked as I sat down in front of Milo's desk.

"Why?" he shot back. "It reminds me of home."

I didn't respond.

"Okay," the sheriff said, flipping to a fresh sheet of legal-size lined yellow paper, "when did you first know of Dylan Platte?"

"I already told you," I said, my more perverse side showing front and center. "Why don't you pay attention?"

"Man," Milo said, "you sure are a pain in the ass when you're hungry. Why didn't you eat lunch?"

"Because," I said, trying to remain civil, "Dylan called me around noon, just as I was going out the door."

"Why did he call you?"

"I thought at first he was returning my call to the motel to talk to him about buying the Bronskys' hideous boondoggle. But I'm not sure if he got the—"

"Hold it." Milo put a big hand up in the air. "Platte was buying Ed and Shirley's place? Was he crazy?"

"Maybe," I said. "Can I finish?"

The sheriff nodded as he lit a cigarette and offered one to me. I declined. "Anyway, Dylan phoned me because he and his wife—Tom's daughter, Kelsey—have taken over Tom's newspaper empire with Tom's son, Graham, and his wife, and wanted to add the *Advocate* to their—"

"I know that part," Milo interrupted. "When did he ask to meet with you?"

"After work," I said. "I told him I was going out of town. He all but ignored my protests and insisted it had to be this evening because he was flying back to San Francisco on Sunday."

"Mrs. Platte wasn't with him, right?"

"So I gathered. How did Dylan register?"

"Alone," Milo said. "He arrived Thursday, according to Minnie Harris. No reservation, just showed up in the early afternoon."

"How did Minnie describe him?"

Milo glared at me. "I'm asking the questions here. How'd Platte react when you kept telling him you couldn't meet tonight?"

"As if I hadn't spoken. Just kept hammering at me about getting together on his terms, selling the paper to him—them—

and so forth. A total self-centered jerk. Furthermore," I added, "he told me not to call him because he wouldn't be in."

"In where?" Milo asked. "The motel?"

I nodded. "When I told Vida about him, she insisted on going over to the Tall Timber. Leo went there, too."

Milo scowled. "I didn't know Vida and Leo got into the act. I'll have to talk to them. What happened when they went to the motel?"

"Dylan didn't—" My cell phone rang. "Sorry, but I've got to see who this is."

"Let them wait," Milo ordered, but I'd already taken out my cell and recognized Rolf's home phone number.

I ignored the sheriff's glare. "Rolf," I said, "I'm being interrogated by Milo Dodge."

"Is that what you two always called it?" he responded. "Cute. Who gets to wear the handcuffs?"

I turned away to avoid Milo's annoyed expression. "I'm serious. There's been a murder. It's a long story, but it involves somebody who wanted to buy the *Advocate*. I'll call you when I get home, okay?"

"I've nowhere to go, no one to enjoy my passionate embrace. What should I do to while away the hours?"

"You've got your dog."

"Even my dog can't compensate for your absence, although his brown eyes and clinging paws remind me of you." He sighed loudly. "As you will. Maybe I'll jump off my balcony. Or phone the hooker service."

I never knew when Rolf was teasing me. "I have to go."

There was a pause. "You said this victim wanted to buy the *Advocate*?" Rolf's tone had become serious.

"Yes." I glanced at Milo, who was stubbing out his cigarette as if he wanted to burn a hole in the ashtray. "I promise to call you as soon as I can."

Rolf resumed his characteristic banter. "What if this is the last phone call you're allowed to make before he arrests you?"

"Good-bye, Rolf." I hung up.

Milo shook his head. "I'll be damned if I know what you see in that guy. He's a real bullshitter, if you ask me."

"I didn't ask you," I retorted.

A tap-tap-tap on the door caught the sheriff's attention. "Yeah?" he called out.

Lori entered, bearing my meal. "Sorry," she said, "I didn't ask if you wanted something, sir."

"Not now." Enviously, he watched me remove the items from the white paper bag with the red barn logo. "Maybe I'll eat some of Emma's salad."

"I could get you one of your own," Lori offered, putting my change of a quarter and three pennies on the desk. "Or go to the Venison Inn. They have a nice shrimp and crab Louis special on Fridays."

"Later," Milo said. "Thanks."

"You really are watching what you eat," I remarked after Lori left. "That's good."

"Like hell it is," Milo grumbled. "Ever since I had my gallbladder out I'm supposed to stay away from grease. Who wants to live forever without a thick steak or a double cheeseburger?"

I tried to look sympathetic. "Don't you feel better since you had the surgery?"

The sheriff made a face. "I don't have those damned chest pains anymore, but as long as I know I'm not having a heart attack, I'd almost put up with them if I could eat what I like all the time." He took his eyes off my burger and looked at his notes. "Okay, so what about Vida and Leo at the motel?"

"Nobody responded to their knock on the door of Dylan's unit," I said, sprinkling the contents of the salt and pepper

packets on my salad. "They went back to the office to tell Minnie, and she told them that his rental car was still parked by his
room, so maybe he'd walked wherever he was going. She
hadn't seen him because she was eating lunch in the back behind the front desk."

"Anything else?" Milo asked, snatching a couple of French
fries from my red plastic basket.

"Nothing," I replied, "until I heard from you. Why did
Minnie go to Platte's room?"

Milo waited until he'd swallowed the fries. "You mean
when she found him?" He saw me nod. "Mel had lost his
glasses. He thought he might've left them in one of the rooms
when he did the cleaning earlier. Minnie didn't get a response
to her knock, so she used her key. You can guess how big a fit
she pitched when she found Platte's body."

"Minnie has always struck me as levelheaded," I said.

"She is," Milo replied. "But Minnie and Mel have run their
two motels for a long time, and they've never had more than
the usual problems with drunks and irate spouses and petty
theft. Besides, the Harrises aren't spring chickens."

"Who is?" I murmured. "Did either of them see anything or
anybody unusual at the motel?"

Milo shook his head. "Mel was at the Cascade Inn earlier in
the afternoon. Later on, they both were pretty busy. It's vacation time, and their summer hires are just getting used to their
jobs."

"Nobody heard the shot?"

"No." The sheriff was looking impatient. "That's not the
quietest spot in town. The mill's close, the railroad tracks are a
block away, and it's just off Front Street. Platte's unit was second from the end, away from the office. Nobody had checked
in yet on either side of him. Besides, the Fourth of July's com-

ing up. Some of the kids are shooting off illegal fireworks. We've had a few calls about them already."

"Yes," I said, rather absently, having noticed the complaints in the police log that Curtis checked every day. "Dylan's wife—has she been notified?"

"No." Milo stole some more French fries. "Dustin Fong tried to call her in San Francisco, but nobody picked up. He didn't want to leave a message. Deputy Dustman is the soul of tact."

"He is," I agreed. "I wouldn't want Dwight Gould making those kinds of calls. The first thing he'd ask is, 'Are you the widow Platte?' By the way, do the Plattes live in San Francisco?"

"That's the address on the vic's driver's license."

"Where in San Francisco?"

Milo's scowl returned. "How the hell do I know? I've been there twice in my whole life. Damned near froze to death at Candlestick Park in August the first time, and when I went with Old Mulehide sixteen years ago for what she called 'a romantic getaway,' she told me she was filing for divorce."

"That's not the city's fault," I said in my most innocent voice.

"Screw it," Milo muttered, still holding a grudge against his ex-wife for having an affair with a high school teacher. "We're done here. Beat it, Emma."

I started to get up from the chair, but the sheriff had a final warning. "Don't leave town."

"Oh, come on, Milo!" I cried. "You're just trying to ruin my weekend! You know I'm not a suspect!"

The sheriff's expression was surprisingly bland. "I'm not trying to ruin anything. You're the primary source of information for this Platte and the rest of the Cavanaugh bunch. What's wrong with you? I'd think you'd be panting with curiosity about Tom's kids and his business. Even when you don't know any of the people involved in a homicide you get all wound up about trying to figure out whodunit." His hazel eyes hardened just a bit. "Is this Fisher really that hot?"

"That's none of your business," I snapped. "I'm going to see him. Now."

I moved so fast that I knocked the chair over. It hit against my right leg, but I wouldn't let Milo know how much it hurt. Trying not to limp, I hurried out of his office but refrained from slamming the door.

Lori, however, eyed me curiously. "Are you okay?"

I nodded and ignored Jack Mullins's smirk. The deputy had a puckish sense of humor and, for all I knew, had been listening at the keyhole. "Thanks for picking up my dinner," I said to Lori with as much dignity as possible. "Dodge is probably finishing it for me right now."

I went through the swinging gate and out of the building. Behind the wheel of my car, I sat still for a few moments, watching the slow flow of foot traffic on the south side of Front Street across from the sheriff's headquarters: Irene Baugh, Mayor Fuzzy's wife, coming out of city hall; a half dozen teenagers heading toward the Whistling Marmot Theatre to catch the early movie; Karl Freeman, high school principal, using the bank's ATM after hours; the town veterinarian, Jim Medved, and his wife, Sherry, leaving the Burger Barn. Ordinary people doing ordinary things. The sameness of it all, the predictability, the mundane lives of Alpine suddenly struck me in a moment of revulsion. *I was one of them.* And I didn't like myself for it.

There was nothing mundane about murder. Someone had killed someone else, and even if I thought Dylan Platte was a self-centered jackass, he hadn't deserved to have his life cut short. But that didn't make it right. If there was one thing I could do, and had done it fairly well in the past, I might be able to figure out that much. Dylan was Tom's son-in-law. I'd do it for Tom. *No,* I thought, *I'll do it for me. Because I can. Because it will prove I'm not ordinary.*

I dug out my phone and reluctantly dialed Rolf's number. "Let me explain," I said after he'd answered and made some smart remark that flew right by me in my self-appointed scales of justice mind-set. Fortunately, he didn't interrupt but listened as I unfolded the tale of Dylan Platte and the Cavanaugh offspring.

"That is the most elaborate and inventive reason I've ever heard for being stood up," Rolf declared when I was done. "I'm not sure whether I want to know if it really could be true. I'd like to leave it as it is, just for the sake of cocktail chatter when I go alone on the cruise tomorrow night."

"You know perfectly well it's true," I retorted. "You can check it on the AP wire when it comes through courtesy of Spencer Fleetwood. In fact, it's probably already there. He had it on the six o'clock news."

There was a fairly long silence at the other end. "Hmmm," Rolf finally murmured. "Do you want me to drive up to Alpine and help you sleuth?"

"Um . . ." I hadn't expected the offer. "No. I mean, that's really kind of you, but—"

"Stop," he interjected. "I'd only be a distraction, right? And the sheriff might arrest me for obstructing justice. I also must admit I rather like the idea of a pleasant cruise on a night in June complete with adult beverages, delectable hors d'oeuvres, and nubile young ladies. You run along now and track down that ruthless killer."

Rolf hung up.

To hell with him—and Milo, and even Tom, who had fathered two of the vipers who seemed hell-bent on ruining my life. To make matters worse, I was still hungry. Deciding to go home and forage in the kitchen, I turned on the ignition and was about to pull away from the curb when I saw Vida's white Buick slowing down in front of me. If my guess was right, she'd been summoned by the sheriff. I shut off the engine and got out of my Honda.

Vida had found a space two cars down from where I'd parked. I waited on the sidewalk for her to exit the Buick. It didn't take long. Vida virtually erupted from her car, looking aggravated.

"I don't see why I couldn't talk to Milo over the phone," she declared as I approached her. "I was just sitting down to dinner with my sister-in-law when he called on my cell phone and insisted I come in to be interviewed. Ella may be addled, but she cooks rather well and had made a lovely chicken and mushroom casserole." She suddenly peered at me from under the brim of her orange straw hat. "I thought you'd gone to Seattle."

"I got as far as Sultan," I said and explained how Milo had called me.

"My, my," she said with a shake of her head. "So you had no idea about this Platte person before you left. How irksome. You must be wild."

"I am," I admitted. "Milo's being a real jerk about this."

"Yes." Vida grimaced. "The worst of it is, I've nothing to tell him. Imagine! For all I know, Dylan Platte could have been murdered while Leo and I were at the motel. Wouldn't that beat all?"

I could sympathize with Vida for having missed out on being a virtual eyewitness to a homicide. My House & Home editor despised not being in the know, regardless of how horrific the occasion might be. No doubt she was also frustrated because she had nothing to add to the sheriff's small store of knowledge.

"I assume you're still going to Seattle," Vida said, moving toward the entrance to the sheriff's headquarters.

I shook my head. "I feel I should stay in Alpine."

"Very wise," she noted. Of course she'd have said the same thing if Alpine had suddenly become a nuclear waste site. Leaving—or as she'd phrase it, abandoning the town—for any reason was tantamount to treason. "I'll call you when I get done with Milo's silly interview. Oh—and after I finally eat my dinner with Ella. She'll warm it up for me, of course. Unless," Vida added with a frown, "she puts it in the dishwasher instead of the oven like she did the last time I was there and arrived a bit late."

I had to smile. "Good luck with everything. By the way," I called just before she opened the door, "any sighting of what's-her-name at the condo?"

Vida turned around and came a few steps closer. "Ginger. Ginger Roth. No. And that's rather peculiar. Granted, Ella isn't always the noticing kind—cataracts, too, I think—but she insists she's never seen this Ginger or her husband. You did say she was a good-looking blonde, didn't you?"

"I did. She'd be hard to miss, even with cataracts."

Vida shrugged. "I suppose it's because Ella is Ella, and has very little curiosity. That can't be helped." She paused. "But it does strike me as odd."

"If Ginger really wants to talk to me about the newspaper business on behalf of her friend, she'll show up eventually," I said. "Do you know if Curtis tried to reach her or the husband?"

"He claimed he did, but had no success." She made a face. "I doubt he tried. So lacking in diligence." Vida disappeared behind the sheriff's double doors.

Her disappearing act was normal.

Ginger Roth's was not.

FIVE

I FINALLY CONNECTED WITH MY BROTHER IN BALTIMORE JUST before nine o'clock Pacific daylight time. "This call better be important," Ben warned me. "It's midnight, and I'm dead tired. These conferences are damned draining. My lack of humility and patience are appalling in a priest."

"So's your lack of charity," I said. "You know I wouldn't bother you this time of night when you've had a long day unless it was urgent."

"Okay." There was a pause. I imagined my brother had stretched out on his hotel bed and was steeling himself for a crisis. "I know it's nothing *really* terrible," he said before I could speak again, "because you sound relatively calm. Therefore, I'll eliminate Adam being eaten by a polar bear or you burning down your little log cabin in the woods. Talk. I may be able to stay awake for at least five minutes."

"Thanks," I said sarcastically. "It all started when Ed Bronsky—"

"Stop. I'm in no mood for an Ed Bronsky anecdote."

"He sold his villa to Tom's daughter and her husband."

"I'm in no mood to hear about somebody sufficiently stupid to buy that ostentatious dump."

I gritted my teeth before speaking again. "Tom's kids want me to sell the *Advocate,* and his son-in-law was murdered at a motel here in Alpine today."

Silence. Then, finally, "Well. That *is* kind of disturbing. I assume you're going to ask me to give you absolution for whacking the guy."

"I didn't do it."

"That's what they all say." Ben cleared his throat, and I had visions of him sitting up and attempting to focus on my problem. "Have you got a favorite suspect?"

"No," I replied. "I never met this Dylan Platte. I only talked to him on the phone. His wife is Kelsey Cavanaugh. She's still in California. At least I assume that's where she is. Dylan was flying back there Sunday after he inspected Ed's house."

"You say he was killed at a motel? Was he robbed?"

"No," I answered. "Milo would've told me if that were the case."

"That doesn't rule out a random killing, though," Ben pointed out. "Botched robbery attempt, a prostitute, a hitchhiker he'd picked up."

"That's possible," I allowed. "The sheriff keeps his own counsel until he's certain about what may or may not have happened. You know he hates any kind of speculation."

"That's smart," Ben replied, "though it's hard on somebody like you, who has an imagination."

I wasn't sure if Ben was teasing, so I ignored the comment. "The other mystery is why Dylan and Kelsey wanted to buy Ed's villa."

"They'd have to live somewhere," Ben noted. "I suppose that kind of flashy style might appeal to Californians. Do they have kids?"

"I don't know," I admitted. "Frankly, I haven't thought much about them over the past few years. I'd feel very awkward about dealing with them in any case, but especially now that Dylan's been killed in the same town where Tom died. It's . . . eerie."

Ben knew better than to make some flippant remark about violence in Alpine. Skykomish County barely averaged one homicide a year among its more than seven thousand residents. The downside was that my job as editor and publisher put me on the front line of any murder investigation, not to mention on the front page of the *Advocate*.

"I understand your reluctance to deal with the Cavanaugh brood," Ben said. "It'd be helpful if Adam was in Alpine. He's part of their peer group, and I assume the Cavanaughs were raised Catholic."

"I can't ask Adam to leave his flock in Alaska and help Mom out of a jam," I declared. "I'm not an idiot."

"Not usually," Ben said, "but the situation is strange, to say the least. In fact, your coverage of this crime leaves you wide open to all sorts of conflicts of interest."

I hadn't thought that far ahead. "I suppose it could," I replied glumly. "Not to mention that I doubt Kelsey and Graham have any warm and fuzzy thoughts about me."

"My point," Ben said, and I heard him yawn. "Call Adam. See what he thinks. With that crazy radio delay, you'll each have time to consider the other's words. Do it now. It's early evening there, isn't it?"

"Evening goes on forever in St. Mary's Igloo this time of year," I said. "Okay, maybe I will. Or could you ask him?"

"I'm not his mother. Love and prayers," Ben said and yawned again.

"You're right," I agreed. "That was cowardly of me. Sorry."

Ben didn't respond. I waited for several seconds before I realized I could hear snoring in the background. My problems
might keep me awake, but it seemed they'd put my brother to
sleep.

I hung up but stayed on the sofa, watching through the
front window as twilight descended over the mountains. It
never quite got dark this time of year where Adam lived. Endless days during summer, endless nights in winter. I wouldn't
like that. But Adam didn't seem to mind. I marveled at his ma-
turity, which I had thought would never come—and when it
did, he decided to be a priest. I still sometimes found that hard
to believe. There had never been the slightest thing about my
son that led me to consider he might be harboring a vocation.
How little, I thought, we knew about the people closest to us.

After fifteen minutes of rumination, I decided against calling Adam. As much as I wanted to hear his voice, my news was
not the sort to deliver over a flawed telephone hookup. I'd
e-mail him instead.

It took me another five minutes to figure out how to explain
what had happened. "Dear Adam," I finally typed, "I had a
very strange day. Don't worry—I'm fine, but around noon I got
a phone call from . . ."

I brought him up to date on all the information I had except
for the bracelet and the enclosed note. I couldn't explain that to
myself, let alone to Ben—or Adam. After mentioning that I'd
talked to Ben, I stopped, fingers poised above my laptop's keys.
Should I suggest—even *hint*—that Adam come to Alpine?

No. That wouldn't be fair. I didn't want to be a burden on
his conscience.

It strikes me as strange that Kelsey and Graham want to
buy the *Advocate,* and even stranger that Dylan and Kelsey are

moving here, where her father died. I would think they'd avoid the place. Yes, dearest Adam, I realize that Tom was your father as well, but you lived here long before your crazy parents re-united. I'm not sure I'll know how to deal with Kelsey and Gra-ham if, in fact, they do come to Alpine as a result of Dylan's murder. Will sign off for now and try to sort out my feelings. As I mentioned, it's been a really odd and upsetting day.

I frowned at the screen. Of course I realized I'd sown the seeds of my maternal martyrdom in Adam's mind. But I couldn't keep this type of secret from my son. Ordination as a priest doesn't cancel the bond between mother and child.

I left the laptop turned on, hoping Adam would reply before I went to bed. At ten-thirty, just as I was about to head into the bathroom, his e-mail popped up.

Mom—Just got in after having supper with a dozen or so of my parishioners. Your news is startling. I understand why you're upset, but it's not your problem except for having to put it in the newspaper. Try to distance yourself from the Cav-anaughs. It isn't as if you ever had any real contact with them, even after you and Dad got engaged. Got to figure out what my homily will be for the weekend. I'll remember Dylan in the Masses. With love, your son who still marvels at the never-end-ing daylight this time of year.

I was disappointed. I didn't know what I'd been hoping for from Adam, but it certainly wasn't this rather peremptory re-sponse. For a few minutes, I sat wondering if I should answer back. Finally I decided to wait until morning. A good night's sleep might alter my mood.

But that didn't happen. I tossed and turned for hours, finally getting up to take two Excedrin PMs. It was going on five o'clock when I drifted off into a series of unsettling dreams that I couldn't remember when I woke up just after nine-thirty.

While drinking my third cup of coffee, I thought more about Adam's e-mail. My disappointment had overshadowed his advice about the murder coverage. Maybe Ben was right— it could be a conflict of interest for me, though more in a personal than in a professional sense. I considered assigning the story to Curtis, but I was reluctant. He simply didn't know his way around the town yet.

Still, I reflected, maybe that was to his advantage. As long as I watched him like a hawk, maybe I should let him handle the coverage. I dialed his number, which was a cell phone. Curtis was temporarily living with Oren and Sunny Rhodes, who had some spare room in their Ptarmigan Tract house while both of their kids were in college. Oren tended bar at the Venison Inn, and Sunny was the local Avon lady. The extra cash came in handy to help pay tuition.

Curtis didn't answer. It was going on eleven. Maybe he'd left town for the weekend without telling me. Then I remembered that I was his boss, not his mother. I called the Rhodes's number. Sunny picked up on the second ring, perhaps hoping I was a customer with a big Avon order.

"Curtis isn't up yet," she informed me, still sounding like her usual cheerful self. "I promised to make breakfast for him this morning because Oren wanted pancakes. Should I wake Curtis?"

I hesitated. "No. But have him call me as soon as he gets up. Thanks, Sunny."

Sleeping in is not a sin. I'd do it myself if I had more opportunities. But I wondered if my new reporter was a bit lazy. While I waited for him to reach a conscious state, I called Milo's cell phone.

"Are you at work?" I asked in response to his gruff greeting.

"Yes," he replied. "How come you didn't ignore my warning and run off to see Lover Boy in Seattle?"

I realized that Milo had seen my home phone number come up on his caller ID. "That's really none of your business," I snapped. "What *does* concern you is that I'm assigning Curtis Mayne to the Platte investigation."

"Curtis is twelve," Milo responded. "Are you crazy? You didn't let Scott Chamoud take on a big story like this until he'd been working for you at least five years."

"It wasn't *that* long," I countered, although it had definitely taken me quite a while to let Scott handle a touchy assignment. "This is different. I'm concerned about my objectivity."

"Yeah, right, okay," Milo said grumpily. "It's your call. But I don't want to have to hold this twerp's hand."

"That's how he'll learn," I declared. "Naturally, I'll edit his copy closely."

"Damned straight you will," Milo shot back. "I don't want some punk fresh out of college making me look like an idiot."

"Of course not," I said. "Is there anything new on the case?"

"It's not your story," Milo retorted. "I'll keep Curtis up to speed when he gets here."

There was no point in arguing with the sheriff when he was in one of his ornery moods. "You'll see him soon," I promised and hung up.

But noon came and the clock kept ticking. I'd gone outside to work in the garden, taking my phone with me. By one o'clock I'd filled a plastic bag full of weeds, leaves, and branches, taking out my increasing annoyance with Curtis by yanking up the English bluebells that were crowding out my summer-blooming plants.

I stood up, brushed the dirt off my old slacks, and surveyed my handiwork. As usual, I couldn't see much of an improvement. My front yard is relatively flat, but out in back of my log house the property slopes upward and is shaded by tall evergreens. I confine my greatest labor to the front, where the garden gets more sun. The rainy climate encourages growth, and for some perverse reason it seems to have a more positive effect on weeds and other undesirable flora than on the flowers and shrubs I've spent my hard-earned money on. I don't have a truly green thumb, but I try. At the moment, I felt as if I was a better gardener than an editor and publisher, given my inability to keep track of my reporter. I went back inside, washed my hands, and called the Rhodes residence a second time.

"Did Curtis ever wake up?" I asked Sunny.

"Yes," she replied. "He came into the kitchen about ten minutes after you called. I told him you wanted to talk to him, and he said he'd call, but after he ate his breakfast, he left. Maybe," she added hopefully, "he's coming to see you."

"Maybe." I sounded far less hopeful. "Thanks."

I dialed Curtis's cell phone again. This time he picked up on the third ring.

"Wow," he said with what sounded like feigned amazement, "would you believe I was just about to call you?"

"No, I wouldn't," I snapped. "I've been trying to get ahold of you for almost two hours." It was an exaggeration, but I was mad.

"Sorry," he said breezily. "I didn't realize I was still on the clock. I thought this was a Saturday."

"Journalists are always on the clock," I said, trying to keep the anger out of my voice. "News actually does sometimes happen on a weekend, even in Alpine. Where are you?"

"Uh . . . Starbucks. Mrs. Rhodes doesn't make lattes."

I couldn't resist sarcasm. "That's a shame. Poor you. Bring it with you and be here in five minutes." I hung up.

It took Curtis almost ten minutes, but he arrived in his aging Nissan just before one-thirty. He wasn't carrying a paper cup, so I presumed he'd finished his latte at Starbucks.

"So what's happening?" he asked after I indicated he should sit in an armchair by the fireplace.

I sat rigidly on the sofa. "You've heard about Dylan Platte's murder, I assume."

Curtis nodded. "It's all over town. He's the guy who wanted to buy the paper, right?"

"He and some other family members," I said. "I'm assigning you the story."

His blue eyes widened. "No kidding! That's great. Byline and all, huh?"

"That's right." I relaxed a little. "Of course I'll go over your copy. This is a huge story, and it has to be handled carefully. Ordinarily, I'd do it myself, but in effect, I'm recusing myself because of the angle about the buyout proposal."

"Oh, yeah." He'd taken a ballpoint pen out of his pocket and was chewing on it. "Gotcha. Touchy. Kid gloves, right?"

"Yes." I leaned forward. "By the time the paper goes to press, a lot of things may've happened, including an arrest. You'll be dealing primarily with Sheriff Dodge, who will tell you only what he thinks you ought to know. How have you gotten on with him so far?"

Curtis shrugged. "Okay. I haven't seen him more than twice. He's usually in his office when I stop by to check the log. I talk mostly with Lorna, the receptionist, or to one of the deputies."

"Her name's Lori," I said, beginning to realize that Curtis seemed to have trouble remembering people's names. "Lori Cobb. Be sure you take plenty of notes and use your recorder."

"Sure. It's a good one. I got it as a graduation present, a

Sony ICD-MS515 Memory Stick Recorder." He grinned at me. "This should be a kick."

"A kick?" I was appalled. "Murder isn't a cheap thrill. This isn't TV, it's real."

Curtis shrugged again. "Sure—like reality TV. Hey," he continued before I could say anything, "newspapers are part of the media, and the media is all about entertainment. The problem is, print journalists don't get it. They're still living in the past, where they were the big sources of information. Then we got the Information Age, one big explosion of ways to communicate instantly, and meanwhile, editors and publishers and reporters are still back in the Dark Ages. Who wants to wait to read the news? So what's to do? Entertain, just like TV and movies and the rest of the media. How many of those handsome and beautiful people on TV have ever dug out a story on their own? The closest they come to real reporting is to stand in the middle of a hurricane and announce that it's really wet and windy. Even a moron can figure that one out."

"My, my," I said dryly, "I don't recall you giving me this philosophy when you interviewed for the job."

"You didn't ask." Curtis leaned back in the armchair and stretched his legs. "Besides, I thought maybe you already knew all this."

"You have some good points about the media," I allowed, "but I believe in journalistic integrity, which means you can't go off half-cocked and not take a story—any kind of hard news story—seriously. You also have to remember to treat your sources with tact and consideration. In a small town, reliable spokespersons are few and far between. Alienating any of them can dry up your sources forever. These people don't tend to forgive and forget."

"Small town, small minds," Curtis said under his breath.

"Okay, I get it. I'm off to see the sheriff. He *is* at work today, isn't he?"

I shot Curtis a reproachful glance. "He was there a couple of hours ago, when I told him you'd stop in almost immediately."

"Got it." He popped out of the armchair and headed for the door.

For the rest of the day, I tried to shake off my misgivings. I even told myself that Milo and Curtis deserved each other. On the rare occasions when I'd allowed Scott Chamoud to deal with the sheriff, my former reporter's good manners and amiable disposition had set well enough with all of the county's law enforcement employees. Curtis Mayne was a different type—cocky and opinionated. But maybe that meant he was also determined and aggressive. Time would tell.

In the early evening, Vida called. "So you stayed on in Alpine," she said in an approving voice. "I thought you might go to Seattle after all."

I explained why I'd decided against the trip and concluded by saying that I'd assigned the story to Curtis.

Vida exploded in my ear. "Are you quite mad?" she shrieked. "He's an infant! You've sent a boy to the mill!"

"I didn't have much choice," I argued. "I didn't feel right about handling the coverage directly."

"Oh, nonsense!" Vida seethed. "Then why didn't you let me do it? My nephew Billy would have been anxious to help me with information."

Bill Blatt was another of the sheriff's deputies and one of Vida's primary information sources. Over the years the poor guy had sometimes divulged tidbits he should have kept under wraps, but his aunt had her ways of making even the most reluctant informant talk.

"I can't ask you to sacrifice your own page for hard news," I said, never wanting to even hint that Vida's florid writing style was acceptable only for the House & Home readers—of which there were many in Alpine.

"Piffle," she said, dropping her voice a notch. "You know I can do both."

"Curtis has to learn the ropes," I pointed out. "He was hired as a reporter, and that's what he's going to do—report. I waited too long to give Scott his head on big stories."

"Perhaps," Vida allowed, but she didn't sound convinced.

"You *will*," I said, "help him with your encyclopedic knowledge of Alpine, won't you?"

"Goodness," Vida replied airily, "I don't see how I can possibly offer any information in this instance. The victim had nothing to do with Alpine except for arriving here two days ago."

"Vida . . ." I was coaxing her, playing the game like a good sport.

"If Curtis needs my help, he can ask for it," she retorted. "I'm not one to meddle or give unsolicited advice."

"Of course you aren't." *Of course you are,* I thought but knew better than to say so. "I'd appreciate it. If Curtis asks."

"Very green," she remarked. "Twenty-two, twenty-three?"

"Twenty-four in August," I said. "I think."

There was a brief pause at the other end. "I stopped by this afternoon to see the Harrises at the motel," Vida said.

I wasn't surprised that Vida had gone to the Tall Timber. "What did Minnie and Mel have to say about their departed guest?"

"Dylan Platte was just over average height, curly brown hair, mid-thirties—thirty-five, to be exact—according to his California driver's license. He was casually dressed, though Minnie thought his watch was quite expensive." Vida's voice had lost its edge as she rattled off the data she'd collected. "He was courteous but not friendly. No time for chitchat. Sometimes Minnie's rather snoopy about guests, even though that's most unwise in the motel industry. Not that I blame her."

"Of course not."

"Dylan had arrived shortly after the lunch hour Thursday," Vida continued. "He was gone for part of the afternoon, returned to the motel—Mel saw his rental car in the parking lot— and then went out again. The Harrises like to play a little game about their guests. They call it 'Guest Guessing,' and when they don't know why someone is visiting in Alpine, if they find out later, whichever of them has come closest to the real reason puts a dollar in a coffee can toward their own vacation."

"Cute." I failed at sounding enthusiastic. "So did they guess?"

"Guess what?"

"Why Dylan had come to Alpine."

"Certainly not," Vida huffed. "They're not ghouls. Mel and Minnie would never guess that someone visited here in order to be murdered."

"I meant to look at Ed's house."

"Oh. Not precisely. Mel thought Dylan might be one of those California land speculators," Vida said. "It wouldn't be the first time they've come sniffing around here to buy up property at absurdly low prices because they think small town people are stupid."

"So," I asked, "when did Dylan tell them why he was here?"

"He didn't," Vida replied. "They never talked to him after he arrived. Not that it's unusual, especially this time of year, with the travel business being in high gear and two motels to keep up."

"Where had he rented his car?" I asked.

"The airport, I assume," Vida said. "Sea-Tac. Minnie and Mel didn't know, and when I asked Billy about it, he pretended he hadn't found out. I do hate it when he tries to put me off with very transparent excuses. Surely he understands I have no intention of making him look untrustworthy or indiscreet."

"Did Bill say it was strange that no one heard the shot that killed Dylan?"

"I didn't ask him about that," Vida admitted. "If Dylan was killed yesterday afternoon and his unit was at the end of the building, I'm not surprised. Front Street is rather noisy that far to the east. So many businesses surrounding the Tall Timber, what with the mill, the railroad tracks, the truckers, and often as not, especially with school out, teenagers racing up and down Front and the Icicle Creek Road. I've never understood why the original motel owners built there in the first place."

"It's close to everything," I pointed out, not wanting to say to Vida that, being so small, Alpine didn't offer many secluded and convenient sites for hostelries, with the possible exception of the venerable ski lodge founded by her father-in-law.

"Speaking of property," Vida said, "with all this murder business going on, I forgot to mention what Ella told me after I got back to her apartment to finish dinner. Sorting through her muddleheaded chatter, I learned that the owner of Pines Villa wants to eliminate the mixed usage concept and turn it all into condos, like Parc Pines. There's room enough to build on that vacant lot at the corner of Alpine Way and Tonga Road. We must run a story about that."

"Yes," I agreed, making a note on the pad I kept by the phone. "Who owns it now?"

"A woman who lives in Everett," Vida replied. "Ella couldn't think of her name. Indeed, it's a marvel Ella can re-member her own name these days. You recall that the apart-ments have changed hands more than once in the ten or twelve years since they were built."

I vaguely remembered running the stories on the sales. "The courthouse will have a record of ownership," I said and then tossed Vida a bone: "Do you want to check it out Monday?"

"Certainly," she said. "Frankly, I think more condos are a ridiculous idea in Alpine. We don't need them."

I didn't argue. Alpine had single dwellings, apartments, duplexes, college dorms, a retirement facility, and a trailer park. Prices were much cheaper than in the more populous cities, and there was still plenty of room to build. Even though the number of residents had grown to almost seven thousand countywide, hordes of newcomers weren't beating a retreat to our mountain aerie.

After I finished talking to Vida, I checked in with Curtis. This time he answered almost immediately.

"Anything new?" I asked, hearing music in the background.

"New? Or news?" Curtis laughed and said something I couldn't catch.

"The sheriff," I said, hearing girlish laughter at the other end. "Are there any new developments in the case?"

"C'mon down," Curtis responded. "I'll tell you all about it. There's an empty bar stool here at Mugs Ahoy. You can meet Cammie. She's new in town." He turned away from the phone, but this time I could hear his words. "Hey, hottie, want to talk to my boss?"

Cammie screeched and then giggled.

"Curtis!" I barked as the music grew louder and was joined by somebody singing off-key to James Brown's "Good Good Lovin'." "Go outside! I can hardly hear you!"

"I can't hear you, Boss," Curtis shouted into my ear. "I'll call you back in a nano."

I waited. And waited. My home phone didn't ring; my cell remained silent. After fifteen minutes, I was really mad. Curtis was off to a wretched start. I debated with myself about going to Mugs Ahoy but thought that might cause some kind of embarrassing scene. Instead, I dialed Milo's number at home.

"Okay," I said after he answered, still sounding grumpy, "I'm an idiot. Has Curtis screwed up at your end as well as at mine?"

"Curtis?" Milo paused. "Oh—the new kid you hired? No. Why?"

"Did he interview you this afternoon?"

"He stopped by around two or so," Milo replied. "He asked if there was anything new going on with the Platte homicide, and I told him not yet, so he left. That was fine with me."

I frowned, questioning my judgment about what I'd perceived as my new reporter's aggressiveness. "Okay," I said, trying to sound casual. "This is his first big assignment. I'm monitoring his progress."

"What's the rush?" Milo asked. "You've got plenty of time to get a story in the Wednesday paper."

Like many other readers, the sheriff didn't seem to understand the process of news gathering. Get facts, type them up, print in newspaper. Their concept was as simple as that, with no need for background information, dealing with uncooperative or deceptive sources, or trying to find the unvarnished truth rather than glib whitewash.

"I want Curtis to get a head start," I said, using an explanation that even Milo could understand. "He's new to the business. I assume you still don't have any fresh information?"

"Nope. That's why I'm not at work." He yawned loudly enough that I could hear him at my end. "Just watching *Band of Brothers*. Again."

"Good series," I said and quickly moved on. "Have you found out anything on the bracelet and note I got in the mail?"

"Nope," Milo repeated. "That has to go to the lab in Everett. You know we can't afford expensive equipment here in SkyCo."

I wasn't surprised that our county lab's expertise couldn't handle the job. I changed the subject. "What about Dylan's wife, Kelsey? Have you talked to her?"

"Not since she got here," Milo replied.

I stifled the urge to scream at the sheriff. "Kelsey's in Alpine?" I finally said, keeping my voice down.

"She got here late this afternoon," Milo said. "She's at the ski lodge. I'll see her tomorrow."

"Is Graham Cavanaugh coming, too?" I asked.

"Graham? Oh—the brother. I don't know. I'll find out when I see Mrs. Platte." Milo yawned again.

"Okay." I still managed to sound unruffled. "Thanks."

Milo hung up. I sat on the sofa with the receiver in my hand and considered my next move. I didn't want to meet Kelsey Cavanaugh Platte. It was bound to be an emotional roller coaster—for both of us. The grieving widow, the orphaned daughter—and the woman who almost married her father.

But I couldn't avoid Kelsey. I finally put the handset back in its base, grabbed my purse, pulled on my linen summer jacket, and drove to the ski lodge to face a stranger who had nearly become the daughter I'd never had.

SIX

Henry Bardeen, the manager of the ski lodge, was in the lobby by the dining room entrance, talking to Mayor Fuzzy Baugh and his wife, Irene. Judging from the furtive look Henry gave me, I figured they were talking about me.

"Emma," Henry said, putting out a hand. "You haven't graced us with your presence lately. How are you?"

"My social life's a bit dull," I said, nodding at the Baughs.

Irene, a tall, still handsome woman in her seventies, smiled. "We were just leaving. It's lovely to see you, Emma. It's a shame you don't golf. We could use some fresh blood at the country club."

"Yes," I said, sufficiently tactful not to mention that the clubhouse was an army surplus Quonset hut left over from World War Two and the food came out of a vending machine. "I'm not very athletic."

"Neither are the rest of us," Irene said graciously. "So nice to see you. Come, Fuzzy, we must get home in time to feed Huey."

Huey was a bull terrier, named for Huey Long in honor of the Baughs' Louisiana roots.

Fuzzy, as ever, was subdued in his wife's presence. "My, yes, sugar," the mayor said to his wife. "Wonderful repast, Henry. Good night, Emma."

Henry turned to me as soon as the Baughs walked away. "Are you here for dinner?"

"No," I replied. "I ate earlier at home. I'm calling on one of your guests, a Mrs. Platte."

A hint of color crept onto Henry's usually pale face. "You mean . . ." He'd lowered his voice and was glancing around the lobby. A young couple occupied the Adirondack chairs by the fireplace, but they weren't in hearing range. ". . . The woman whose husband was killed yesterday?"

I nodded solemnly. "Yes."

"She asked not to be disturbed," Henry said, barely above a whisper. His usual self-effacing manner was far different from that of his brother, Buck, an intrepid retired air force colonel who had been Vida's social companion for several years. "Mrs. Platte seems very distraught," Henry murmured.

"Did she come alone?" I inquired, wondering where Kelsey's brother, Graham, fit in this mix.

"Yes, very brave of her," Henry replied. "Heather offered to keep her company, but Mrs. Platte insisted that she preferred to be alone."

Heather Bardeen Bavich was Henry's daughter, who worked as her father's assistant. She had been married for several years and had a small child but still put in long hours at the lodge.

I hesitated, trying to figure out what was the best approach to take with Kelsey Cavanaugh Platte. I couldn't shirk my professional responsibilities because of personal concerns. And I was curious.

"Henry," I said, speaking almost as softly as he had, "this

young woman is Tom Cavanaugh's daughter. I feel I have some kind of obligation to see her."

Henry looked stricken. "Oh! Emma, I . . ." Any color he'd had in his face drained away. "I didn't know. . . . You mean . . . What was her husband doing here?"

"It's a long story," I said, realizing that neither Milo nor Spencer had leaked the reason for Dylan's presence in Alpine. I hated having to be grateful to them, but they had a thank-you coming. "I've never formally met Kelsey," I admitted, "but I can't pretend I don't know who she is."

Henry looked thoughtful. "I could send her a note. Or you could."

"Well . . ." I was afraid Kelsey would refuse to see me, no matter how tactfully Henry or I composed the missive. "Would it upset you if I went to her room and explained who I am?"

Henry grimaced. "If you didn't tell her you talked to me, I suppose I could turn a blind eye. But," he quickly added, "she'll know somebody gave her your room number."

"No." I spoke emphatically, causing Henry to give me a curious look. "You have three suites here, and it's June, so chances are all of them aren't taken, but Kelsey's rich—she'd want a suite. Let's see if I can guess. If I'm right, don't say a word and don't watch me go to the elevator."

He considered my idea for several seconds. "All right. Go ahead. In fact, don't even tell me what you're guessing."

"Fair enough." I smiled at Henry and went to the two elevators in the lobby, one for guests, the other for service. I pressed the button for the third floor, which was the highest in the lodge and where all three suites were located. There was the King Magnus Suite, the Queen Margrethe Suite, and the Prince Haakon Suite. I went straight to the Margrethe and rapped the brass knocker three times.

I waited, wondering how long it would take for Kelsey to peer through the peephole and decide if I looked like a crook. A full minute passed—I'd checked my watch. A few seconds later, I heard a tentative voice say, "Yes?"

"Ms. Lord," I announced. My voice seemed to echo along the empty corridor, with its Norwegian hooked rugs and framed photos of skiers tackling the slopes around Stevens Pass.

I was about to give up when the door opened a couple of inches, the chain still in the guard. A familiar pair of blue eyes stared out at me from a pale face framed by long fair hair.

"Yes?" Kelsey repeated, more softly this time.

"You know who I am?" I asked, also very quietly.

"Yes." She bit her lip. "You're the newspaperwoman."

The newspaperwoman. Not her father's fiancée, not his bride to be, not even a friend of the family. I felt something very like a brick sink in my stomach. But what was I expecting? That Kelsey would throw herself into my arms and sob her heart out for missing out on having me as a stepmother? No. Still, her response was so impersonal that I felt as if I'd played no part in her father's life.

"May I come in?" I asked stiltedly.

Kelsey looked uncertain. From what I could see of her, she seemed to exude a waiflike air, a slim, fine-boned young woman devoid of makeup and, except for her blue eyes, bearing no resemblance to Tom. *Sandra's child,* I thought and wondered if she had also inherited her mother's unstable mental condition.

Thin fingers with very short nails coped awkwardly with the chain. "Please." Kelsey stepped aside to let me enter. "It'd be better if you waited until Graham was here," she said, sinking gracelessly into an armchair.

"When is your brother arriving?" I asked, sitting down unbidden on the sofa. As I recalled, the suite had a sitting room, two bedrooms, and two baths. I could see an open suitcase on the floor in the nearest bedroom. Kelsey was barefoot. A pair of Juicy Couture brown suede and gold snake sandals lay not far from the sofa. A pale yellow cashmere cardigan was draped over the back of the chair where Kelsey had sat down. She wore what I assumed were designer jeans, a honey-colored tee, and a diamond ring with a marquis-cut stone as big as a cat's eye.

"Graham will be here tomorrow," she said, picking up a bottle of water from the side table by her chair. "He's coming from New York."

"He lives there?"

"No. He's boating with some friends at Glen Cove." She drew farther back in the armchair and tucked her feet under her bottom. I sensed that she was wary of me. I didn't blame her.

"I see." I hoped I looked sympathetic. "I'm terribly sorry for what's happened to your husband. I never got to meet him."

Her gaze was off into space. "No?"

"We were trying to set up a meeting," I said.

"Yes."

There was an uncomfortable pause. At least it was uncomfortable for me. Kelsey was staring up into the exposed pine beams of the cathedral ceiling. There was no sign of recent tears, but probably she was beyond that by now.

"It's very brave of you to come to Alpine," I finally said.

Kelsey shrugged.

"I'm sorry we have to meet in these circumstances."

Kelsey nodded.

I was running out of platitudes—even if they were true— and I wondered how I could get her to talk. "Would you like to see a doctor?"

She blinked several times. "A doctor? Why? I'm not sick."

"You're in shock, I think."

"I don't believe in medical doctors," she said. "Natural remedies are best."

If that was what she was using, Mother Nature had struck out. Or perhaps Kelsey preferred cocaine or some other illegal substances for medicating. Yet her eyes seemed as clear as they were dry. I tried another query. "Do you have any . . . plans?"

"Plans?" She finally looked at me again. "You mean for the funeral?"

"That, of course, and with regard to your move."

She shook her head. "Dylan did all the planning. I'm not very organized."

Getting two entire sentences out of Kelsey felt like a small victory. "Do you and Dylan have children?"

She shook her head again. "We talked about it, but . . ." Her voice trailed off.

I recalled Tom telling me, some years earlier, that Kelsey had gotten pregnant by the boyfriend she was living with. Maybe she'd miscarried. Maybe she'd had an abortion. Maybe she'd given the baby up for adoption. Maybe she'd forgotten that she'd ever had a baby. Of course I realized that she was probably still in a state of shock. Her husband had been dead for only a little more than twenty-four hours. "You live in San Francisco?"

Kelsey nodded yet again.

Another long silence hovered over us. Did I dare mention Tom? Not yet. Kelsey seemed very fragile. Perhaps she'd inherited her mother's emotional instability after all. Still, I reminded myself, she was Tom's daughter. Although I could make little physical connection between the two, I wanted to help her. So many what-ifs raced through my mind.

"Is there anything I can do?"

Kelsey looked at me curiously. "In what way?"

"Have you eaten since you arrived in Alpine?"

She took another swig from her water bottle. "No. I couldn't."

"You can't starve yourself," I pointed out. "You need to keep up your strength." *More platitudes.* I was a walking compendium of clichés.

She shook her head. Again.

"Do you know anyone in town? That is, have you had personal contact with anybody here?"

Another head shake. "Dylan did all that."

I felt like asking her why she'd bothered to make the trip. Was she planning to sit in the ski lodge suite until the county released Dylan's body? "Who notified you about Dylan?"

"A man," she replied. "I think he was from the sheriff's office."

"That was Deputy Fong," I said. "Would you like to talk to him?"

"Why?"

"To learn the details," I said. "To find out how to . . . make arrangements."

"Graham can do that when he gets here." She swallowed more water before standing up and crossing the room to open the doors of a rustic armoire that held the television and the bar setup. "Do you want to watch TV?"

"Ah . . . no, thanks." I also stood up. "I should be going."

With the remote control in one hand, Kelsey studied the TV program guide. "Saturdays are bad nights for good shows. You don't get HBO here?"

"Not at the lodge," I said, moving to the end table. I picked up a pad and pen that were next to the phone and wrote down my name and numbers. "If you need me for anything, call. I mean it, Kelsey."

She accepted the slip of paper and shoved it into the pocket of her jeans. "Thanks."

I left. Kelsey hadn't bothered to move from the spot where she was standing by the TV.

I didn't know what to make of her. She didn't seem to be plugged into the rest of the world. Heredity, grief, shock—I supposed there were explanations. But I definitely found her odd. Maybe her brother would be an improvement.

After ten o'clock Mass the next morning, I cruised by Vida's house. She attended the Presbyterian church, where the services usually ran almost two hours. There was a fellowship gathering afterward, which provided Vida with ample opportunity to catch up on any gossip she'd missed during the week. It was probably wishful thinking that she'd come home before one o'clock.

I waited in front of her house for over ten minutes with no luck. I was about to drive away when a horn honked behind me. My rearview mirror showed Ed Bronsky's Mercedes pulling up alongside my parked car. I'd avoided the Bronsky bunch at church, an un-Christian thing to do, but I wasn't in the mood to face him about his hard luck with the house sale.

All eight of his bulky family members were jammed into the sedan because they'd sold Shirley's matching Mercedes. Ed had rolled down the window on the passenger side and leaned across the youngest of the brood, Christina, and his wife to call out to me.

"Is that lawyer woman at church any good?" he shouted.

"Marisa Foxx?" I called back. "Yes, she's very competent. I thought you had a lawyer from Everett."

"He's unavailable," Ed replied as Shirley tried to keep smiling despite being crushed by her husband's weight. I couldn't see Christina at all. Maybe she had been wedged between the seats. "I'll give her a call today," Ed added. "She didn't stick around for coffee and doughnuts after Mass."

I was sure that the Bronskys had stayed on, stuffing them-selves with as many free goodies as they could clutch in their pudgy hands. "Why," I asked, knowing the answer was going to be something I didn't want to hear, "do you need a lawyer?"

"I want advice on how to handle this sale of the house," Ed said. "A deal's a deal."

Despite my vow to avoid his harebrained schemes, I asked another question: "Has money crossed hands?"

Ed glowered at me. "Verbal agreements stand up in court, you know."

I mentally kicked myself for not keeping my mouth shut. "Since when?"

He leaned even farther across his daughter and wife. I won-dered if either of them could breathe. "Since I've got a witness who heard me talk to Dylan Plate," Ed declared as Shirley uttered a little groan. At least she hadn't been smothered to death.

"His name is Platte," I said, spelling it out, though I figured that Ed's mistake indicated he still had food on his mind. "You met him?"

"No," he retorted, "but I talked to him on the phone this week. Snorty Wenzel was on the extension in the study. Plate— I mean *Platte*—told us he'd put the earnest money down as soon as he got to Alpine. He thought it'd be best to set up an account and deal with a local bank."

"Probably," I allowed. "Did you talk to Platte after he got here?"

"No," Ed shot back. "I told you that. You think I offed the guy?"

"Of course not," I replied. "You'd be killing the goose that laid the golden egg."

"You got that right," he muttered. "In fact," he continued, "I'm going to drop off Shirley and the kids and go see Mrs. Platte. She's at the ski lodge."

"That's not a good idea," I informed him. "She's not receiving."

"Receiving what?" Ed demanded.

"Never mind," I said. It was useless to argue. "Good luck."

Ed finally sat up. I saw Shirley take a deep breath and try to offer me a smile before the Mercedes headed east on Tyee Street. There was still no sign of Vida, so I went home. I called Henry Bardeen at the ski lodge and asked if Graham Cavanaugh had checked in yet.

"No," Henry replied. "His sister wasn't sure of his arrival time."

"That figures," I murmured. "She struck me as rather vague."

"Understandable," Henry said.

"Yes. By the way," I added, "Ed Bronsky is coming to see her. Brace yourself."

"Oh, my!" Henry exclaimed. "Why?"

"The Plattes were buying Ed's villa," I replied. "Ed, of course, is hatching plots to unload the place."

"That puts me in a bind," Henry said. "Very awkward, being caught in the middle."

"I don't envy you. Maybe Kelsey won't let Ed in."

"You know how he . . . Well," Henry amended, "Ed can be very determined."

Not when he sold advertising for me, I thought. "Good luck. Say," I said, "would you ask Kelsey if she has a picture of her husband? I just realized we don't have any photos for the newspaper."

"Can that wait until tomorrow?" Henry inquired. "Heather will be here then. It's my day off, you know. Maybe a woman's touch would be better."

"Sure," I said. "I'm sorry to bother you, but we should run a picture, even if it's just one she carries in her wallet."

"I'll make a note," Henry promised. "Ah! Here comes Ed."

I thanked Henry and hung up. Feeling at loose ends, I opened my laptop and checked to see if Adam had sent me a new message. He hadn't. I felt vaguely resentful about the way he'd responded Friday night. He certainly understood how upset I must be, given the painful memories that recent events had resurrected. After all, Kelsey and Graham were his blood siblings. The more I thought about it, the more annoyed I became.

Of course I was also irked at Rolf, who should have been more sympathetic. He was in the news business, too, and ought to understand the demands of a breaking story. I'd expected—hoped, actually—he might call to apologize. But by four o'clock the phone had remained silent. I was beginning to get mad at the entire world, at least the half occupied by men.

The rest of the day passed uneventfully. I couldn't bother Ben. He'd be on his way back to his temporary parish in Cleveland, where he was filling in for a priest who'd gone on sabbatical. I didn't want to pester Milo. I wasn't the designated reporter on the murder investigation. I shouldn't bother Curtis. If he'd been working on Sunday, which I doubted, he would've brought me up to speed on any new developments. Or would he? I'd wait to find out in the morning.

Monday brought a drizzling rain to the mountain slopes of Alpine. I arrived at the office before anyone else except Kip, who was already finalizing his report on the new software we needed for the back shop.

"It's going to cost around four hundred dollars," he informed me. "Is that okay?"

"It has to be if we need it," I said. "Go ahead."

The rest of the staff—Ginny, Vida, Leo, and Curtis—trickled in.

"Where are the bakery goods?" Leo asked, looking a bit forlorn after pouring out a mug of coffee.

Vida turned her gaze to Curtis. "I believe it's your day to go to the Upper Crust," she said in a reproachful tone. "Did you forget?"

Curtis made a face. "Darned if I didn't. Who wants what?"

Vida wasn't letting him off the hook easily. "You know how we do it," she asserted. "This will be your third trip since you started here. It's your responsibility to determine which products look best on any given day. And never get doughnuts on a Monday. It's likely that they're left over from Saturday. The Upper Crust is closed on Sunday."

"Wow," Curtis said under his breath. "I never guessed I'd have to take a course in pastry before I went to work for a newspaper." He sauntered out of the newsroom.

"Much too cheeky," Vida remarked. "What's wrong with young people these days?"

"Spoiled rotten," Leo said, sitting down at his desk.

"Definitely," Vida agreed as Leo lighted a cigarette. "But at least Curtis doesn't smoke."

"Oh, Duchess," Leo lamented, "and just when I was beginning to think you liked me after all these years."

Vida snorted before taking a sip of the hot water she drank at work instead of coffee.

I leaned against Curtis's desk and told Vida and Leo about my Saturday visit to Kelsey Cavanaugh Platte. Leo was intrigued; Vida was outraged.

"You went without me?" she cried. "How could you?"

Leo ignored her comment. "Kelsey was still a teenager the last time I saw her. It was summertime. She and Graham were on a tour with their dad to visit his newspapers in Southern California. I wonder if she'd remember me. It's a wonder I remember her—I was semidrunk at the time."

"I assume she looks like her mother," I said. "She does have her father's blue eyes, but that's it."

"Graham doesn't look much like Tom, either," Leo noted. "In fact, Adam bears a closer resemblance to his father than Kelsey and Graham do."

"Maybe," I suggested, "you should be the one to talk to Graham. He was supposed to get here yesterday."

"Wouldn't that be stepping on Curtis's toes?" Leo asked.

"I meant," I said, trying to avoid Vida, who was now glaring at both Leo and me, "as an old friend of the family."

"I was never that," Leo pointed out. "I was an employee. I probably only saw the Cavanaugh kids two or three times in all the years I worked for Tom."

"Still," I began, "at least you have an entrée into—"

"Oh, bosh!" Vida exclaimed. "Either Curtis is covering this story or he isn't. Of course it's none of my business, but it makes good sense to give him his head, Emma."

I looked at Vida. "Or enough rope to hang himself?"

She bristled. "Certainly not. You seem to have confidence in him, or you wouldn't have assigned him the story in the first place." Vida turned away, studying some photos she'd received from one of the food syndicates she used on her page.

Leo shot me a knowing glance. I shrugged and went into my cubbyhole. Half an hour later, when I went back into the newsroom to refill my coffee mug, I realized that Curtis hadn't yet returned from his bakery run. Vida and Leo were both gone, off on their various rounds. I went into the front office to ask Ginny if she'd seen Curtis.

"Not since he left about eight-fifteen," she answered in a doleful voice. She sat up straight in her chair and pressed a hand to her back. "I don't remember hurting this much the other two times, at least not this early on."

"Can you take anything for it?" I asked.

Ginny shook her head. "I don't think it's a good idea. You never know how pills can hurt the baby."

I didn't argue. A lot of things had changed in obstetrical practice since I'd had Adam, thirty-odd years earlier. I made no further comment on the subject. "Did Curtis say if he was going anywhere except to the bakery?"

"No." Ginny shifted around in the chair and made some grunting noises. "Do you want him to see you when he gets back?"

"Yes. Please," I added and went back to my office.

Kip had come into the newsroom from the back shop. "What happened to the bakery stuff?" he asked, sounding disappointed. "Is the Upper Crust closed today?"

"The runner du jour hasn't run back with the goodies," I replied. "Curtis forgot, and he hasn't shown up since he went to the bakery. What do you make of him, Kip?"

"Too soon to tell," Kip replied and grinned. "He makes me feel old, though."

I smiled. Kip had started working for the paper in his early teens as a delivery boy. After he graduated from high school, he'd taken over the job of driving the weekly edition to the printer's in Monroe. Later, when I finally decided to enter the late twentieth century, he'd had enough computer savvy to manage the whole operation on-site. Now in his thirties and married with two small children, Kip had proved himself a reliable and knowledgeable employee. Some time ago I'd told him that if I ever sold the paper, he'd be at the top of my list as a potential buyer. It suddenly dawned on me that he might have seen the Cavanaugh offer as a threat to his own future as well as to mine.

"I hope you didn't spend the weekend worrying about the

Advocate being sold," I said. "As I told everybody last week, I've no intention of packing it in just yet. When I do, you'll be the first to know."

Kip grew somber. "Thanks. But you know how it is these days," he went on, stroking his neatly trimmed auburn goatee, a gesture that was a sign of anxiety. "These big whales swim around gobbling up all the little fish in the sea. They make offers that nobody can refuse."

"I never even asked what the offer would be," I assured him.

He nodded. "Maybe now it doesn't matter. If this Dylan Platte was the main man, the rest of them may be scared off."

I was slightly taken aback. "You think Dylan was murdered to prevent the acquisition of the paper?"

"Well . . . no," he finally said. "But what happened to him might change their minds, especially since . . ." He sighed. "Alpine can't have good memories for the Cavanaugh kids."

"I wouldn't think so," I agreed.

"Sorry." Kip looked embarrassed. "I mean, I didn't want to bring up what must be rough on you, too."

"My hide's thicker than it used to be," I said grimly. I needed no external stimuli to remember how Tom had died at my feet.

Kip looked as if he'd like to believe me. "It still seems like a bummer that those Cavanaughs wanted to buy the *Advocate*. Do you know if they own any other papers in Washington?"

"Platte told me Alpine was going to be their foothold in this part of the world."

Kip shrugged. "It doesn't seem right."

"How do you mean?"

He shrugged again. "I don't know exactly. It just . . . strikes me as . . . wrong." Kip gave me an uncertain smile. "Hard to understand people sometimes, isn't it?"

I laughed ruefully and shook my head. "You bet it is."

"I know I'm a small town boy," Kip said, "so I guess I don't understand people wanting to get richer and richer. How many fancy cars and big houses and expensive clothes and Swiss watches does anybody really need? You can only drive one car at a time and wear one shirt. It doesn't make sense to me."

"I suppose," I replied thoughtfully, "that it depends on how big the hole is inside the person. Everybody has one, and we tend to stuff it with whatever we think will fill it up—cars, houses, jewelry, food, booze, drugs, whatever. Of course it never works, because it's a spiritual void."

Kip looked at me as if he thought I, too, might be a little peculiar. "Oh—yeah, right," he said. Like Milo, Kip dealt only with what he could see and hear and touch.

An hour later, Curtis finally showed up, clutching a pink bakery bag. "Better late than never," he announced in the breezy manner that was beginning to irritate me. "I got it all—glazed doughnuts, cinnamon rolls, three kinds of Danish."

Vida was still gone, but Leo had returned and Ginny was making more coffee.

"No elephant ears?" Ginny said in a disappointed voice. "I don't know why, but I've had a craving for elephant ears this whole pregnancy."

Curtis cocked his head to one side. "Maybe your kid's going to be the size of an elephant. Better watch it. Doc Louie might need a crane to deliver him."

"His name is *Dewey*," Ginny snapped. "If you must know, I'm very careful about my diet. But sometimes I have these natural cravings, which must mean I'm lacking something in my regular foods." Ginny did a fairly good imitation of flouncing from the newsroom without bothering to check out the baked goods.

"Touchy, touchy," Curtis murmured. "Remind me never to get married."

Leo chuckled. "Getting married isn't the problem. Staying married is the hard part."

Curtis had left the bakery bag on the table without putting the items on the tray. I quickly did the task for him, handed Leo a blackberry Danish, and grabbed a glazed doughnut for myself. "Come into my office," I said to my new reporter.

"Sure." He followed me into the cubbyhole. "What's up?"

"That's my question," I said, sitting down at my desk. "What took you so long? Were you working on the Platte story?"

Curtis sprawled in one of my visitors' chairs. "I decided I might as well check the police log while I was out. Nothing big. The usual weekend traffic stuff and a couple of minor accidents."

"What about the homicide?"

"The sheriff was in a meeting," Curtis replied. "Guess he has a staff get-together on Mondays."

"That's news to me," I said. "Milo hates meetings." I leaned closer and fixed my eyes on Curtis. "What the hell were you doing for the past hour and a half?"

He winced. "How can I put it?" He paused and stared off into space. "I was getting my bearings. Finding my groove. You know—trying to get a feel for this place. It's pretty weird, this small town atmosphere. I need some time to make it real."

"It *is* real," I retorted. "Get a grip, Curtis. You've got a murder story to cover, and we've got a deadline tomorrow afternoon. Forget acclimating and do the job."

Curtis looked offended. "That's what I'm saying. I can't do the job unless I feel as if I'm part of this town. It's like . . . culture shock. A time warp. You know what I mean, like how in old movies everything looks grainy and not quite in focus. I have to adjust."

It was useless to argue the obvious with him. "Okay," I said, trying not to sound as aggravated as I felt, "how's the story shaping up?"

Curtis held up his hands as if he were measuring something. "A stranger comes to town. Wise in the ways of the big city's mean streets. But he's out of his element. The forest, the mountains, the rivers—to him they seem menacing. But he has a goal, a plan, an offer to make that can't be refused. And then Fate steps—"

"Whoa!" I cried, waving a hand to shut him up. "Are you writing a movie treatment or a news story? Skip the useless crap and give me the facts you've got so far."

Curtis frowned. "That's what I was doing. You got something against creativity?"

"Yes." I nodded vigorously. "Don't they teach you how to write a who-what-when-where-why-and-how story anymore in journalism school?"

"I told you," Curtis said doggedly, "readers don't want that tired old stuff. They want excitement, entertainment. TV has made them eyewitnesses to events. Newspaper reporters have to make it personal to make it real."

"Not our readers," I said. "Not *my* readers. Come on, let's hear what you *know*."

Curtis looked pained, as if I'd asked him to give me one of his kidneys. "Dylan Platte, thirty-five, of San Francisco, California, was shot and killed sometime between noon and five o'clock last Friday afternoon at the Tall Timber Motel. Details aren't available until Sheriff Milo Dodge gets the results from the Snohomish County medical examiner's office. Platte was reportedly in Alpine on business and was making an offer to buy *The Alpine Advocate* from editor and publisher Emma Lord."

I waited. But Curtis didn't say another word. "And?" I finally coaxed.

"And?" He looked puzzled.

"I knew that Friday night," I said calmly. "What did you find out over the weekend?"

Curtis wouldn't meet my gaze. "I told you—I got a feel for the story. I talked to Dodge, but he didn't have much to say. I went to the motel and looked around. You know, to see the setting."

I nodded. "Did you talk to the Harrises?"

"The owners?" Curtis finally looked at me again. "Just Mrs. Harris. Her husband was at the other motel. But she didn't want to say anything because she had guests checking out. Trying not to let on what happened, I guess. Bad for business."

"What about Graham?" I asked.

Curtis's expression was blank. "Graham?"

"Graham Cavanaugh," I said, trying to be patient. "Kelsey Platte's brother. Dylan's brother-in-law." I considered making shadow puppets to better explain the connection but decided a family tree would be more appropriate. "Tom Cavanaugh's children are Kelsey and Graham. Dylan is married to Kelsey. Graham's wife is Sophia. Graham was scheduled to arrive in Alpine yesterday. Did you try to contact Kelsey Platte at the ski lodge?"

"I called, but whoever answered told me Mrs. Platte wasn't taking calls or seeing visitors."

I didn't know whether or not to tell Curtis that I'd managed to meet with Kelsey. I didn't want to rub it in for fear of ruining whatever now seemed to be his slim chances of covering the story. On the other hand, he had to learn that reporters can't take no for an answer.

I was still mulling when Vida burst into the newsroom and headed straight for my office, oblivious to the one-on-one talk I was having with Curtis.

"You won't believe this," she announced in a trumpetlike tone. "My sister-in-law Ella has had a stroke. Or a fit. Or something." Vida leaned against the back of the vacant visitor's chair next to Curtis. "Her neighbor at Pines Villa, Myra Koenig, called me about an hour ago and said Ella had been taken to the hospital in an ambulance. I checked with the emergency room, and learned I couldn't do anything until Doc Dewey had seen her, so I decided to go to Pines Villa and have Myra let me in to gather up some things Ella needs if she stays in the hospital overnight, which I suspect she will." Vida paused for breath. "While I was there," she went on, "I went to Ginger and Josh Roth's unit. No one responded. I asked Myra if she knew them. You'll never guess what she said."

"What?" I asked after Vida paused for dramatic effect.

"That unit has been vacant for weeks. Ginger and Josh Roth apparently don't exist."

SEVEN

"WHAT DO YOU MEAN?" I DEMANDED. "I MET GINGER ROTH in this very office!"

"Yes, yes," Vida retorted. "But that doesn't mean she ever lived at Pines Villa. Or that her real name is Ginger Roth."

Curtis scrambled up from the chair. "I'll put my notes together," he murmured and dashed out of my cubbyhole.

I held my head. "Sit, Vida. Let me absorb this a little more slowly."

"There's nothing to absorb," she asserted. "You were tricked."

I thought back to the previous Wednesday, when the lovely Ginger had parked her shapely carcass in the same chair where Vida was now sitting. "It was a bit odd," I admitted. "She was doing research—supposedly—for a friend in Arizona who was working on an advanced journalism or communications degree. Ginger was quite vague, but in retrospect, it could've been an act. At the time, I was reminded of the beautiful but dumb blonde cliché from the movies."

"What if," Vida said with a frown of concentration, "she

was actually studying you and the newspaper operation for the Cavanaughs?"

"That makes sense," I agreed, "but why the subterfuge?"

"Why not? To find out what you're like. To survey the premises. To get the upper hand. These Californians are very sharp when it comes to business practices."

Vida's rationale made some sense. "Is that the unit where Scott and Tamara Chamoud lived before they moved?"

She nodded. "The last I heard, they thought they'd sublet it to a retired couple from Everett, but I don't know if the deal fell through. We should call Scott and ask him. If it was still vacant, there's no reason that these devious Californians couldn't have simply slipped a card with the names of Ginger and Josh Roth into the building's directory. It's right there by the main entrance."

I nodded. "I'll call Scott. Of course, just because these people never lived at Pines Villa doesn't mean they don't exist."

Vida rose from the chair. "True. But it all sounds rather theatrical to me. Hollywood, you might say."

"San Francisco," I pointed out. "That's the Cavanaugh family's base of operations."

Vida shrugged. "It's still California. I believe I'll call that woman in Everett who owns Pines Villa. I may have her name somewhere."

I had Scott's new number in my Rolodex. He and Tamara had found a rental house in Burien, just south of Seattle, where prices were somewhat lower than in the rest of the city. Tamara had signed a teaching contract at Highline Community College, and Scott was trying his hand at freelance photography, working out of their home.

Tamara—or Tammy, as Scott called her—answered on the third ring. "Emma!" she exclaimed. "How nice to hear from

you! Scott told me that someone had been killed over the weekend in Alpine. He saw a small article in *The Seattle Times'*
Northwest news wrap-up."

"Unfortunately," I said, "that's true. In fact, it's a long story.
Want to be bored?"

"Why not?" Tamara laughed. "I don't start teaching until
fall quarter, and that doesn't begin for almost three months.
I've been revising my lesson plans, and I'm already bored."

When I'd finished my account of the Dylan Platte homicide,
Tamara was aghast. "Those Cavanaugh kids wanted to buy
you out? That's dreadful! They sound like vultures."

"I only met them once," I said. "I didn't even know until
now that this Dylan Platte existed."

"Still . . ." Tamara paused. "I can't wait to tell Scott. He's
out taking some pictures for his portfolio. It was raining a little when we got up, but it's clearing off now. How's your new
reporter working out?"

"Let's say that it's early days," I replied reluctantly. "Let's
also say that I wish your husband were still working here."

"I get it," Tamara said. "Oh, Emma, I hope Scott can make
a go of his freelancing. Things are pretty tight these days.
Sometimes I wonder if we did the right thing."

"You'll be fine," I said encouragingly. "It takes time, and
Scott's a very good photographer." I had a sudden idea. "Have
him call Rolf Fisher at AP. Maybe he can give Scott some leads
or even buy a photo from him."

"Rolf Fisher? Isn't he the guy you've been seeing?"

"On and off," I replied but didn't add that, at the moment,
the relationship seemed more off than on. "I've got a question
for you—did you sublet your apartment?"

"No," Tamara answered, sounding a bit grim. "That's one
of the reasons we're in a financial hole. We're paying rent for

two places because our lease doesn't run out until October first. The couple who planned on retiring in Alpine changed their minds and decided to move to Ocean Shores. I guess they prefer waves to mountains. Do you know somebody who's interested?"

"Unfortunately, no," I said and then explained about Ginger and Josh Roth.

"That is so weird," Tamara declared. "I don't suppose they were like . . . squatters?"

"I suspect they never got inside the building. But Vida's going to check with the owner. Is it still that woman in Everett?"

"Mrs. Hines? Yes, as far as I know. Do you want her number?"

I said I thought Vida might have it but to give it to me just in case.

Vida not only had found Mrs. Hines's number but was talking to her on the phone when I came out of my cubbyhole after my chat with Tamara.

"Yes," she was saying into the receiver while showing me a scribbled note with the landlady's name, number, and address, "I'd very much enjoy a cup of tea. Shall we say three o'clock at the diner? Lovely. I'll see you then." Vida hung up and smiled triumphantly. "By chance," she said with her Cheshire cat grin, "Mrs. Hines is coming to Alpine this afternoon to consult with Dick Bourgette about the possibility of converting Pines Villa. She seemed quite intrigued when I told her about the Roths using the address as camouflage. I got the impression that she enjoys a mystery. We're having tea after her meeting with Dick." Vida became somber. "Of course I realize that I may be treading on Curtis's toes. I'd be the last person to interfere with his assignment."

I kept a straight face. "We don't know that there's any connection between Ginger and Josh Roth and the Platte homicide," I pointed out. "After all, you wanted to interview them for a new-comer feature."

Vida nodded once. "That's so."

"Then go ahead and talk to Mrs. Hines," I said and filled her in on my conversation with Tamara. Glancing at my watch, I saw that it was going on eleven. "I hope Curtis found out if Graham Cavanaugh arrived in town."

"Surely," Vida said, "Curtis can do at least that much in a single morning."

The sarcasm wasn't lost on me. But before I could comment, Ginny entered the newsroom carrying an envelope with the ski lodge logo. "Heather Bardeen Bavich sent this to you, Emma," she said. "Do you mind if I take a little extra time this noon? I want to go home and have a nap. I hardly slept a wink last night."

I hesitated. "Would you rather leave early? We don't have many front office visitors after four-thirty."

Ginny toyed with a long strand of her luxuriant red hair. "Well . . . if I can stay awake that long."

"Okay," I said. "Drink some more coffee."

"Caffeine isn't good for the baby," she said. "I'll just force myself to stay alert." Shoulders slumping, Ginny trudged out of the newsroom.

"Oh, for heaven's sakes!" Vida exclaimed after Ginny left. "Where's her gumption? She's worse this time than she was with the other two. And all this nonsense about what you can and can't eat! I'm very disappointed with Doc Dewey for giv-ing in to these current fads."

"I don't think they're all fads," I pointed out. "It's always better to err on the side of caution."

"Oh, piffle!" Vida yanked off her glasses and rubbed fiercely at her eyes, a sure sign that she was annoyed. I swear I could hear her eyeballs squeak. "Moderation is always wise.

But these days, the medical practitioners seem to have abandoned common sense."

I decided to forgo an argument. Opening the envelope from Heather, I saw a note and a small photograph. "Emma," the note read, "this is the only photo Mrs. Platte had. It was taken last winter at Lake Tahoe."

The wallet-size color picture showed a man and a woman in ski togs, posing under a snow-covered pine tree. There was no identification or date on the back. "Let me borrow your magnifying glass," I said to Vida. "This is allegedly Mr. and Mrs. Platte."

Vida got the magnifying glass out of a desk drawer. "Let me see when you're done," she said.

I peered at the photo. Kelsey was barely recognizable, probably because she was smiling and looked relatively animated. Her appearance was far different from that of the young woman I'd talked to at the ski lodge. The dark-haired man was also smiling. He appeared to be about six inches taller than his wife and could have qualified as handsome. "Here," I said, handing over the photo and the magnifying glass.

"A rather nice-looking couple," she said after a long pause. "A shame, of course. They look very happy here. But then you never know, do you?"

"No," I agreed as she handed the photo back to me. "I hope Kip can enlarge this and still keep it in sharp focus."

Back in my office, I called Heather at the ski lodge to thank her for sending the picture.

"No problem," she said. "Dad left me a note about it. I feel so sorry for Mrs. Platte. She seems totally out of it."

"Did her brother get in yesterday?" I asked.

"Yes," Heather replied. "Late last night. I haven't seen him yet. He's staying in the suite with Mrs. Platte."

"Did Graham's wife come with him?"

Heather paused. "I don't know. Carlos was working the front desk last night. You know—the cute guy from the college who wants to go into hotel management."

I didn't know Carlos. "Look," I said to Heather, "I know I'm prying, but that's my job. I'm also trying to be a hands-on boss with a new reporter. Has Curtis talked to Mrs. Platte or her brother?"

"Curtis?" Heather sounded puzzled. "Oh—the one who took Scott's place. Gosh, I'm sorry Scott moved away. He was real eye candy. Every time he came to the lodge all the girls started having the wildest fantasies!"

"Yes, Scott was a dream walking," I said, wondering if his replacement was going to become a nightmare. "But what about Curtis?"

"I'm not sure," Heather said. "I spent most of the morning in the office. Dad told me Ed Bronsky stopped in to see Mrs. Platte yesterday, but she refused to let him in. I guess Ed got all pissy about it."

"That sounds like Ed." I backtracked to my previous question. "Did Graham Cavanaugh register for two people?"

"I'll have to check. Can you hang on?"

"Sure." I was trying to be patient. In fact, I realized that if Alpine weren't a small town and I was calling a stranger who worked at a big city hotel I'd never get any personal information about guests. One of the benefits of life in SkyCo was that everybody knew everybody and had a tendency to band together against strangers.

"Yes," Heather said, sounding as pleased as if she'd found a pearl in one of the ski lodge's Quilcene oysters, "Mr. and Mrs. Graham Cavanaugh, and their home address is on Clay Street in San Francisco."

"Thanks, Heather," I said and plunged ahead. "Could you ask Graham to call me at the *Advocate*?"

"Sure. I'll put your request in his voice message box."

I thanked Heather again. I knew I was interfering with Curtis's assignment, but after all, Graham was Tom's son, my son's half brother. At least that was my excuse.

The phone rang soon as I'd hung up. Dustin Fong's polite voice was at the other end. "I've got some information for Curtis," he said, "but Sheriff Dodge thought I should let you know in case Curtis isn't in."

"He isn't," I responded. "Have you seen him today?"

"Yes," Dustin answered, "he was here a little before nine. I haven't seen him since, though."

"Go ahead," I said. "What's new?"

"We got the preliminary report back from the Everett ME," Dustin replied. "The victim was killed with two shots from a .38 caliber Smith and Wesson. One bullet severed a major artery near the heart, and the other went into his left lung. Death wasn't necessarily instantaneous."

"But no weapon was found at the scene, right?"

"Right. We may have the full report by the end of the day."

"Good," I said. "You'll let us know?"

"Sure." Dustin paused. "Should we call you or Curtis?"

"Either of us," I said, somewhat grudgingly. "By the way, was there any sign of a struggle?"

"No," the deputy answered. "The sheriff and Sam Heppner responded to the call from Mrs. Harris."

"You didn't see the crime scene for yourself?"

"No." Dustin sounded apologetic. "I've only seen the pictures Sam took. Nothing seemed to be disturbed in the unit, and as far as I know, the victim didn't have any marks on him except for the gunshot wounds. He was lying on the floor between the bed and the desk."

I tried to visualize the scene. I hadn't been in any of the Tall Timber rooms in years, but my recollection was that they were

standard fare—one or two double beds, desk with TV and telephone, a small table, two chairs, an open space for hanging
clothes, and the usual bathroom accommodations, with tub or
shower.

"Not much room to maneuver," I remarked.

"Pardon?" Dustin said.

"The lack of space in a typical motel room," I explained. "If
someone pulls a gun on you and your back is to the door,
where do you go?"

"Oh—I see what you mean." The deputy was probably
nodding. Of all the employees in the sheriff's office, Dustin had
the best people skills by far. "I'll let you—or Curtis—hear of
anything else we learn today," he added.

I thanked him and hung up. By the time I'd dashed off a
couple of brief page one stories about street resurfacing and
annual maintenance of the high school's football field, it was
time for lunch. Vida had already left, Leo was out on his
rounds, and Curtis was still AWOL. Maybe I was misjudging
him. I hoped so. Not only was his learning curve steep but it
could be perilous on his new assignment.

The sun had come out, so I decided to walk the six blocks
to Pie-In-The-Sky Café at the Alpine Mall. They had the best
sandwiches in town, although the Grocery Basket's deli featured an excellent tuna salad—but only on Fridays. As the
owner and my fellow parishioner, Jake O'Toole, put it in his
verbose, malapropian style, "Most discernible people only eat
the *fruits de mer* on Friday, Vatican dictums slackening the
rules for fasting and abstinence notwithholding."

I was walking by the sheriff's office when Doe Jameson, the
county's only female deputy, came out. "Ms. Lord," she called
to me, "got a minute?"

"Sure," I said. "I'm headed for the sandwich place. Want to
join me?"

Doe peered beyond me toward Alpine Way and the mall. I wondered if she were visualizing the display cases to figure out if she could resist temptation. A solid and also stolid young woman in her late twenties, Doe was part Native American and had a no-nonsense manner that bordered on being abrasive.

"No, thanks," she said, "but I'll walk to the mall with you. I have to buy some summer socks at Barton's Bootery."

We crossed at the corner of Second and Front, walking past the forest service and the post office. Doe didn't speak again until we'd almost reached the end of the block.

"I just took a call from the Associated Press in Seattle," she said. "Dodge had already left for lunch, so I had to field the questions." She shuddered. "I don't like doing that. I shouldn't be the official spokesperson for the sheriff's office."

"What questions?" I asked as we waited for a truckload of shingles to turn the corner from First to Front Street.

"About the Platte homicide," Doe replied. "Usually the Seattle media pays no attention to anything that happens up here. Oh, they might run a small story in one of the papers or even mention whatever is happening on the TV news, but they almost never contact us."

"Who called you?" I had a feeling that I already knew.

"His name is Fisher," Doe said, confirming my suspicion. "He mentioned that it might be a developing story for their wire service because it might involve the local weekly newspaper. He'd gotten a call from some organization that wanted information."

"Organization?" We'd reached Alpine Way, where we had to wait for one of the town's three stoplights. "Did he say which one?"

Doe frowned. "Washington State Newspaper Publishers . . . Alliance? Association? Assembly? It begins with an *A*."

"Association," I said. "I belong to it." We hurried across the street and turned up past Old Mill Park to the mall. "Gossip doesn't just travel fast in small towns," I murmured. "It invades every industry. Damn!"

Doe shot me a sidelong glance as we crossed Park Street. "Should I tell this Fisher to call you?"

"No!" I barked and immediately was remorseful. "Sorry." Seeing the surprise on Doe's usually stoic face, I tried to smile. "Cooperate with him. It's a legitimate story for the wire service. Somebody at the WNPA must have recognized Platte's name. I don't know how, but of course there'd be some interest in his murder, even if it's just insider stuff." I'd been talking too fast, trying not to expose my wrath at Rolf for going behind my back. Doe and I stopped at the mall's parking lot. "What did you tell . . . Fisher?" I almost gagged on his name.

"Just the facts we've given you," Doe replied, still looking put off by my outburst. "Won't he call you for the details?"

Trying to act nonchalant, I shrugged. "Maybe. All I can say is what I told Dodge. I wasn't interested in any offer, no matter how lucrative. And I never met the victim. As far as the sale of the *Advocate* is concerned, it's a nonstory."

"Okay," Doe said. "If he should call back, I'll send him to you."

"Sure." I hoped my expression was noncommittal.

We parted company then. She headed off to Barton's Bootery, and I went into Pie-In-The-Sky. The café was busy, and I had to stand in line. While I waited, I wondered if the sandwich menu listed gall on rye with a side of bitter almonds. That was what I'd like to send Rolf. Instead, when my turn came, I ordered the turkey breast on white bread with lettuce and mayo. I felt like a turkey. Maybe I looked like one, too.

Feeling sorry for myself, I walked back to Old Mill Park

and sat down at one of the vacant picnic tables. Several people of all ages were enjoying the warm day. A half-dozen young boys were kicking a soccer ball. An elderly couple holding hands were looking up at the statue of the town founder and former mill owner Carl Clemans. A trio of teenagers swooped up and down the recently installed skateboard ramp. There were a few loners like me, drinking coffee from plastic cups or eating their noon meals out of foam cartons or paper bags. An old woman tossed bread crusts at the robins and sparrows and cedar waxwings. Abruptly, the birds all scattered as a Steller's jay sailed out of a tall cedar, uttered its harsh, guttural cry, and claimed the bounty for its own.

I regarded the jay with a wary eye, but the bird was busy devouring the old woman's bread. Halfway through my sandwich, I saw a vaguely familiar figure walking toward me. It wasn't until he was about six feet away that I recognized Ed's real estate agent, Snorty Wenzel.

"Emma Lord," Snorty said in greeting. "I see you're enjoying the sunshine. Mind if I join you?"

"Go ahead," I said, even though I didn't mean it. "Have a seat."

Snorty sat down a couple of feet away from me on the wooden picnic table bench. He was a stocky man of indiscriminate age with a rather wizened face that would have suited an ex-prizefighter. His thinning hair appeared to be dyed, a curious color that I recalled from Adam's Crayola box as burnt sienna.

"Looks like Ed's had a little glitch in his real estate plans," Snorty remarked, opening his battered faux alligator briefcase and taking out what appeared to be a ham and cheese sandwich. "Not to worry, though. I've got people lined up to buy that drop-dead gorgeous villa." He took a big bite of his sandwich—and snorted. Twice.

"Great," I said, noticing that Snorty's round nose actually looked like a pig's snout. "So why is Ed threatening a lawsuit?"

Snorty chuckled. "Oh, you know Ed! Always figuring out the angles. Covering all the bases. Pretty shrewd, that's Ed."

I couldn't look Snorty in the eye. It was just as well because he'd taken another bite of his ham and cheese—and snorted a couple of more times. "Had you met Dylan Platte?" I asked, watching the jay fly off and perch atop the old mill building that now housed Alpine's museum.

"A couple of times," Snorty replied, still chewing lustily. "Played some golf with him just to get acquainted. I was supposed to meet him at the villa around seven Friday night. Fact is, I went there and he didn't show. Ed and Shirley and the kids were just finishing dinner." He paused to take a bag of Fritos out of his briefcase. Munch, crunch, snort. "Want some?" he asked, holding the bag out to me. I declined. "Anyways, Ed and Shirley asked me to come in. They were having what they call 'the dessert course.' Classy, that's Ed and Shirley. So we all tied in to these terrific Dairy Queen Blizzards." Snorty licked his lips. Unfortunately, he didn't lap up the bit of Frito on his chin. "Just after seven-thirty I called Platte's cell number," he continued. "No answer, so I phoned the motel office and Mrs. Harris gave me the gruesome news." Snorty shook his head. "I couldn't believe it. Neither could Ed and Shirley." He stopped speaking and reached again into his briefcase, this time removing a plastic bag filled with chocolate chip cookies that looked store-bought.

"Have you spoken to Platte's widow?" I inquired.

"No," Snorty replied with a cookie halfway to his mouth. "She's pretty upset, I heard." He shrugged. "Who knows? She may still want to buy the villa." He bit into the cookie. And snorted.

I'd finished my sandwich. "Good luck," I said, standing up and brushing some crumbs off my slacks. "I'd better get back to work."

"Me, too," Snorty said. "When I finish here." He saluted me before delving once more into his briefcase and coming up with a bottle of juice. As I walked away, I wondered if there was anything in that case besides food and drink. Clearly, Snorty and Ed were well-matched.

As I walked in front of the sheriff's office, I paused, wondering whether I should see if Milo was in. His Grand Cherokee was parked in its usual spot. I decided to pay him a visit.

Doe Jameson, apparently having completed her purchase of summer socks, was behind the counter, sipping from a bottle of cranberry juice. "Is Dodge available?" I asked.

Doe shook her head. "He's interrogating a suspect."

I was startled. "In the Platte case?"

"Yes." Her face remained expressionless.

"Who?"

Doe frowned. "I'm not sure I should say. Sorry."

"If," I pointed out, leaning my elbows on the counter, "the sheriff is questioning someone, it's official. Therefore, you can give me the name."

Before Doe could respond, Jack Mullins appeared from the corridor that led to the restrooms. "Hey, how's Lois Lane today? Waiting for the mild-mannered sheriff to change his clothes in a phone booth and turn into Superdude?"

"Milo's not exactly mild-mannered," I pointed out. "I'm trying to get the name of his suspect out of Deputy Jameson, but she enjoys a secret."

Jack put an arm around Doe's broad shoulders. She winced but didn't move. "Hey, Doe," Jack coaxed, "give this newspaper lady a break. Tell her who Dodge has on the hot seat."

Doe looked uncertain. "Are you sure?"

Jack removed his arm and nodded. "You bet." He hesitated, staring at me. "Or is this a test? I thought your cub reporter, Jimmy Olsen, was covering the Platte case."

"He is—allegedly," I replied in a weary voice. "But he's still operating with training wheels."

Jack nodded once. "Okay." He turned back to Doe. "Out with it, darlin'."

Doe winced again but looked me straight in the eye. "We shouldn't say this is a suspect so early on in the investigation." Even though there were only the three of us in the front part of the office, she lowered her husky voice. "His name is Dylan Platte."

EIGHT

MY FIRST THOUGHT WAS THAT MY HEARING HAD GONE. But I could tell from Jack's puckish expression and Doe's somber face that I'd heard the name correctly.

"Okay," I said at last, trying to unscramble my brain, "either there are two Dylan Plattes or the victim was somebody else."

"You're a genius," Jack declared, his eyes twinkling and his tone droll. "I picked this guy up for speeding just this side of the county line. California driver's license. The photo matched the speeder. Imagine my surprise!"

"Hold on," I said, wanting to make sure I understood. "Didn't the victim have a California driver's license, too?"

"Oh, yeah," Jack replied. "But those things are easy to forge. In fact, I think there's someplace on the Internet that can make up one for you if you want to be somebody else for a change. You know those Californians—they're like chameleons, always wanting to try on a different skin."

I was still confused. "So how do you know which one is the real Platte and which one is the phony?"

"That's what Dodge is trying to find out now," Jack said. "If we have to, we can run their fingerprints through the database and hope that at least one of them is a match."

"What," I asked, "did this Dylan have to say for himself when you pulled him over?"

"Not much," Jack answered. "He agreed that he'd been speeding but said it was a habit he'd acquired driving Highway 1 in California, which, I guess, is even trickier than Highway 2 up here."

My next question was so obvious that I wondered why I hadn't yet asked it: "Can't Kelsey Platte come down to identify her husband?"

Jack made a face. "We couldn't get her to make a positive ID on the victim. She absolutely refused. We want her brother to do it, but so far he hasn't showed. What's his name? Graham?"

"Yes." I rubbed at my forehead. "This is all very weird. I don't know what to make of it, let alone print in the *Advocate*."

Doe nodded. "It's the strangest case I've been on. It makes me wonder if this Kelsey woman is really Kelsey."

"True enough," I agreed. "But now you'll have to get one of those Cavanaughs in here."

Jack made a disgusted noise. "Oh, sure. But how will we know if they're lying their heads off?"

"You can sort through all that," I said. "What bothers me is why these people seem to be impersonating each other. Or whatever they're doing." I recounted Josh and Ginger Roth's apparent subterfuge. "I'm assuming there's a connection between that pair—if they ever were a pair—and this other bunch. It can't be a coincidence."

An older man I vaguely recognized entered the sheriff's headquarters and held up his hands. "I surrender. I've just killed a mama black bear."

Doe looked crushed. Jack swore quietly. "Oh, man. How the hell did you do that, Gus?" he asked the newcomer.

"With my .30-.30 Winchester," the man called Gus replied. "I only meant to scare her off, but she came at me. No bluff, like they do sometimes. I saw the two cubs afterwards. Do whatever you need to do. I feel like crap."

Jack sighed. "Come on around here, sit down, fill out some forms. Jeez, Gus, that's rough."

"What about those cubs?" Gus said. "That's what really gets me. They probably haven't learned what to eat or how to find a den."

Jack had led the shooter to the far end of the counter. Doe's dark eyes followed the two men. She seemed on the verge of tears. "I can't believe," she said to me, "that the state licenses five hundred permits every year to hunters for certain parts of the state where they can kill those bears in the spring. It doesn't seem right."

"I suppose the numbers have to be thinned in certain areas or the animals will starve," I said, feeling a bit sorry for the dead bear, the cubs—and Gus. The irony didn't escape me, however. No one in town had seemed unduly disturbed by Dylan Platte's death. *If* he were Dylan Platte. But whoever the murdered man was, he hadn't lived in Alpine. Strangers didn't seem to count. Local bears did.

I turned as another newcomer arrived. To my surprise, it was Curtis Mayne. He looked equally surprised to see me.

"Whoa!" Curtis exclaimed and grinned. "Did I just flunk the trust test with my employer?"

I smiled wanly. "This is more of a social call," I lied. "I was coming back from lunch." *Why,* I asked myself, *do I feel a need to make excuses to Curtis?* "In fact," I went on, though with reluctance, "I was about to go back to the office. Jack and Doe have some news for you."

"All *right*!" Curtis's grin grew even wider. "Start dishing," he said to Doe, who looked wary.

I left. It wasn't easy, but I had to force myself to keep some distance and allow Curtis to justify my hiring of him. By the time I got back to the newsroom, Vida was hanging up the phone.

"Ella is doing as well as can be expected," she announced. "I'll drop in to see her at the hospital after work." Vida peered at me through her big glasses. "What's wrong? You look like a pickle."

"I'm trying to figure out if *we're* in a pickle," I replied, leaning on her desk as I regaled her with what was going on at the sheriff's headquarters.

"Well now," she said, taking in the tale of two Dylans far more calmly than I'd expected, "that's most intriguing. And you just walked away. My, my!"

"What else could I do? It's Curtis's story, and he actually showed up. Besides," I added, "I didn't know how long Milo was going to interview this second Dylan. We've got a front page to fill before tomorrow's deadline."

"And I still have to do 'Scene Around Town,' " Vida said, frowning. "I've been very lax about my snippets of town gossip this week. Surely you have something for me?"

Off the top of my head, all I could think of was the local gathering in Old Mill Park that I'd seen while eating lunch. Unfortunately, although I'd recognized several of the people by sight, I wasn't sure of their full names. "Oh," I said suddenly, "Gus Somebody-or-Other just shot a bear."

"Really?" Vida tapped her pencil on the desk. "That's probably a brief article. "Gus who? Gus Lindquist from the A-frame off Disappointment Avenue?"

I grimaced. "I think so. I'll check with Jack Mullins."

Back in my cubbyhole, I called the deputy before I forgot about the incident. My brain seemed to be operating on overload. All those questions of who really was who weighed me down.

Lori was back on duty and transferred me immediately to Jack. "No charges filed against Gus Lindquist," he said. "Self-defense. Gus insisted on seeing what he can do about those cubs. If he can find them, I figure they'll be his new family pets."

"That's a story in itself," I remarked. "Thanks, Jack."

"That it?"

"Ah . . . yes." I grimaced as I exerted supreme self-control.

"You sure?"

I caught the taunting note in Jack's voice and sighed. "I have to let Curtis try his hand at a big story. I'm not thrilled about his performance so far, but backing off is the only way I can show any faith in his ability."

"You're the boss," Jack said.

"Is Curtis still at headquarters?" I inquired.

"He's talking to Dodge even as we speak," Jack replied.

I shut my eyes tight, battling with the urge to ask if Dylan Platte II was still there, too. "Okay. I'll talk to Curtis when he comes back."

I hung up just as Vida left the newsroom. Leo came in a couple of minutes later, looking worried and heading straight into my cubbyhole. "I just ran into Dick Bourgette," he said, standing in front of my desk. "He's a stand-up guy, isn't he?"

"Yes," I replied, regarding my ad manager with curiosity. "The whole family is first-rate. Why do you ask? Is it something to do with our roof project?"

"No." Leo hesitated, his weathered face still etched with concern. "We got to talking in front of the post office, and he mentioned that he was going to the Tall Timber Motel to see Minnie and Mel Harris about doing some repairs on the room where Platte was shot. Dick and one of his sons did quite a bit of work on the motel in the off-season."

I nodded. "I remember. The usual wear and tear after the tourists leave."

"Right. Anyway, he let something slip about 'you go to see a fellow in his prime, and then he's dead.' I asked what he meant, and Dick got flustered and tried to make a joke of it. It bothered me. That's not like him."

I was puzzled, too. "The only thing I can think of is Dick told me something about dropping by the motel to drop off a business card in case the Plattes wanted to renovate the Bronsky house."

"So why get flustered?" Leo shook his head. "Don't think I'm suspicious of Bourgette. I'm not, as far as Platte's murder is concerned, but his attitude was damned odd. Did he see something or somebody he doesn't want to mention?"

"Maybe he saw Platte," I said. "But Platte may not be Platte."

"What?"

I explained what I'd learned at the sheriff's office. Leo looked bemused. "I suppose everybody's blaming all the evils of the world on us poor Californians."

I smiled grimly. "It's part of the locals' birthright around here."

Beyond Leo, I saw Curtis enter the newsroom. He had an iPod in his ear and was doing a little dance step as he approached his desk.

"Here's the once and future reporter now," I murmured. "I'd better talk to him."

"I'll eavesdrop," Leo said, leading the way out of my cubbyhole.

Curtis saw me and yanked the iPod plug from his ear. "Truth or dare?" he said, looking pleased with himself.

"Truth is good," I said. "It's what journalists always seek."

"Aha!" Curtis grinned. "But one person's truth may not be another person's, right?"

"Curtis . . ." I leaned a hand on the edge of his desk. "Just say it."

"Two dudes named Dylan Platte—or so it seems." Curtis paused, obviously enjoying his little game. "One dead, one alive. The wizards in Sacramento stared into Dumbledore's Mirror of Erised and saw the real Dylan behind Door Number Two. Driver's license picture matches the guy who was flying his broomstick over the speed limit."

"You read Harry Potter," I remarked, slightly surprised that anyone under fifty read anything resembling a real book.

Curtis shrugged. "I've seen the movies," he said, bursting my bubble. "Anyway, the guy on the slab is now a John Doe."

"What about Mrs. Platte?" I asked.

"She's thrilled to pieces," Curtis replied, "and can't wait for the resurrected Mr. Platte to join her in making big whoop-de-do in her fancy suite."

"Kelsey hasn't come down from the lodge?" I asked in surprise.

Curtis shook his head. "I imagine she's tossing rose petals all over the marital bed, awaiting his arrival."

"What about Graham?" I inquired.

"Graham?" Curtis looked blank. "Oh—the brother? No clue. I'll interview all of them, of course," he added hastily. "They need time to absorb the shock."

Leo was sitting at his desk, shaking his head. "Why," he muttered, "do I think I'm too old for all this?"

"Don't feel bad," I said. "I can't figure out this bunch, either. You'd think Kelsey would rush right into Dylan's arms." I had a sudden thought. "The picture . . . let me take another look." I scurried over to the back-shop door and called to Kip, asking him to give me the photo of Kelsey and Dylan at Lake Tahoe.

"Did you see this allegedly real Dylan?" I asked Curtis, showing him the picture.

"Just a glimpse," Curtis said. "Not up close. He was going from the interrogation room to the men's can down the hall."

"So you didn't talk to him?"

"Not yet. I will," my reporter responded, on the defensive.

"ASAP," I insisted. "Kelsey and Graham, too, and Mrs. Graham—that is, Sophia Cavanaugh. Now."

"Hey," Curtis said, looking offended, "I have to give them all some time. I'm not a ghoul."

"This isn't being a ghoul," I pointed out. "They should be elated, and therefore talkative. Get your butt up to the ski lodge, okay?"

Curtis sighed. "Sure, sure, I'm on my way." He stalked out of the newsroom.

Leo was lighting a cigarette. "You shouldn't have to kick his ass to get him to cover this kind of story."

"You think I don't know that?" I glanced at Vida's empty desk. "Now where did *she* go?"

"I saw her on my way in," Leo answered after expelling a couple of smoke rings. "She had an interview with somebody at the retirement home, and then she was meeting a woman from Everett named . . . Hines? Yeah, Hines about Pines Villa, that's it."

"I forgot," I admitted. "Vida's trying to find out about Josh and Ginger Roth, who claimed to be living at Pines Villa, which this Mrs. Hines now owns."

Leo held up his hands. "Don't tell me anything more."

My phone rang. I hurried back into my office and picked up the receiver.

"Caught your killer yet?" my brother asked.

I sank into my chair. "No. Where are you?"

"In my temporary office at my temporary Cleveland parish where I'm serving temporarily," he replied. "It's after five here, and I'm about to wrap it up for the day. What's happening in one of my former temporary parishes?"

Ben was referring to his six-month posting at St. Mildred's in Alpine a couple of years back, when he'd filled in for Dennis Kelly, who had gone on sabbatical. "It's so confusing that I'm not sure I can explain it to you," I said.

"Then don't," Ben said. "Send me an e-mail when you get it sorted out. No arrests, I gather?"

"No."

"Did you talk to Adam?"

"No."

"You didn't?" Ben sounded surprised. "How come?"

"It was less awkward to e-mail him," I replied.

"And?"

I hesitated. "He didn't sound exactly concerned about his mother's predicament."

"Ouch! I hear the wounding of maternal pride."

"Yes, you do."

"Hey, give the kid a break," Ben said. "You've never walked in his mukluks. Can you imagine what it's like to live in such a remote part of the world and just try to keep your head straight? Hell, I remember when you first moved to Alpine. You made it sound as if you were living on Saturn. Bitch, bitch, bitch, that's what you did for the first year or two. A small town eighty-odd miles from a big city isn't Siberia. And by the way, Adam's got a flock to tend, and not just minister to their spiritual needs."

My brother was raising my hackles. He'd had plenty of practice over the past half century. "Does that mean he has to forget he's got a mother?"

"Of course not." Ben sounded exasperated. "It means he has priorities. You're not at death's door, you've got a roof over your head, you're fully employed, and whatever's going on with Tom's kids may be a pain in the ass, but in the long run it's not going to ruin your life. Maybe you're feeling guilty because you never had a chance to be a stepmother to these poor misguided wretches. If so, that's stupid. It's not your fault that you and Tom didn't get married."

"I don't feel anything toward this Cavanaugh bunch," I declared.

Ben chuckled. "Maybe that's the problem. They're orphans. They're pitiful. That upsets you because, whatever else they may be, they're an extension of Tom."

I looked up to see Leo going out of the office. He'd probably overheard part of the conversation and felt a need to make himself scarce. At least Leo knew the Cavanaugh family. Maybe Ben had sunk his teeth into a kernel of truth.

I sighed. "Look," I said, "I really don't want to argue with you. I've got a paper to put out. Will you be around this evening?"

"After the parish council meeting," Ben replied. "I should be done about six, six-thirty your time."

"I'll call you at the rectory, okay?"

"Probably," Ben replied, "unless I'm temporarily out."

"Right." I hung up.

I sat staring at the computer monitor, trying to put some passion into my editorial on resurfacing Railroad Avenue. The street paralleled the train tracks and ran in back of the *Advocate* office. We used it only for loading the newspapers and for large deliveries. Except for the one remaining mill west of the Sky River bridge, most of the industry—a relative term—covered the nine blocks from Alpine Way to the Icicle Creek Road. These businesses included a couple of small warehouses, all the public utilities, a used car lot, a trucking facility, a public storage building, and the department of motor vehicles. Heavy loads and hard weather chewed up the road almost on an annual basis. The potholes and ruts were three years old, due to lack of funds. A cardinal rule for editorial writing was to make people care by enflaming enough passion to goad them into action. The problem was that I didn't care. Living at the edge of the forest forced me to accept the occasional bump or dip or crack or washout. I seldom drove on Railroad Avenue. If Fuzzy Baugh had any spare cash in his wall safe—which he kept behind a much-retouched portrait of himself in city hall—it could be put to better use.

Off the top of my head, I couldn't think of a worthy project. I still felt overwhelmed by the events of the past few days. Then inspiration struck: Why not let our readers tell us where they wanted their tax dollars spent?

I was off the hook, tapping out two hundred and fifty words to fill the editorial space and fudging a bit by listing general topics, such as education, parks, tourism, and sidewalks.

Relieved of my weekly burden, I got out a magnifying glass and studied the photo of Kelsey and Dylan Platte. Not that it did me much good. The smiling young woman didn't bear much resemblance to the hapless wraith I'd visited at the ski lodge. I'd never met either of the men who'd claimed to be Dylan Platte, so there was no basis for comparison.

I went into the back shop and asked Kip if he could enlarge the photo.

"I was going to do that a little later," he said, "but if you need it, I'll do it now."

"Thanks," I said. "I want to show it to Milo."

Twenty minutes later, Kip brought me an eight-by-ten blowup of the wallet-size picture. It was a little fuzzy but revealed much more of the details, such as hair color and maybe the eyes. I was heading through the newsroom when Vida and a woman I'd never seen before came in.

"Ah!" Vida exclaimed with her toothy smile. "How nice! You're here. This is Diana Hines."

Diana, a petite and pretty woman about my age, held out her hand. "So you're Emma Lord," she said with enthusiasm. "I read your paper whenever I get a chance. It's a welcome relief to see newspaper headlines that aren't full of war and terror and scandal."

"Unfortunately," I said, shaking her hand, "we do have some crime around here. I understand you own Pines Villa apartments. It's just a couple of blocks from my house."

"Really?" The remark seemed to please her. "I inherited the building from my uncle, Harry Sigurdson, a couple of years ago. He owned quite a bit of property in Skykomish County, though you'd never have known it to see him."

"No," Vida agreed pleasantly. "Harry was rather close with his money." Her smile became brittle as she glanced at me. "You may recall, Emma, that he always wore overalls and a favorite straw hat."

Vida herself was wearing straw, with a big turned-up brim and voluptuous yellow roses. I translated her description of Harry as meaning dirty old clothes and beat-up headgear that looked as if a hungry goat had chewed on the straw.

Diana laughed merrily. "Oh, Uncle Harry was a true character! He didn't drive, you know. He'd had an old Model A Ford before the Second World War, and he kept that car going for almost forty years. I remember it—holes in the floor and the seats so worn you couldn't sit comfortably and always breaking down on the highway. I was just a little girl, but I thought it was great fun. After the car finally gave out for good, he never bought another one. He walked everywhere, even as far as Sultan and sometimes Monroe. None of us knew how much money he had until after he died. We were flabbergasted."

It was obvious that Vida wanted me to have a sit-down with Diana Hines. I invited her to come into my office. Naturally, Vida came along.

When we were all seated, I offered coffee, but Diana shook her head. "Mrs. Runkel and I just finished having tea. She told me the most fascinating story about someone who pretended to be living at Pines Villa. I couldn't believe it."

"It's very odd," I agreed. "What we want to know is who they are and why they did it."

Diana nodded. "I stopped at Pines Villa before I met Mrs. Runkel. When I checked on the unit, it was empty with no sign of life. The former tenant worked for you, I understand. I was so afraid we might have had squatters. It happens, you know."

"You can't be too careful," Vida said darkly.

Diana nodded. "That's so true. It's why," she went on, growing very serious, "my husband, Murray, and I've decided it might be smart to convert the apartments into condos."

Vida couldn't keep her disapproval to herself. "As I told you earlier, I don't think that's a good idea. In Everett, maybe, but not in Alpine. Our residents simply aren't the condo type."

Diana's expression was sympathetic. "I think I know what you mean," she said quietly, "but what *is* a condo type? There's really no such thing as a . . . single category." Vida opened her mouth to say something, but Diana kept talking. "People who buy condos are old, young, middle-aged, married, single, and usually without young children. They don't want to take on the upkeep of a home or a garden. If they own a house, they're better off financially buying a condo. While we were having tea, you mentioned how much you enjoy gardening but that sometimes it's difficult to keep everything under control, especially in the spring." Vida again started to say something, but Diana wasn't finished. "I can see you're a high-energy person. I'll bet you can work circles around people half your age. But you must know plenty of folks in your peer group who aren't as vigorous or conscientious. Take your sister-in-law Mrs. Hinshaw for example. When she recovers from her stroke, she'd be so much better off in her own condo than in a rented apartment."

Vida finally managed to break in, her voice gloomy. "If she survives."

Diana laughed softly. "Oh, Mrs. Runkel, if she spends time with you, I'll bet she has some spunk!"

"I don't know about that," Vida said skeptically.

"The thing is," Diana continued, "my husband's health isn't as good as it might be. Murray had to take early retirement. I'm the one who's had to do the actual managing of Pines Villa during the past year. We've got two grandchildren now, and in the long run, it'd be better for us if we renovated and expanded exclusively for condos. Frankly, the drive from Everett to Alpine can be nerve-racking, especially in bad weather."

"Why don't you move here?" Vida asked.

"Oh, no!" Diana exclaimed, wide-eyed. "Our two daughters and the grandchildren live so close to us now. I couldn't possibly move." She laughed again. "I was born to be a grandma."

"Grandchildren are a joy," Vida declared. "Though," she added, "only one of mine lives in Alpine, and he's so busy these days finding a summer job." She sighed heavily and pushed the straw hat back farther on her gray curls. "Roger's going through a difficult time, trying to decide on his major."

In my opinion, the spoiled brat's major was to avoid working. I often wondered if his role model was Ed Bronsky. But I kept my mouth shut.

Diana was nodding. "Youngsters these days face difficult challenges. Housing, of course, is one of them."

Vida's gray eyebrows lifted. "Housing? Roger lives at home with his parents."

"I meant in general," Diana said, looking faintly apologetic. "Traditional family dwellings have become so expensive, particularly in the Greater Seattle area. That means most young couples have to move farther away from their workplace, and those commutes are very time-consuming as well as stressful."

I finally decided to stop playing my frequent role as Vida's stooge. "We understand that shift. Monroe, even Sultan and Gold Bar and Startup have had an influx of people fleeing the high prices in and around Seattle."

Vida nodded. "Very wise of them to do so, but that doesn't mean they wouldn't prefer a single dwelling with some property to a boxlike condominium or even one of those so-called town houses. So confining, I think, and not enough room to swing a cat."

Diana's expression was neutral. "There is an interesting new factor. I'm referring to the person who works for a big company but stays home. This means that very soon Alpine should expect some kind of population boom. That's another reason why Murray and I want to convert Pines Villa."

Vida looked mulish. "If that happens, it'll come very slowly. Not," she added hastily, "that Alpine isn't a wonderful place to live."

Diana smiled at Vida. "My point exactly. You'd be surprised at how many people around the area have inquired about buying a condo."

"Yes," Vida said, unconvinced, "I certainly would. I suppose you can name names?"

Diana nodded. "One of your county commissioners, Alfred Cobb, and his wife, Bertha."

"Hunh. Alfred is senile and Bertha is only a step behind him."

Diana wasn't daunted. "Edna Mae Dalrymple, the librarian."

"She's extremely dizzy," Vida asserted. "Apparently her eyes have gone from reading so many books. Her garden is a disaster."

Still unfazed, Diana rapidly ticked off the names of other would-be condo buyers on her slim fingers. "Derek and Blythe Norman, Marisa Foxx, Buck Bardeen, Rosemary—"

Vida lurched forward in her chair. "*What?*"

I tried to maintain an impassive expression, as Diana responded. "Buck Bardeen, a retired air force colonel who owns a small house in—"

"I know," Vida barked. "Buck is . . . a good friend. He certainly never told me anything about wanting to buy a condo. This is most unlikely."

"Goodness!" Diana exclaimed. "I didn't mean to upset you, Mrs. Runkel. I feel terrible."

"Never mind," Vida said brusquely. "Excuse me," she added, getting up from the chair. "I must make some phone calls before the workday is done."

Diana didn't watch Vida stalk out of my office, but kept her eyes cast down on her lap. "I am so sorry," she said softly.

"Don't worry about it," I advised, lowering my voice. "Mrs. Runkel doesn't like change." I didn't dare say much more, given Vida's acute hearing. "I assume," I said, in my normal tone, "that no one at Pines Villa knows anything about the mystifying Josh and Ginger Roth."

"No." Diana remained apologetic. "I asked some of the tenants who were at home today if they'd heard of them." She shook her head. "I'm afraid I've made a bit of a mess out of this meeting."

"It's not your fault," I assured her. "The fact that Josh and Ginger Roth clearly don't want to be found could mean that they don't exist."

Diana sighed. "It's way out of my league." Her hazel eyes roamed around my cubbyhole. "I suppose I should start back to Everett. The commuters will be on the road by now."

"I think we sent you on a fool's errand," I said as we both stood up.

"Oh, no." She smiled, but not as brightly as before. "When I heard about Mrs. Hinshaw's stroke, I wanted to talk to Debbie Murchison, who lives next door. You probably know Debbie—she's a nurse at the hospital here."

I nodded as we strolled out of my office. "I've run into her a few times."

"Unfortunately," Diana explained, "Debbie took a long weekend to visit a young man she's been seeing who lives in Mount Vernon. She isn't expected back until this evening. But she's working tomorrow, so she'll find out about Mrs. Hinshaw. I'd like to have her keep an eye on the poor lady when she gets home."

"That's very thoughtful of you," I said, noting that Vida was on the phone but her eagle eyes flicked in our direction as we passed her desk.

I walked Diana to the front entrance and waved her off. She hadn't been able to shed any light on the Roth puzzle, but there was an interesting story in her proposal for condo conversion of Pines Villa. I'd save it for next week, after I talked to some of the people who'd expressed an interest in changing lifestyles. I'd even risk facing Vida's wrath by calling Buck Bardeen.

I didn't realize that it was what Diana Hines hadn't been able to tell me was a piece of our homicidal puzzle. I wouldn't find out why until it was almost too late.

NINE

CURTIS AMBLED INTO THE NEWSROOM JUST AFTER FOUR-thirty. "You still got that picture of Dylan Platte?" he asked, leaning in the doorway to my office.

"Kip took it back," I said. "He blew it up."

"He might as well," Curtis said. "That's not the dead guy. Mrs. Platte wants the original."

"You mean," I said, "there's no doubt that the real Dylan Platte is the one who got picked up for speeding?"

Curtis looked annoyed. "Didn't I say so earlier?"

"Yes," I agreed, "but you must attribute that statement to the Sacramento DMV. This is a very touchy story, and we don't want to take the fall in case somebody else has made a mistake."

"I know, I know," Curtis said impatiently. "You think I want to get sued?"

"Of course not." I tried to be pleasant. "Any idea who the victim really is?"

Curtis shook his head. "The only ID he had on him was the driver's license and a couple of phony credit cards in Platte's name. The vic—I pick up cop talk real fast—used the credit cards for the motel and the car rental at Sea-Tac Airport."

"But not for his flight?"

My reporter shook his head again. "Dodge or whoever is going to check flights out of the Bay Area that came into Sea-Tac just before the car was rented."

"Maybe the dead man didn't come from there," I suggested.

Curtis shrugged. "Dodge is sending the airlines a photo of the Mystery Man. Kind of grim, isn't it? I mean, since he's dead."

"That can't be helped," I pointed out. "I wonder if we should run it?"

"Won't the readers get all squeamish and complain?"

"Maybe," I said, "but it's possible that somebody around here knows him or at least has seen him—besides the Harrises at the motel."

"Oh—I don't know." Curtis scratched his cheek. "It seems gruesome to me."

"Murder is pretty gruesome," I remarked. "We can run the pix on page three. Kip can give you the original. Are you going to see Mrs. Platte, or have you already interviewed her?"

"She didn't come down to the station," Curtis replied. "I talked to her brother, Grant, for a couple of minutes."

"*Graham.* Graham Cavanaugh." I paused to let my irritation seep into my reporter's foggy brain. "What kind of quotes did you get?"

"He didn't have much to say, except that he'd never seen the dead guy before in his life. Hey," Curtis went on, gesturing with his thumb, "I should sort through my notes and get out of here. It's going on five."

"Whoa." I motioned for him to come closer. He took a couple of reluctant steps and fidgeted with a loose button on his shirt. "How did Graham explain why Kelsey didn't know that her husband was alive and well and driving too fast on Highway 2?"

Curtis looked peeved. "He didn't. He told me his sister was a real ditz. She's lucky to know where *she* is, let alone anybody else."

I pressed my lips together. "Fine. Go sort your notes."

Curtis sauntered off. I shut down my computer, grabbed my purse and yellow cardigan, and hurried out through the newsroom. Curtis was slouched behind his desk; Vida was on the phone again; Leo was heading to the back shop.

"I'm gone for the day," I announced over my shoulder.

Vida's head snapped up. "What?" she called, putting her hand over the phone's mouthpiece.

I kept moving, my hiring of Curtis Mayne gnawing at my brain. How in the hell had he ever gotten out of the University of Washington? I wondered. Had standards fallen *that* far? Or was he smart enough but just plain lazy and unmotivated? By the time I reached the sheriff's office, I'd worked up a full head of steam.

"Where's Dodge?" I demanded.

"Oooh!" Jack Mullins exclaimed. "Somebody looks a little crabby." He whistled and rolled his eyes at Lori Cobb. "Better buzz the boss man, kiddo. The lovely Ms. Lord looks fit to spit."

"I'm not mad at you," I declared. "I'm mad at myself. You must all be wondering if I lost my mind."

Jack chuckled. "You refer, I think, to your recent hire. You're right—he's probably not up for a Pulitzer Prize real soon."

"I should never have allowed him to cover this story," I grumbled as Milo loped out of his office, coffee mug in hand.

"What's up?" he asked, looking vaguely bemused.

"My temper," I said. "I'm an imbecile."

"No," Milo countered, "but you can be a pain in the ass. What's wrong?"

"Curtis Mayne," I snapped. "You haven't noticed?"

Milo drained the dregs from his mug into a coffee can under the front counter. "You hired the last one for his looks. This one doesn't have that much going for him. He doesn't seem to have shaken off his frat boy mentality. Give him time."

"Exactly," I agreed. "It was way too soon to let him take on a homicide story. Can we talk?"

Milo glanced up at the big clock on the far wall. "Give me ten minutes and I'll buy you a stiff drink. Give me twenty minutes and I'll buy you a steak at the Venison Inn."

I considered the offer. "Okay. I'll meet you there. But could you bring that picture of the victim with you? I want to run it."

Lori flinched. "Ugh."

"Hey," Jack pointed out, "the dead guy doesn't look half as bad as any of our three old fart county commissioners."

"Jack!" Lori cried. "You're talking about my grandfather!"

"Oops!" Jack put one hand over his mouth and the other on Lori's shoulder. "Sorry. I forgot he put you on the dole."

I rushed outside, leaving Milo's employees to their own personnel problems. I all but ran to my car two blocks away, got in, and drove off to the Tall Timber Motel. I had yet to see the murder site. I also wanted to talk to Minnie and Mel Harris.

At almost five o'clock, Minnie was busy behind the desk, checking in at least two separate parties. A woman holding a fussy baby was sitting in one of the small lobby's armchairs while a toddler boy tried to pull the leaves off a potted philodendron. I caught Minnie's eye. She acknowledged me with a quick smile; I pointed in the direction of Dylan Platte's unit;

she nodded once; I went outside and walked to the end of the two-story building.

There was no crime scene tape, but the door was locked and the drapes on the single window were pulled shut. I presumed the unit was still off-limits. There must have been blood on the carpet or the furnishings, but Minnie and Mel could take care of that problem rather easily. Meanwhile, I guessed that the Harrises had pleaded with Milo to remove any outward signs of the homicide that could deter business.

A logging truck rumbled by, coming off the Icicle Creek Road and headed for Jack Blackwell's mill. The load of second-growth trees was made up of depressingly small trunks compared with the virgin timber I recalled from my youth. But the smell of the freshly harvested evergreens was just as sweet.

A dozen cars were already in the motel parking lot, half of them from out of state. I looked across Front Street to the liquor store, Taco Bell, and Bayard's Photography Studio. A couple of years ago, Kip MacDuff had acquired the technology to develop our own newspaper pictures instead of farming them out to Buddy Bayard. He and his wife, Roseanna, had never quite forgiven us for our defection. Furthermore, I hadn't lived up to my promise to run some of Buddy's photos in the *Advocate*. As long as Scott Chamoud was on the staff, I hadn't needed freelance work. So far, Curtis hadn't proved to be more than adequate in his approach to photographs. Maybe it was time to make peace with Buddy.

But not just yet. The family with the baby and the toddler were unloading their luggage from an SUV with Idaho plates. No one else had pulled into the parking lot. I went back to the office just as Minnie was handing two keys to a middle-aged couple wearing matching golf outfits including jackets and caps with Eagle Vines Golf Club embroidered into the fabric.

Minnie dispatched them politely and efficiently. I approached the counter while she tucked in a few strands of graying brown hair and took a deep breath. "I'll bet you're not here to spend the night," she said. "How are you, Emma?"

"I've been better," I replied. "The last few days have been a pain. For you, too."

She nodded. "What's this world coming to? And why here?" Minnie's plump hand took in what might have been the motel, the town, or anything else she considered her personal sphere. "Oh, we've had the usual problems associated with this business, but never a murder or even a serious assault. And now it turns out this fellow wasn't who he said he was. I heard that on the news this afternoon."

"Yes," I said, silently cursing Spencer Fleetwood for his predictable victory over the *Advocate*. "Nobody knows who he really is. *Was*. Tell me, Minnie," I went on, quickly because I knew that more guests would be showing up momentarily, "was there anything—anything at all—that was different about this guy?"

Minnie leaned on the counter and fingered her dimpled chin. "Not really. A typical Californian—that's what I told Sheriff Dodge. Good-looking, well-dressed, smooth, self-confident." She shrugged. "You look back, you'd like to think you noticed something that'd help figure out why he was shot. But nothing. Just another visitor from California."

"I know what you mean," I said. "I don't suppose there was anything about his car or his room that wasn't quite right?"

"I don't pay much attention to cars," Minnie said. "Mel does, but he didn't mention anything unusual. Dwight Gould checked it out, but he didn't seem to find any of what you'd call clues."

"Any visitors?"

Minnie tapped a finger against her cheek. "I'm not sure. Unless someone asked me for this man's room number, I wouldn't see who went to his unit so close to the end of the building."

A pretty woman wearing huge sunglasses and a sky blue halter dress entered the office. I knew that was my cue to leave, but I had one more question. "He got here Thursday, right? Who made up his room Friday?"

"I did," Minnie replied after giving the new arrival a welcoming smile. "Our summer help isn't in full swing yet."

"Nothing odd about the room?" I asked, moving aside so that the woman in the halter dress could take my place at the counter.

Minnie was placing a registration card in front of her guest. "No. Nothing untoward—if you know what I mean."

I assumed she meant no sign of an unusual sexual romp, drugs, or booze. I nodded absently while the pretty woman began filling out the form.

Minnie took a couple of steps closer to where I was standing. "There was one little thing—really little, that I just thought of now." She nodded discreetly at the woman, who had taken a small notebook out of her purse while she delved inside for what I assumed was her driver's license. "We keep those little tablets in each room," Minnie said softly. "Mr. . . . Whoever had used his up. There wasn't any paper in the wastebasket. I don't suppose it means anything, but it was kind of strange, especially since I noticed he hadn't used any of the new notepaper the day he was killed." She turned away from me. "Oh, you're a fellow Washingtonian, Ms. Pierce. Aren't our licenses the darnedest things to try to read when they're still in your wallet? The DMV ought to make the serial numbers bigger. I'll have to take this out. I'm so sorry."

This time I took my cue and left. My usual spot in front of

the *Advocate* building was still vacant, so I pulled in and walked down the street to the Venison Inn. The dining area was beginning to fill up, but I saw no sign of Milo. I looked into the bar. He wasn't there, either. I went back and stood near the entrance. It was almost five-thirty.

Sunny Rhodes, wife of the inn's bartender, Oren, greeted me. "Do you want a booth?" she asked with the bright smile that had long ago prompted her nickname.

"I'm waiting for the sheriff," I said. "Maybe I should get a booth."

"He'll smoke," Sunny reminded me. "I wish he wouldn't, especially when he sits by the sign in the dining room that says 'No Smoking.' It's a poor example. I thought he might quit after that siege he had in the hospital a while back."

"That was his gallbladder," I said.

"I know," Sunny replied, "but I hoped it would give him a scare about keeping a healthy lifestyle. Oren says Dodge almost never orders anything but steak when he comes here."

"Well," I said, looking out of the corner of my eye, "here he comes again. We'll sit in the bar to ease your conscience."

Sunny's big smile was lost on Milo, who glowered at her. Obviously, they'd had some previous run-ins. "We'll be in the bar," he declared and led the way.

"Damned do-gooder," the sheriff grumbled after we'd arrived at a table for four and he'd lowered his long-limbed frame into one of the captain's chairs while I sat on the banquette. "She'd be better off watching where she parks that car of hers when she's peddling Avon stuff. I'd guess she pays at least three hundred bucks in fines every year. Can't she read a loading zone sign when she sees it?"

"Sunny *is* loading," I pointed out. "Or unloading, as the case may be. She's usually delivering her orders."

Milo snorted as he signaled Oren to bring what he knew was our usual request—bourbon for me, Scotch for the sheriff.

"Speaking of a different kind of case," I said, "is there anything I should know about the phony Dylan Platte's homicide?"

"You mean that Curtis either hasn't asked about or isn't telling you?" Milo leaned back in his chair. "I doubt it. Not," he added, "that I think your new guy can walk and chew gum at the same time. At least Scott and Carla were better-looking."

"Not only do I wish I still had Scott on the staff," I admitted, "but I even yearn sometimes for Carla, typos and all."

"She's cute, even if she has put on some weight," Milo noted. "Still teaching journalism at the college?"

"Alas, she is," I said. "I almost think Curtis could have had her for a teacher. Her last story for the *Advocate* was about her replacement. She spelled Scott's name S-c-o-o-t."

"I'm going to let Jack or one of the other deputies handle Curtis from now on," Milo said. "I don't need any more aggravation on the job."

"I've decided to yank Curtis from the story," I confessed. "He can do some sidebars, but he isn't ready for a big assignment. I should never have given it to him."

Milo waited for Oren to deliver our drinks. "How are you two doing?" he asked in his friendliest bartender's manner. "Sounds like you've both got a big job on your hands with this murder at the motel."

"We're working on it," Milo responded in his laconic manner.

Oren nodded. "I bet I know that guy who got shot. He came in here Thursday night and ordered a Mind Eraser. Who else but a Californian would ask for that? His girlfriend wanted one of those energy drinks, you know, Red Bull and vodka. Crazy, huh?"

"Girlfriend?" I said, surprised.

Oren nodded. "A real knockout. Could've been a movie star. Beautiful, blond, and with a figure that—" He stopped, looking embarrassed. "Sorry. Not supposed to make cracks like that these days according to the little woman."

"You're not supposed to call your wife 'the little woman,' either," I pointed out, although I frankly didn't give a rip if he called Sunny his ball and chain. "Tell us more. I'm sure the sheriff would like to hear about your conversation with the victim."

The sheriff, however, was lighting a cigarette and exhibiting his usual laid-back attitude when listening to a witness. No rush, in Milo's opinion. Sooner or later, you'd hear what you wanted to know. Just let people talk.

But the bar was getting busy. Oren had an assistant, a petite brunette named Julie, who was working her way through Skykomish Community College after her ill-fated teenage marriage had ended in divorce. She was pleasant, but not very efficient.

"I'll be back," Oren said, looking anxious. "You want menus?"

The sheriff told him we did. Oren hurried away.

"Why do we need menus?" I asked. "We always know what we're going to order."

"It makes Oren feel like he's earning his tip." Milo tapped ash into one of the inn's new glass ashtrays, which had replaced the old black plastic variety. "So how are you going to grill him about the knockout blonde?"

"She sounds like Ginger Roth," I said. "I've had a feeling there was a connection all along between the Roths and the homicide."

Milo groaned softly. "Oh, God, please, not women's intuition!"

I made a face at him. "It's not that. I'm always wary of co-incidences that aren't."

"Whatever that means," Milo muttered as Oren appeared with our drinks and menus. "Hey," the sheriff said, "what time was this Eraser guy here Thursday?"

Oren thought for a moment. "Seven, seven-thirty. The blonde came in a few minutes later."

"How long did they stay?"

"An hour or so," Oren replied, adjusting his bar apron over his paunch. "They had a couple of those screwy drinks, and then I think they went into the dining room and had dinner. Ask Sunny. She's been working for the past week or so filling in for Tracie, who's on vacation."

"How'd they act?"

"Friendly," Oren said, "but not all over each other. They just talked, kind of serious, now that I think about it."

"Hear any of what they were saying?"

"Not really."

"Think."

Oren cracked his knuckles, a habit that irked me no matter who the cracker might be. "Uh . . . no, I honestly didn't catch anything. They'd clam up when I came along." He nodded toward a small, round, and currently empty table in the far corner. "I suppose maybe they didn't want to be overheard."

Milo nodded once. "Thanks, Oren," he said, handing his unread menu back. "I'll have the T-bone medium well done, with the salad and blue cheese and a baked potato, but not with any of that goop that comes in the little cups."

The bartender looked at me. "Emma?"

"The same, only rare, with all the goop for the potato."

Oren took both menus and went off to the bar.

"Business, not pleasure," I said.

"Sounds like it." Milo puffed on his cigarette. "They're going to change the state laws about smoking, you know."

"Yes," I said, "late this year. No smoking in any eating or drinking establishment."

"Freaking Nazis," Milo muttered. "If anybody expects me to enforce that rule, they can think again or meet me out back by the Dumpster. Don't these morons have anything better to do? It's not like there aren't any real crimes in this country. And don't tell me that these motherjumpers who come up with this crap aren't snorting coke or puffing on some funny stuff and being so self-righteous I could puke."

"You done?" I asked sweetly.

"Hey," Milo said sharply, "aren't you a journalist? Aren't you supposed to get all wound up over people's rights being trampled? How come all of you dinks suddenly shut the hell up when it comes to smoking?"

"How come you don't read my editorials?" I retorted. "I already wrote one a couple of months ago saying that even if I weren't a smoker—usually—I felt this new law was a serious infringement and only more chipping away at personal freedoms. You missed that?"

The sheriff looked faintly sheepish. "Must've. Write another one."

"I might." We'd gone off the rails. "About the dead man and the blonde," I said. "If she posed as Ginger Roth, a real or imaginary person, where was she holed up while—let's call him Josh for now—was at the Tall Timber?"

"Maybe she wasn't staying around here," Milo suggested. "Maybe she's from somewhere nearby."

Maybe she's been here all along, I thought. But I didn't say so out loud. It seemed like a preposterous idea. Nobody in Alpine resembled the beautiful young woman who'd called on me.

"Are you going to talk to Sunny on the way out?" I asked.

"Might as well," Milo said without enthusiasm.

"What's Graham Cavanaugh like?"

"The son?" Milo frowned. "Long ponytail, goatee, harp tattoo on his left hand, probably the artsy type."

"He's supposed to have a good head for business," I said. "His wife is a writer. Was she with him?"

The sheriff shook his head. "I guess she stayed behind at the ski lodge. I'll talk to her and Kelsey tomorrow."

"Let me know what they have to say."

"How come you're not going to see them?"

"I'll have to. I can't trust Curtis to find out anything crucial."

Julie brought our salads. Milo requested another drink for each of us. After she'd gone on her way, the sheriff shifted awkwardly in his chair and posed a question for me: "Did Tom talk much about his kids?"

"Some," I said, thinking back and remembering all sorts of things that had nothing to do with conversation. "There were so many years that Tom and I had no contact, so I knew next to nothing about them as children." *Nor had Tom known anything about Adam's early years,* I thought with too familiar regret. "By the time I . . . we got back together, Kelsey and Graham were in their late teens. Then he'd talk about their off-and-on-again attempts at college and the phases they were going through with careers and interests." I paused. "What's odd now that I think about it is how seldom Tom mentioned any interaction between his kids and their mother, Sandra. Maybe, given all her emotional and mental problems, she didn't play any kind of traditional mother's role."

Milo was rearranging the salt and pepper shakers, an old habit he'd never shed. "She spent some time in nuthouses, didn't she?"

I couldn't help but smile. "Well, Tom never called them that, but yes, she took the occasional trip to a clinic or hospital. It must've been very hard on Graham and Kelsey—and Tom, of course."

"Right." Milo almost sounded sympathetic. "He had to bring home the bacon, too. At least he didn't have to fork it out in child support."

I knew the sheriff referred to his own situation when his ex-wife, Tricia, had moved to Bellevue and taken their teenage kids with her. Between his work-related duties, which often kept him on the job during weekends, and his kids' frantic schedules, he hadn't seen them very often. I also knew that it had been a relief to him, having been spared many adolescent crises.

I had a different slant on Tom's relationship with his son and daughter. My conscience bothered me because I'd seldom probed too deeply into Sandra's problems—or those that she must have caused her family. I didn't want to know. I didn't want to hear about her. I suppose I preferred to pretend she didn't exist.

Our second round of drinks appeared, courtesy of Julie. I mentioned Minnie's remark about the used-up note tablet at the motel. As I expected, Milo didn't seem interested. Somehow the conversation drifted away from the homicide investigation. I assumed the sheriff wanted to forget his responsibilities for a while. I didn't blame him. He was always on duty, even in his nominal leisure time.

He picked up the bill, having offered to buy me drinks and dinner. I didn't argue. Milo often ate at my house, expecting dessert that wasn't served in the kitchen. He was almost as often disappointed. Even though we were compatible in bed, I didn't want to give him false hope about a permanent future together. I valued Milo's friendship. I just wished his previous efforts to find a new woman in his life hadn't all turned out badly.

We caught Sunny Rhodes just as she'd seated Scooter Hutchins and his wife in a booth near the front of the restaurant. Milo asked our hostess about the beautiful blonde and the Californian.

"I certainly remember them," Sunny said, keeping one eye on the door. "So good-looking. But I didn't get a chance to talk to them much. We were fairly busy that night."

The sheriff didn't press Sunny for further information. The arrival of a party of four, none of whom I recognized, interrupted the brief interview, so we left. Outside, I suddenly remembered that I'd asked Milo to bring a photo of the victim.

"Oh, shit," the sheriff said. "I forgot. Want to come back to the office and get it?"

The short trek took less than three minutes. At almost seven o'clock, it was still broad daylight, with the sun not yet setting over the Skykomish River valley. A couple of cars and a camper bearing out-of-state license plates cruised along Front Street. In the distance, I heard a train whistle, probably Amtrak's eastbound Empire Builder running a few minutes behind schedule.

Sam Heppner was alone behind the counter. He greeted us with a wary eye. "Checking up on me, boss?" he asked Milo.

"You're staying awake," the sheriff responded, opening the gate in the counter and leading me to his office. "I had copies made of the vic's phony driver's license," he explained, moving papers and files around on his desk. "I figured you might not want to run the postmortem photo in the paper."

"Not unless that were the only way he might be identified," I said.

"Here." Milo handed me a manila envelope. "Don't worry about prints. The originals are in the evidence file."

I looked first at the black-and-white head shot of the victim. Eyes closed, no expression, could have been asleep. But postmortem photos aren't misleading. There is something cold and distant about the faces of people who have died. They're not there, it's just an image, and all I see is the absence of life.

The driver's license was another matter. There were two versions, one the actual size of the license, and the other an enlargement of just the head shot. I gasped when I saw the full-color, smiling face of the handsome young man.

I instantly recognized him.

TEN

"WHAT?" Milo asked, surprised at my startled reaction.

"I've seen him." I stared at the enlarged photo. "I'm sure of it. I . . ." Pausing, I searched my memory. "Stella's beauty parlor," I finally said. "He came in while I was there and asked for directions."

Milo frowned. "When?"

"Wednesday, our pub day," I replied. "Midafternoon."

"You sure?"

"Yes, of course." Suddenly I realized what Milo meant. "This guy supposedly didn't arrive until Thursday."

The sheriff moved from behind his desk to stand beside me and gazed at the photos. "How close a look did you get?"

"Twenty feet," I said. "Maybe a little more. Stella was the one who talked to him. You'd better ask her where the guy was going and get her to ID these head shots."

"Is she still at work or gone home?"

"That depends on how busy she is," I replied. "Want me to come with you?"

Milo shrugged. "Why not?"

Stella's Styling Salon was directly across the street from the sheriff's office. We could see that the closed sign wasn't hung on the door. Jaywalking across Front, we entered and found Stella alone, toting up the day's receipts.

"Good Lord," she exclaimed as we walked in. "Am I under arrest for stealing my own hard-earned money?"

"You get to be a witness," I said. "Dodge is going to grill you."

"Been there, done that," Stella said bitterly, referring to a murder several years earlier that had occurred on her premises. She turned to Milo. "That was no picnic for you, either, was it?"

"No." The sheriff and Stella exchanged beleaguered looks. The victim had been related to one of his former girlfriends.

"So now what?" Stella asked, one fist on her hip. "Has this something to do with your latest corpse?"

Milo showed her the enlargement of the driver's license. "Look familiar?"

Stella studied the photo carefully. "Yes." She glanced at me. "You saw him, too, last Wednesday. Oh, God, Emma, what have you done to your hair this time?"

"Skip the shoptalk," Milo said. "What did he want?"

"Directions," Stella answered, apparently taking no offense. "He asked how to get to the golf course."

"That's it?" Milo looked disappointed.

Stella nodded. "I told him, he thanked me and left."

"Okay," Milo said. "Thanks, Stella. Sorry to trouble you."

"No problem." Stella again looked at me. "The real problem is that my client here can't seem to find her brush, comb, or product. Did you *do* anything with your hair today?"

"I washed it," I replied, on the defensive. "I even used the dryer."

"The one that sits next to the washer?" Stella retorted. "Next time try tumble dry. It couldn't hurt."

After we'd closed the door behind us, Milo scowled. "What was that all about? I think your hair looks nice."

"It doesn't look the way Stella thought the cut should be styled," I said. "Her criticism doesn't bother me. I'm used to it, and she's right. I'm inept when it comes to hair. Are we going to the golf course?"

"*We?*" Milo echoed, standing with one foot on the curb and the other in the street. "Oh, why not? We'll take our own cars, so I'll head straight home after that."

We parted company in front of his headquarters. By the time I walked back to the *Advocate* office and got in my Honda, Milo had already made an illegal U-turn on Front Street and was heading for the Icicle Creek Road. I didn't catch up with him until his Grand Cherokee turned right onto Railroad Avenue. We crossed Icicle Creek before making another right into the golf course. As I turned, I glimpsed Casa de Bronska to the east, its bright pink stucco mass erupting from the hillside with all the elegance of used bubble gum.

The parking lot—which had finally been paved a couple of years ago—was three-quarters full. It was a pleasant evening, a good time to get in nine holes after work. I had just turned off the ignition when my cell phone rang. Reluctantly, I answered while Milo loped toward the homely clubhouse.

"Emma?" Minnie Harris said. "Mel just got back from his stint at the Cascade Inn. I told him about your visit, and he remembered seeing Dick Bourgette's truck in the lot Friday afternoon around two or so. Is that any help?"

"It can't hurt," I replied.

"Don't get me wrong," Minnie pleaded. "I'm not accusing Dick of so much as wishing somebody ill, let alone actually doing it. In fact, I can't be sure he was calling on the poor man who got killed. But Mel did notice that Dick's truck was parked close to the end of the building."

"I think the world of all the Bourgettes," I asserted, "but every scrap of information might help. Dick mentioned dropping off a business card for the man he thought was Dylan Platte, the potential buyer of the Bronsky place. Maybe that's what he did."

"Oh." Minnie paused. "Of course. I'm sure you're right. Some latecomers are just pulling in. I must dash. We've only got two vacancies left. Three," she added dolefully, "if we could use the dead man's unit."

I rang off, thinking that, for the Harrises, the corpse without a name had merely become an impediment to their motel's full occupancy. Life went on in Alpine. Still, somebody somewhere must miss the victim. Who? Where? Would we ever find out?

Milo had already gone into the clubhouse. When I entered, he was in the pro shop talking to the manager, Van Goleeke.

The sheriff glanced at me and turned back to Van. "Meet my new deputy, Emma Lord," Milo said wryly. "Be good to her. She's just learning the ropes."

I smiled at Van, a clean-cut, good-looking man in his thirties with wavy auburn hair and rather long sideburns. He was a nodding acquaintance, though not from the golf and country club. Van and his wife, Arlette, had moved to Alpine a couple of years earlier. She taught music full-time at the community college, and Van was a part-time instructor in golf and tennis. I'd run into him on campus once or twice. I couldn't even remember the last time I'd been to the golf course.

"Van tells me that our body was here Thursday," the sheriff said in a neutral voice. "He shot a few holes with Snorty Wenzel."

"The real estate guy?" I blurted.

Van chuckled. "Right. Odd little character. He's not a bad golfer, though. He told me he usually plays at the Blue Boy West Golf Course in Monroe."

Again, I spoke before the sheriff could say anything. "He lives in Monroe?"

"I guess so," Van said. "He's only played this course three or four times, usually with Ed Bronsky."

Milo practically elbowed me out of the way. "So how did this guy sign in? The Californian, I mean."

"As Dylan Platte from . . . San Francisco, as I recall," Van replied. "You want to check the guest register?"

"I'll take your word for it," Milo said.

Van looked bemused. "So he was an impostor?"

Milo nodded. "We're running him through the system to see if he has a record, but all we have are fingerprints. No match in this state. You talk to him?"

"No," Van said. "Not much chance for that. Any talking was done by Snorty. Not to mention the snorting in between sentences." Van chuckled again. "He's a real motormouth. Say, Sheriff, how come you never swing a club around here? You could walk here from your backyard."

"Not my game," Milo replied. "I fish and hunt. I like the outdoors best when I'm alone."

"Golf's a great game," Van declared. "You can play until you're a hundred."

"And get a score a lot higher than that," Milo retorted. "No, thanks. The only holes I care about are the ones I can punch out on my fish and game card."

Van grinned. "Suit yourself."

Milo thanked Van and we left.

"Damnit," the sheriff muttered as we walked into the parking area. "Now I'll have to track down this Snorty dink. I'll be damned if I'll call Ed and ask for his number."

"You don't have to," I said. "If you ever *really* read the *Advocate,* you'd know he runs a small ad every week. I think his number is a cell phone."

Milo stopped and gazed skyward, where puffy white clouds moved slowly up the river valley. A faint mist was beginning to rise out of the meadow between the golf course and the Icicle Creek development where Milo lived. "I've got last week's paper somewhere. I'll call this Snorty from home." He looked down at me. "You want to come in for a nightcap?"

"It's still daylight." I smiled faintly. "I'll take a rain check, okay?"

"Sure." He didn't look too disappointed.

I stood on my tiptoes and kissed his cheek. "Later, big guy. Take care."

"You, too."

He headed for the Grand Cherokee; I got into my Honda. On the way home, I decided to make my own call to Snorty Wenzel. I'd give Milo half an hour of lead time. Meanwhile, I'd update Vida on what little I'd learned about the homicide case. I considered calling Curtis, but my irritation with him hadn't gone away. He should have been following his own leads. Realistically, I figured he was probably sitting on his butt drinking beer and listening to iTunes.

Vida's line was busy when I called her a little after eight o'clock. After listening to her usual lengthy message commanding the caller not only to leave a name and number but to include details of information, news, gossip, or anything else that could possibly provide fodder for her immense store of local knowledge, I disobeyed and simply asked her to call me back.

Ten minutes later my phone rang. "Well?" Vida demanded. "What is it?"

I tried to be succinct. My House & Home editor was intrigued. "This Snorty person," she mused, "may be the key. I'm suspicious of anyone who conducts business from his car. Nor do I know anything about his background. He seems to have sprung up from nowhere."

To Vida, that was tantamount to being an unnatural creature spawned by evil spirits. Her lack of knowledge was an insufferable condition that had to be remedied as soon as possible.

"You know people in Monroe," I said in my most innocent voice.

"Oh, yes, of course," Vida agreed. "Buck has friends there, too."

"By the way," I said casually, "have you talked to Buck about his interest in buying a condo in Alpine?"

"I haven't spoken to him since Saturday," Vida replied, somewhat strained. "I'm certain that Mrs. Hines has confused Buck with someone else."

That struck me as highly unlikely, but I held the thought. "You realize," I said, "I'm pulling Curtis off of the homicide story except maybe for sidebars."

"You have no choice," Vida declared. "Your conflict of interest ended when the murdered man turned out to be someone other than a Cavanaugh kinsman. The entire *Advocate* issue could be a hoax."

"That seems pointless," I said. "He must have some connection to the Cavanaughs or he wouldn't know about the family, the newspapers, and me. And what about that bracelet and note?"

"A front man, perhaps," Vida murmured. "I must admit,

it's very puzzling." She paused. "Are you going to call this Snorty tonight?"

"Yes."

"Why not see him in person?"

"I don't know where he is."

"You've met him," Vida said. "Didn't you say he came into the front office to place an ad?"

"Yes."

"I wasn't there at the time," Vida said. "He wouldn't know me. I could be a stranger. I could be"—she paused again—"from somewhere other than Alpine." Obviously, the mere idea of living elsewhere disturbed her. "I might tell him that I'd heard the purchase of the Bronsky house wasn't going through and that I was interested in seeing it."

"But Ed and Shirley know you," I pointed out.

"Yes, yes," she said impatiently, "but I'd ask to look at it only from the outside, perhaps have him drive me around town."

I turned her plot over in my mind. "No," I said firmly, "I don't like it for several reasons. Snorty may not in fact hold the key, as you put it, except, of course, to the Bronsky house. And while you may not have met the man, that doesn't mean he wouldn't know who you were even if you used an assumed name. Let's face it—you are well-known in Alpine, and any number of people, including Ed and Shirley, may have pointed you out to Snorty."

"My hats," she muttered. "Well now. You do have a point. Still . . ."

"No," I repeated. "A simple phone call, which I'll make in the next half-hour. I'll let you know if he has anything of inter-est to say."

I heard her sigh. "If you insist."

"I do."

I checked Snorty's number in his one-column, three-inch ad. "Win with Wenzel! Flexible Mortgages! Dream Homes Our Specialty! Creative Financing! Act Now!!!" ran the copy. Leo must have cringed when he put that one together. The featured home of the week—in very small print with no photo—was described as "Three glorious rooms with river view, natural landscaping, and small outbuilding needs your TLC." I deciphered that as somebody's abandoned cabin and privy in the woods so close to the Skykomish that the next spate of high water would wash the whole mess all the way to Puget Sound.

Before I could dial Snorty's number, my phone rang. Somewhat to my surprise, Mary Jane Bourgette's brisk voice greeted me.

"I'm glad I caught you at home," she said. "This is just a reminder about the parish potluck picnic this Thursday at Old Mill Park. You're a salad or fresh fruit."

I had forgotten, despite the announcement from the pulpit at Sunday Mass, the notice in the bulletin—and the small article we'd run in the *Advocate* along with a listing in the Alpine events calendar. "Oh—sure, six o'clock, right?"

"Five-thirty," Mary Jane said dryly. "With school out, we're having the Teen Club set up so we can get an early start in case it rains."

I knew Mary Jane well enough to admit I was slightly addled, especially since I could tell from her voice she'd already figured that out for herself. "Too much going on," I said by way of explanation.

"The murder at the motel," Mary Jane said. "You must feel a lot of pressure when we have something like that happen around here."

"That's true," I admitted, well aware that Mary Jane had

given me the perfect opening to ask a nagging little question. "Say, when I talked to Dick about our repair projects last week, he mentioned planning to stop by the Tall Timber to drop off a business card for the man we thought was Dylan Platte. Did he meet the guy or decide to wait?"

Mary Jane didn't answer right away. "Hang on," she said at last. "Dick's in the garage. I'll ask him. Or do you really want to know?"

"It'd be helpful if your husband had a chance to size up this guy," I explained. "He's a John Doe at present, and that stymies a murder investigation."

"Okay." Mary Jane didn't sound enthusiastic. "Hang on. I'll be right back."

Five minutes passed before I heard Mary Jane or any sound at the other end of the line. She'd apparently pressed the mute button so that I couldn't listen to her conversation with Dick.

"He did swing by the motel that afternoon," Mary Jane informed me. "But he didn't see the guy from California."

"So he didn't leave his business card?"

"No."

I realized that Mary Jane's usual candor was missing. "Gosh," I said, feigning shock, "does he think the victim was already dead?"

"I don't know what you mean," Mary Jane said, now sounding downright defensive.

"I'm trying to piece together the sequence of events Friday afternoon," I said, sounding bewildered, which wasn't hard to do. "Time of death isn't always exact. I thought maybe Dick saw something or somebody suspicious and decided to get out of there. You know how we sometimes have these strange feelings that can creep us out."

"Dick's not like that," Mary Jane replied, her voice resuming its familiar dry tone. "My husband isn't imaginative. Hammer and nails, saw and boards—that's his métier."

"Yes, I can understand that," I said, "since that's what makes Dick so good at what he does for a living." I paused, wondering how far I could press my developing friendship with Mary Jane. The road to real camaraderie had been rocky for me in Alpine. I didn't want to ruin a growing sense of trust between us. "That," I said, taking the plunge, "would indicate Dick definitely saw something very real that put him off."

Mary Jane uttered a big sigh. "Oh, damn, Emma, you're putting me in the middle! I told Dick I wouldn't say anything to anybody. It's all too stupid anyway."

"What is?"

Another sigh from Mary Jane. "Look. It's not a big deal, I'm sure of it. And unlike most people in this town—remembering that we're latecomers to Alpine—I don't flap my jaws about things that can be misconstrued. I'm not going to start now. Oh, I realize you're only doing your job, but I have to draw the line. I won't break my word to Dick."

I was disappointed, but I understood. "That's okay, Mary Jane," I said resignedly. "I'd probably do the same in your place. But if Dick ever decides what he saw might help nail a killer, he ought to talk to the sheriff, not to me."

"I know, I know," she said impatiently. "I actually mentioned that to him already, but then we agreed that it . . . Never mind. I'd better shut up. He's coming inside, and I don't want him to think I blew it."

I hung up and sat on the sofa trying to think what—or maybe who—Dick Bourgette had seen at the Tall Timber. It could have been anyone, including our pastor, Dennis Kelly; Mayor Fuzzy Baugh; or even Averill Fairbanks, our resident

UFO freak, who thought he'd seen a space pod land on top of the motel's neon sign.

I phoned Vida again and told her about the call from Mary Jane Bourgette. "She refused to tell me what or who Dick saw at the motel."

"Nonsense!" Vida exclaimed. "How could she be so reticent when it comes to a murder investigation?"

"She called whatever he saw 'stupid,' " I said, "implying that she didn't see any way that it was connected to the homicide. I figure the Bourgettes are protecting someone. Mary Jane didn't want to start a rumor that would lead to gossip racing all over town."

"Oh, for heaven's sakes!" Vida was utterly exasperated. "Did she believe you'd put whatever it was in the paper? How ridiculous!"

"Probably," I agreed, "but it does make me want to eliminate possibilities. Are you certain either you or Leo didn't notice anything when you went to the motel?"

"Of course," Vida declared. "We'd have said so. When Dylan didn't respond to our knock, we left. Both of us had better fish to fry that afternoon."

"Okay," I said. "I'm going to call Snorty now."

"Very well." Vida sounded prickly. "By the way, did I tell you I had three-way calling on my phone?"

"If you did, I forgot. Are you suggesting that you call me back and then dial Snorty's number so you can listen in?"

"What harm would it do?"

"None, I guess." *As long as you keep your mouth shut.*

"Good. I'll hang up now."

"Please do."

My phone rang fifteen seconds later. "I have Snorty's number," Vida said. "I'm dialing it now. Be ready."

To our mutual annoyance, we got Snorty's recording. "Snorty Wenzel here, glad you called, but I'm unavailable at the moment." A faint snort followed. "Our real estate firm has got just the right home for you in the right place at the right price." Another faint snort. "I'll get back to you as soon as I can, so please leave your name and number." Snort, snort. "If you're calling to order Play Hard to Get, my special fast-acting vitamin supplement for men, give me your name and address so I can mail you a free trial supply. Discretion is my middle name. Wait for the beep." Snort, beep, click.

"Oh, good grief!" Vida shrieked after quickly disconnecting. "He's also a quack?"

"I suppose," I mused, "there's a story in that somewhere, but I don't think I want to go near it."

"I should hope not!" She paused. "You didn't leave your name and number."

"That's because I don't want him to call me at home," I replied. "I'll try again from work tomorrow."

After I'd hung up, I contemplated my next move. Tomorrow was Tuesday, our deadline. Although I didn't want to do it, I felt compelled to interview whichever Cavanaughs I could run down before they left town. Unless Milo had some solid evidence, I assumed he couldn't order any of them to stay in Alpine. I was certain that the entire clan would probably head back to California as soon as possible. In fact, I was surprised they hadn't already gone.

Or had they? Feeling panicky, I called the ski lodge. The young man named Carlos who was working his way through the community college answered.

"The Plattes and the Cavanaughs are still here," he informed me, "but Mr. Platte told Mr. Bardeen they'd be checking out early Thursday morning."

"Are they at the lodge right now?" I asked.

"They're finishing dinner in the Viking Lounge," Carlos replied. "Do you want to leave them a message?"

"Um . . . no. Thanks, Carlos. I think I'll drop by to pay them a visit."

I hadn't yet changed out of my work clothes. It was going on nine, not the usual hour for me to still be out and about in Alpine on a work night. But I didn't want to change my mind about meeting Tom's children. I applied fresh lipstick, ran a brush through my hair, heard Stella's voice saying, "That didn't help much, Emma," and grabbed my purse.

Eight minutes later, I was entering the ski lodge lobby. Carlos recognized me from behind the front desk and nodded toward the restaurant area.

Only a handful of diners were still seated amidst the ersatz greenery and stone statues of Norse gods and goddesses. I spotted the Cavanaugh group immediately, only because they were the youngest guests in the lounge. I stopped halfway to their table, virtually lurking behind an artificial tree trunk. Kelsey's appearance had improved since I last saw her, though she still looked wan.

One of the men had slicked-down black hair; the other man's brown hair was in a ponytail. Recalling Milo's description, I figured he must be Graham. Despite his coloring, he, like Kelsey, seemed to take after his mother rather than his father. I assumed the woman with the mass of black curls was Graham's wife, Sophia. Taking a deep breath, I approached their table. Except for the dark-haired man, whose back was turned, the others all stared at me. Nobody spoke.

"I'm Emma Lord," I said, gazing at Kelsey. "Remember me?"

Kelsey pressed her lips together. Finally, she nodded. "Yes. Hello."

The ponytailed man half-rose from his chair and put out a hand. "I'm Graham Cavanaugh. Would you like me to pull up a chair for you?"

The gesture was unexpected. "That would be nice," I said, shaking his hand. "Thanks."

The other man also offered his hand. "I'm Dylan Platte." He chuckled as he clasped my hand in a very firm grip. "Dylan Platte, alive and well. My pleasure." He waved a hand at the young woman with the raven curls. "My sister-in-law, Sophia Cavanaugh."

Sophia nodded and smiled. She was more striking than beautiful, with strong features and sea green eyes that seemed to bore into me. "I didn't get to Alpine until this afternoon," she said in a husky voice. "I'm a writer who had a deadline. You know how that is."

"Oh, yes," I agreed. "Tomorrow is ours for the *Advocate*."

Graham had brought the extra chair. I sat down between him and Sophia. "Amazing," he said, settling back into his own seat. "We'd just decided to set up a meeting with you for tomorrow evening. You read our minds."

"I did?" I said in surprise.

Dylan Platte put aside the folder that apparently contained the dinner bill. "We were about to leave, but may I suggest a round of after-dinner drinks? I assume you've already eaten, Ms. Lord."

"Yes." I felt stupid. Dylan's voice had a grating quality, not at all like that of the person who had claimed to be him during our phone call. My gaze kept flitting from Graham to Kelsey and back again. I simply couldn't see much of Tom in either of his children, except perhaps for their blue eyes. Graham was about six feet, almost as tall as his father, but his build was slighter. Maybe, I thought, I didn't want them to resemble

Tom. Maybe I had a problem with Tom having had children by someone else. It was only Adam who had inherited his father's chiseled profile and strong build. My sole contribution was the color of my son's brown eyes.

"Then," Dylan said after signaling for their server, "you want to talk business."

"Business?" I echoed.

"The purchase of your newspaper," he responded, looking as if he thought perhaps I wasn't the local publisher but the village idiot.

The server, one of the lodge's several blond and often buxom girls of Scandinavian extraction, arrived to take our orders. I asked for a Drambuie straight up. Suddenly I felt as if I needed a stiff drink.

Graham spoke up after the waitress left. "It's understandable," he said in a kindly voice, "that you'd think the man who called you last week was part of a hoax. The sheriff explained to me that this poor devil who was killed had contacted you about buying the *Advocate*. We've tossed that bombshell around the past day or so and can't figure out who he is or why he made the offer. All we can suggest is that he must've been someone who'd gotten wind of our proposal and decided to act on his own. I can't think why."

Dylan smirked. "Hey, Graham, you of all people know why. Business is a cutthroat world, now more than ever."

Graham was unabashed. "You can't blame me for thinking that people who still love newspapers have to have higher standards. My dad always taught me that's the way it should be."

My dad. I could barely keep from cringing.

"Such an absurd stunt," Sophia declared. "It's a wonder it didn't get him killed."

I was confused. My brain didn't seem to be functioning.

Maybe I didn't need a drink as much as to stick my head under an ice-cold water tap. All the memories, good, bad, and horrendous, weighed me down. I felt so close to Tom and yet even further away, as if these four people had erected some kind of wall between us. "Excuse me," I said, sounding like Emma the Meek and Humble. "He *was* killed. What do you mean?"

Dylan waved a slender hand. "Of course. But it had to be some sort of shakedown or a robbery, a hooker, a vagrant. Who in this town would want him dead?" He paused for a scant second. "Unless," he said with a crooked smile, "it would be you, Ms. Lord."

ELEVEN

I TRIED TO PRETEND THAT DYLAN PLATTE'S REMARK WAS A joke, but my laugh was hollow. "I haven't gotten to the point where I have to create my own headlines," I said.

Graham's smile was deceiving. His blue eyes were hard as glacier ice. "That's not entirely true, is it? You had quite a big story when my father was shot in front of your eyes."

I gasped. "That's a terrible thing to say! It ruined my life!"

Graham slowly shook his head. "Did you ever think what it did to us?"

Before I could respond, our waitress delivered the round of drinks. Only Kelsey had abstained from an alcoholic beverage. She'd ordered a Diet Coke and stared warily at her soda, as if she suspected I'd had it spiked with arsenic.

I started to lift the small flutelike glass of Drambuie but realized that my hands were shaking. "I never knew you. How could I understand . . . what you felt?" My voice cracked.

Sophia swirled her brandy snifter with a languid hand. "I gather my father-in-law wasn't anxious for his children to meet you. Unfortunately, I didn't know Mr. Cavanaugh. He died before I met Graham."

The hostility that surrounded me stiffened my backbone. I was tempted to retaliate with my own hurtful words, but escalating the situation seemed foolish. I'd only reinforce the conflict of interest that I'd felt from the start.

"Look," I said, folding my hands in an effort to steady them, "I don't want to go to war over any of this. Let's get one thing straight once and for all. I am *not* selling the *Advocate* to you or to anyone else."

Graham leaned back in his chair. "Well. I guess that concludes our meeting."

I was finally able to pick up my glass without spilling any of the liquor. "So I assume you won't be moving here after all," I said, looking at both Dylan and Kelsey. She turned away from me and gazed questioningly at her husband.

"Oh, I think we probably will," Dylan said, taking Kelsey's hand in his. "We're going to go through the house tomorrow. Apparently, the present owners want to do some fixing up before they show it to us."

I could imagine the disarray at Casa de Bronska. A shovel and a match would probably have been the best way to clean up Ed and Shirley's vulgar mansion. What I couldn't imagine was Kelsey and Dylan's move to Alpine.

"Why?" I asked, not bothering to disguise my incredulity.

"Change," Dylan replied easily. "The Bay Area is obsolete, overcrowded and overpriced. We want some room to roam. A house like the Bronskys' costs a fortune in San Francisco. The Bronskys are asking 1.1 mil, but we figure they'll take 850 and kiss our feet in gratitude. I'm told the place needs work."

Work. Not a word Ed had ever understood. "Good luck," I said, focusing on my drink instead of the company I was keep-

ing. The silence that followed seemed uncomfortable to me—
but I sensed that no one else felt that way. They were enjoying
themselves at my expense. Except, perhaps, for Kelsey, who
struck me as being withdrawn from the others even though her
husband still held her hand. "I'm going now," I announced and
took a last, fiery sip of Drambuie. "Thanks for the drink."

"Of course," Graham said softly.

I got up with my usual lack of grace, though at least I didn't
drop anything, trip, or walk into a wall. I heard a woman's
throaty laugh—Sophia's, I was sure—as I moved out of the
dining area. As soon as I got into the Honda, I regretted my
hasty retreat. There were dozens of questions I wanted to ask
that foursome, and not just about the allegedly unknown murder victim. Did Kelsey and Dylan have children? What about
the child she'd been expecting before she got married? Had she
and Graham sold Tom's condo on Nob Hill in San Francisco
or the house in Pacific Heights? What were their memories of
their father? Or their mother? Had Tom talked to them about
the marriage we were planning before he was killed? Did they
know or care about their half brother, Adam?

I sat in the parking lot for several minutes, watching the sky
darken as night descended over the mountains. Just before I
was about to turn the key in the ignition, I was startled by a tap
on the window of the passenger door. Anxiously, I looked to
see who was trying to get my attention.

"Open up, Emma," Leo called, looking a bit sheepish.

I unlocked the door. My ad manager scooted inside. "I was
afraid you'd already left," he said.

"You were at the lodge?" I asked, still feeling unnerved.

He nodded. "I was spying from the bar. I wanted to see
what those Cavanaugh kids looked like now that they're
grown up. You came in just before I was going to leave. They

didn't recognize me, of course. But then I wasn't trying to be seen."

"Carlos should have told me you were there when I talked to him at the front desk," I said.

"Carlos is fairly new on the job. He doesn't recognize me." Leo rolled down the window and took out his cigarettes. "Do you mind?"

"No," I said, opening my own window halfway. "What did you think?"

Leo lighted his cigarette before he answered. "I don't know. Graham's changed the most, gone from gawky boy to manly man. Kelsey seems to have lost her bounce."

"She bounced?"

"She was what I'd call perky," he said. "Graham was more reticent, sometimes a little surly. But he was at that awkward age, between twelve and twenty. Frankly, I'm not even sure how old those kids were when I last saw them. A permanent alcoholic haze will do that to a fellow." Leo shifted in his seat to look at me more closely. "Are you okay? I had the feeling your get-together wasn't a bundle of fun."

I laughed weakly. "True. I don't know what I expected, but they put me on the defensive from the start."

"Not surprising. It seems that Dylan Platte is the little group's driving force."

"I'm not sure," I said. "He *seems* to be, but Graham's no slouch, and his wife, Sophia, strikes me as fairly tough. Kelsey's the only one who doesn't quite fit in. I have to admit, I wonder if she's inherited some bad genes from Sandra."

"It's possible." Leo tapped ash into the small tray under the dashboard. "Did they badger you about selling the paper?"

"They tried." I shrugged. "I told them to forget it."

"They won't."

"What do you mean?"

"I have a feeling they're in this for the long haul," Leo said. "The waitress who was serving them—Britney, Brandy, Brianna, whatever—told me she'd overheard them talking about moving to Alpine. I assume that means Ed still has a buyer."

I sighed. "Dylan insists they're going ahead with the deal." I turned to look Leo in the eye. "Do they think they can wear me down with a war of attrition?"

"That's my guess," he replied. "I suppose Dylan and Kelsey figure that if they're living here and they keep upping the ante, eventually you'll give in. You're not at retirement age, of course, but down the road, in a couple of years, you might start thinking about it."

I made a face. "Not likely. What would I do with myself? The only close relatives I have are Adam and Ben. Neither of them is around here and probably never will be. I won't ever have grandchildren. I'm not a joiner. I have no intentions of writing the Great American Novel. My whole life is the *Advocate*." I clapped my hand to my forehead. "Oh, God! That makes me sound pathetic!"

Leo grinned. "That's probably what they're counting on. Then they can rescue you and be heroes. Hey," he said, tugging on the sleeve of my cardigan, "don't ever let the bastards see you sweat."

I smiled at Leo. "I'm not sweating. But that whole encounter temporarily unhinged me. I thought I was doing okay, putting Tom into some quiet corner of my mind after all this time. Then his kids come along and . . ." I made a helpless gesture.

"Neither of them is much like Tom," Leo remarked. "If you didn't know who they were, you'd never guess they were related. Kelsey looks kind of like her mother, but Graham doesn't take after either of his parents."

"Adam doesn't look like me," I pointed out.

"No, he doesn't. He's mostly Tom." Leo took another puff off his cigarette and shook his head. "My kids look like both their mother and me, though the gene pool actually improved. You never can tell what goes into a kid's makeup. Throwbacks, sometimes." He opened the passenger door. "I'd better let you get home. Tomorrow's deadline day. You'll need all your strength."

"You will, too," I said. "Thanks, Leo."

"Sure." He patted my back and got out of the car but leaned down before shutting the door. "Hey, just remember Walsh's Famous Maxim—'Things can always get worse.'"

I laughed. Sort of. "I know."

Of course Leo was right.

I didn't call Vida after I returned from the ski lodge. I was too tired, and couldn't cope with a rehash of my unsettling encounter with what I was beginning to think of as the Cavanaugh Gang.

By the time I got to the office at a couple of minutes before eight the next morning, I felt better despite a series of chaotic dreams, none of which I could remember after I woke up. That was probably for the best. Real life seemed harrowing enough.

Kip was already on hand, but Ginny hadn't yet arrived to start the coffeemaker. "I can do it," Kip said. "Is she sick?"

"Not that I know of," I replied. "She's just . . . pregnant."

Kip laughed. "I'd forgotten what she was like the other times."

"She wasn't quite as bad," I said, "but she didn't already have two other kids making demands on her time and energy."

Just as Kip was about to measure out the coffee, Vida entered the newsroom. "Think, think, think! I need four more

'Scene Around Town' items. Emma, Kip—what have you got for me?"

Kip held up a hand. "Norm Carlson went out yesterday looking for those two cubs that lost Mama Bear. No luck, but he told his dairy truck drivers to get an early start on their routes so they could help him search the woods near Gus Lindquist's place on Disappointment Avenue."

"Excellent," Vida declared, then looked at me. "Or is it a small story?"

"Yes," I said, "but there's no reason you can't put it in 'Scene' as well. I wouldn't list all the searchers for fear of leaving someone out and making them mad at us. There's bound to be more than Norm and his Sky Dairy employees around here, given the number of people who love animals."

"Very true," Vida agreed. "Now you give me an item for 'Scene.' "

My mind was blank. All I could think of was the Cavanaugh Gang. It suddenly dawned on me that, if they had been anybody else, I'd toss the tidbit into Vida's hat—which, this morning, was a white and purple striped turban. "Bay Area visitors at the ski lodge enjoying dinner while taking a respite from house hunting in Alpine."

Vida gaped at me. "What?"

"I saw them last night," I said. "I got home too late to call you."

"Nonsense! You know I stay up past eleven! How late could you possibly have been?"

Kip wisely decided to withdraw and retreated into the back shop. "Frankly," I said, looking Vida straight in the eye, "I was too damned worn out and frazzled."

Her ire evaporated. "Truly? Were they unbearably rude?"

"Smug's more like it," I said. "I'll tell you all about it later. And yes, Kelsey and Dylan still plan to buy Ed's house."

"Oh, for heaven's sakes!" Vida cried, throwing her hands up in the air. "Smug indeed! 'Stupid' describes them better."

"Maybe," I murmured. "Here's Leo with the bakery goods. Ask him what he thought about the Cavanaugh Gang." I greeted my ad manager and hurried into my cubbyhole.

Several minutes later, as I was going into the newsroom to pour my coffee, Ginny plodded through the door. "Sorry," she said in a forlorn voice. "Our hot-water heater blew up."

"Good," Vida said, swinging around to her keyboard. "That goes in 'Scene.' Let me see . . . 'Expectant parents run out of hot water for their two youngsters who—' "

"Don't," Ginny pleaded. "We never mention our staff in 'Scene.' "

"I'm not using your names," Vida responded. "It'll be one of my little teases."

Shoulders drooping even more, Ginny surrendered. "Really, Emma, I'm sorry I was late. I've already checked the calls. You have one from a Mr. Weasel." She took a slip of memo paper out of the pocket of her baggy cardigan. "Here's his number."

"Thanks. I think his name is Wenzel." I glanced at the clock above the coffee and bakery table. It was eight-thirty. "Anybody seen Curtis?"

Leo looked up from the Grocery Basket layout on his computer screen. "Yes, I saw his beater pulling out of Cal's Texaco when I stopped to get gas just before eight."

"Then where the hell is he?" I demanded.

Vida swiveled around in her chair. "Emma, please! Watch your language. You're out of control this morning."

For once, I ignored her comment. "Ginny," I said before our office manager could escape to the sanctuary of the front office, "did your husband have anything more to say about the man who came into the bank and called himself Josh Roth?"

"Not really," Ginny responded. "The only reason Rick

talked to him was because Jodie—that's the new teller—thought a manager had to sign off on a traveler's check from out of state."

"Did you show Rick the picture we're running of the dead guy?"

"No." Ginny looked puzzled. "Why should I?"

Ginny is fairly smart and usually very efficient, but she has no imagination. "To make sure the guy on the driver's license is the same one who Rick saw at the bank. Why don't—" I stopped. Asking Ginny to go to the bank now would get her off to an even later start in the workday. "I'll have Curtis do it when he gets in."

Ginny nodded. "The bank doesn't open until nine-thirty, you know." She slouched out of the newsroom.

"I'll go to the bank," Vida volunteered. "I must get a money order for some bulbs I'll plant after Labor Day. They're twenty percent off now in the catalog I like, but they don't take checks and I refuse to give out my credit card numbers to anyone unless I know them personally."

"Okay," I said, knowing that Vida was using the bulb purchase as an excuse to talk to Rick. Little by little, Curtis was losing his grip on any part of the homicide coverage, but he had no one to blame but himself.

Ten minutes later my new reporter arrived, seemingly full of enthusiasm. "Time to beat those deadlines with those headlines," he said, rubbing his hands together before selecting a couple of doughnuts from the bakery tray. "Hey, boss," he called to me, "how much room for my page one story?"

I'd been standing in the doorway of my office, talking to Kip. "None," I replied. "Come in here and talk to me. Close the door behind you."

I stalked over to my desk and sat down. Curtis hadn't

worked for me long enough to know that the closed door meant serious business was at hand. Still, he already looked abject, his usual cockiness gone.

As usual, I felt guilty over causing pain for anyone else. I am basically softhearted, a trait that had kept Ed Bronsky on the payroll during my early years with the *Advocate*.

"Look," I said, resting my elbows on the desk and leaning forward, "I made a big mistake. I should never have assigned you to this homicide story so early on in your job here. In fact, I didn't give Scott much responsibility for complicated and potentially touchy coverage until the last year he worked for the *Advocate*. That was a mistake, too, though of a different kind. If necessary, I'll still have you do some of the sidebar or background stuff, but I feel this is a burden I ought to take on myself. It's not fair to weigh you down with this murder investigation."

"Okay." Curtis's chin was practically on his chest. "Maybe crime's not my strong suit. It's politics that interests me. Like I could do a series profiling the average voter in this county. It's an election year, so it'd be timely." He raised his head and suddenly regained some of his swagger.

"We might consider that," I allowed. "There'll be issues, of course. Any levies or bonds will be on the primary ballot in September. In fact, my editorial this week involves asking residents what they'd like to see happen in SkyCo. Your articles could tie in with that."

Curtis frowned. "That isn't exactly what I had in mind. I was thinking more about national and international problems facing the whole country. It'd be kind of a forum."

I had the feeling that somewhere along the way in college Curtis had written a poli-sci paper on the subject and planned to take the easy way out by using it to fill up space in the *Ad-*

vocate. "We'll figure out the angle later," I said. "We've got over two months until the primary. Meanwhile," I continued, sitting up straight and pushing my chair away from the desk, "we have a paper to get out. You've turned in a story and two photos already about Mayor Baugh's wood carving. What else is ready to go to the back shop?"

"The sheriff's blotter is almost done," Curtis replied. "Not much new this morning."

"What about the bear?" I asked. "Do that story and how some of the locals are searching for the motherless cubs."

Curtis looked askance. "That doesn't exactly have global implications, does it?"

"We're not global," I asserted. "We're local, small town. This isn't the *Guardian,* it's the *Advocate.*"

Curtis didn't look pleased, but he refrained from arguing. "You want to use my lead for the homicide story?"

"I haven't seen it," I said. "Let me have a peek."

"Sure." He got up from the chair. "I'll zap it in to you."

I watched him leave the cubbyhole. From where I was sitting, I could see only the front of his desk. After he disappeared out of sight, I waited. And waited. Finally he came back into my office.

"Sorry," he said ruefully. "I must've deleted it by mistake. Oh, well. Too bad. It was a real grabber."

I didn't ask if he could remember what he'd written. Or *if* he'd written anything. "That's okay. I'll wing it."

As soon as Curtis left, I dialed Snorty Wenzel's number. He answered—and snorted—on the first ring. "The local media," he said, chuckling and snorting. "First KSKY, now the newspaper. Not to mention the local law enforcement last night. I feel like a celebrity."

"You've done a radio interview?" I asked as Spencer Fleetwood's hawklike face sprang before my eyes.

"Just coming from the station," Snorty replied. "Fleetwood's playing it on the half-hour turn at nine-thirty. You ought to tune in."

"Right," I said without enthusiasm. "Could you stop by the newspaper office? I'd like to do a face-to-face interview."

"Sure. I can be there in five minutes. Hold the presses."

I tried to ignore the several snorts he'd made during his part of the conversation. It might be even worse up close and personal. But I thanked him and rang off.

I went into the newsroom. Leo had left, Curtis was on the phone, and Vida was tapping away at her keyboard. "Snorty Wenzel's on his way," I announced, glancing up at the clock. It was nine-fifteen. "He'll be here in time for his taped session with Fleetwood at nine-thirty."

Vida looked up. "Oh, dear. I suppose that was to be expected. Spencer would naturally want to follow up on the murder. Which reminds me, I need a guest tonight for 'Cupboard.' Maud Dodd has come down with a virus. A shame, since I could've helped promote her senior citizen column for the paper."

"Vida's Cupboard" was a weekly fifteen-minute radio program of local lore and gossip. The ratings were excellent, and Vida never used items that should have run in the *Advocate*. In April, the time slot had been changed from Wednesdays to Tuesdays in order to beat the multiple grocery chains' mailings and thus bring in more ad revenue for KSKY.

"Have you got a backup for Maud?" I asked.

"Not yet," Vida replied.

"What about Mrs. Hines?" I suggested. "I'm doing a brief front-page article about the possibility of converting Pines Villa into condos."

Vida scowled. "Must you? It seems so out of place."

"That doesn't mean it won't happen," I pointed out.

"She might not want to drive back to Alpine this evening."

"You could do it over the phone," I said. "Spence can hook you up."

Vida shook her head. "No, no. I dislike that sort of thing. So impersonal. Maybe I'll try Reverend Nielsen. He and his wife are going to Scandinavia this summer. Again."

Ginny trudged in carrying the mail. "Catalogs!" She shook her head. "Why do we get so many catalogs? Most of them have nothing to do with newspapers, and they're so heavy."

"Get on one list, get on all lists," I said. "I'm told you can request that individual companies stop mailing them to us."

"I tried it," Ginny said, putting a six-inch stack in Vida's in-basket. "Three times. The catalogs keep coming. Marlowe Whipp gets really annoyed when he has to deliver all of them. His back's going out."

"Oh, piffle!" Vida cried. "Marlowe is a chronic complainer. The last I heard was that he wanted the post office to get him one of those contraptions that big city employees use on hills, like meter readers in Seattle do. An elaborate and expensive sort of motorized tricycle. So silly. The hills here in Alpine are good exercise."

A short, stocky, balding man stopped in the doorway and rapped on the frame. "Anybody home?" he inquired—and snorted.

I hurried to greet him. "Mr. Wenzel," I said. "Come in."

Snorty's handshake was on the weak side; his skin felt very soft. He turned toward Vida. "You must be the famous Ms. Runkel. Your popular radio show airs tonight, I hear. Spence absolutely raved about you."

Vida's guarded expression didn't change. "He did, did he? He ought to. I bring in a goodly sum of advertising for him. And please call me *Mrs.* Runkel."

Snorty made a little bow. "I am delighted to do you that honor . . . *Mrs.* Runkel. You are, I understand, one of the brightest stars in Alpine's firmament."

"Really." Vida looked less than pleased.

Snorty—who, naturally, had snorted his way through all this fulsome verbiage—turned to look at Curtis, who had hung up the phone and was obviously trying to keep a straight face. "And this dashing young man?" Snorty inquired of me.

"Curtis Mayne, our new reporter," I said, noting that Ginny was furtively leaving the newsroom after finishing her mail delivery.

Snorty saluted. "Truly pleased to make your acquaintance. Ah, youth! I remember it well. So encouraging to see that newspapers still attract the younger set. I'm sure you're on your way to making a name for yourself in the business." He paused and glanced up at the clock. "Nine-twenty-five, I see. Where shall we listen to the broadcast?"

"Right here," I said. "Have a seat." I indicated Leo's empty chair. "I'll get my radio. There's coffee and baked goods on the table under the clock."

Snorty snorted with pleasure and made a beeline for the freebies. By the time I returned with the radio and plugged it into the outlet by Vida's desk, he was in Leo's chair with two doughnuts, a cup of coffee, and several napkins.

After turning the radio on, I sat on the edge of Vida's desk. Curtis was sitting with his head propped up by his fists; Vida's posture was ramrod straight as she stared straight ahead; Snorty was smacking his lips over a jelly doughnut. KSKY's "Morning Medley" was playing Connie Francis's "Stupid Cupid" from the fifties. It was one of those oldies that convinced me popular music had gotten better, not worse, over the years. Snorty, however, was rocking in Leo's chair and wagging his head.

A canned commercial for Safeway followed. Then Spence's mellifluous radio voice floated over the airwaves. "This is your 'Mid Morning' host, Spencer Fleetwood. We promised our listeners in beautiful Skykomish County an interview with a local Realtor, Snorty Wenzel, who had business dealings with the unidentified man shot to death last Friday in Alpine. However, due to technical difficulties, we're unable to air that segment at this time." Brief pause. "Now let's take another stroll down Memory Lane with Dean Martin's 'That's Amore' . . ."

I clicked off the radio. "That's too bad," I said. "Maybe Spence will run it later."

Snorty looked crushed. Curtis was still trying not to laugh. Vida scowled at the radio.

"Spencer better not have technical difficulties when I do my show this evening," she declared. "Two weeks ago my chair broke. Fortunately, it was during a commercial." She turned her gaze on Snorty. "You might as well recount what you said in the interview."

I kept my eyes averted. Leave it to Vida, I thought, to make sure she got in on my interview. Not that I minded—she'd be a help, not a hindrance.

"Well . . ." Snorty used a napkin to brush a bit of doughnut off his lower lip. "It's kind of complicated. Want me to begin at the beginning?"

Vida nodded. "If that's necessary, please do."

"It is." He scratched his thick neck. "I met Ed Bronsky at the country club a while back. He was thinking about selling that amazing house of his. I told him I was in the real estate business and would be glad to handle it for him. A couple of weeks later, he agreed and we made a deal for an exclusive listing." He tugged at the collar of his green, blue, and white-striped too-snug Polo shirt. "Now let's face it—there aren't many people in SkyCo who'd be able to afford or maintain a fine property like Ed's, so I listed it on the Internet."

He paused and grimaced at me. "Sorry about that, but your paper's circulation doesn't attract a large readership of wealthy buyers. Location, location . . . it cuts both ways in real estate."

I nodded. "Go on."

"I got a couple of hits the first week, but nothing solid until about the second week of June. This Dylan Platte guy sounded really interested. We e-mailed back and forth for a few days, and he finally said he'd come to Alpine toward the end of the month and have a look. Then he called me a week ago Monday . . . no, it was Tuesday . . . and said he'd be here Thursday. I met him at the diner and we played a little golf before I took him to look at the site. We didn't go inside because Ed and Shirley needed more notice to get everything shipshape for viewing. Anyway, I'd given him kind of a virtual tour on the Internet, you know, showing all the highlights. The next thing I know, the poor guy's dead." Snorty shook his head. And snorted, of course. "I was stunned, I can tell you."

I couldn't look at Vida, who'd winced almost every time Snorty had snorted during this lengthy account. Curtis, meanwhile, was half-listening in. The other half apparently was intermittently typing on his keyboard.

"Are you sure," I said to Snorty, "that this so-called Platte didn't arrive until Thursday?"

Snorty seemed taken aback. "That's what he told me. Why?"

"I'm positive I saw him in Alpine Wednesday afternoon," I said. "So did Stella Magruder at the salon. He was asking for directions to the golf course."

Snorty put a chubby fist to his cheek and pondered. "That might explain it."

"What?" Vida broke in.

He swerved to look at Vida. "When I took him on that drive, he mentioned the swimming pool and that he'd replace those poplar trees around it with some sort of cypress. I didn't think about that until later, but we hadn't gone by the pool area on the east side of the house yet, and my virtual tour only showed the pool itself, not the trees."

"Meaning," I said, "he'd been there earlier. Or maybe he saw them from the golf course, if that's where he'd gone on Wednesday."

Snorty shook his head. "I don't get it. Why would he do any of those things, including impersonate Dylan Platte? It sounds like a practical joke or something to me. Not," he added, wagging a finger, "that I don't appreciate a good laugh like anybody else."

"I'm sure the sheriff would like to know the answers, too," I told Snorty. "And the real Dylan Platte as well. The sale is going through, though, isn't it?"

Snorty frowned. "I hope so. I'm on my way up to the ski lodge to take a meeting with Mr. and Mrs. Platte. Ed and Shirley ought to have the house ready for viewing by now."

"Don't count on it," Vida muttered.

Snorty grimaced. "It's not easy with a place that big. Hard to get hired help around here, too." He eased himself out of Leo's chair. "Guess I'll be on my way. Say," he said, eyeing me with what I assumed was his friendliest smile, "you'll be sure and mention in your story that I'm a real estate agent dealing primarily in residential property all around Skykomish and Snohomish counties?"

"This isn't an ad," I said, trying to sound kind. "It's news. Of course I'll identify you as the agent for the Bronsky house."

Snorty nodded once. "It never hurts to dress that kind of

thing up, you know. I mean, small town people like to feel as if they're doing business with a neighbor."

"True." I was noncommittal. "Thanks, Mr. Wenzel."

As Snorty went out, my phone rang. I hurried into my cubbyhole to answer it.

"We got a hit on the dead guy's prints," Milo said. "NICS IDed him as Maxim Roth Volos, thirty-five, of New York City. Rap sheet includes a couple of fraud charges, dealing in illegal firearms, and some minor stuff. No convictions, though."

"New York?" I said in surprise. "You mean he's listed as a current resident there?"

"Last known address was somewhere in Manhattan," Milo answered, "but that was three years ago. I don't know much about New York, but the street where he lived then is called Amsterdam."

"I'm not familiar with the city, either," I admitted, "but I think it's one of the main drags."

"Like Alpine Way?" Milo said.

I figured he was kidding. "Everything in this world is relative. They both begin with an *A*. I don't know what to make of this news, but I'm glad you found out who he was before we go to press."

"I'm glad you're glad," he said dryly. "All it does for me is muddy the waters."

"I assume you'll ask the Cavanaugh Gang if they've ever heard of this guy," I said.

"Oh, sure. But if they have, they probably won't admit it. Talk to you later." The sheriff rang off.

Vida, naturally, had been eavesdropping. She'd headed my way as soon as I put the phone down. "Well?" she said.

I related what Milo had told me. "A little strange, isn't it?"

She pursed her lips and frowned. "Yes. But there must be

a connection." Vida pointed to the enlargement I'd had made of the victim's driver's license picture. "I can't think what it could be."

"I can't, either," I said.

We didn't know that the answer was staring us in the face.

TWELVE

FOR THE REST OF THE MORNING, I HURLED MYSELF INTO finishing my tasks for the front and editorial pages. I'd already completed my copy for the special Fourth of July four-page insert. We were going to run a photo from 1917, when Alpine had sold the highest ratio of World War One Liberty Bonds per capita in the state. The original pictures had been taken on the old mill's loading dock, with the residents proudly displaying a huge American flag donated by the once-great Seattle department store Frederick & Nelson. Vida had contributed a feature on previous Independence Day festivities and a "where-are-they-now" article about some of the descendants of the participants in the patriotic Liberty Bond drive. She featured a trio of young boys in the photo—two Dawson brothers, Louie and Tom, and a cousin, Bill Murphy—who had all served during World War Two. Louie had been in the Coast Guard, Tom was with General Patton in North Africa and Sicily, and Bill had been a naval officer in the South Pacific. All three had survived the war and returned to the Seattle area.

Curtis's contribution was an attempt at humor—not entirely

successful—on what might have happened if the colonists had lost the Revolutionary War. Leo, of course, was responsible for all of the extra-revenue ads that supported the additional four pages.

My homicide article proved tricky, but I managed to get in all the pertinent facts. I let Curtis write the cutline for the head shot and ask if anyone had seen the dead man during his brief stay in the area. If so, they should contract the sheriff—or the *Advocate*.

I stayed in for lunch to ride herd over the copy—as well as the ads—that were going to the back shop. I'd eaten two doughnuts and figured I could last until the lunch bunch had left the Burger Barn so I wouldn't have to wait in the take-out line.

At a quarter to one, I took a break to check my personal e-mail. I'd been too tired and upset the previous night to see if there were any messages after I'd gotten back from the ski lodge.

To my surprise—and initial delight—Adam had sent me a message just after ten PDT. "Hi, Mom," it read.

> Just sent an e-mail to Father Den Kelly in Alpine, telling him about the need for a new heater in our little church and also a new outboard motor for the boat I use during these summer months. Heater costs about $1,800, the motor runs (or doesn't run, in the case of the current one) almost $9,000. Thought Den might take up a special collection, and you could do an article in the paper that would reach not just the local residents but the retirees and other people who've moved out of the parish. I know many of them still subscribe to the *Advocate*. We'd really appreciate the help. Thanks—Love and prayers, Your Landlocked Son.

I sat very still for almost a full minute, staring at the screen and trying not to be furious. No mention of my dilemma, no reference to his half siblings. It was as if he'd forgotten all about what was going on with his mother. Finally, I typed my terse answer:

Adam—Have Father Den give me the details. We're up against deadline. Love, Mom.

I hit the Send button and immediately felt a pang of guilt. At least I'd signed the message "Love." Of course I knew my son was in a far-off place with huge demands upon his time and energy. But the kind of distance I sensed wasn't in terms of miles, it was emotional detachment. He'd taken vows of chastity, poverty, and obedience. Or, as his uncle Ben had put it, "No honey, no money, just the Boss." Unlike the sacrament of Matrimony, Holy Orders did not ask him to forsake all others, including his mother. Adam had hurt my feelings, and I couldn't help but be resentful.

While I was still licking my wounds, Leo sauntered in. "Emma," he called, approaching my cubbyhole, "guess who I ran into at the diner."

I tried to pull out of my bleak mood. "Who?"

"Fleetwood," Leo said, grinning. "Guess why he didn't run that interview with Snorty Wenzel?"

"Why?"

"Too many snorts," Leo replied. "When Fleetwood tried to edit them out, he ran into some technical problems and . . . What's wrong? You look pissed."

Denial was futile. I'm not very good at hiding my feelings. "I am. My son is being a pain in the butt." Seeing Leo's surprised expression, I held up a hand. "Don't get me wrong. I understand he has tons of problems to tackle every day, and a child assumes a parent can weather his or her own little storms. After all, that's what parents do and keep their mouths shut."

"Actually," Leo said, leaning on the back of one of my visitors' chairs, "we don't. Not after they get to be about six. Otherwise, they aren't ready for the real world. I ought to know. My ex and I knocked ourselves out keeping my drinking problem a secret from our kids—right up until I fell off the stage during the Christmas pageant at St. Elizabeth's in Van Nuys. Our oldest was in sixth grade at the time. 'Daddy's sick' didn't cut it."

"You have a point," I conceded. "In many ways, I didn't shield Adam from grim reality. I couldn't—not when he got old enough to wonder where his father was."

"What did you tell him?"

"That his dad lived in California." I thought back to that awkward moment when my son had just turned four. "Adam had heard of California. I showed him on a map and told him it was a long way from Portland. In fact, I hadn't known myself that Tom had moved from Seattle until I heard it a few months earlier through the grapevine at *The Oregonian*."

Leo nodded. "There must have been more questions when he got older."

"Oh, yes." I shook my head. "That got harder, but I was candid. When Adam was ten, I gave him the birds-and-the-bees talk. Luckily, I had Ben to help steer him through that from a male's standpoint. I told Adam then that his father and I had made a mistake, that I couldn't marry Tom because he already had a wife and children, and that it was best for us—I meant Adam and me—to stay out of Tom's life. I tried very hard to not describe his father as a villain, even though I had dark moods of resentment and anger."

"Not surprising." Leo regarded me with an inquisitive expression. "I . . ." He shrugged. "Never mind."

"What?"

"Hey, it's none of my business," he said, looking embarrassed.

"Oh, come on," I urged. "If it isn't, I'll tell you to stick it."

Leo uttered a big sigh. "I've wondered if Tom ever offered to help with Adam. Financially, I mean."

"He called me a couple of times at first. I hung up on him. Then he wrote me a letter. I threw it away and never answered it." I made a face. "That was it—until he showed up eighteen years later."

"So Adam really had only . . . what? An off-and-on relationship of five or six years with Tom?"

"A bit more," I said, finally realizing why Leo was quizzing me. "I know what you're thinking. Adam and Tom saw each other maybe a dozen times at most. Not enough to really bond. Ben was the surrogate father."

"Not to mention Adam must resent those half siblings, who, in effect, held his father hostage while they lived a life of luxury and you toiled away to keep food on the table and a roof over Adam's head. Hell, Emma," he said, straightening up, "your son may be a priest, but he's still human. He could be having his own struggles with this situation."

"Maybe," I allowed, noting that Vida had returned and was casting an inquiring eye in our direction. "I guess I should make allowances for that, but Adam's apparent indifference still hurts."

Before Leo could respond, my phone rang. Figuring Ginny wasn't yet back from lunch, I picked up the receiver.

"Ms. Lord?" the cheerful voice at the other end said. "This is Diana Hines in Everett. I called Debbie Murchison last night to inquire about Ella Hinshaw. She hadn't yet gotten back from Mount Vernon, but I left a message, and she called me on her lunch break a few minutes ago."

Leo had gone back to his desk. Vida had poured herself a mug of hot water and was standing in the middle of the newsroom. "Yes, Mrs. Hines," I said, making sure my House & Home editor could hear me. "How's Ella doing?"

The question rocketed Vida into my cubbyhole. "Malingering, probably," she muttered.

"She's doing fairly well," Mrs. Hines said, "and please call me Diana. Ella's going to need help when she's discharged, though. Her right side is paralyzed, though the prognosis is good."

"I'll let Mrs. Runkel know," I said, gazing innocently at Vida, who had settled into a chair. "She'll be so pleased to hear how her sister-in-law is getting along. Thanks for calling."

"That's not all," Diana said hastily as Vida glared at me. "I asked Debbie about the Josh and Ginger Roth thing. She had actually seen Mr. Roth—she presumed it was Mr. Roth—slipping his name into the mailbox slot a week or so ago."

"She had?" I scribbled a note for Vida and pushed it across my desk. "Did she talk to him?"

"Yes," Diana replied. "She asked if he was moving in. He told her he was, along with his wife. And then he left. Debbie was coming off the night shift and was dead tired, so she went straight to her unit."

"Did you ask her what he looked like?"

"She said he was very good-looking, thirties, well-dressed, brown hair. Is that any help?"

"It could be," I said, noting that Vida was shifting impatiently in the chair. "Maybe we can show her some pictures." Thanking Diana, a second time, I rang off.

"Well now!" Vida huffed. "What's this about?"

I gave her the details. "Do you want to see Debbie?" I inquired. "You could look in on Ella."

"I already did, after work last night." Vida made a face. "Ella ought to have more spunk. Therapy should restore the use of her arm and leg, but dollars to doughnuts, she won't stay with the regimen. She'll expect everyone to wait on her."

"Luckily," I pointed out, "Ella has quite a few relatives in town."

Vida looked askance. "I refuse to be numbered among them."

Having no intention of getting into a Runkel family feud, and never exactly certain of how each was related to the others, I changed the subject. "What about talking to Debbie?"

"You mean to show her the picture of the victim?"

I nodded. "If she doesn't recognize him as the man at Pines Villa, get a description."

"Very well." Vida stood up. "First, I must finish 'Scene'. I could use one more item."

"It looks like the squirrels have been digging in the planter boxes on Front Street," I said. "There was dirt all over the sidewalk by the one where I parked this morning."

"Nasty creatures," Vida murmured. "So destructive. And prankish. They ate almost all of my daffodil bulbs this winter. I don't know why I'm buying more to plant this fall. At least they left some of the tulips."

She started out of my office, but the mention of bulbs was a timely reminder for me. "Hey," I called out, "you never told me what Rick Erlandson said when you went over to the bank to get your money order. Did he recognize the victim's picture?"

Vida turned around and scowled. "Rick was in a meeting. I'll check with him when I go to the hospital to see Debbie. And," she added grudgingly, "Ella."

"You might check at the Venison Inn with Oren and Sunny Rhodes," I said. "The blonde known as Ginger was there with a man last week. They'll remember—Milo and I already talked to them, but we didn't have a picture of the victim with us."

Vida looked disapproving. "I prefer not going into the bar. Midafternoon drinkers are often alcoholic. And Sunny doesn't ordinarily start work until the dinner hour."

"Okay, I'll do it myself," I said. "Or send Curtis."

"Good luck with that assignment." Vida stalked off.

Curtis returned shortly after she'd left. Leo was in the back shop with Kip. Ginny was languishing behind the front desk.

"I'm going to get some lunch," I informed my reporter. "I won't be gone long."

"Anything I can do?" he asked in a rather plaintive tone.

"All of your copy is in?"

He nodded. "All six inches of it."

I felt guilty for having lost confidence in his journalistic ability. "Okay. You can go to the diner and talk to Terri Bourgette. Ask if she remembers the guy who came in Thursday with Snorty Wenzel. Then stop by the sheriff's office and find out if there are any last-minute facts they've uncovered." I figured there probably wouldn't be anything new or Milo would have let me know. On the other hand, the sheriff sometimes forgot about our Tuesday deadline. "Oh—get a copy of the victim's enlarged driver's license head shot and check in with Oren Rhodes. If Sunny—his wife—happens to be there, ask her, too."

"Got it," Curtis said, all but leaping out of his chair. "Race you to the door."

I let him win. Short of firing him, the only thing I could do was try to offer encouragement and hope he improved as a reporter. After all, he'd been on the job just a few weeks, and he was young as well as inexperienced. Over thirty years ago, I'd traveled that same road. My internship at *The Seattle Times* had helped me adapt to the real world of newspapers—and, in the process, it had broken my heart. My mentor had been Tom Cavanaugh. At least I didn't have to worry about Curtis falling in love with Vida.

Shortly after two, my House & Home editor returned, her gray eyes snapping behind her big glasses. "Well! That was most interesting!" she declared, confronting me as I was coming out of the back shop. "Rick Erlandson and Debbie Murchison identified the victim as the same person they'd seen at the bank and Pines Villa."

"Maxim Volos," I said. "Pretending to be Josh Roth. So who is Ginger?"

Vida frowned. "*Where* is Ginger?"

"She's not around here." I paced a bit. "It couldn't be Kelsey, even if she is blond. I doubt very much that Kelsey could carry off an impersonation of somebody like Ginger. And Sophia's very dark. Unless . . ."

"Unless what?"

"Unless," I said, leaning against the filing cabinet, "Sophia was disguised. Come to think of it, Ginger had green eyes. So does Sophia. She strikes me as far more aggressive than Kelsey. You saw the so-called Ginger when she was here. What did you think?"

"Hussy. California. Not a genuine human being."

"In what way?"

"In . . ." Vida paused. "Oh. I see what you mean. Physical attributes as opposed to personal. Both. The hair, the makeup, the very large sunglasses, the skimpy clothes—rather theatrical, I thought. I didn't speak to her but would assume she was . . . acting. Is that not a California type?"

"Often a cliché," I allowed. "But you're right about Ginger. It seems obvious now that she wasn't real."

"You're certain Kelsey couldn't have played the part?"

I nodded. "Very certain. She couldn't have done it unless she's the greatest actress to not yet win an Oscar, and because she'd also have to be pretending now that she's a very passive and probably troubled young woman."

Vida stuck a stray hairpin into her unruly gray curls. "Yes . . . and I really should meet her. How do you think she'd respond to my request for an interview about moving here?"

"I don't know," I admitted. "First, they haven't moved yet. We've no idea if they took one look at the Bronsky house up close and ran as fast as they could back to . . . San Francisco, I guess. I suppose Snorty or Ed could tell us."

"They'd lie," Vida asserted. "Or at least hedge. What about Sophia? A visitor's reaction to Alpine."

"That might work," I said. "We don't have room for it this week."

"Then next."

"Go ahead. Have you time to do that this afternoon?"

"My, yes," Vida said. "I've sent everything to Kip. I'll call the ski lodge to set a time." Sniffing the scent of new quarry to stalk, she went on her splayfooted way.

Curtis returned a little before three. "Same guy," he informed me, handing over the driver's license photo. "Terri Burdette and Oren Rhodes both agreed this was who they saw at their restaurants."

"Bourgette," I corrected. "Terri *Bourgette*." I paused to let the name sink into Curtis's skull. As usual, he seemed unfazed by the correction. Either he was used to being wrong or he chose to reject any criticism. "Okay, we've confirmed that much. Did you ask the sheriff if he'd done the same?"

"Dodge wasn't in," Curtis replied. "He was out with the bears."

"The bears?"

"Right. Those cubs. I guess they found them by some old mine shaft."

Taking a deep breath and staring at my bobble-head doll of Edgar Martinez in his Mariners uniform, I refrained from screaming at Curtis. Edgar wasn't just a two-time American League batting champion but an icon of patience at the plate. And I needed patience, lots of it, in dealing with my exasperating reporter. Finally, I looked up at him. "Can you get a picture and some information so we can put the cubs in this week's edition with its five o'clock deadline?"

"I guess. Sure. Okay." Curtis started to turn around but stopped. "Where *is* that mine shaft?"

"If it's the one by Disappointment Avenue," I said, getting up, "it's off of the Icicle Creek Road, otherwise known as Highway 187." I pointed to the spot on my wall map. "If it's a different old mine shaft, then it's somewhere else around here," I went on, biting off each word more sharply than the last, "but you can find that out by asking one of the deputies."

"Will do. I'm outta here."

Curtis rushed out of my office and straight to the newsroom door. "Hey!" I shouted after him. "Camera?"

"Oh, snap!" He laughed lamely and went over to his desk to get his camera. I turned my back and looked again at Edgar. *Patience, patience, patience.* The young and the feckless were fraying my nerves.

"Five o'clock," Vida called to me. "Sophia wants to join her for cocktails at the ski lodge."

I walked to the newsroom doorway. "Are you going to order a drink with actual alcohol?"

Vida looked uncertain. "I have upon rare occasion done such a thing, as you know," she mused. "Perhaps I should, if only to demonstrate that I'm not utterly opposed to liquor.

That might get us off on the wrong footing. A Tom Collins— I always remember that cocktail. Years ago, there was a bucker by that name at the Alpine Mill. But I can't linger. I should be at KSKY by six-thirty for my program."

"Frankly," I said, "I'm surprised Sophia agreed to the interview. Did she mention if Dylan and Kelsey are really going to buy the Bronskys' atrocity?"

"She told me they were in negotiations." Vida grimaced. "I hope that involves demolition."

"We'll see," I murmured, heading into the back shop to see if Kip had enough room for a front-page picture of the bear cubs. *If* Curtis managed to take it.

My production manager was uncertain. "If the shot's any good," he explained, "we should run it three columns by six inches. That means the photos of Fuzzy Baugh's carving have to be cut way down, and probably the head shot of the dead guy, too."

"We need the head shot to run large enough so that anyone who's seen this guy can recognize him," I said after a moment's consideration. "Can we eliminate the pix Curtis took at the carver's studio and put Fuzzy and his porcupine on the back page?"

Kip stroked his goatee and shook his head. "The mayor won't like that."

"The mayor isn't in charge of the *Advocate*," I retorted. "If he bitches, we'll tell him our only other choice was to hold the picture off until next week."

Having made that decision, I returned to my office and called the sheriff. He might still be with the cubs, but I wanted to make absolutely certain that we weren't overlooking anything involving the homicide investigation.

Milo was in. "Just got back," he said. "The Dithers sisters found the cubs. They ride their horses on a trail that follows

Carroll Creek. One of them stayed with the cubs while the other went back to notify us."

I wasn't surprised that Judy and Connie Dithers had managed to corral the cubs and keep them from running off. The sisters led lives that were all about animals, especially the half-dozen horses they owned. One of their few diversions was playing in our bridge group, but even then, they spoke only if necessary, and I always expected them to whinny or neigh when it was their turn to bid.

"Curtis is taking a picture," I said. "He probably didn't get there until after you left."

"Didn't see him," the sheriff remarked. "Doe Jameson told me he'd been in a while ago to see if there was anything new on our murder. There isn't."

"I figured as much," I said, "but I'm trying to train Curtis in very small doses. Anything new on this Maxim Volos?"

"I'd have told you if there was," Milo shot back. "Don't nag."

"Okay," I agreed. "But there must be a connection between him and the Cavanaughs. How else would he have known about me and the paper and Tom?"

"I checked with Graham earlier," Milo replied. "He claims they never heard of him."

"Do you believe that?"

"How can I prove they don't?"

Even as I talked to Milo, I went online and looked up Volos. It was a town in Greece, although I got hits on a couple of Americans with that last name. "From New York, huh?"

"Yeah. So what?"

"I'm trying to think of a connection."

"To what?" Milo was beginning to sound irked. "Wes Amundson just came into my office to tell me what the forest service is going to do with the cubs. Put your jigsaw puzzle together on somebody else's time." The sheriff hung up.

I made a quick note to call Wes, one of our local forest rangers, before deadline. It would be too much to expect that Curtis might find out about the cubs' future on his own.

I went to talk to Vida, who was flipping through her large file of recipes. She didn't look up when I approached her desk but beckoned for me to sit. "Kip informs me," she said in a vexed tone, "that Nucoa isn't around anymore, at least not under that name, and that even if it is, you no longer have to add the yellow color packet to make the margarine look like butter."

"How old is that recipe?" I asked.

Vida finally looked at me. "I'm not sure. Right after World War Two? It was left to me by my predecessor, Mrs. Debee."

"Isn't that a bit dated?"

Vida shrugged her broad shoulders. "A tasty dish is still tasty despite the passage of time. Now I must find a substitute." She pulled a three-by-five card out of the file. "Pottsfield pickles. That sounds interesting. Or this one," she went on, extracting another card. " 'How to Can a Tuna Fish.' "

I didn't offer any more advice. Vida couldn't cook a decent meal to save her soul. I shuddered at the mere thought of her wrestling with a tuna fish—or even pickles.

"Tell me," I said, "what am I missing on this Cavanaugh thing? How could Maxim Volos of New York City know about the *Advocate* and Tom's children?"

She frowned. "Well now . . . I suppose there's a social or a work connection somewhere. I assume Milo has asked the Cavanaughs."

"Yes. They claim ignorance."

"They would, wouldn't they?" Vida drummed her fingers on the desk. "Dylan and Kelsey live in California, correct?"

"San Francisco," I said. "Graham and Sophia also live there."

"Are any of them living in Tommy's former home?"

Even after so many years, I could never get used to Vida referring to Tom as "Tommy." It had never bothered him, but it always sounded incongruous to me. I tried to remember the address Graham and Sophia had given when they registered at the ski lodge. "No, not the house in Pacific Heights. Tom planned to sell it after Sandra died because it was too big—and maybe held too many memories. I'm not sure if he ever put it on the market, though. He'd already bought a condo on Nob Hill." Pausing, I tried to remember the street name that the younger Cavanaughs had registered at the lodge. "Clay Street. I'm not sure, but I think Clay cuts across Nob Hill."

Vida stroked her chin. "So no New York residents."

"I'm trying to remember," I said, certain that some vital fact was buried in my brain. "One of Tom's kids moved to New York for a while. Yes, it was Kelsey. She was in love with a guy who got her pregnant."

"Dylan Platte?"

"I don't think so," I admitted. "She told me they didn't have any children together. I'm not sure Tom ever mentioned the father's name. In fact, I don't even know if Kelsey had the baby. She had a difficult pregnancy. You may recall that Tom had to cut one of his visits here short when Kelsey appeared to be having a miscarriage." I tried to think, to remember, to bring back Tom's voice in my head. "Maybe I never really wanted to hear about Tom's kids. It was hard enough to listen to Sandra's problems. And there was such a lapse of years before we got back . . ." My voice trailed off. I was close to tears. Clenching my fists, I cleared my throat. "For a couple of writers, we never wrote to each other. Everything was on the phone or in person."

"Of course," Vida said. "Too risky for him, at least to receive anything at his home while Sandra was alive." She waited for me to pull myself together. "Something may come back to you."

"Maybe."

"Birth records," Vida said with a snap of her fingers. "If Kelsey didn't marry that boyfriend, then her child's birth would be recorded under her maiden name in San Francisco."

"True," I agreed. "Although that really wouldn't help much in figuring out who killed Maxim Volos."

"Probably not," Vida responded, "but aren't you curious? What about marriage certificates?" she went on, obviously gathering steam. "Dylan and Kelsey, Graham and Sophia. There could be a connection that Milo, with his limited imagination, would never search for."

"We could do that on the Internet, though I'm sure they'd charge us for a search."

"It's a business expense," Vida pointed out.

"Yes," I replied, "but we have other extra business expenses these days." I pointed upward. "The roof, for example."

"Oh, for heaven's sakes!" Vida cried, fists on hips. "You're being evasive. I don't think you want to know anything about these people, criminals or not! Where's your curiosity? If need be, I'll pay for a search myself." She stopped speaking and frowned. "Though I must admit, I'm not sure how to go about it. You know I'm decidedly ignorant when it comes to anything with the computer that goes beyond typing. I've never seen any reason why I have to learn all those silly functions just to write my articles."

"Okay, okay, check it out. Here." I leaned over her shoulder. "Go online . . . like this." I clicked the mouse to get Vida on the Internet.

"Now what?" she asked as I typed in "California birth records."

"We find a good site." I chose the first of many listings. "There. Go ahead and type in the name Kelsey Cavanaugh."

"In that blank box?"

"Yes."

"I could do this for anyone I was curious about?"

"Yes."

"Hmm. Perhaps I should learn some of these things after all."

"It can be very helpful," I said, knowing that Vida was already hooked. I could imagine her brain firing up with endless possibilities. It wouldn't have surprised me to see smoke coming out of her ears.

"Ah!" Vida exclaimed as Kelsey's name appeared along with her age as thirty-two. The city listing was San Francisco. "Now what?"

"We have to agree to pay the forty bucks to check further," I said. "We might as well. We'll need to go through a bunch of hoo-ha to register and pay with a credit card. I'll get my purse."

By the time I'd returned with my Visa card in hand, Vida had brought up Dylan, thirty-four, San Francisco, CA. She seemed quite proud of herself.

"We can find out when they were married," Vida said. "Shall we?"

"Okay, but why don't you move so I can type in all this other stuff?"

Vida got up, and I sat down. "This is quite fascinating," she declared, adjusting her navy blue skirt to cover the hem of her slip. "I had no idea there were so many ways to learn about people. I may try this to find out information about . . . say, former Alpine residents and where they're living now. Strictly work-related, of course."

"Of course," I agreed, deadpan. It took a few minutes to enter the required information. Vida stood by the small window next to her desk, watching the passing parade on Front Street.

"Barney Amundson's limping," she murmured. "I wonder why. A mishap at Alpine Meats? Marisa Foxx . . . where is she going? The courthouse? That reminds me, Judi Hinshaw is her legal secretary. Perhaps she could stay with her aunt Ella for a while."

"How is Ella?" I asked, waiting for credit card approval.

"Exactly as I'd expect," Vida replied. "Feeble. Wan. Feeling sorry for herself. I prescribed a good dose of gumption."

"A stroke can be serious," I pointed out, relinquishing the chair to Vida. "Ella is fairly old."

"Old," Vida declared, "is a state of mind, not a number." She waved a hand in apparent dismissal of Ella's problems. "Exercise, that's what she should have done. I walk all over town, I work in the garden, I keep up a house. Ella simply sits in her apartment and watches TV. I've no time for that kind of laziness." She slapped her hand down—unfortunately, on the keyboard. The search site disappeared.

"Oh!" I blurted, then realized that I was overreacting.

"What?" Vida asked.

I pointed to the screen, which now showed the wedding cut-line Vida had been writing. "No problem. We'll just have to go on the Internet again."

"Oh, dear." Vida sighed. "I'm so sorry. Maybe I'm hexed."

"No, no," I assured her. "Go ahead and sign on—"

Curtis's arrival interrupted us. "Ta-da!" he cried in triumph. "Great cubs pix, ready to go on page one."

"Let's see," I said.

Vida joined me at Curtis's desk, where he transferred the photos to his computer. "See?" He grinned with pride. "Cute, huh?"

Two fuzzy black bear cubs stared at me with wary eyes. Or maybe they were hungry eyes, sad eyes, lonely eyes, motherless eyes. "Very good." I waited while he went through the other shots. "The third and seventh ones are best," I decided. "You and Kip figure out which one. What are they going to do with the cubs?"

"I dunno," Curtis replied. "Let them loose? Give them to a zoo?"

I pointed to his phone. "Call Wes Amundson or the sheriff now and find out. It's going on four o'clock. We don't have much time."

"Gotcha." Curtis picked up the receiver and stopped. "Who's Wes Amundson?"

"One of the forest rangers," I informed him and marched over to Vida's desk. "Okay, let's get back on the Internet. We'll try for birth records first and see if Kelsey's baby—" I stopped. "My God, it just came back to me! How could I have forgotten?"

Vida regarded me curiously. "What?"

I perched on the edge of her desk and pressed my fingers to my forehead. "Maybe it's all this talk about abandoned baby bears, but I suddenly remember that Kelsey had her baby and was trying to raise him—it was a boy—on her own with Tom's help. He was named Aidan, for Tom's father. I think he'd be about six by now."

"Well." Vida nodded several times. "You see? You did pay attention. Do you think Dylan is the father?"

"No, he's not." I shook my head in dismay. "I can't believe how much of what Tom told me has been pushed way back in my brain. The boyfriend he mentioned was named Thor, who wasn't suitable husband or father material. He was a musician, maybe—or some other kind of creative type earning a subsistence income. I'm not sure if she met him in San Francisco or somewhere else." I shook my head in frustration. "I simply don't remember."

Curtis hung up the phone. "Wow! Ever hear about the man who talks to bears?"

Vida and I both stared at him. "No," I said. "Who is he?"

Curtis indicated the phone. "I talked to Doe Jameson at the sheriff's office. She's part Native American, I guess, and into all this forest lore. This guy's called the Bear Whisperer, though he talks to other animals, too. He saw the cubs not far from where he lives and wants to raise them. He's done it before with deer and even birds."

Vida had yanked off her glasses. "Who is this person?" she demanded. "I've never heard of him. Are you sure he exists?"

"Oh, yeah, he's real," Curtis asserted. "He lives someplace in the woods and hardly ever comes to town. You know—some kind of crazy hermit or recluse. His name's Craig Laurentis."

THIRTEEN

Vida's mouth dropped open; I was stunned. "Craig Laurentis is an artist," I said. "I own one of his paintings. He's actually quite brilliant."

"Really?" Curtis looked skeptical. "He sounds like a wacko to me."

"He's eccentric," I said. "An aging hippie, who isn't fond of civilization as we know it. Did you see him?"

Curtis shook his head. "I guess that's the thing with this guy. He likes hanging out more with animals than with people."

"It'd be wonderful if we could get a picture of him," I said, "but I doubt that Craig would let us. He prefers to keep to himself. I respect that. His talent earns him the right to be as antisocial and nonconformist as he pleases."

Vida had put her glasses back on. "We should mention his name in the paper, though," she pointed out. "That's assuming Craig gets permission to nurture the cubs."

"That may take a day or so to work through," I said. "I'll write the cutline to say that Craig has offered to care for them. I doubt that he ever reads the *Advocate*, so he shouldn't be upset."

Curtis looked puzzled. "You care if he's upset?"

"Yes." My expression was defiant. "I do care. Not only do I get great pleasure from his painting but he helped me once when I had an accident on a trail near Icicle Creek."

Curtis shrugged. "Takes all kinds, as they say." He sauntered off to the back shop.

Vida gestured at her computer screen. "Shall we go on with the Internet whatever-you-call-it?"

"Not just now," I said. "I have to write that cutline, and I should check with Kip to make sure the front page will be okay now that we have the cub picture."

My House & Home editor seemed disappointed. "I might experiment trying to get on the Internet after I finish my own cutline. The Anderson wedding wasn't dropped off until this afternoon. Why do people wait so long? They were married in mid-May, and not in Alpine but at the San Diego Zoo. Why on earth would they do such a thing? There's a hippopotamus in the background." She peered more closely at the photo. "Or is that the bride's mother?" I left Vida to figure it out for herself.

An hour later we were officially at deadline. As far as the nuts and bolts of the paper were concerned, everything was ready to go. But I was uneasy. Our coverage of the murder investigation was too sketchy. It also had required great delicacy and far too many *allegedly*s and *possibly*s. The victim was just a name. I wouldn't mention any details of the buyout offer because it was a moot point. I'd written that "Volos apparently had impersonated an owner of a large western newspaper chain." I didn't even say that the name the victim allegedly had used was Dylan Platte. As for Dylan and Kelsey's proposed move to Alpine, that was a separate story, if and when they put down earnest money on the Bronsky manse. I'd wrestled with how to handle the connection but decided that including the

Plattes in the homicide story might suggest that I was fingering them as suspects.

Having turned over the rest of the publishing task to Kip, I left the office at ten after five. I was heading for my car when someone called my name from half a block away.

It was Marisa Foxx. "A quick question," she said, hurrying to join me. "Is it true that you told Ed Bronsky I'd be glad to handle a lawsuit for him on a pro bono basis?"

"Good Lord, no!" I uttered an abbreviated laugh. "He asked me if I thought you were a good attorney. I told him of course—or words to that effect. But I'd never suggest that you'd take on his case, especially pro bono."

Marisa's expression was wry. "I thought not. I'm sorry to have bothered you."

"I can't believe Ed knows what *pro bono* means," I said.

Marisa smiled slightly. "He knows what it means, all right, but he called it pro bueno. I guess he thought it was Spanish, not Latin. He told me once after Mass that he'd served as an altar boy. You'd think he might have remembered *some* Latin from the old days."

"He's lucky he remembers English," I responded. "Oh, I shouldn't be so hard on him, but Ed can be a trial. Say," I went on impulsively, "have you got time for a drink?"

"Well . . . yes," Marisa answered, obviously surprised by the invitation. The fact was, I'd been meaning to get to know her better ever since she'd moved to Alpine not too long after I arrived. Our relationship had been strictly professional, although we occasionally chatted briefly before or after Sunday Mass. We had a good deal in common, though, both being single career women and not having much in the way of social lives.

"Venison Inn?" I said, pointing just down the street to the restaurant's entrance.

The wry expression returned. "Where else?"

I laughed. "We could go to the liquor store, buy a cheap fifth of something, and drink under the statue of Carl Clemans in Old Mill Park."

"That would end up in Vida's 'Scene,' " Marisa said.

"Not while I'm editor," I retorted as we headed down the street.

We made casual chitchat until we were seated in the bar and had given our orders to an effusive Oren Rhodes.

"Is he always like that?" Marisa inquired after Oren returned to the bar. "I don't come here very often."

"I think he saves the flattery for women of a certain age," I replied. "Maybe that's what they taught in bartending school thirty years ago."

"That sounds about right," Marisa remarked, her shrewd gaze moving around the rapidly filling room. Her voice was low and rather soft but well-modulated, probably a valuable asset in trials. "So. What kind of off-the-clock legal advice do you need?"

I was surprised and faintly offended. "I don't. Is that something you're used to being asked for?"

"Of course." She looked amused. "Just like doctors get cornered by people with symptoms whenever they're out of the office or the clinic or wherever." Before I could respond, she waved a slim hand. "Sorry. I'm not used to life as a social animal."

"I can understand that," I said. "Alpine isn't really suited for single professional women. So why do you stay?"

Marisa shrugged. "I grew up in a small town. Omak, on the other side of the Cascades, in what is quaintly called high desert country." She smiled. "But you know all that. It's about the same size as Alpine, but even farther away from a big city.

My parents moved to Arizona a few years ago. Then my father died and Mom had to go into a nursing home, so I found a place for her in Everett. I've thought about moving there to be closer, but her health is very fragile. My practice is fairly good because there are so few lawyers in Alpine, and property is much cheaper here. So I stay." She shrugged again. "Maybe that's a mistake."

"I can't offer any advice on that," I said and waited for Oren to set down Marisa's vodka martini and my bourbon and water. Briefly, I wondered if Vida was nursing her Tom Collins cocktail at the ski lodge with Sophia Cavanaugh.

"Anything else, lovely ladies?" Oren inquired, bending down a bit, maybe assuming that we were both deaf. "Dinner menus?"

I shook my head. "Can't. It's Tuesday, Vida's night to howl."

The bartender straightened up, and his beaming face turned serious. "You don't have to tell me that. This place is really dead when her show is on the radio." He gazed around the bar and fingered his chin. "Do you suppose Vida'd like to do her broadcast from here? What do they call it? A remote?"

"Probably not," I said, "but," I went on, feeling impish, "you could ask her the next time she comes into the restaurant."

"I just might," Oren replied. "You never know."

"So," I said to Marisa after Oren had again gone on his way, "you went to law school at the UW. I take it you didn't want to stay in Seattle?"

"I was fine while I went through the U," Marisa said. "Focused on my studies, lived on campus in one of the dorms until my final year, and then I moved to a boardinghouse nearby. But the big city kind of frightened me. I worked for the state in Olympia for several years, and that wasn't too bad. Then I decided to go into private practice, and the opportunity came up here in Alpine. I took it. And I haven't budged in all these years, despite a couple of tempting offers."

"In bigger cities?"

She nodded. "One in Seattle, but the firm was *too* big. I'd have felt lost. The other was in San Francisco, and it was a much smaller firm. I was tempted because it was fairly prestigious. But when I found out I'd be replacing a lawyer who'd been murdered, I didn't feel right about it. That was three or four years ago, and I suppose I'm not really sorry I said no. 'Kill all the lawyers' suddenly seemed like more than a mere quote from Shakespeare. Silly, huh?"

"Maybe not," I allowed. "Walking in a dead lawyer's shoes might not be comfortable. Did an outraged client do the dastardly deed?"

Marisa shook her head as she swallowed a sip of martini. "The last I heard, the case was never solved."

"I hope the sheriff has better luck with our current homicide," I remarked.

"Dodge seems very competent," Marisa said without expression. No doubt she knew that Milo and I had an off-and-on-again affair.

"He is," I agreed, "though he tends to go by the book. Still, that's important these days. I imagine that lawyers, especially prosecutors, prefer law enforcement types who are sticklers for going about their jobs the right way."

"Oh, certainly," Marisa said. "Not that I do any serious criminal law. DUIs, speeding tickets, a rare burglary or assault. Even some of those are often frivolous from a defense attorney's viewpoint. Myra Sundvold's husband, Dave, insists that I represent her every time she's charged with kleptomania. The last case I had to take to court involved her stealing a three-pack of boxer shorts from the men's store in the mall. Dave said she had no reason to take them because he wears briefs and she wears bloomers. The prosecuting attorney, Rosemary Bourgette, suggested that Myra might have a lover. That's when the fur began to fly. But you know more about crime in Alpine than I do since you have to publish the offenders' names."

I admitted that naming names in the paper was always very touchy in a small town. "They can't sue because the police log is a matter of record," I pointed out. "But that doesn't mean they can't harass me by phone, mail, or even in person. Not to mention their irate friends and relatives. Sometimes I feel very unpopular."

"I understand," Marisa said. "I've had some ugly reactions—even threats—when I win a judgment for one local against another. What makes it worse is that sometimes the two sides are related to each other. Talk about family feuds!"

We spent the rest of our drinking time discussing the various perils of our professions. It was almost six-fifteen when we left the Venison Inn. "We should do this another time," I said just before we parted company on the sidewalk.

"I'd like that." Marisa smiled. "We should have done it a long time ago."

"I know. But life—or maybe I should say the rut we get in— often seems hard to change. Next time we'll do dinner, but not at a time that interferes with Vida's program."

"Right." Marisa's smile seemed genuine, though she immediately sobered. "You know something? Talking about that job offer in San Francisco made me think that I should follow up and find out whatever happened to that lawyer I was supposed to replace. I completely lost interest after a couple of months went by. Now I'd like to find out if they ever solved the case."

"And if the lawyer they hired instead of you turned out to be a dud?"

She laughed, a sort of low little chuckle. "Oh, they probably got some eager beaver from Stanford or Cal who's now making big money. Most of that practice was probate, and frankly, I'd find it very limiting. I'd have gone stale in six months."

After we made another vow to get together, she headed for her office in the Alpine Building, across the street from the *Advocate*. I considered checking with Kip but knew that if he'd had any problems he would've called me on my cell phone. With only a glance at the front door to our modest digs, I got in my car and went home to my equally modest log house.

The mail I removed from my box by the side of Fir Street was all junk, with the usual couple of promos for credit cards. No phone calls awaited me. Except for a batch of advertising messages, there were no new e-mails of interest. The refrigerator and freezer were bereft of any tempting items. I took out a frozen chicken and noodle casserole and a handful of little peeled carrots. The casserole went into the oven. I might take shortcuts in food preparation, but with some muddled rationalization that I wasn't completely lazy, I rarely microwaved frozen entrées. Then, despite already having downed a preprandial drink, I poured a half-inch of bourbon over ice and added some water. Now I was set to enjoy my evening's big event, listening to Vida chat her head off from her gossipy cupboard.

The casserole wasn't done by the time the usual sound effects of creaking hinges announced that Vida was opening her cupboard. She immediately launched into her usual "Good evening to all my dear friends and neighbors in Alpine and the surrounding area of Skykomish County. As ever, I take my hat off to each and every one of you for . . ."

The rest of the salute varied from week to week. This time

her apparent theme—not that she always had one—was the Fourth of July or, as Vida insisted on calling it, Independence Day, and her hat was doffed to everyone who appreciated the American way of life, especially those who had the good sense to live within the range of her trumpetlike voice.

She continued her holiday theme by talking about more of the descendants of the early town settlers and the mill workers. Ruby and Louie Siegel had moved to Sultan and raised three sons; one of the mill owner Carl Clemans's three daughters had married her fellow Alpiner Payson Peterson and settled in Snohomish; the former logging camp cook Webster Patterson and his wife, Clara June, had two sons, one of whom had become a doctor and the other a Jesuit priest. And so on, names from the distant past that still seemed to resonate across the river valley from Mount Baldy to Tonga Ridge.

During the commercial break, I took my casserole out of the oven and began to eat. The substitute for the ailing Maud Dodd was Vida's nephew, the SkyCo deputy sheriff Bill Blatt. As was her custom, she called him "Billy," despite the fact that he was now in his mid-thirties and probably would've preferred just plain Bill. The interview was about observing a countywide restriction against setting off fireworks except in Old Mill Park or on the high school football field. The law was aimed not only at preventing careless people from blowing off their fingers but also preventing forest fires. There were always several arrests and fines for those who ignored the ordinance. The previous year our resident UFO spotter, Averill Fairbanks, insisted that his teenage grandson had launched several mortars in the backyard to prevent a half-dozen hostile spaceships from landing on top of First Baptist Church across the street. Milo didn't buy the argument, and the Fairbanks family had to shell out—so to speak—two hundred bucks in fines.

My mind wandered during the interview. Bill Blatt was reit-

erating much of what we were running in the *Advocate,* as
we'd been doing for the last few years since the ordinances had
gone into effect. I had finished my meal by the time Vida closed
her cupboard—more creaking hinges followed by Spencer
Fleetwood's recorded message to return next week when "Vida
Runkel is back at this same time on KSKY with all the news
that isn't fit to print."

I shut off the radio and tidied up the kitchen. Feeling at
loose ends, I turned on the TV to catch the Mariners playing
the Texas Rangers at home in Safeco Field. My brain, however,
wasn't focused on the game. Vida probably would call me as
soon as she got home to tell me about her chat with Sophia
Cavanaugh. Remembering Adam's request, I started to dial
Father Den's number at the rectory but stopped on the third
digit. Tuesday was our pastor's night for conducting a class on
St. Matthew's gospel. I'd phone him in the morning.

Ten minutes later, I heard a knock on the door. *Vida,* I thought
and hurried to let her in. But she wasn't my visitor. Graham Cavanaugh stood on the small front porch, smiling pleasantly.

"I decided it was time to talk," he said. "Do you mind if I
come in?"

"No," I said, stepping aside. "I'm not very busy."

I offered him the armchair by the hearth and asked if he'd
care for something to drink.

Graham shook his head. "I'm good," he replied, surveying
my living room with its exposed logs and rafters. "So this is the
little log cabin in the woods."

"Yes," I said, resuming my place on the sofa. "Can you picture your father living here?"

"No, I really can't," Graham said after a pause. "He'd become a true San Franciscan. No offense, but we never believed
he'd move away after thirty years."

"Really." My tone was skeptical.

"Oh, I realize that's not what you like to hear," Graham said matter-of-factly, "but Tom was all about business and profit margins. That was his life. He enjoyed the action."

"Maybe."

Graham leaned forward, hands clasped on his knees. "Look, I understand you may have a different take on my father, but we all have our own perceptions. How many years did you hold on to the dream?"

"Too damned long," I snapped. "It was no dream. We finally had definite plans. Adam—your half brother—and my own brother were going to concelebrate our nuptial Mass."

"That sounds wonderful," Graham remarked, "and I'm sure that's what you wanted. It's quite touching—romantic, too. But that wasn't going to happen." He slowly shook his head. "I'm sorry, it's tough to demolish someone's illusions, but the real world is often harsh."

"Why have you come to see me?" I asked, trying to control my distress and at the same time searching for something—anything—about Graham that reminded me of Tom.

Graham sat back in the armchair, crossing one leg over the other and giving his designer slacks a little tug to keep the crease straight. "To settle this business with the *Advocate*. We've reworked our offer and want you to stay on as long as you wish as the editor."

I started to protest, but Graham held up a hand. "Please, hear me out. We're making a generous offer, and we'll also give you a salary that will be considerably more than you take home now. We can do that because we own over three dozen newspapers west of the Rockies, up by fourteen percent in the three years since Tom died. Almost all of them are in the black. We manage to make a profit because our specialty is advertising on a very broad basis, not just local or even regional, but including national and even international advertisers. In some instances, we can give the newspapers away because of the lucrative ad revenue. You can see for yourself not only that this setup would provide you with a comfortable income until you're ready to retire but that the buyout money will give you a fat nest egg."

The offer made some sense. *Some,* I thought, yet not enough to make me jump at the prospect.

My hesitation was Graham's signal to chuckle softly. "Don't give me an answer now. Think about it, sleep on it. You know from your own experience that our little empire is solid and has a fine reputation. We're staying for another day while Dylan and Kelsey make up their minds about that house they're considering." He got to his feet and smiled benignly. "I'll go away now and let you cogitate. Thanks for hearing me out. We're not villains, we're businesspeople, trying to make a successful enterprise prosper even more." He reached out to shake my hand.

I couldn't refuse the seemingly polite gesture. "I should do some research," I said, realizing that Graham had yet to name his buyout price. I decided not to press him. I was afraid that, if it was large enough, I might be tempted. Instead, I informed him that I couldn't promise an answer overnight.

"That's fine," he said, letting go of my hand. "Take your time."

The phone was ringing. "Yes. Okay. I must get that call," I said.

Still smiling, Graham left.

I'd already grabbed the receiver and answered as I closed the door behind him. It was, as I'd expected, Vida. She explained that she'd stopped off on the way home from KSKY to visit with her daughter and her husband.

"I'd hoped Roger would be home," Vida went on, "but he was working out at his friend Davin's basement gym. Davin just returned from Western Washington University in Bellingham. Naturally, Roger is glad his chum is home again. He's so keen on keeping fit but doesn't want to impose on the family when Davin's away at college."

Davin was the son of Oren and Sunny Rhodes, Curtis's temporary landlords. The only basement apparatus I knew the family owned was an old pinball machine that had been taken out of the Venison Inn's bar when the restaurant had been renovated. As far I could tell, keeping fit meant that Roger could still ease his large rear end into an even larger chair.

I went straight to the point. "What did Sophia have to say?"

"She was very vague about the Bronsky house," Vida replied, "emphasizing that the decision quite naturally was up to Dylan and Kelsey. She and Graham came to give moral support after Dylan was supposed to have been murdered."

"That sounds odd," I said.

"Oh—I don't know," Vida responded thoughtfully. "They *are* family."

"I suppose so."

"Anyway," Vida continued after a pause, "I found out about Kelsey's little boy. He's staying with Sandra's sister in San Rafael."

"I didn't know Sandra had a sister," I said. "Or if I did, I forgot."

"Understandable," Vida remarked. "I gathered," she went on, lowering her voice, "they still want to buy the *Advocate*."

"That's right," I informed her. "Graham stopped by to make an offer only an idiot like me could refuse."

"What was that?" Vida's voice sharpened.

I recounted the proposal. "Frankly," I said, "it makes sense—right up until I realized that I wouldn't have control of

the paper anymore. Judging from how he described their operations elsewhere, they publish gigantic shoppers instead of newspapers. I've seen some of those. Local news is a low priority."

"I know. What's the point?" Vida's words shook with indig-
nation. "Making money is a very unfulfilling way to live. I
can't imagine that Tommy would approve. From what Leo
says, Tommy's papers were filled with local information."

"That was then, this is now," I said, hearing a siren in the
distance and hoping that, if it were a fire engine, nobody's house
was burning down after our deadline. "Let's face it, the media
has changed drastically in the short time since Tom . . . died."
Short time? It seemed like forever. "I'll tell them no, of course."

"Of course. I can't imagine Alpine without a hometown
newspaper."

I couldn't imagine Alpine without Vida's contributions.
"Their revised offer is a bribe. If they want a foothold in Washington, there are some other weeklies around that are still inde-
pendent."

"Not as many as there used to be, though," Vida pointed
out. "Oh—before I forget, I saw Leo arriving as I was driving
away from the ski lodge. Was he calling on those Cavanaughs?"

"Not that I know of," I said. "Maybe he was meeting one
of our advertisers there for a drink or dinner."

"He must've missed my program," Vida murmured. "Oh,
well. I suppose business comes first with Leo."

Vida and I wound up our conversation just as I heard the
westbound Burlington Northern freight whistle as it rumbled
through town. I left my House & Home editor to reflect on
how our advertising manager would explain his dereliction of
duty to her cupboard. Glancing at my watch, I saw that it was
eight-fifteen. I could e-mail Ben. Or write a couple of real letters, a habit I'd fallen away from in recent years.

Standing by the sofa, I gazed at Craig Laurentis's *Sky Autumn* and wondered if he'd be permitted to adopt the bear cubs. I hadn't seen Craig since I'd gotten the painting, almost a year ago. Darlene Adcock had reported a sighting of him by her husband's hardware store in February. Most of the locals still called Craig by his nickname, Old Nick. His long gray beard had made him seem much older than he really was. According to Donna Wickstrom, who ran the local art gallery, he was in his mid- or late fifties and had dropped out early on, when even a hippie's alternative lifestyle had proved too burdensome.

The phone rang, interrupting my reverie. I took my time picking up the receiver, sensing that it might be Graham Cavanaugh adding more plums to the pie he'd offered.

Milo's voice was at the other end, sounding odd.

"Emma?" he repeated hoarsely.

"Yes, it's me. You don't sound like yourself. What's wrong?"

"It's Leo Walsh," the sheriff replied with pain in his voice. "He's been shot. His chances don't look good."

FOURTEEN

I COLLAPSED ONTO THE SOFA. "No!" I CRIED. "NOT LEO!"
"Calm down, Emma," Milo said quietly. "I'm at the hospital. You stay put. I'll call as soon as I find out anything."

"I'm coming," I said, my voice shaking.

"Don't," the sheriff insisted. "You can't do a goddamned thing. You're in shock, you'll drive your goddamned car into a goddamned light pole."

Dimly, I realized that Milo must be in shock, too, or he wouldn't have been cussing so much. "I'll wait to collect myself." I hung up. And realized I didn't know how or where or anything else about Leo's shooting.

The siren. I remembered hearing it, thinking idly about its source. Vida. She'd seen Leo arrive at the ski lodge. When? As she was leaving before six-thirty to get to KSKY in plenty of time for her program. Had Leo been shot at the lodge? The *Advocate*. Kip wouldn't have started printing the papers yet. Still trembling, I picked up the phone and misdialed three times before I got it right.

"Kip?"

"Emma? You sound weird."

"I am. Leo's been shot."

"What?"

"Leo. He was shot. He's in the hospital. It sounds . . . bad."

"Who shot him?"

"I don't know. I'm going to the hospital. Milo's there. Where are you?"

There was a pause before Kip answered. "Oh—you mean with the paper." He sounded relieved, probably thinking that I'd lost my mind, which wasn't far from the truth. "Just finishing up the front page. Shall I hold a spot open?"

"Yes. I . . ." How long before we knew if Leo would live? I couldn't imagine anything worse than coming out with a bulletin tomorrow that said he'd been shot and, before the paper could be delivered, learning that Leo had died. "I'll call you from the hospital. It may be a little while, okay?"

"Sure. Do you want me to come with you?"

"No. Hold down the fort."

"This is unbelievable," Kip said, the tremor in his voice indicating that my horrible news had sunk in. "Leo? Why?"

"I don't know. I've got to go." I hung up.

I had to call Vida, but suddenly I felt drained. A terrible sense of urgency came over me. I couldn't waste time before getting to the hospital. Not bothering to grab a jacket or a sweater, I ran out to the carport and got into my Honda. At least I had sense enough to take a deep breath and make sure that I'd put the car in reverse. Milo was right: I wasn't in very good shape to drive.

The fastest way was along my own street for a couple of blocks and then down Third to Cedar. It was still light outside, and traffic was minimal. That was lucky because I ran the arterial turning onto Cedar. There was an open parking spot in front of the dental and chiropractic clinic across the street from the hospital.

I hurried through the emergency entrance, heading for the waiting room. Milo wasn't there. I went up to the counter where the receptionist, Bree Kendall, sat with her usual hostile expression.

"Mr. Walsh is in surgery," she said with what I thought was something akin to pleasure at the opportunity to give me bad news. Bree and I had a brief but acrimonious history resulting from my dogged determination to interview her about a previous murder investigation. "That's all I know."

"Where's Sheriff Dodge?" I asked.

"I've no idea." Bree turned away.

I hesitated, then stomped straight through the emergency area's double doors.

"Wait! You can't do that!" Bree shouted after me.

I didn't bother to look in her direction. She might have been taller, younger, and more athletic than I was, but my mood brooked no interference. If she tried to stop me, I'd deck her.

Fortunately, it didn't come to that. Dr. Elvis Sung came out of one of the examining rooms and quickened his step to meet me.

"Dodge went out front for a smoke," he said. "Leo's being operated on by Doc Dewey and Dr. Weinberg."

"Dr. Weinberg?" I didn't recognize the name.

"We got lucky," Dr. Sung said with a grim little smile on his broad, good-looking face. "He's a crackerjack surgeon visiting from New York. He and his wife are staying at the ski lodge and were coming from dinner when they heard about the shooting. Trust me, this guy's good. I've heard of him, even read a couple of his articles in medical journals."

"Then Leo may be okay?" I asked, feeling breathless.

"Let's say that his chances improved with Weinberg on the case. Not," Sung added quickly, "to take anything away from Doc, but we couldn't ask for a better surgeon in the OR."

"Where was Leo hit?"

"Two bullets in the back, one close to his kidneys, the other just missed a lung." Sung, a Hawaiian native, ran a hand over his smoothly shaved head. "One of the ski lodge valets heard the shots and found Leo in the parking lot. The young man at the desk called 911 and then got Weinberg out to tend to Leo. Luck of the Irish, you might say."

"Not so lucky to get shot in the first place," I murmured. "How long will Leo be in surgery?"

Sung shrugged. "It's hard to tell. A couple of hours, maybe more." He lifted his hands in a helpless gesture. "Excuse me, Emma. I've got to finish up with Dixie Ridley. She broke her ankle playing tennis. Rip says he should've benched her a long time ago."

Dixie was married to the high school football and basketball coach. On the verge of any other last-minute deadline, I'd have called in her mishap to Kip so he could put it on page three. But not tonight. Leo was my priority.

I didn't want to go back through the waiting room and face Bree Kendall a second time, so I slipped out through the rear exit. Sure enough, Milo was pacing and smoking on the corner of Third and Pine across from the Clemans Building.

"Emma." He dropped his cigarette, ground it out with his heel, and loped toward me. "A hell of a thing," he said, putting an arm around me. "You okay?"

"I'm better now that I talked to Dr. Sung," I said. "He didn't scare the crap out of me like you did."

"I didn't know about this Weinberg guy," Milo admitted.

"He rode with Leo in the ambulance, but I thought he was just another citizen tourist doing a good deed."

"Has Leo said anything?" I asked, grateful to lean against Milo's solid presence.

"No," he replied. "Jesus, do you think this is connected with the other shooting? It can't be random, can it?"

"You're asking *me*?"

"Yes. No." Milo looked up into the summer sky, where ribbons of pale gold and purple crept earthward to the west. "Still, you know more about this bunch than I do."

"Not a lot," I admitted. "They're virtual strangers." I paused, my head still resting against Milo's chest. Last January it had been the sheriff who had given me—and everyone else who knew him—a dreadful scare with what had finally been diagnosed not as a series of heart attacks, as we'd all feared, but as gallstones. Now it was Leo. Life's uncertainties were taking a toll on me. "I'm helpless, incapable of changing the world around me. I feel remiss, almost as if I purposely neglected Tom's kids. Crazy, huh?"

"No crazier than a lot of stuff," Milo said, clumsily patting my back before he let go of me. "We should check in, see if there's any news."

"There won't be this soon," I said. "Do you know how long Leo's been in surgery?"

Milo glanced at his watch. "Twenty, thirty minutes. I got here from home right after the ambulance pulled in. Jack Mullins and Dustin Fong were on duty, so they went to the ski lodge. They're still there, processing the scene."

"Vida," I blurted. "I must call her."

"Oh, hell!" Milo exclaimed. "Do you really want her roaring around here like a wounded elephant?"

I looked up at the sheriff. "Better than having her roaring at me for the next few days if I don't tell her. After all, Leo *is* her coworker. Despite their bickering, I think they actually like each other."

Heading for the hospital door, Milo shrugged. "Your call."

"Literally," I said and took out my cell phone. "I'll do it here. Sometimes they won't let you use a cell inside the hospital because of all the sensitive equipment."

The sheriff loped back inside while I dialed Vida's number. Her line was busy, so I left a message telling her to call me as soon as possible. I've never felt right about delivering bad news to a machine instead of a person.

My next call was to Kip. I told him to wait a bit to run anything but the bare facts. We should have more news after Leo came out of surgery.

"How long?" The usually unflappable Kip sounded anxious.

"I've no idea," I told him.

Milo was pacing in the waiting room. The only other people in the area—except for the surly Bree Kendall behind the counter—were a young woman I didn't recognize and her two-year-old boy, who had a runny nose and was coughing his head off.

I joined the sheriff by the tropical fish tank and reduced my voice to a whisper. "Did you ask Bree how long it might be before we have any news?"

"She doesn't know," Milo replied, not bothering to speak any more quietly than he usually did. "Does anybody who works in a hospital ever know anything?"

I glanced at Bree, who was turned away from us. Then I glanced at the fish tank, noticing that a neon tetra was floating upside down. I hoped it wasn't an omen. "Not very often," I finally said, having to raise my voice to be heard over the coughing kid.

"I can't stick around here," Milo declared, frowning in

Bree's direction. "I'm going up to the lodge. Where's Vida? She lives only five blocks from here. Or didn't you call her?"

"Yes, I did," I replied. "Her line was busy. She usually spends the hour or two after her show talking to people who call to offer ideas or criticism, or want their five minutes of fame in an interview."

Before Milo could respond, his cell phone rang. He took it out of his shirt pocket. "Dodge," he said.

Bree had finally turned around. "Would you please take your cell outside? We don't permit them inside the hospital."

Milo lifted his chin above the phone and glowered at her. "I don't see any fancy equipment in here except you. Keep it down or the cell you're talking about'll be the one I put you in." He spoke again to his caller. "Go ahead, Dustman. I'm about to arrest somebody for interfering with a law enforcement officer."

I discreetly looked in Bree's direction. Her fair skin had turned pink, and her piercing blue eyes were narrowed. But she kept her mouth shut. Unfortunately, the toddler with the cough began to hack his way into a hysterical crying jag. His mother tried to soothe him, but he wouldn't, maybe couldn't, stop.

"Shit!" Milo bellowed and headed for the exit. "I can't hear a . . ."

I followed him outside, although I moved far enough away so as not to appear to be eavesdropping. I was, of course. I couldn't help it unless I went across the street. From Milo's end of the conversation, I surmised that Dustin and Jack had finished up at the ski lodge.

However, I was only half-right. After clicking off his phone, the sheriff waved at me. "I'm heading out. Jack's still at the lodge, but Dustin got called in on a possible break-in by Cass Pond. My car's around front by the Clemans Building."

"Hey," I yelled, "can I tag along?"

"What for?" Milo called back.

"What do you think? It's my job."

For once, Milo didn't argue. "Okay. You can't do anything around here except worry yourself into a knot. It's better to keep busy."

I went off in the opposite direction to my Honda. I followed Milo's Grand Cherokee after catching up with him at the arterial on Alpine Way. He turned left, and so did I, making a right onto Tonga Road, which led to the lodge. Twilight was settling in over the mountains, and lights were on in some of the rooms, as well as the lobby and the parking lot.

The first thing I saw was Leo's Toyota Celica hitched up to Cal Vickers's tow truck. Cal, who owns the local Texaco station, was at the wheel, carefully hauling the car over the lot's speed bumps. I waved to him as he passed by. Pulling into a vacant space not far from where Leo's car had been parked, I spotted Jack Mullins talking to Heather Bardeen Bavich. Milo had parked in the loading zone and was coming toward his deputy and Heather.

Seeing the crime scene tape already stretched over a large swath of the parking lot and into the trees beyond, I suddenly realized that I hadn't asked Curtis to take a picture. In fact, I hadn't thought about Curtis at all.

Hurriedly, I called Kip. "The news is better about Leo," I said. "His surgery is being performed by Doc Dewey and a world-class surgeon from New York. I don't know when he'll be out of the OR, but I'm at the ski lodge now with the sheriff. If I asked Curtis to take a picture, would we have any room for it?"

"Oh, boy!" Kip sounded frazzled. "I mean, that's great about Leo—if it all turns out okay. But a photo? I honestly don't know where I'd put it. I assume you want at least two columns. Is it worth pulling anything we've already got?"

"I assume you mean Fuzzy's wood carving," I said, gazing around the lot to consider possible angles. "I wouldn't mind dumping that until next week, but a photo of Jack Mullins scratching his ass in front of a bunch of parked cars maybe isn't worth the trouble. I'll call Curtis now and get him up here. We can always run it next week."

Kip agreed that was the best way to handle the late-breaking news. I clicked off and went over to where Milo was crouching on the ground. There was no chalk outline where Leo had fallen, but marks had been made by the deputies to show the position of his body. A dark, still-wet patch of blood on the pavement provided a grim reminder of the shooting. I closed my eyes for a moment, and when I opened them, I forced myself to look away.

The sheriff stood up. "Walsh's car was parked in this third spot from the end of the row," he explained. "The shooter probably stood behind those trees." Milo pointed to the second-growth Douglas fir and western cedar that surrounded the ski lodge complex. "The two end slots in this row were empty, according to the valet who heard the shots and found Leo."

"Who's the kid and where is he now?" I asked, nodding at Jack and Heather as they walked toward us.

"Andy," Milo replied. "Andy Andersen, a college kid. His dad, Kent, works in the Sears catalog office. He's inside, recovering from what happened."

I looked at Heather. "Is your dad here?"

"Yes," she answered, looking rather pale. "He got here a few minutes ago. He's trying to reassure our guests that this kind of thing has never happened here before. Naturally, some of them are thinking about checking out."

"Can't blame them," Jack Mullins said in his usual flippant style. "First the Tall Timber Motel, now the ski lodge. Makes Alpine look like Destination Death."

Heather shot Jack a dirty look. "That's not funny."

"Hell, no," Jack retorted. "Even less funny to the dead guy at the motel and poor Walsh fighting for his life. Loosen up, Heather. Life's just a bunch of crap. Worse, if you're married to my wife."

Heather appeared shocked but didn't respond. Milo and I were used to Jack's caustic remarks about Nina Mullins, who had always struck me as a kind and pleasant woman. Either she was a saint or she had a sense of humor that put her husband's comments in perspective.

I turned my attention to Milo. "Has that area in the trees been searched?"

"Dustin didn't find anything, but we'll give it another look." He ambled over in that direction. I followed him. "See?" he said, pointing to the ground just beyond the parking lot. "No underbrush to trample. I guess they clear it out regularly to protect any wandering guests from nettles or devil's club or anything else that might be a nuisance. Not enough rain lately, and all these big trees protect the dirt. Oh, there are some partial footprints, but too damned many to give us anything. I called in the state patrol just to make sure, though. They should be here pretty soon."

"No witnesses?"

Milo shook his head. "Just the Andersen kid, who heard the shots. Two, just like the guy at the motel. Leo had his back turned, so he probably didn't see anything."

I winced. "Poor Leo!" With great effort, I tried to push him into the back of my mind. "Who's been questioned at the lodge?"

The sheriff regarded me with an ironic expression. "You mean how many of your Cavanaugh crew have an alibi?"

"Yes." I looked Milo straight in the eye. "Who else?"

He shrugged. "Ed Bronsky? He's got a motive for shooting Leo."

"Get real. Ed was always just one small step ahead of even a dead man when it came to hard work."

Milo didn't comment. He looked thoughtful as he watched Jack walk toward the lodge with Heather. "So," the sheriff finally said, "you think Leo knows something you don't?"

"I honestly have no idea," I replied. "You know Leo—he's pretty open when it comes to his past life. Over the years, he's talked about working on Tom's papers in California. But he really never knew Tom's kids except for seeing them once in a while. The last time was when they were in their early teens. I suspect that Tom was a bit guarded when it came to his family problems, especially Sandra's mental health."

"Probably," Milo said. "If Leo pulls through, maybe he can tell us why he was shot. That is, if this is tied in to the motel murder."

"It must be," I asserted. "We can't have two homicidal maniacs on the loose."

"Doesn't seem likely," Milo murmured and heaved a sigh. "I'd better go talk to that bunch myself." The sheriff must have seen the spark in my eyes. "No, Emma, you can't come with me. Don't even think about it. This is official business stuff."

I knew he was right. I'd have to rely on Milo's interrogative abilities, which, I had to admit, weren't all that bad. He might conduct an investigation by the book, but he had a certain amount of instinct about people after his years in law enforcement. "Okay," I conceded. "I have to call Curtis anyway."

The sheriff loped off to the lodge. I felt somewhat uneasy

about standing alone in the parking lot where Leo had been shot, so I got into my car and phoned Curtis. He didn't pick up. I got his usual glib recording that he might be working or partying or "Who can tell with the Mayne Man?"

Idiot, I thought but left a terse message to call me. Not that it mattered whether Curtis took the photographs tonight or tomorrow as long as we couldn't use them in this week's edition, but he had to learn that a journalist's life isn't strictly nine to five.

Next, I took my chances with Bree Kendall and dialed the hospital's emergency number.

"No word yet," she snapped when I asked if Leo was out of surgery. I thanked her and hung up. It was, I mused, unfortunate that Bree was not only too old for Curtis but dating a CPA from out of town. Otherwise, I felt they'd make a perfect match, being different kinds of jackasses.

In the rearview mirror I saw a middle-aged couple coming out of the lodge and heading for a nearby car with Oregon plates. Apparently the lodge's guests weren't being ordered to stay put. It wasn't fair to inconvenience the innocent. I hoped the Cavanaughs wouldn't be allowed that kind of freedom. In my mind, at least one and maybe all of them were suspects.

My cell phone rang. Maybe it was Curtis, finally getting around to checking his messages. Instead, it was Vida, and she was in a dither. "Good heavens!" she shrieked into my ear. "Leo! I can hardly believe it!"

"You know?"

"Of course." She paused for breath. "My nephew Billy was called back on duty an hour or so after he left the radio station. Milo is suddenly shorthanded. Where are you? What do you know? Who shot Leo? Is he out of surgery?"

I informed Vida that I was in the ski lodge parking lot and knew just as much as she did. "The good part," I pointed out, "is that an excellent surgeon from New York happened to be staying at the lodge and is assisting Doc Dewey."

"David Weinberg?" Vida said. "Yes, I had my niece Marje look him up in her AMA directory. She assured me he's outstanding, judging from his medical credentials. Oh, I hope so!"

As usual, Vida knew more than I did, having relatives well-placed in the sheriff's and the clinic's offices. "Milo's questioning the Cavanaughs," I said. "I think I'll go inside and nose around, though I don't know what I expect to learn before he's finished."

"There's always something to learn," Vida declared. "In fact, I'll join you. Meet me in the lobby by the statue of Leif Eriksson."

"Okay," I agreed. "By the way, bring your camera. I can't get hold of Curtis."

"Oh, for!—" Vida stopped herself. "Fine, I'm on my way."

A family of four pulled into the lot as I got out of my car. They spotted the crime scene tape and stopped their SUV. A moment later, they reversed and left. I supposed I couldn't blame them. If they were tourists looking for overnight lodging, I felt like telling them they might want to skip the Tall Timber Motel as well and keep going until they got to Leavenworth.

It was almost dark as I walked into the lobby. Heather and Carlos were both behind the desk, apparently catching up on paperwork. A young couple pushed their sleeping infant's stroller out of the recently added coffee shop and headed for the elevator. One of the custodians—I recalled that he was known as Swede—was sweeping up some debris by the pay phones. Two older men were seated in comfortable armchairs, chatting in a subdued manner. Everything might have seemed normal to the casual observer. But a few clusters of people were standing around looking anxious and wary, as if they sought company to ward off the threat of more havoc.

There was no sign of Milo, Jack, or any of the Cavanaughs. I approached Heather, smiling at both her and Carlos. "Where's the inquisition?" I asked, keeping my voice down.

Heather pointed to the hallway that led to the meeting rooms. "They're in the Tonga Room. Sheriff Dodge also has some people waiting with Jack next door in Valhalla."

I glanced at Carlos, who had stopped what he was doing to listen to us. "Did either of you see Leo come into the lodge?"

Heather shook her head, but Carlos nodded. "He got here around six-thirty and wanted to know if any of the Platte or Cavanaugh party were around. I told him that I thought Mrs. Cavanaugh was still in the Viking Lounge, where she'd met Mrs. Runkel. Mr. Walsh thanked me and went off to the bar. I already told Deputy Fong that. He took notes."

According to Milo, Dustin's notes were not only always precise, but they were very legible. "So he joined Mrs. Cavanaugh there?"

Carlos nodded again. "Brianna said he sat down with her. Then, after she'd served them, Mr. Cavanaugh went into the bar, but he came back out a few minutes later."

Mr. Cavanaugh. The name conjured up Tom, not Graham. "I see," I said absently, wishing that this situation didn't bring back so many painful memories. "Did Graham Cavanaugh leave the lodge or go back to his room?"

Carlos frowned. "I don't know. I had to answer the phone and didn't notice."

I knew, of course, that he'd left—if not then, a few minutes later—because he'd showed up at my house shortly after Vida's program was over. "How long did Leo stay in the bar with Mrs. Cavanaugh?"

Carlos looked at Heather. "What did Brianna say? Half an hour, forty-five minutes?"

Heather frowned. "I think so."

"Where's Brianna now?" I asked.

"In the bar," Heather replied.

"Maybe I should talk to her," I said. "Are you very busy in there?"

"Well . . . yes." Heather grimaced. "Word about the shooting got out, and everybody seemed to want to be with other people. Safety in numbers, my dad told me. Of course, a few of the guests refuse to leave their rooms. It's . . . scary."

A sudden thought came to me. "Has Spencer Fleetwood been here?"

"No," Heather said. "Mrs. Runkel mentioned that he was leaving town right after her program. He had to go somewhere on business because he's expanding the station's power or whatever you call it."

"Ah, yes. He told me about that." Ever since Rey Fernandez had quit KSKY for greener—and richer—pastures, Spence had been forced to hire students from the community college. No doubt he was having his own problems with the younger generation. I sympathized. It appeared that whoever had been left in charge hadn't been paying attention to the police scanner. "Okay," I said, "I'll talk to Brianna. If Mrs. Runkel comes in, tell her where I am."

Heather looked startled. "Mrs. Runkel is coming back to the bar?"

I smiled. "Once she gets started, there's no stopping her."

Heather looked shocked; Carlos seemed bemused. I left

them and went into the Viking Lounge, where I found the blond and buxom Brianna working at the register. The bar was filled almost to capacity. One of the dining room waitresses had been brought in to help serve the anxious customers. There was, however, no sign of the Cavanaugh Gang.

"Excuse me," I said apologetically to Brianna. "I know you've already talked to one of the deputies, but I need to find out exactly what happened, since Mr. Walsh is one of my employees."

Brianna's blue eyes widened. "I know." Her voice was very soft, almost like a child's. "Isn't it awful? He's such a nice man, too. What's going on around here? I'm totally terrified. I don't want to go outside alone after I finish my shift, so my boyfriend is coming to get me."

"The sheriff will probably leave someone to protect everybody at the lodge," I assured her, even though I had no idea if Milo would in fact put his sparse manpower on an all-night watch. "Can you tell me exactly what happened after Mr. Walsh arrived in the bar?"

She sighed. "It seemed so . . . normal. He came in and started for the bar, and then I guess he saw Mrs. Cavanaugh and went over to her table. She was just leaving. Mrs. Runkel had left a few minutes before that. Anyway, he sat down, and I went to get his order. Mrs. Cavanaugh said at first that she didn't want another drink, but she changed her mind before I walked away." Brianna paused. "Do you need to know the time?"

I inferred that Brianna had already been asked that question by Dustin Fong. "Yes," I said, "if you can remember."

She uttered a short laugh. "Of course I can. I always watch the clock. I'm taking a full load of classes at the college, and I get tired in the evenings, especially since I know I have to go home and study for another couple of hours. Mr. Walsh and Mrs. Cavanaugh talked for about twenty minutes, and then Mr. Cavanaugh came in, but he didn't stay long. In fact, he didn't sit down, so I figured he wasn't going to order a drink."

I nodded. "Yes, I know. He came to see me. What happened next?"

"A little after seven I asked Mr. Walsh and Mrs. Cavanaugh if they wanted another drink. He said yes, she said she'd wait—the rest of her party was going to meet in the lobby later on and go to Le Gourmand to have dinner. After another few minutes, she got up and left. That was around seven-twenty. Mr. Walsh went to the restroom—you know there's one off the King Olav Restaurant—and when he came back, Jake and Buzzy O'Toole had come into the bar. It was Buzzy's birthday, and his brother was buying him a drink. Leo invited them to join him at his table, and he bought Buzzy a drink later, about a quarter to eight. Mr. Walsh was sort of nursing his along, and after he finished, he left. That was a couple of minutes before eight. The O'Tooles didn't leave until after they heard about the shooting. They were both really upset."

"Yes," I said, "I would think so. Leo has gotten to know them quite well because Jake's Grocery Basket is a big advertiser for us. I take it you didn't see any of the other members of the Cavanaugh party in the bar after Sophia took off?"

"You mean Mr. and Mrs. Platte?" Brianna shook her head. "No. Not tonight. I mean, not until much later, after Mr. Walsh was shot. They all found out about it when they came to the lobby to leave for dinner. I guess they had a late reservation. People from California seem to eat later than the rest of us."

"Sometimes," I murmured. My mind had gone back to Leo, lying helpless in the parking lot. Shock and fear were being displaced by anger.

My mood must have been contagious. Brianna suddenly clenched her plump fists and looked as if she might cry. "Oh, Ms. Lord, who'd do such an awful thing to Mr. Walsh? He's such a really nice man."

"That," I said slowly, "is what I want to find out."

FIFTEEN

VIDA MARCHED THROUGH THE LOBBY JUST AS I WAS
coming out of the bar. "Good grief," she said, not bothering to lower her voice, "I just saw where it happened." She
shuddered in an exaggerated manner. "So gruesome, and right
here in Alpine! A terrible day, and still no word on Leo. He's
not out of surgery yet."

The handful of people in the lobby—including Heather and
Carlos behind the desk—were trying not to stare at Vida. At
least, I thought, nobody had started to scream or run off in a
panic.

I steered Vida over to the luggage room door and I hoped
out of earshot. "Did you get a picture?"

"Yes, several," she replied, "but they aren't very dramatic.
No sign of Leo's car. No people to include."

"Cal Vickers towed Leo's Toyota away," I said. Briefly, I recounted what the lodge employees had told me. "We have a
solid idea of the time line. It doesn't seem that any of the Cavanaugh bunch has an alibi."

Vida nodded. "They'll provide alibis for each other, of

course, but that won't hold any water." She sighed. "Poor Leo. Why was he shot?"

"Maybe," I said hopefully, "he can tell us."

"He knows something," Vida declared. "Something he may not realize, that makes these awful people afraid of him. Generally, I find conspiracy theories to be so much hokum, but perhaps this is an exception. They seem like a tight little circle."

"They *are* family, remember," I noted dryly.

"Yes, yes," Vida responded, "but Californians aren't always the wholesome variety from my point of view. The trick, I think, would be to cut one from the herd."

I regarded Vida with interest. "You're right. I nominate Kelsey. She strikes me as very vulnerable."

"Then do it," Vida said. "You've met her. You could have been her stepmother. But of course you must be careful. She may be unhinged like her mother. She may even be dangerous."

"I realize that." I paused, trying to figure out an angle to get Kelsey alone. "I have some photos that Tom took when he was here. A couple of them are in Leavenworth when we went over there to do the Bavarian village setting. I'll say I want to give her some copies." I paused again, considering my options. "Breakfast tomorrow at the diner. I have to find the pictures first. I couldn't bear to look at them for a long time, so I put them away . . . I'm not sure where. Adam's old room, maybe."

"The diner is a good choice." Vida nodded several times. "Much safer to meet in public. You must insist she come alone."

I went to the front desk. "Heather, could you please ring Mrs. Platte's room? I'd like to talk to her or give her a message."

Heather rang Kelsey's suite. "No answer," she said, hanging up. "I think Mrs. Platte is with the others in the Valhalla Room waiting to speak to Sheriff Dodge."

"Oh. Of course. I should've thought of that. I'll leave a note," I said. "Tell her it's important and I'd appreciate a call this evening. I'll be up until at least eleven."

Vida was pacing the lobby. "Well?" she asked as I approached her.

I explained how I'd had to leave a message for Kelsey. "I'm not sure I can do much more here, and I have to find those pictures," I went on. "Do you want to stay and see if there's any information we can use? That is, if Milo can tell you."

"He'd better," Vida said in a steely voice. "Yes, you run along. I'll hold down the fort."

I was a block from home when my cell phone rang, so I let it ring twice more while I pulled into my driveway. Elvis Sung's voice came through loud, clear, and encouraging. "Leo's out of surgery and in the ICU. His chances look good. He lost a great deal of blood and he's very weak, but Doc Dewey and Dr. Weinberg are optimistic."

"Thank God," I said. "And thanks for letting me know. I'll spread the word so you can get back to your patients."

I called Kip as soon as I went inside. He, too, was vastly relieved and ready to insert another couple of lines into the front-page bulletin. "That was worth waiting for," he said. "I may get out of here before midnight."

I wished him well and phoned Vida. She was elated, saying she'd pass on the news to Milo. "I wonder how soon Leo will be able to talk."

"Tomorrow, maybe," I said. "Anything going on at the lodge since I left?"

"Hardly," Vida replied. "You've only been gone ten minutes, though I just saw Dylan Platte go into the Tonga Room."

"Who came out?"

"One of the female guests I didn't recognize," Vida informed me. "I assume she's the last of the witnesses, though what she may have seen or heard, I certainly don't know. The employees have all been interviewed. Milo must have saved the Cavanaugh group for last. Making them squirm, I hope."

"Not to mention hungry," I noted. "They were supposed to have dinner at Le Gourmand this evening."

"It serves them right for missing it. Starving them into submission might be an excellent idea."

I didn't argue. After hanging up, I went into Adam's old room, which had, over the years, become something of a storage area. Having only a carport and no basement, I lacked space for items I wanted to get out of the way but still save on the vague premise that someday I might need them. Although it was after ten o'clock, I was wide awake and knew I wouldn't go to sleep for a long time. The nightmare of Leo's shooting had made me feel wired and edgy. I decided I might as well use the time to find the photos of Tom, and also try to cull out some of the useless junk. Armed with a couple of big garbage bags, I went to work.

The first to go were Adam's old skis. He'd bought new ones before his assignment in Alaska. Out also were two pairs of well-worn tennis shoes, a bunch of unmatched socks, my old hair dryer, my portable typewriter, and three *World Almanacs* dating back to the nineties. Half an hour later I found the pictures in a Nordstrom gift box with some other photos that had been taken during the last decade.

It was painful to sort through the disorganized pictures, and not just because of seeing Tom's smiling face and twinkling blue eyes. There was Adam, a carefree college student, veering from campus to campus and major to major. Ben, ten years younger, a few pounds lighter, back in the days when he was stationed in Tuba City, Arizona. And me, arm in arm with

Tom, strolling the streets of Leavenworth with all the ersatz Bavarian shopfronts in the background. I looked so happy. So did he. *Oh my God,* I thought, *what a blessing that we can't see into the future.* Life hadn't treated us kindly. But then it seldom does.

I decided on three shots of Tom, none of them including me. Two were from Leavenworth, and one was from the picnic area by Deception Falls. I had the negatives, so I could make copies for myself.

Suddenly I was overcome with fatigue. I made a slapdash attempt at putting everything back into order. I returned the rest of the photos to the Nordstrom box. As I was shoving it onto a closet shelf, I dislodged a letter-size envelope that fell at my feet. Picking it up, I saw Tom's typed name and the address of the condo he'd bought after Sandra's death.

I remembered that it was a list of all the numbers I might need to know in case of an emergency. Tom had given it to me a year or so before he died. When he'd been killed, I was in such a state of collapse that I didn't remember getting it from him, let alone where I'd stashed it. Leo and Milo had handled the initial calls to the family while I languished in the hospital overnight. I set the envelope aside and hurriedly finished putting things away and hauling the garbage out to the carport.

It was going on eleven when I sat down on the sofa, staring dumbly at the envelope. Reluctantly, I opened it. Except for Tom's note at the top, the rest was typed.

"Emma," he'd scrawled in his large, almost illegible handwriting. "Just in case—this is a copy of the info I've given to Graham and Kelsey. Hope you never need it."

The names and addresses included his family doctor, Charles Burke; the law firm that represented both his personal and business interests, Bowles, Vitani & Mercier; his financial adviser, Kenneth West; his four accounts at the California Avenue branch of Bank of America; his pastor at the Old Cathedral of St. Mary of the Immaculate Conception; and the names, addresses, and phone numbers for all of the newspapers he owned. If I'd ever studied the list, I didn't recall anything about it. I certainly didn't need it now. But just as I was about to put it in the trash, I stopped. It was a link to Tom, and I had damned few of those. I'd keep it, at least for now.

By eleven o'clock, Kelsey hadn't called and neither had Curtis. The younger generation seemed hell-bent on trying my patience. A quarter of an hour later I was about to crawl into bed when the phone rang. To my surprise, the caller was Dylan Platte.

"Sorry to bother you so late," he said in his grating voice, "but I understand you wanted to talk to my wife. She's exhausted and has gone to bed."

"Is there any chance she could meet me for breakfast tomorrow around eight at the diner off of Alpine Way?"

"I doubt it," Dylan said. "She's been through a terrible ordeal the past few days, and she needs to regain her strength. I expect her to sleep in. She should after all that's happened."

He had a valid argument. Maybe lunch would work as well. "Could you please have her phone me tomorrow morning at the office? I have some things concerning her father that I think she might want."

"What things?" Dylan demanded sharply.

"The sentimental variety," I said, wondering what he expected. "Thanks for getting back to me. Good night." I disconnected, not wanting to give Dylan an opportunity to probe further.

The phone rang again almost immediately. "I'm home," Vida announced. "You weren't in bed, were you?"

"Not quite," I said. "Anything new?"

"Not anything startling," she replied, sounding testy. "Milo finished up with the Cavanaughs shortly before ten-thirty. They'd insisted on having room service bring them their dinner in the Valhalla Room. Henry Bardeen was much put out but forced to do their bidding. I'm afraid Henry's out of his depth with these people. I'd like to see them try to boss Buck around. That would be a far different kettle of fish."

"Buck's military background would serve him well," I remarked, wondering as I always did who bossed whom in Vida's relationship with the retired air force colonel.

"Having failed to elicit much from Milo, who can be so annoyingly tight-lipped," Vida went on, "I left and stopped by the hospital. Leo is still in ICU, but they said his condition had been upgraded from grim to mediocre."

"I don't believe that's medical terminology," I pointed out.

"Of course not," Vida huffed, "but it's much more understandable. All this 'serious,' 'unsatisfactory,' 'satisfactory,' and 'fair,' is gibberish. I also peeked in on Ella. She was awake and watching television. That's the worst thing for her. She should be up and doing, especially since she's probably being discharged tomorrow. Really, people don't use good sense. I sometimes wonder if I shouldn't write an advice column, though most readers wouldn't have sense enough to do what I suggest."

"Actually," I said, "that's not a bad idea. Are you serious?"

Vida hesitated. "Well . . . it *has* occurred to me now and then. I'll think about it. Now I'm going to bed."

Before she could hang up, I told her about Dylan's call.

"Typical," Vida said. "No spunk, a younger version of Ella. Whoever got the ridiculous idea that human beings were evolving into a better species?"

She hung up before I could deny ever having made such a statement.

I didn't get to sleep right away. I was still worried about Leo and upset over all the memories that had been stirred up during the past week. I finally dozed off around one a.m. and didn't wake up until ten after eight. I'd forgotten to set the alarm. It was a good thing that Kelsey hadn't been able to meet me for breakfast.

I didn't bother to eat or even make coffee but phoned the office while I was getting dressed to tell Ginny I'd be in by eight-thirty.

"Who is this?" she demanded, almost in a whisper.

I was puzzled. "It's me, Emma. What's wrong?"

"Emma who?"

The question exasperated me. "Emma Lord, your boss, the one who signs your paycheck."

"What's the name of your son?"

"Ginny!" I shouted. "It's Adam, of course. Have you lost your mind?"

"No," she replied in a more normal tone. "But you can't be too careful around here after what's happened, especially to Leo. I'm screening all calls until the killer is caught."

"I see. Okay, fine, I'm on my way. Speaking of Leo, is there any news?"

"Vida says he had a decent night," Ginny replied, then added darkly, "one of us could be next."

"Thanks for getting my day off to a happy start," I retorted and hung up. It wasn't until I was pulling out of the driveway that I realized Ginny might have a point. What if Leo had been shot because he had some knowledge that might identify the motel victim's killer? What if the killer was some sort of maniac who thought the only way to get hold of the newspaper was to knock off the staff one by one? It seemed too far-fetched, but I could almost understand Ginny's fears.

"Sorry, Ginny," I said upon entering the front door. "No coffee yet. I thought I was still dreaming."

"A bad dream," she said morosely. "Here's a real one. Ed's here."

"*What?*"

She gestured toward the newsroom. "He got here just a couple of minutes ago. He'd heard about Leo and offered to fill in. We do need the help, of course. It's just weird having him . . ."

I didn't wait for her to finish the sentence but burst through the door. Sure enough, Ed was at the coffee table, chomping on a cinnamon roll. Vida was glaring at him from behind her desk, and Curtis had his face hidden behind *The Seattle Times*.

"G'monyema," Ed greeted me with his mouthful. A trickle of butter ran off his chin. Or chins, to be precise.

"Good morning," I responded. "You're here to . . . work?" I could hardly get the word out.

Ed swallowed. "You bet. Seems like old times, doesn't it?" He popped the last chunk of cinnamon roll in his mouth and chewed lustily.

"Yes," I said slowly, "it does." Rational thought began creeping around in my foggy brain. Ed was better than nothing—and nothing was what we had with Leo in the hospital. "Well," I said, trying to sound enthusiastic, "you know the drill. Wednesdays are always a good time to think ahead to the next issue and figure out if there are any new revenue sources. KSKY may be upping its power to broadcast as far west as Monroe. You should probably look into that market, since it's fairly new territory and we have an understanding with Fleetwood about co-op ads."

Ed swallowed again and looked surprised. "We do?"

"Yes. *The Monroe Monitor* comes out on Tuesdays, so we already have the most recent edition. Check with Ginny." I forced a smile as I poured coffee and grabbed a cinnamon roll before Ed devoured all of them. Turning to Curtis, I spoke in a frosty voice. "Could you please come into my office?"

He peeked out from behind the *Times*'s sports section. "Me?"

"Yes. You." I walked briskly to my cubbyhole, managing to splash a few drops of coffee on the floor. If Curtis slipped on it and broke his neck, it'd serve him right. Obviously, my day's bad start was getting worse.

I didn't bother to have him close the door or even sit down. "Why didn't you return my call last night?" I demanded.

Curtis looked blank. "What call?"

"About Leo," I snapped. "About taking a picture up at the ski lodge."

"I knew about Leo," he mumbled, shifting from one foot to the other. "It blew me away. It's way too scary around this town. What's wrong with this crazy place?"

Looking at Curtis's suddenly pale face, I realized he was genuinely shaken. "How did you hear about the shooting?" I asked, softening a bit.

"I . . ." He looked away, drumming his fingers on the back of one of my visitors' chairs. "I was at the ski lodge."

I was startled by his response. "You were?"

He nodded, glancing anxiously at me before looking away again. "I met a girl who works there." He swallowed hard. "Brenda. She's a waitress in the coffee shop. She gets off at eleven, but she takes a break around eight."

I had a vague idea of who Brenda was—a fairly pretty strawberry blonde with an earsplitting giggle. "When did you hear about Leo?"

Now Curtis's pale face showed some color. "In the break

room. The storage room, really, but . . . sometimes Brenda goes there to . . . chill. The fry cook came looking for her and told her somebody'd been shot in the parking lot. She left after that, and I waited a couple of minutes and then took off out the back way. I didn't want to go to my car in case the shooter was still there, so I just hung out by the exit for a while. Then I tried to go back in, but the door locks from the inside. I heard the sirens, so I figured the coast was clear, but I had to go around to the front. Somebody—I think it was one of the EMTs—said it was Leo who got shot. I got in my car and peeled out of the lot before anybody could stop me." He hung his head. "I guess I lost my cell phone, maybe in back of the lodge. Or the storage room. Guess I'm not much of a hero, huh?"

"I don't expect you to be a hero," I said quietly, remembering my first bout with professional cowardice, almost thirty years earlier. I'd been driving back to *The Oregonian* from an interview in the suburbs of Portland when I encountered an accident involving a boy not much older than Adam. The kid had been hit by a car while riding his bicycle and was on the pavement, where the emergency personnel were tending to him. I didn't know if he were dead or alive, and I didn't stop to find out, despite having my camera with me. My crusty old buzzard of a city editor demanded to know why I hadn't done my job. I told him honestly that I was too frightened—all I could think of was my own son in a similar situation. To my surprise, the editor understood, though he warned me to stiffen my backbone the next time. Because, he insisted, there would always be a next time. "I do, however," I emphasized to Curtis, "expect you to act responsibly. You'd better find your cell phone or get a new one."

"I will," Curtis promised, finally looking me in the eye. "If only I'd seen the shooter. That would've saved the day, right?"

I agreed. "But it seems nobody else did, either." I smiled slightly. "Now get out there and go to work. And by the way, I'm not overly thrilled about Ed's return to his old job, but as long as he's here, do whatever you can to keep him moving."

Curtis saluted. "Aye, aye, captain."

My phone rang just as he left. It was Father Den, saying that he'd gotten an e-mail from Adam about a special collection. "I guess," my pastor said, "he e-mailed you a reminder last night, but I told him what had happened with Leo and that maybe you hadn't had a chance to check your computer."

"That's right," I said. "I hadn't."

"That's okay," he assured me in his usual affable voice. "I've got the details. By the way, I went to the hospital last night and gave Leo the Last Rites when he came out of surgery. Of course it's called the 'Anointing of the Sick' these days, because that's not so frightening. In fact, I figure someday it'll be known as the 'Sacrament of the Not Feeling as Good as I Should.' Anyway, I'll be including Leo in the intercessions for the next few days. I just wish he'd show up for Mass more often than at Christmas, Easter, and the occasional Sunday. Adam's going to be offering prayers for him, too. Have you contacted Ben?"

"No," I admitted, "but I will. Leo can use the prayers. We all can."

For a Wednesday, the morning seemed busier than usual. I e-mailed both my son and my brother, checked with the hospital to make sure Leo was still making progress, and offered more suggestions to Ed about pursuing ads. Vida was clearly avoiding Ed by being away from the office, so when she returned around eleven, her phone messages had piled up.

"Oh, for heaven's sakes!" she exclaimed while I was pouring more coffee. "I'm supposed to go to the hospital and help get Ella home! Why me? What's wrong with the rest of the family?"

Fortunately, I didn't have to answer that question because my phone rang. I scurried back into my cubbyhole and grabbed the receiver. Kelsey Platte was on the line.

"Ms. Lord?" Her voice sounded uncertain. "Dylan told me you wanted to meet me for lunch. He said you had some things that belonged to my father. Could you please send them to the lodge? I really don't feel at all well."

"I'd rather not," I said. "How about this? I'll come pick you up around twenty to twelve. That way we can beat the lunch rush at the diner and find a nice quiet booth."

"Oh . . . I don't know . . . I really shouldn't . . ."

"You need a break," I said, trying to sound confidential, warm, fuzzy, and whatever else might motivate the young woman to trust me. "I feel really lax about you and your brother. I should have kept in touch, but I wasn't sure how you'd react. Let me buy you lunch. It can't make amends for not having reached out sooner, but I'm trying to do that now. Please, Kelsey. It's important to me, for the sake of your dad."

"Ah . . . okay, I guess." She paused. "What are you driving?"

"A green Honda Accord," I said. "Twenty to twelve in front of the lodge. See you." I hung up before she could change her mind.

Not two minutes later the phone rang again. "Emma," Marisa Foxx said. "I thought this might be a good time to call, since it's the day the paper comes out and you're not under pressure. How is Leo?"

"Improving," I said. "Thank God."

"Amen," Marisa said. "He seems like a very decent man."

"He is," I said. "By the way, your would-be client Ed Bronsky is filling in for Leo."

"Oh." Marisa's laugh was very soft. "Is that good or bad news?"

"I'm not sure," I admitted, lowering my voice. "Ed's one step ahead of being better than nothing. I think."

"I'd prefer not representing him," Marisa said, "so I hope the house sale goes through. Of course, he should have an attorney look at the contract. There are some real horror stories out there these days with the high price of real estate. I just heard one of them last night from an old friend in San Francisco. And by the way, I called her because of our chat about the attorney who was murdered. After we'd talked, my curiosity got the better of me. I thought I'd find out if the case were ever solved and figured she would've heard, being a prosecutor for the city."

"Was it?" I asked.

"No. But that's not the only unsolved homicide in San Francisco—or anywhere, for that matter," Marisa said. "No apparent motive, no witnesses, no weapon found. It was just one of those seemingly random murders. Mr. Vitani's wife had warned him about walking home late at night and taking shortcuts down dark alleys. It was so sad. He left four young children behind. Angela—my friend—heard Mrs. Vitani was getting married again this summer. Maybe she'll have better luck."

"Yes." Something Marisa had said distracted me. "Vitani? That name's familiar. Did you mention it before?"

Marisa paused. "I might have. Why?"

"I don't know."

"It's probably not that uncommon a name," she said, before changing the subject. "Do you play poker?"

"Yes, but I haven't played in years," I said. "I don't know all of the newer games, except for watching the tournaments on TV. Why?"

"I belong to a group—mostly lawyers, but they're a fairly lively bunch—and we get together twice a month," Marisa explained. "It's one of my rare social outings. We usually play in Monroe because it's a central meeting point for our six regulars. Would you be interested in sitting in sometime? We have dinner first."

"I might, if you're all very generous about my ignorance," I said.

"Good. In the summer we often have some open chairs with people going on vacation. I'll call you before the next get-together, the second week of July."

"I'd appreciate that," I said. "Thanks, Marisa. I—" The name Vitani suddenly struck me. "I remember," I blurted. "Was this Vitani in a law firm with somebody else? I can't think of the other names."

"Yes," Marisa replied. "Bowles and Mercier. It's now Bowles, Mercier and Fitzsimmons. How do you know of them?"

I explained about seeing the firm's name among some papers I'd found recently. Marisa and I might be nourishing a budding friendship, but I was reluctant to reveal too much all at once. "When was Mr. Vitani killed?" I asked.

"Four, five years ago?" Marisa responded. "I'm not sure exactly, but it was in the summer. I suppose it was still fairly light out and Mr. Vitani felt safe. Unfortunately, he was wrong." She paused. "Was he someone connected to your newspaper business?"

"No," I said. "I don't know anything about him, except what you've told me. He represented someone I knew."

Marisa was very sharp. "Your fiancé?"

"Yes." There was no point in evading the issue now. "Mr. Vitani's firm may have represented the newspaper chain that Tom owned."

"I doubt it," Marisa said. "Good Lord, what are you think-

ing? That these people who've come to town have some connection with Mr. Vitani? I don't mean to pry, but I've heard rumors, of course, including that they're somehow related to
Tom. How painful this must be for you!"

"Yes," I confessed, "it's been tough. Very tough. But I'm not
selling, and that's that. Why did you say that Mr. Vitani
wouldn't have represented Tom's business? His name was on a
list of emergency contacts."

"Mr. Vitani—his first name was John, I think—handled
mostly estates, probate, that sort of thing," Marisa explained.
"And high-profile divorces, which might have seemed like a
motive for murder, though no serious suspects were ever
found. Why kill the attorney instead of the estranged spouse?
Anyway, one of the other senior partners, either Bowles or
Mercier, could have handled Tom's business. They're both
more into corporate law, if I recall correctly."

"If that's so," I said, keeping my eye on the time, which was
almost eleven-thirty, "then the firm may still represent the Cavanaugh children."

"That's very likely," Marisa agreed. "Does that mean if you
get involved in some legal complications, I could be going up
against those high-powered San Franciscans?"

"I doubt it'll come to that," I said. "They can't sue me for
not selling them the *Advocate*. Still, it's very curious how
linked everybody seems to be. It *is* a small world sometimes."

"It is," Marisa replied, "particularly if you limit it to the
West Coast. Even here in Alpine I find myself dealing with
firms from Mexico to Canada. The law is a bit like a big frater-
nity, though often as adversaries, not allies."

"I suppose that's true," I said. "And speaking of adversaries, I have to pick up Tom's daughter in a few minutes and
take her to lunch."

"Ah." Marisa uttered a little laugh. "That should be interesting. Or," she added, sounding more serious, "will it be awkward?"

"Both," I said. After a couple of cliché pleasantries, we rang off.

Coming back from a quick trip to the restroom, I found Vida arguing fiercely with—I guessed—one of her relatives. "You're not a working woman," she asserted, tapping the desk with a pencil and making a sound like an angry woodpecker. "And don't tell me how much you do around your house or your garden. I have all that to keep up, too. Just because you worked two jobs and raised a family a hundred years ago doesn't mean—" Vida stopped talking. "Well!" She banged the receiver down in its cradle. "The nerve! Mary Lou hung up on me!"

Mary Lou Hinshaw Blatt was another sister-in-law, and equally strong-minded. The two women had never gotten along. "I gather," I said, "you're stuck with Ella."

Vida leaned back in her chair, fists on hips. "That's right. Ella's related to I don't know how many able-bodied people around this town, and yet I'm the one who has to get her home and settled in. It's simply not right!" Suddenly she sat up, whipped off her glasses, and began that ferocious habit of grinding away at her eyes with her fists. "Ooooh! If this doesn't beat all!"

I had moved closer to Vida's desk, trying to ignore the unsettling sound of her eyeballs squeaking when she punished them so harshly. "So Ella won't be going to rehab?"

Vida stopped the irksome rubbing and looked up. "Rehab? Oh, for goodness' sakes! It wasn't that serious a stroke. More like the vapors, if you ask me." She sighed, her big bosom heaving and her broad shoulders sagging. "I'd better go fetch Ella now. She's already been discharged."

I got out of the way as she put on her glasses, plopped the big orange straw hat on her head, grabbed her purse, and sprang from her chair. "I'll be back by one," she called over her shoulder.

The newsroom was empty, except for me. Curtis and Ed had both gone out, though where I didn't know. I could only hope they were actually working. After getting my own purse, I headed outside, passing Ginny, who was on the phone taking a classified ad.

On the short drive to the ski lodge, I thought back to what Marisa Foxx had told me about John Vitani's unsolved shooting death. I couldn't help but wonder if there was any connection between that case and our local tragedies. It seemed unlikely, though, so I put it out of my mind. Dealing with Kelsey Cavanaugh Platte was my priority. I sensed that our lunch date was going to be painful for both of us. I decided there was no point in trying to connect the dots between Mr. Vitani, Maxim Volos, and Leo.

That, of course, was a big mistake.

SIXTEEN

KELSEY PLATTE STOOD NEXT TO ONE OF THE GRANITE pillars that supported the lodge's porte cochere. She looked forlorn and maybe apprehensive. I stopped my car and waved at her. After peering at me for what seemed like a long time, she walked over and opened the passenger door. Before getting in, Kelsey glanced into the backseat. Maybe she was checking to see if I had an accomplice stowed away.

"I'm not very hungry," she announced before I could offer a greeting. "Does this diner serve a lot of grease?"

"It *is* a diner," I said, slowly driving away from the lodge and trying not to look at the crime scene tape that still marked the spot where Leo had been shot. "They have nice salads, though."

"I'm into the Kushi Macro Diet," Kelsey said. "It's been a nightmare up here. Nobody knows about *Gobo Misso Itame* or even azuki beans and konbu algae."

"That's a shame," I said, wondering what the hell she was talking about. "How will you manage when you move here?"

"Mr. Bardeen told me there was a really big Asian food store in Seattle called . . . I forget. I wrote it down."

"Uwajimaya, I'll bet. It's in Seattle's Chinatown," I said as we headed down the road that led to Alpine Way. "It's huge and has all sorts of items you can't get anywhere else."

"That's a relief," Kelsey said with a little sigh. "I can't get over this town. It's so . . . remote. I feel like I'm in a time warp. What do people *do* around here?"

"That's an interesting question," I replied, attempting to encourage her to talk to me. "In the early days, Alpine was a logging camp. There was no road into the town. It could be accessed only by train or climbing a mile up Tonga Ridge. Families were allowed to live in the camp, and while there were never more than two or three hundred people, they managed to come up with their own entertainment. The winters were harder and longer in those days, too, but Alpine was always a closely knit—"

"Who's that?" Kelsey interrupted, pointing to the statue of Carl Clemans in Old Mill Park.

"The town's founder and mill owner, Carl Clemans," I replied. "He'd come west to attend Stanford and organized the first Sigma Nu chapter on campus. He was also the quarterback and captain of the first Stanford football team that—"

"Hunh," Kelsey said. "Why would somebody from Stanford become a logger?"

"He was a businessman," I explained. "He bought other parcels of land around the state, including—"

"A couple of my friends went to Stanford," Kelsey said. "I never wanted to go there. I took some classes at Mills for a while, but I couldn't see the point. Life's about living, not just learning." She turned to look at me as I pulled into the diner's parking lot. "Where did you get those tan slacks?"

"I don't remember," I admitted. "I've had them for several years. Nordstrom's, maybe."

"I like Nordstrom's," she said. "I go to the one on Market

Street." Kelsey pointed to the sleek chrome structure that had been built to resemble a fifties roadside diner. "Is that it?"

"Yes." I felt like asking her what else it might be, especially with the bright red neon sign proclaiming "THE DINER— Good Eats."

As I'd expected, the restaurant hadn't yet begun to fill up at ten to twelve. Terri Bourgette seated us toward the rear and shot me a questioning glance. I looked back at her with an I-think-I-know-what-you're-wondering expression but couldn't say anything to identify my companion. I figured that Terri, who is a very sharp young woman, had probably already guessed.

Kelsey ordered iced tea; I asked for a Pepsi. For the next few minutes we studied the menu in silence. Or rather Kelsey did, as I already knew I wanted the rare beef dip.

"This is really awful," my guest said with a deep frown. "I'm going to order the navy bean soup with a side of whatever greens they've got."

Our waiter, a young man named Royce, took the orders without argument. "Carrots, radishes, celery, and black olives on the side," he repeated in an amiable voice. "Got it."

"So," I said, leaning forward in the booth, "you're definitely buying the Bronsky house?"

"I guess," Kelsey said vaguely. "Dylan wants to. He skis."

"Do you?"

"Sometimes. I don't really enjoy it." Her blue eyes gazed at our booth's divider panel. "Why do they have all these pictures of old-fashioned people? Are they from around here?"

Given that she was referring to black-and-white still shots of *Leave It to Beaver, Dragnet,* and *The Honeymooners,* I was appalled at her ignorance. "Those were popular TV shows in the fifties," I replied. "All the decor here is from that era, including pictures of movie stars and singers."

"Oh." Kelsey seemed uninterested, preferring to concentrate on pulling a stray thread from her sleeveless yellow blouse.

I decided to broach a topic that might interest her. "You have a son, I believe. How old is he?"

"Aidan? Almost seven. He starts second grade in September."

"Do you have a picture of him?"

She shook her head. "I did, but I lost it. It was out-of-date anyway."

"Yes, they grow so fast." I racked my brain for something, anything that might get Kelsey to open up. "Have you gone through the Bronsky house?"

She shook her head again. "Dylan did this morning. He was supposed to do it . . . I forget when, but he didn't then. It's up to him." She shrugged. "Dylan thinks it needs work, but that's okay. We probably won't move in until fall." She frowned. "Oh, gee, that means Aidan will have to go to school here. I never thought of that."

My Pepsi and her iced tea arrived. "We have two grade schools here, one private, one public," I explained. "I assume you're raising Aidan Catholic?"

"What?" She looked startled, her thin hands gripping the tall glass. I sensed that she'd drifted to some far-off place, perhaps the school he'd been attending in San Francisco. "Catholic?"

"Yes."

"Dylan says children should choose for themselves," Kelsey replied. "Aidan was baptized because my father insisted on it, but I don't go to church anymore. What good does it do? It didn't do much for my father, did it?"

"I can't judge that," I replied, beginning to feel not just frustrated but annoyed. "Nobody can. It wasn't religion that got your father killed, it was politics."

"It was both," Kelsey insisted, showing a bit of animation. "I hate religion and politics. They only cause trouble and pain and wars and death."

I didn't know what to say. Kelsey didn't appear capable of rational thought. Nor could she seem to focus for very long. ADD, maybe or, as Vida would say, an excuse for people who lacked the self-discipline to concentrate on any one thing for more than thirty seconds.

I changed the subject. "Before our meal arrives, I'll show you what I brought along."

Kelsey frowned. "Something that belonged to my father?"

"Well," I said, opening my handbag, "not exactly. It's some photographs of him taken when he visited Alpine."

"Oh." She looked away, exhibiting no interest whatsoever.

I hesitated, my fingers touching the envelope in which I'd put the pictures. "You don't want to see them?"

"No. I remember what he looked like. I've got photos at home somewhere." She stared at the black-and-white glossy of Wally and Beaver Cleaver. "I wish Graham were here. It'd make me feel better."

"You should've told me you wanted him to join us," I said. "He's more than welcome." That wasn't part of my plan, of course, but I realized now that Kelsey might have been more forthcoming in her brother's company.

"No, no," she said, shaking her head. "You don't understand."

"Understand what?" I said, letting go of the envelope containing Tom's pictures and zipping up my handbag.

"I feel better when he's with me," Kelsey murmured. "I miss him."

"Of course," I agreed. "I miss my brother, too."

"Maybe soon," she said, so low that I barely caught her words.

"Right." I was flummoxed. I'd dealt with plenty of airheads in my time, but Kelsey was in the extreme. I couldn't tell what was wrong with her, at least not in any clinical sense. Maybe she had built up so many barriers to protect herself that no one could get through to her. No one, it seemed, except Dylan. Admittedly, I've got my own thick walls, so I understood—to a degree. But Kelsey seemed utterly beyond reach.

Our orders arrived before I could speak again. Even after Royce had left us, I couldn't figure out what to say. Finally, I made a desperate lunge.

"Kelsey," I said, leaning even closer, "I almost became your stepmother. You must know that. We met at your father's funeral in San Francisco. Do you recall that?"

"The funeral?" She nodded. "It was in that huge church with all the white marble. I thought it was ugly."

"Do you remember my son, Adam?"

Her whole body tensed. "He was one of the priests you brought along."

Kelsey made me sound like some sort of traveling bereavement circus. Fighting for control of my temper, I fixed my gaze on her face, which seemed frozen. "Have you no curiosity about me or your half brother? Haven't you ever wondered why your father was going to marry me?"

"I know why," she replied, tight-lipped. "Dylan told me. He wanted your newspaper."

"That's a lie," I declared. "We loved each other. Your father was my son's father. Surely you know that."

"Another lie." She relaxed slightly and tasted her soup. "This isn't very good."

It was hopeless. I'd lost my appetite. Kelsey was a mess, impossible for me to deal with, maybe the pathetic victim of her mother's heredity. I tossed my napkin on the table and slid out of the booth. "Good luck," I said. "Good-bye."

Incredibly, Kelsey registered surprise. "How do I get back to the lodge?"

"Don't know, don't care," I retorted. Maybe she expected a Cinderella coach with four white horses and a clutch of footmen. I hurried up to Terri Bourgette, who was at the register. "How much? I'm leaving, but I'm also paying."

Terri looked startled. "You just got your meal. Are you sick?"

"Yes—at heart." I glanced back toward where Kelsey and I'd been seated. There was no sign of her. She hadn't cared enough to try to follow me. "That's Kelsey Cavanaugh Platte," I told Terri. "She's either crazy or so far into denial that there's no way of reaching her. I can't stand another minute in her company."

Terri sadly shook her head. "That's terrible," she said. "You must be really upset. You're not the type to give up easily."

"This is different." I tried to smile but couldn't quite manage it. "Sorry. It wasn't the food that put me off. I just couldn't eat." I told Terri what we'd ordered. It came to just under twenty dollars, so I gave her two tens and a five for Royce's tip. "Next time, I'll come here with a more congenial companion. Maybe one who isn't nuts."

By the time I got back to the office, the latest edition of the *Advocate* had hit the streets. It always gave me a sense of satisfaction to see people putting their quarters into the newspaper boxes and checking out the front page. The home deliveries were made later, though only by about an hour in the summer because our carriers weren't in school.

I immediately called the hospital to check on Leo and see if he could have visitors. Debbie Murchison answered. "Mr. Walsh has been moved out of the ICU. In fact," she went on, "Mrs. Runkel was here a few minutes ago to see him. She's gone now. She took Mrs. Hinshaw home. That was very nice of her."

"Mrs. Runkel has a deep sense of family obligation," I said, wondering if Ella's ears were being seared by Vida's scolding. "Maybe I'll stop by to see Leo in a few minutes. Is he able to eat lunch?"

"I think so," Debbie replied. "The trays were delivered about five minutes ago. I haven't had a chance to check."

It wasn't yet twelve-thirty, so I decided to walk the four blocks to the hospital. Leo was on the second floor. As I got out of the elevator, I steeled myself, not knowing what to expect.

It could've been worse, I suppose, but the IVs and the oxygen mask were enough to unsettle me. Leo was propped up in bed with his eyes closed. The lunch tray sat on a table next to the bed. Since the steel lids were still on all of the items, I gathered that he hadn't tried to eat anything yet.

"Leo?" I said softly, approaching the bed.

He stirred slightly and mumbled something I couldn't catch. His usual leathery skin was pale, and somehow he looked as if he'd already lost weight. I had a sudden urge to cry but stiffened my spine once more and pulled the single visitor's chair closer to the bed. As I sat down, I wondered if Vida had actually spoken to him. If anyone could get a response out of a semiconscious patient, it'd be her.

I sat quietly for five minutes, saying a couple of prayers and wondering if Leo would sense my presence and wake up. Suddenly I was hungry, having skipped both breakfast and lunch. I lifted the lid off one of the smaller bowls: tapioca pudding, lumpy and unappetizing. I continued to sit and stare around the room. The other bed was empty. Disinfectant hung on the air, along with the odor of food that probably smelled better than it tasted.

Five minutes passed. Leo was still breathing, but otherwise he showed no sign of life. I supposed I couldn't expect much more. Feeling useless, I got up and went out to see Debbie at the nurses' station.

"I'd like to leave a note for Doc Dewey and Dr. Weinberg," I said.

"Dr. Weinberg was leaving for Portland today," Debbie informed me. "His son lives there. I can give Doc a note, though."

"Oh . . . I'll tell him myself," I said. "By the way, Leo's asleep and hasn't touched his lunch."

Debbie seemed unmoved by my report. "That's fine. Trays are delivered whether the patients want them or not. Mr. Walsh needs to rest. I'll check on him shortly."

I felt as if I were being dismissed. But as I was about to walk away, she smiled at me. "I know this sounds stupid, but I can't get over the fact that I actually saw the man who was murdered at the motel. And now Mr. Walsh gets shot." The smile had disappeared. "It's horrible, isn't it? I feel spooked. I wonder what happened to his wife."

"His wife?" I echoed. "You mean the bogus Mr. Roth's wife?"

Debbie nodded. "Mrs. Runkel said you met her in your office. I only saw her once, from a distance. Is she still in town?"

"I don't think she ever existed," I said. "That is, there was no Ginger or Josh Roth. That's all in today's *Advocate*. The dead man's body was never claimed by anyone. His real name was Maxim Volos."

Debbie's round face looked puzzled. "I don't get it. If this Ginger came to see you and I met Josh, what's that all about? I mean, the dark-haired woman I saw may not have been the man's real wife, but she must have known him well enough to be sorry he'd gotten killed."

"She may have left town before—" I stopped. "Did you say a dark-haired woman? I didn't realize you'd seen her."

"From my apartment," Debbie replied. "I looked outside after I got home that day and saw him getting into a car with this woman. I assumed she must be the wife—or the pretend Ginger."

"You're sure she was dark?"

Debbie's laugh was soft. "Definitely. She had wonderful curly black hair. Of course I didn't see her face."

"Interesting," I murmured. "My Ginger was blond."

Debbie's hazel eyes widened. "Two pretend wives? No wonder he got killed!"

"I think maybe only one," I said. "I also think maybe I've been an idiot."

"What?"

"Never mind," I said, seeing that three of the patients' rooms had their call lights on. "You've got some folks who need help and I have to get to work. I'll explain if and when I figure it all out. Give Leo my love."

I hurried away from the hospital, convinced that Debbie Murchison had seen Sophia Cavanaugh with the dead man. Going down Third Street, I crossed at the corner and headed along Front to the sheriff's office. Milo had just returned from lunch and was standing behind the counter talking to Dwight Gould.

"Care to hear one of my wacky ideas?" I asked.

"Sure don't," the sheriff replied. "I'm on my way to check out those bear cubs."

Exercising my tattered self-restraint, I decided it was best to humor Milo. "Where are the cubs now?" I inquired, leaning against the counter.

"Up by one of the old mine shafts," Milo replied. "That Laurentis guy is trying to coax them to wherever the hell he lives. This puts me in a bind because it's illegal to feed wildlife. Still, the cubs need help."

"Curtis should get another picture," I remarked. "Is it okay if he meets you up there?"

"I don't give a damn, but Laurentis may not like it," Milo replied. "I've got a sneaking suspicion these cubs aren't the first bears he's taken on. If that's the case, he's asking for trouble, not just for himself but for everybody else, and even the bears. There's an old saying, 'A fed bear's a dead bear.' "

"They're damned unpredictable," Dwight Gould put in. "Damned near so as humans. That's the problem. Bears get used to being fed, go looking for a meal from some stranger, scare the hell out of whoever, and get themselves shot. Just like this mama bear. I blame Gus Lindquist for panicking. Crazy fool. He should've known better."

I understood the problem. "Do you know where Laurentis lives?" I asked.

Milo shook his head; Dwight snorted. "He's not handing out calling cards," the deputy said. "Still, it's got to be around that mine shaft somewhere. I'll bet he's got a gun, too."

Lori Cobb entered the office, apparently returning from her lunch hour. Milo nodded at her. "I'm outta here. I should be back in an hour or so." He came through the swinging gate in the counter and walked right by me.

"Hey!" I called, following him to the double doors. "You're going to hear my wacky idea if I have to get in the Grand Cherokee and go with you."

With an impatient sigh, Milo stopped, one hand on the door. "Make it quick. What is it?"

"I think Sophia Cavanaugh was somehow involved with

Maxim Volos." As concisely as I could manage, I told the sheriff what Debbie Murchison had said.

Milo frowned. "She's sure it was Sophia?"

"No," I admitted. "She doesn't even know her, but it was a woman with lots of curly black hair. Who else could it be, at least as far as this case is concerned? It makes sense. I have a feeling Sophia may also have been the blond Ginger who came to see me."

Milo looked skeptical. "You couldn't tell they were the same person?"

"Not at the time," I said. "I mean, this Ginger was probably wearing a wig, had dark sunglasses, and plenty of makeup. It did strike me that she was overdone, like something out of Hollywood."

"Woman's intuition," the sheriff muttered. "Jeez."

"Okay, don't take me seriously," I snapped, "but I'm not seeing you pull any rabbits out of a hat. You'd rather chase a couple of bears around the side of Tonga Ridge."

"I'd rather be fishing," Milo stated. "It's a nice day. The river's clear, running almost green down about a half-mile. I'd like to be able to leave an hour early and head out to try my luck with some rainbows, fish until almost dark while the mist rises out of the meadows."

"Dream on," I retorted, pushing open the other door. "And don't let those bears take a bite out of your butt. Not that you couldn't afford to lose it."

I walked swiftly along Front Street to the *Advocate* office. Ginny, still looking suspicious, handed me my phone messages. "Ed went to lunch with Mr. Wenzel," she explained, "so he may be a little late getting back."

"Surprise." I sighed and went into the empty newsroom and on to my desk. The first message was from Grace Grundle with the notation "Re: kittens." Grace had probably befriended more feline companions to add to her already large menagerie. No doubt she had pictures. Bad ones. I moved on to the next message.

It was from Rolf Fisher. He'd called from the AP office. I assumed he'd heard about Leo. I hesitated before dialing his number. It'd been five days since I'd had to cancel my weekend with him in Seattle. I hadn't heard a peep from him since. On the other hand, the phone worked both ways. With a resigned sigh, I called him.

"Aren't you going a little too far with this shooting spree to avoid me?" he asked in his ironic tone. "First strangers, now your employees. Who's next? The sheriff?"

"Probably," I replied. "He may be the only person I know who's a bigger jackass than you are."

"Hmm. Let me think," Rolf said in that musing tone that irked me as often as it amused me. "I'm strangling here on swallowed pride and you're being nasty. It makes a fellow wonder why he bothers."

Maybe he was serious. I could never be sure. "Hey, it's been an awful week. Not only have I temporarily lost an invaluable employee but I seem to be alienating all sorts of people, including my own kin."

"Surely not your priestly brother or your equally priestly son? How can a good Catholic girl manage that? Or is that part of the guilt thing with you people? I only know about my own Jewish guilt. Which, I suppose, is why I called."

"It's these Cavanaughs," I said, ignoring his comments. "They're mixed up in all this, and it's making me crazy."

"More Catholics. Tsk, tsk. You people should really try to get along."

"I'm not sure this bunch is Catholic," I said. "But I'm convinced they're greedy crooks."

"So why can't they also be Catholic?"

"Please. Don't." I paused, frantically scratching my head. "If you were here, I'd tell you all about it." I saw Curtis stroll into the newsroom. "Can I call you back this evening?"

It was Rolf's turn to pause. "Okay," he finally replied. "Make it after eight. I won't be home before that. I'm rekindling an old flame after work."

"It can't take much of a flame if you need only a couple of hours," I shot back.

"That's pleasantly true. Until then." He rang off. I felt like wringing his neck. He hadn't bothered to ask how Leo was getting along. It seemed that Rolf's sole reason for calling was to needle me.

Vida returned just after Curtis left to try for another shot of the bear cubs. "Such a bother!" she exclaimed, tossing the straw hat onto the top of her filing cabinet. "Ella is the fussiest woman I've ever met. 'Would you please open the drapes just a tad, Vida dear? No, not that much. No, no—too far shut. I need a teensy bit more light.' 'My ficus should be watered, poor thing. Lukewarm from the tap. Not *too* warm and not *too* much. Oh, goodness, I think you're drowning it!' 'The bed needs changing and I'm so weak. Would you make sure you put on the sheets with the three-hundred-thread-count cotton?' Now who on earth counts the threads in their sheets? You order them from Sears on sale and pick them up at the catalog office a week later. As for drowning her pitiful-looking plant, I was very close to drowning Ella."

"Surely," I said, and not without sympathy, "other family members will rally around her now that she's home."

"They'll have to," Vida said grimly. "I simply cannot devote my life to caring for Ella." She glanced around the newsroom. "Where's Ed? Don't tell me he's out soliciting advertisers."

"I won't tell you that because he isn't," I replied irritably. "He's lunching with Snorty Wenzel. I hope it's *some* kind of business, because he's been gone for over an hour and a half. Maybe the house sale is actually going through."

Vida sniffed with disdain. "More fools than sense. Moving to Alpine is understandable. Buying Ed's house is not."

"Let's face it," I pointed out. "That house would cost six or seven times as much in California. It *can* be altered into something tasteful."

Vida looked dubious. I informed her I was going to get fish and chips from the Burger Barn, having struck out with Kelsey—and, in a different way, with Leo.

"Kelsey is mental," Vida declared. "A pity. As for Leo, he was sleeping when I was there, too. Maybe that's all for the best. If he can't smoke in the hospital, he may quit. That would be something good to come out of this nightmare."

"Speaking of which . . ." I murmured as Ed bustled into the newsroom.

"Hey, hey, hey!" he exclaimed, waving his hand-tooled leather briefcase. "It's a done deal. We sold the house. Woo-woo!"

"Great," I said as Vida glowered at Ed. "Did you get your price?"

Ed had waddled over to Leo's desk. "Almost," he replied, lowering both his voice and his head. "Nothing but the formalities and legal mumbo jumbo now." He opened the briefcase. "The offer and all that is right—" He stopped, removing a take-out menu from Itsa Bitsa Pizza. "That's not it." He stuffed the menu back into the briefcase and took out several other sheets of paper, one at a time. "Got to call Marisa Foxx. She'll know what to do with these hotshot San Francisco attorneys." He picked up the receiver and paused, stubby finger on one of the buttons. "You got her number handy?" he asked me.

"Not off the top of my head," I replied. "Try the phone book."

"Oh. Yeah, right."

I left for the Burger Barn. I didn't want to listen to Ed torturing Marisa. When I returned fifteen minutes later, he was on the phone, but he wasn't talking to a lawyer. It was obvious that Shirley was on the other end of the line.

"Furniture and all," Ed was saying. "Gosh, Shirl, where would we put all that stuff in our new place? It's expensive to store it."

I went to Vida's desk. "Did he get hold of Marisa?" I whispered.

Vida shook her head. "She was busy."

Ginny appeared in the newsroom doorway. "Ms. Foxx is on your other line, Ed."

"Hey," he said into the phone, giving Ginny a thumbs-up gesture, "gotta dash. Later, Shirl, okay?"

Cradling my bag of fish and chips, I went to the coffee table to get a couple of napkins. Ed delivered his big news to Marisa. I tried to tune him out as I headed back into my cubbyhole. "Names?" he responded. "Uh . . . Bowels and somebody-other-else."

I stopped in my tracks.

"Oh," Ed said, "you're right. It's *Bowles*. Sorry about that. When can we get together?"

I waited by the door of my office, reaching into the Burger Barn bag and taking out a couple of French fries.

"Not until then?" Ed said, disappointed. "It shouldn't take long." He paused; I waited some more. "Okay, Tuesday, ten o'clock. Sounds swell. Bye."

Going back to Leo's desk, I kept my late lunch close to my chest, fearing that Ed might try to steal it. "Bowles, Mercier

and . . . Fitzsimmons?" I said, unsure of the newer senior part-
ner's name.

Ed nodded. "How'd you guess?"

"It isn't a guess," I replied as Vida turned in our direction.
"That's the firm that handled Tom's business and personal af-
fairs."

Ed shrugged. "Makes sense. Keeps it all in the family."

"True."

And at last, something else was beginning to make sense, a
sense that caused me to lose my appetite all over again.

SEVENTEEN

CURTIS CAME BACK A LITTLE AFTER THREE, LOOKING DISAPpointed. "No luck," he said, and I realized his woeful expression was genuine. "The cubs didn't show, neither did the Bear Whisper guy. Dodge was pretty pissed off."

Vida glared at Curtis. "Please! Could you not use such crude language?"

"Huh?" he stared at her. "Oh. Sorry." He frowned. "What's wrong with 'pissed off' anyway?"

Vida made a face. "If you don't know, you're beyond help."

Seemingly perplexed, Curtis shook his head. "Okay, whatever."

"Maybe," I said, trying to keep the peace, "we'll get another chance at the cubs. We can't print anything for a week."

Curtis nodded and held up his copy of the *Advocate,* pointing to his picture of the cubs. "Not bad, though, huh?"

"Very nice," I said and headed back to my desk to avoid listening to Vida, who was now on the phone and apparently haranguing one of Ella's other relatives.

I'd barely sat down when Ginny buzzed me on the intercom, a method of communicating with me that she'd rarely used until she got pregnant again. "What," she asked, "do you want me to do with all these ideas for improvements?"

It took me a few seconds to realize what she was talking about. So much had happened since I'd written my editorial asking readers to make suggestions for improving the county and the town that I'd put my half-assed effort in the back of my mind. "Oh. Yes," I said. "Don't connect them to me if they call. Just take down the name and the idea, okay?"

"Okay." Ginny sounded unenthusiastic. "We've already had four calls. Donna Wickstrom suggested an August outdoor art show on Front Street, Evan Singer thinks we should have a film festival in January at the Whistling Marmot Movie Theatre, Reverend Poole wants to know if there's countywide support for him to hold a Baptist Bible camp for children in Old Mill Park during the summer, and Nell Blatt wants Vida to leave town."

I figured Vida had already talked to Nell about Ella. "Just write it all down for me, okay?" I said.

"Okay." I could hear Ginny sigh over the intercom before she clicked off.

For the past hour I'd been arguing with myself about calling the Cavanaugh family's law firm in San Francisco. I knew that lawyers are notoriously reticent about discussing their clients—and justifiably so. But my curiosity was driving me crazy. What was worse, I represented the press. And, of course, I had a vested—possibly even adversarial— interest in the Cavanaughs. I didn't really believe I could learn anything helpful from Mr. Bowles, Mr. Mercier, or the relative newcomer, Mr. or perhaps Ms. Fitzsimmons.

I had two other options: Milo and Marisa. The sheriff would scoff at me; Marisa might balk at the idea. Scoff or balk. I tapped my foot and tried to make up my mind.

Marisa won—or lost, depending upon her perspective. I got up and closed my door. This was one of those rare occasions when I didn't want to be overheard. Luckily, Marisa was available.

"You heard from Ed," I began. "I'm sorry about that, but I couldn't stop him."

"It's fine," Marisa responded. "He's not my only client who's a . . . *challenge.*"

"I suppose not," I remarked and then voiced my concerns.

After listening without comment to my rather rambling recital, Marisa spoke in a matter-of-fact tone. "So you think that Mr. Vitani's murder may somehow be linked to Mr. Cavanaugh's estate. That's an intriguing idea."

"You don't think I'm nuts?"

"I have to examine the facts," Marisa said after a pause. "Mr. Cavanaugh is killed—please excuse me for stating it so baldly—shortly before his marriage to you. It's possible that he'd made arrangements with Mr. Vitani to alter his will so that, in the event of his death, you wouldn't be excluded from the estate. Did he ever talk to you about that?"

"No," I said. "We hadn't yet gotten to the point of discussing money or business. We were waiting for Adam to be ordained so he and my brother, Ben, could concelebrate our marriage. Tom was always generous to me, within limits. He appreciated the fact that I didn't want to be seen as a kept woman. I even insisted that I pay him for the Lexus he bought after my old Jaguar was ruined. The amount was minimal, and after he died, I sold the car. It was too painful to keep it."

"I understand." There was sympathy in Marisa's voice. "Then there never was any provision for you as far as you knew."

"That's right," I agreed. "Although Tom did give me that letter with all of his contacts, including the law firm."

"But you never followed up?"

"No," I said bleakly. "I never thought about it. I was too shattered to even remember I had the letter."

"Of course," Marisa said. "But let's say that, if Tom had changed his will, then there was a motive for the Vitani murder. Unfortunately, it's not the kind of thing the police—or even Mr. Vitani's coworkers—might know. This is where legal practitioners play things so close to the chest that it can be detrimental. I'll be frank—I'm not sure how I could go about talking to anyone in the firm."

"Or," I suggested, "you mean that the only people who knew what Tom intended are both dead?"

"Yes," Marisa agreed—and then contradicted herself. "No, actually. Assuming your theory's right, someone else knew, probably the killer or an associate."

It was encouraging to have Marisa basically endorse my theory, but I felt helpless. "Then it wouldn't do any good to press the sheriff about making inquiries at the law firm?"

"That's right," Marisa admitted. "It'd be tricky in any event. The Vitani case is outside his jurisdiction, he hasn't charged anyone with the Volos homicide or the attempt on Leo's life, and he can't tie the two murders together except on the flimsiest of pretexts. As I understand it, Dodge isn't keen on conjecture."

"That's the truth," I said ruefully. "And I completely botched it in my attempt to cut Kelsey loose from the herd. Our lunch was a debacle."

"That poor child," Marisa murmured. "It sounds as if she's being severely manipulated, virtually brainwashed."

"Exactly," I said, ignoring the red light on my second line. "In some deluded moment, I thought I could help her, and thus help solve this whole mess. Delusions of grandeur on my part is more like it."

"That's part of your job," Marisa said. "Crusading for truth and justice."

"I call it filling up the front page. Thanks, Marisa, I appreciate—" I stopped as someone pounded on my closed door. "Got to run. I'll talk to you later." I hung up. "What is it?" I asked impatiently.

"Visitor," Ginny's muffled voice responded.

"Okay, open the door," I said wearily.

Ginny was cowering behind an angry Dylan Platte. "Sorry," she mumbled and slunk back out through the newsroom.

Dylan leaned on my desk, looming over me. "What the hell kind of stunt was that you pulled with my wife? Hasn't she got enough problems without you abandoning her at that third-rate diner? How did you think she'd get back to the lodge, you thoughtless bitch?"

My initial reaction was to hurl insults right back at him. But that wouldn't do any good. Besides, I felt a twinge of guilt. "Stop shouting and sit down," I said coldly. "Please."

Dylan, who had narrowed his eyes and looked fairly dangerous, froze for an instant—then yanked out one of my chairs and sat. "Well?" he demanded, still glaring at me.

"What," I asked with a calm I certainly didn't feel, "are these other problems your wife has?"

Dylan flung a hand in the air. "Both parents dead, an unstable mother, a misguided train wreck of a father, a kid to raise on her own until I came along—not to mention being told that I'd been murdered. We came here to find some peace and quiet, and now . . . this." He slammed his hand down on my desk. "To tell us her father intended to marry you! I don't believe it."

I glanced out into the empty newsroom. My entire staff seemed suddenly to have deserted me. I felt vulnerable, if not frightened. "I'm very sorry I walked out on Kelsey," I said, trying hard to keep eye contact with Dylan. "Frankly, I found it virtually impossible to carry on a conversation with her. Are you certain she's not on medication or other kinds of drugs?"

"Of course!" Dylan retorted indignantly in the voice that rasped on my ears like sandpaper.

"Maybe she should be," I said. "She's clearly suffering from an emotional disorder. You know that her mother was highly unstable. It's very likely that Kelsey inherited some of those flawed genes." I noticed that he was about to interrupt, but I held up my hands. "Hey, I'm not telling you anything you don't know. Is it possible that this latest turn of events, including the erroneous report of your death, may have sent her over the edge?"

"Kelsey's fine," he asserted, still belligerent. "Yes, yes, I know she's gone through plenty of bad stuff, but she's tougher than you think."

"Basically sound," I murmured.

"What?" he snapped.

"Never mind." It dawned on me that there was a method to his particular kind of madness. No doubt Kelsey, as well as Graham, would have to sign off on any legal papers involving their father's newspaper empire. If one or the other of the siblings could be proved incompetent, the gravy train for Dylan—and Sophia—would come to a grinding halt. I kept my hands in my lap so that Dylan couldn't see they were trembling. "I've apologized. Now what?"

Dylan leaned back in the chair. "We wait."

"For what? My demise?"

His smile struck me as sinister. "Your decision to retire."

"I'm nowhere near that."

"You will be." He stretched and yawned, his black muscle shirt revealing taut biceps. He suddenly switched gears. "Hey," he said, almost pleasantly, "nobody wants to work forever. In the meantime, Kelsey and I'll be chillin' in that Alpine villa with the heavenly view."

"So you really are buying the Bronsky house," I said, trying to convince myself that I was merely interviewing a newcomer to town. "Do you plan on renovations?"

Dylan chuckled. "Oh, yes. The basic structure is good, the decor is abominable. But that kind of a property . . . Well, it goes without saying that it's a virtual steal compared to California."

"And you won't mind living eighty-five miles from a big city?"

He shook his head. "No. It'll be good, especially for Kelsey."

"Yes," I said, nodding. "That may be true." The transition into a normal conversation was having a calming effect on me. "As long as living in the town where her father was killed doesn't upset her."

Dylan chuckled again. "You don't have a plaque marking the spot, do you?" He noticed my stricken expression and sobered. "Sorry. I keep forgetting, he was your fiancé."

The words were uttered with a hint of sarcasm. I didn't respond but waited for him to resume speaking.

"It's harder for Kelsey to be in the places where she knew her father," he explained. "She has no memories of Alpine because she's never been here before. In many ways, my wife's very good at blocking out unpleasantness."

"I noticed," I said, recalling my first meeting with the young woman who hadn't quite seemed capable of taking in her husband's alleged death. "We'll want to do a story about the house sale and your move here, of course. Let us know when the deal is closed." Not that Dylan would need to tell me—Ed would be trumpeting his self-styled coup from one end of Front Street to the other.

But Dylan was shaking his head. "No, that's not necessary.

Or desirable. We want peace and quiet. No drumrolls, no fanfare."

I tried to smile. "But it *is* news," I pointed out. "In a small town, everybody is interested in their neighbors. There's no anonymity. Gossip and curiosity are standard pastimes."

He stood up, smiling enigmatically. "I'm sure that's true. But I have to put my foot down. For Kelsey's sake, you see. We simply want to be left alone."

Although he spoke lightly, that grating voice and those piercing eyes made the request sound like a threat.

Ed returned around four-fifteen. "Golly," he said, chomping on a Nut Goodie, "I'd forgotten how fun it is to go out there and meet the merchants. But once I started on my route, everything came back to me, just like riding a bicycle. I didn't skip a— Oops!" He frantically reached for the rest of the Nut Goodie, which had fallen out of his hand and landed on his paunch.

"Did you sell any ads?" I inquired as Vida frowned at Ed, who was shoving the rest of the candy into his mouth.

"Nawfet," he said, chewing hurriedly.

I couldn't understand him. "What?"

He swallowed and wiped his mouth with the back of his pudgy hand. "Not yet. This was what I call reconnoitering. Have to see the strengths and weaknesses in how Leo has handled the job in my absence."

"*Absence?*" Vida yelped. "Good grief, you've been gone for ten years!"

"You know what I mean," Ed asserted, looking away from Vida's baleful glance. "Anyways, it felt good." He pointed to Curtis's empty desk. "How's this new kid doing?"

"Too early to tell," I admitted, wondering where, in fact, our reporter had spent the last hour or so. "I'm going to phone the hospital to check on Leo."

"Tell him not to rush back," Ed called to me as I went into my cubbyhole.

I heard a faint growling sound from Vida but ignored both of my staffers. It seemed like old times—bad old times, with Vida and Ed sharing space.

I was put through to Debbie Murchison, who was in the middle of changing shifts. "Mr. Walsh is doing as well as can be expected. He's been conscious off and on this last hour or so. I'm sorry, but I must dash. We're going over charts."

Vida had overheard me and tromped into my office. "Well?"

"Leo's improving," I said.

"Good."

I noticed a gleam in her gray eyes. "What's with you? Is that smugness I see or," I added, lowering my voice, "a plot to get rid of Ed?"

She sat down and all but simpered. "I did some research this afternoon. Not easy, I assure you. I simply couldn't follow all of your Internet instructions, so I went to the library and asked Edna Mae Dalrymple to help me with their computer. Edna Mae seems so terribly dizzy sometimes, but she's actually very efficient as long as you don't take her out of her element."

"I know," I agreed, trying not to sound impatient. "And?"

"And," Vida said, squaring her broad shoulders and projecting her imposing bust, "I learned something about Sophia Cavanaugh."

"You did? What was it?"

Vida leaned forward. "She's from New York, and her maiden name is Volos."

My mouth dropped open. "As in Maxim Volos, motel murder victim?"

Vida nodded, her thick gray curls flopping every which way. "Her brother. Do you think Milo knows?"

"No." I paused. "Or if he does, he isn't telling us."

"True." Vida frowned. "It's the sort of thing he'd keep to himself, as it isn't something a law enforcement person would put on a warrant."

"Sophia doesn't act heartbroken," I remarked. "Is that because . . . ?"

Vida shrugged. "We can look at this several ways. First, a conspiracy involving Sophia and Maxim. Second, the entire Cavanaugh ménage including Maxim was conspiring together, but something went terribly wrong. Or third, Maxim was some sort of loose cannon, on the outs with his sister and the rest of the Cavanaughs." She grimaced. "Unfortunately, this gets very complicated to pass along to Milo."

"We'll have to," I insisted, standing up. "Now. Let's walk down to his office."

"He's not there." Vida frowned. "I just called. Lori told me he left ten minutes ago to go fishing."

"Damn!" I sank back into my chair. "What's wrong with him? He shouldn't take off early in the middle of a murder investigation."

For once, Vida failed to rebuke me for using what she considered vulgar language. "I suspect that fishing helps him think things through. All that solitude and just the river and the trees. Very soothing when it comes to inner reflection."

"I know, I know," I said, annoyed. "But we're finally getting somewhere and the sheriff's off chasing trout God only knows where. He probably has his cell phone turned off." I had a sudden thought of my own. "Milo's not fishing."

Vida looked taken aback. "What?"

"It's too early, the sun's still on the river," I explained. "I should've realized that when he told me he might go out this afternoon. So what's he up to?"

Vida looked thoughtful. "Dare we hope he's following up on his lines of inquiry?"

"We wish," I said. "What would he be doing that he couldn't do from his office?"

"A good point," Vida noted. "Interviews, I suppose. Witnesses, suspects. But why make it a secret?"

We were both silent for a few moments, lost in our own ruminations. "Leo," I finally said. "If he's awake off and on, maybe Milo's at his bedside."

Vida was skeptical. "Not his sort of thing. But someone should be there. Shall I?"

"Go ahead," I urged. "If Leo's lucid, he may be able to tell us something helpful."

Vida looked at her Bulova watch, with its slim gold band and rectangular face. It had been a tenth wedding anniversary present from her husband, Ernest, and she swore it had never had to be repaired. "It's twenty to five. I won't be back here today, of course."

"Of course. Good luck," I said as she rose and went out to the newsroom.

I sat in my chair for the next five minutes wondering about Sophia Volos Cavanaugh and her late brother, Maxim. Sophia certainly hadn't behaved like a grieving sister when I saw her. Obviously, she—and maybe the rest of the nefarious crew—had something to hide. But if Maxim had been part of the plot to buy the *Advocate,* why had he been killed? And why was he impersonating not only Dylan Platte but the allegedly fictitious Josh Roth? None of it made sense.

At five to five, Ed stuck his head—and his paunch—in my doorway. "I'm taking off for the day. See you tomorrow." He smacked his fist into his palm. "Revenue City, here I come! Hubba hubba!"

"Right, Ed." I tried to sound enthusiastic.

As soon as he'd toddled out the door, I went into the news-room. Curtis still hadn't returned. His camera and tape recorder were sitting on a carton of printer cartridges by his desk. I was puzzled. Wherever he'd gone, apparently he wasn't pursuing a story. I began to worry.

In the front office, Ginny was gathering up her belongings. I asked if Curtis had told her where he was going.

"No," she answered. "I was on the phone when he left. He just waved."

I glanced out into the street. Curtis's car was nowhere in sight. When I went back inside, Kip was talking to Ginny. I interrupted and asked if he knew where Curtis had gone.

"I haven't seen him since before lunch," Kip said. "Sorry."

"I'll call him," I said and went back in my cubbyhole.

There was no answer except for the message that "the cus-tomer at this number is not currently available." I remembered then that Curtis had lost his cell phone at the ski lodge. Maybe he'd gone there to find it.

My new reporter had lingered outside after he heard about the shooting. Had he seen something or someone that he didn't realize was dangerous to know? *Maybe,* I thought, with a rush of fear, *before he could find his phone, someone had found Curtis.*

EIGHTEEN

I CALLED THE SKI LODGE, ASKING FOR HENRY BARDEEN. WHEN he came on the line, I tried to keep my tone light. "You haven't seen my new reporter, Curtis Mayne, in the last hour or so, have you?"

"No," Henry replied, "but I spent most of that time in my office. I was just about to go home. Do you want me to ask around?"

"If you would," I said and tried to remember the name of the waitress who had holed up with Curtis in the storeroom or wherever the hell they'd been doing God knows what. "He knows one of your coffee shop waitresses. Her name begins with a *B*—"

"Don't they all?" Henry said with that dry humor that was seldom in evidence, at least when guests were present. "The coffee shop, you say? Bernadette or Brenda?"

"Brenda. Thanks, Henry. I'm sorry to bother you."

"Shall I call you back at the newspaper or at home?"

"Home," I said. "It's quitting time for me, too."

After hanging up, I grabbed my purse and headed out to the

car, locking the office door behind me. Curtis had a key if he needed to get in. Driving home, I took a detour, crossing Alpine Way and turning onto Railroad Avenue, heading west to Ptarmigan Tract, where Curtis was temporarily bunking with Oren and Sunny Rhodes. Except for Oren's pickup, there were no other vehicles parked in front of the split-level house. Both Rhodeses were probably working at the Venison Inn. As for Curtis, he was still among the missing.

I got home shortly before five-thirty. Two messages were waiting on my answering machine. The first was from Rolf Fisher. "Wednesday, five-oh-six p.m.," he said, imitating a recording. "Just missed you. Must be nice to be your own boss. Got your cub reporter's pic of the cubs from the current edition. We're running it on the wire, so this Mayne kid's already on his way to fame and fortune. Be sure to let him know. Until later."

I wished I *could* let Curtis know. But his whereabouts were a mystery. Of course, it was possible that he'd simply gone to a bar or a tavern or even someone else's home. I kept trying to tell myself he might be out in that famous secluded spot on Cass Pond making like a mink with Brenda or Bernadette or Brianna or Sweet Betsy from Pike. He was not my son, he was an employee and presumably a grown-up.

So was Leo. Definitely grown up, and able to take care of himself, though he'd done a poor job of it. I sighed wearily and listened to my second message.

Mary Jane Bourgette's recorded voice sounded uncharacteristically tentative. "Hi, Emma, it's Mary Jane. Just had a chance to sit down and read the *Advocate*. It doesn't sound like much progress has been made on finding the killer. We're so sorry about Leo, by the way. Anything we can do now or when he gets out of the hospital? Dick just got home from work, and we talked about you know what. Call me when you can. It's nothing important, really, but we decided you were right when you said every little bit helps. Give me a buzz when you have time. Thanks."

It took me a few seconds to remember what she meant by "you know what," but finally I recalled that Dick had seen someone at the Tall Timber Motel on the afternoon of the murder but that neither Bourgette had been willing to say who, lest they start ugly rumors. Mary Jane's message had come through at five-twenty-five, so I immediately called her back. She answered on the second ring.

"Oh, hi," she said in her usual outgoing manner. "Do you want to talk to Dick? He's right here, popping the top on a Bud Light."

Dick came on the line. "I got to thinking," he said, sounding apologetic, "that when we moved here and were building the diner, we got involved right off the bat with a homicide when that body was found on the construction site. Don't try to kid me, I know you had a big role in solving that case. You even put yourself at risk to catch the killer. So I figured we owed you one—not that it's probably much help."

"Every detail's a help in these investigations," I said. "Maybe you should be talking to the sheriff."

"No, no," Dick insisted. "Really, it's very minor, and from what I know about Dodge, he'd probably blow me off. I wouldn't blame him. Anyway, the person I saw at the Tall Timber was that new reporter of yours, Curtis Whatever."

"Ah." Curtis again. "What was he doing?"

"He was going into one of the units," Dick said.

I was surprised. "Was it the one where the shooting took place?"

"No. It was more in the middle on the ground floor. Maybe

the third or fourth unit from the office." Dick uttered a rueful chuckle. "I didn't think much of it at the time because I figured maybe he was staying there until he found a place to rent. Then Oren Rhodes mentioned that Curtis was rooming with them. All kind of silly, huh?"

"Did he have a key?" I asked.

"I'm not sure," Dick admitted, without his usual aplomb. "It was all so . . . ordinary. I wouldn't have recognized the kid if I hadn't seen him when I was putting together my estimate for your roof. I'd just pulled into the parking lot, saw him walking toward the room, and then he went in and closed the door."

"The Harrises have records of who was staying where and when they checked in," I said, thinking out loud. "As usual, the motel didn't fill up until later in the day. You didn't see if anyone was in the room waiting for him?"

"No. I pulled out then. Say," Dick said, sounding more like himself, "are you ready for me to start on the roof, about Thursday the eighth?"

"Sure, that's fine. Thanks, Dick. You're right, by the way. It probably has nothing to do with the murder. It's odd, though, that Minnie Harris didn't mention Curtis being there."

"Maybe she didn't know," Dick said. "It could be . . . Well, boys will be boys."

"True, but," I went on, "the Harrises don't cater to the hooker crowd."

"Also true," Dick agreed. "Still, if there's a girl involved, she needn't be a hooker. That occurred to me at the time, which is why I didn't want to say anything. You know how everybody around here likes to spread gossip. I know you won't, though, especially when it involves one of your own. See you at the parish picnic."

I hung up, wondering how well I knew my latest hire. The phone rang before I could head for the kitchen.

"You're home," Marisa Foxx said. "I feel like a spy."

"How so?" I asked, sitting down on the sofa.

"I could term it 'networking,' I suppose," she said. "I called another old law school chum who works for the city in San Francisco. He verified what my other old friend, Angela, had told me. The Vitani case was never closed, his widow is indeed remarrying in August, and so on. I like to make sure I'm not dealing in rumors. Anyway, Lawrence—the city attorney—is living with a much younger man who's a paralegal for a firm in the same building as Bowles, Mercier and company. Naturally, there's gossip traded at lunch or whenever these employees get together." Marisa paused. "The Vitani murder was a hot topic for some time, but Lawrence's live-in never heard any mention of the Cavanaughs in connection with the case."

My shoulders slumped. I'd been prepared for something juicy. "Damn!"

"I know," Marisa said. "I'm sorry. But maybe no news is . . . interesting news."

I frowned. "Meaning?"

"Lawrence checked the police department's case notes on Mr. Vitani's homicide. No mention was made of the Cavanaughs, including Tom. On the day Mr. Vitani was killed, he'd seen four clients, including two older widows, one younger couple who were adopting a baby from Asia, and an eighty-six-year-old woman who was divorcing her fifth husband. None of them were ever considered suspects."

I hadn't paid close attention to Marisa's account of Mr. Vitani's last workday. Instead, I was trying to figure out if every possibility to make a connection between the Cavanaughs and Mr. Vitani's slaying had been exhausted. "Okay," I finally said,

"how about this? Could your pal, or your pal's paralegal pal,
find out the last time Tom had an appointment with Mr. Vitani?"

"Possibly," Marisa replied. "You aren't pushing too hard
on this angle, are you, Emma?"

"Probably," I admitted. "I'm a pest, I know. But I'm not a
great believer in coincidences."

"You're not a pest," Marisa said kindly. "I must confess I
find this rather fascinating, as long as I'm viewing it from a safe
distance. I'm fond of puzzles."

"So am I," I said as someone knocked loudly on my front
door. "I've got company. Thanks again. I'll talk to you later."

My caller pounded a second time, harder. On guard, I
peered through the peephole and saw an enormous straw hat.
"Vida," I said in relief, opening the door. "Why didn't you use
the bell?"

She burst across the threshold like a whirlwind. "Because
nobody has one that works," she asserted. "I assume that includes you."

"You know better," I said as she virtually fell into the armchair by the hearth. "How's Leo?"

"Hazy," Vida said. "I had to stop at the Grocery Basket on
my way home. Since it's out of my way and closer to your
house, I decided to deliver personally what little information I
have about Leo. I sat at his bedside for nearly an hour, and he
woke up briefly twice. I'm not sure he even knew I was there.
The nurse—someone new, I have no idea who she is or even if
she's a real nurse—how could I not hear of her? All this current
vogue of nurses taking on rotating assignments for six months
at a time is such a poor idea. No continuity, no attachment to
patients or the community. What's wrong with people these
days? They can't stay put." Vida whipped off her hat, displac-

ing several hairpins and a small tortoiseshell comb. "What was I saying?"

"The nurse," I reminded her. "She told you . . . something."

Vida bent down to collect the hair accessories. "Oh, yes. This so-called nurse—very haughty—informed me that Leo was heavily medicated and visitors shouldn't tire him. How can you tire someone who's unconscious most of the time?" She poked pins back into her coiffure, which didn't do much to tame the errant gray curls. "I actually think this nurse—her name tag was handwritten and utterly indecipherable—thought she could make me leave. Nonsense, of course. I wouldn't budge."

"Of course not," I murmured. "Was Leo at all coherent?"

"Not really," Vida said, finally settling back in the chair. "The first time he opened his eyes, he muttered. I thought he was thirsty, so I tried to give him a sip of water. It spilled all over. Later—oh, goodness, it must have been another half-hour—he woke up again, and he did look at me, but as I mentioned, I don't know if he knew who I was or where he was and how he got there. I asked him, in fact. He just lay like a lump with his eyes half-closed and then finally—and this was rather curious—he said, 'Not game.' What on earth do you suppose that means?"

I shook my head. "To me, it's only a term we use in playing bridge. Or to describe someone who isn't willing to participate in something, especially sports."

"He said it three times," Vida said, frowning. "It never became more distinct. Then he went back to sleep, so I finally left."

"That sounds as if he was trying to tell you something important," I suggested.

"Well . . ." She looked thoughtful, resting her chin on her fist. "Maybe so. But what?"

"Who shot him?"

"Wasn't his back turned?"

"We don't know for sure," I replied, unable to block out the mental image of Leo being hit by a bullet. "He might have been able to move after he was shot."

Vida nodded. "True. 'Not game,' " she repeated. "What does that sound like?"

"Not same?" I suggested. "Not lame? Not blame?"

Vida shook her head. "It was *not* and something beginning with a *g*, because each time Leo said it, he had difficulty getting it out."

My mind was blank, so I changed the subject and told Vida that I couldn't run down Curtis. "It worries me. It's as if we all have targets on our backs. You're being careful, I hope?"

"Oh, piffle!" Vida exclaimed. "Why would anyone except you want to shoot Curtis?"

"Because he was at the ski lodge when the shooting took place," I said. "I just told you that."

"I don't think so," Vida responded. "He's not the noticing kind."

"The killer doesn't know that," I pointed out.

"Perhaps." She still didn't look convinced. "Are you going to see Leo this evening?"

"I hadn't thought that far ahead," I said. "I might." Then I launched into the phone calls from the Bourgettes and Marisa Foxx.

"Curtis at the motel?" Vida definitely looked puzzled. "You must call Minnie to find out who had that unit."

"I will," I promised, glancing at my watch. It was twenty after six. "But they're probably busy now, registering guests. Do you want to stay for dinner?"

"Well . . . that would be nice. If it's no trouble," Vida added.

"Of course not," I assured her. "I'll thaw some lamb steaks. Come join me in the kitchen." I got up, with Vida following me so closely that I was afraid she'd step on my heels. "I've got some fresh corn in the fridge, too," I said, opening the freezer section. "I was about to make a drink. Do you want something?"

Vida shuddered. "I've had quite enough alcohol for one week after having a drink with Sophia Cavanaugh. Ice water will be fine, thank you. I wish I'd known at the time that Sophia's brother was the slain man at the motel. Have you told Milo?"

I shook my head. "I couldn't reach him, either, and I haven't tried since I got home. I'm so afraid that this whole gang will leave town and disappear before the sheriff solves the case."

"Dylan and Kelsey aren't going far if they're buying Ed's silly house," Vida reminded me.

"If," I emphasized, putting the lamb steaks in the microwave and hitting the Defrost button. "Or is that a smoke screen? As for Sophia and Graham, I . . ."

Vida looked at me curiously. "What is it? You were saying?"

"Graham," I said softly. " 'Not Graham.' Is that what Leo meant?"

Vida's mouth formed a big O. "Oh, my!" she finally said, also very softly. "Yes, indeed. But what does it mean? Not Graham who shot Leo?"

"Maybe." I thought in silence as the microwave's timer ticked off the seconds. I felt as if it might be counting down to doomsday. "It's got to be one of them," I finally said. "The Cavanaughs, I mean. There are only four suspects, assuming Ginger Roth and Sophia Volos Cavanaugh are the same person."

"I suppose you're right," Vida agreed after a long pause. "There's no connection to anyone around here. Except, of course, for you."

"Thanks." I was washing a couple of potatoes under the tap. "I do not, however, own a Smith and Wesson. Nor was I in San Francisco when Mr. Vitani was shot. And I would never, ever shoot Leo. Not when the penalty is putting up with Ed Bronsky in the office. That's cruel and unusual punishment for any crime."

Vida nodded absently. "While you do that," she said as I put the potatoes in a baking pan, "I'm calling Minnie Harris. She can't be *that* busy. I don't mind having to wait on the phone as long as I can hear what's going on at the other end. Now tell me again where Dick Bourgette saw Curtis at the motel."

I recounted his not quite precise recall of the unit. Vida stalked off into the living room, where I'd left the phone. I tried to eavesdrop but couldn't catch much of what she said. She returned while I was shucking a couple of ears of corn.

"Well now." She offered me her owlish expression. "Minnie says only one of those middle units was occupied that afternoon. The name on the registry is Camille Whitson from Colville. She stayed two nights and checked out the day after the murder. Young, rather pretty, as Minnie recalled, and blond. She mentioned that she'd come to Alpine to be with her boyfriend."

"Colville?" I echoed, referring to the small town northwest of Spokane. "Did she have proper ID?"

"Yes, a Washington State driver's license. Of course it could be faked, as was that one from California."

The microwave bell rang. "Did Minnie ever see this girl with her boyfriend?" I asked, removing the lamb steaks.

Vida, who was hovering next to me by the stove, shook her head. "She only saw the girl when she checked in and when she left. May I help you?"

"There's nothing much to do," I assured her, well aware of Vida's ineptitude in the kitchen, despite her reams of copy offering advice to Alpine cooks. "I'll get our drinks, and then we can sit for a bit. See if you can reach Milo."

"I doubt that Curtis is in any kind of—" Vida began, but the phone interrupted her. "I'll get it," she offered and hurried to the living room.

The fridge's ice maker drowned out Vida's voice, but before I could finish putting cubes into our glasses, she came through the kitchen door with the phone plastered to her ear. "I can't believe it!" she cried, apparently for my benefit as well as that of whoever was on the other end of the line. "It's absurd. Yes, I'll tell her." Shaking her head, she clicked the phone off. "That was Milo. He's arrested Curtis, charging him with one count of homicide and another of attempted homicide."

"No!" I shrieked. "I can't believe it!"

"You'd better," Vida said grimly. "Curtis confessed."

"Why? How? Are you sure?" I demanded, setting the two glasses on the counter.

Vida nodded in a series of agitated jerks. "Milo doesn't joke about murder."

"No," I murmured, leaning against the counter for support. "Oh, my God! Fleetwood will pick this up!"

Vida had removed her glasses and was breathing on the lenses. "Milo was decent enough to say that he isn't going public until he has to make the log available tomorrow morning."

"For who?" I retorted. "Not Curtis. Fleetwood or somebody working for him usually just calls in every morning."

Vida wiped off her glasses with a piece of paper towel. "Shall we go?"

"Go?" I was still rattled. "Where?"

"To the sheriff's office," she replied. "Curtis needs us."

I was incredulous. "I thought you'd prefer having him locked in a cell."

"What I'd prefer and what's right are two different things," Vida asserted as she put her glasses back on. "He really doesn't know anyone in town. Where are his parents?"

"I think they live in Seattle, near the University of Washington," I said, turning off the oven and making sure the burners weren't on. "Maybe I should call Marisa Foxx."

"Very well. I'll go on ahead while you do that," Vida volunteered. "I'll see you there."

She left as soon as she could put on her sweater and hat. I stood motionless at the counter, trying to absorb the latest catastrophe. On the surface, it made no sense. As far as I knew, there was no connection between Curtis and the Cavanaughs. The word *conspiracy* was haunting me. Maybe all of this was an elaborate plan involving the newspaper's acquisition. It seemed ridiculous, but human nature is unpredictable, especially so when the cast is a bunch of relative unknowns.

Armed with a small shot of Canadian whiskey on the rocks, I dialed Marisa's number and relayed my bombshell.

"I'm not a criminal lawyer," she protested after expressing her shock. "But I suppose I could at least make sure that Curtis's rights aren't being violated. He is over twenty-one, isn't he?"

"He's almost twenty-four," I said. "I think he has an August birthday. I'm going to try to track down his parents now. Will I see you at the sheriff's office?"

"Yes," Marisa said. "I'll be there in about fifteen minutes. I'd already changed into my robe."

I thanked her profusely and dug out my Seattle telephone directory. There were only a handful of Maynes listed, and none of them lived near the university. I opened my laptop to see if I had any information about Curtis's family stored in my files. I was still searching when the doorbell rang.

"Now what?" I muttered, getting up from the sofa.

It was still broad daylight outside. Looking through the peephole, I saw a young man standing on the porch. He looked vaguely familiar, though I couldn't recall his name. At least he wasn't holding a weapon.

"Hi," I said a bit breathlessly after opening the door. "Are you looking for me?"

"I am if you're Emma Lord," he said in a serious voice.

"I am," I responded, wondering where I'd seen the visitor. "You're . . . ?" I let the question dangle.

"I'm Graham Cavanaugh. May I come in? My sister, Kelsey, is in grave danger."

NINETEEN

I WAS STUNNED. NO WONDER MY CALLER LOOKED FAMILIAR. He was no spitting image of Tom but was almost as tall, had the same blue eyes, and, like his father, faintly chiseled features. Graham—if this was indeed Graham—had lighter brown hair and wasn't as broad.

"Do you need ID?" he asked in a weary voice as I stood there in the doorway looking, I'm sure, like an idiot.

I shook my head. His face—no, I realized, it was his mannerisms that evoked his father. "Come in," I urged, stepping aside. *Not Graham.* That was what Leo had been trying to say. The man calling himself Graham Cavanaugh was another impostor.

He moved swiftly to the hearth and took a deep breath. His eyes darted around the room, searching, studying, as if he were taking inventory. At last his gaze steadied, fixed on me. I could imagine what he was thinking. *So this is the woman my father loved.* I couldn't help but wonder if he were judging my worthiness. But when he spoke again, his words had nothing to do with my credentials. "Have you seen Kelsey in the last few hours?"

"No," I replied. "Is she . . . missing?"

"I don't know." He rubbed at the back of his head. "She's not at the lodge."

"Please," I implored, indicating the armchair nearest to him. "Sit. What's going on? If you're Graham, then who's—"

He waved an impatient hand and remained standing. "I don't know. Frankly, Kelsey was somewhat incoherent, and I was stupefied when I heard Sophia was here. We separated six months ago, when she told me there was another man and she was planning to move in with him after he got rid of his wife. Anyway, I took an early flight out of New York this morning after Kelsey called me in a panic last night to tell me what was going on around here. Good God," he said with fervor, "has everybody lost their minds?"

I had to sit down. "How long have you been in town?"

"An hour." He looked at his watch. "Closer to two hours now. I've lost track of time."

"When was Kelsey last seen?"

"This afternoon," Graham replied, pacing the hearth. "Or so the manager at the ski lodge told me."

"Have you talked to anyone else in their party?"

He shook his head. "They've gone to ground. That's why I'm here. I thought if anyone might know where Kelsey was, it'd be you." He grimaced. "You were, after all, about to become our stepmother. I thought Kelsey might come to you for help."

I couldn't hide my surprise. One of the Cavanaughs had finally acknowledged my existence in Tom's life. With effort, I tried to regain some composure. So much had happened so fast. My brain was being pelted with revelations.

"You must notify the sheriff," I said, reluctant to tell Graham that a suspect was in custody. "Why do you think Kelsey's in danger?"

He looked at me with disbelief. "Why do you think? Because she knows too much. Because these crooks can't get their hands on your newspaper without her. Damn!" Clearly on edge, he moved around the room, pausing only to look out the front window, to touch the fireplace mantel, to glance at some books I'd piled on top of a shelf. "Okay," he finally said. "I'll call the sheriff. I don't know what else to do."

"Here." I handed him the phone. "Before you do, I have to ask you a question. Do you know someone named Curtis Mayne?"

He frowned. "No, I don't think so. Why?"

"He's confessed to murdering Maxim Volos and taking a shot at Leo Walsh. Curtis works for me."

Graham looked startled. "As what? An assassin?"

I couldn't help it. I started to laugh and tried to stop before I became hysterical. "No, no," I finally managed to get out. "I hired him recently as a reporter."

"Leo Walsh?" A light seemed to go on in Graham's blue eyes. "I remember Leo, but I forgot that he works for you. He was shot?"

"Last night," I said. "Now I know why. He knew that the person posing as you wasn't. That is—"

"I get it," Graham snapped. "Holy Christ!"

"I should've known," I said ruefully as recollections of two separate conversations flashed in my brain. "When Kelsey and I went to lunch, she kept saying she wished you were here. I thought she meant with the two of us at the diner, but in fact, she was telling me you weren't in Alpine. And whoever impersonated you referred to your father a couple of times as Tom, not Dad."

"Some kids do that," Graham said with a shrug. "Maybe I should see the sheriff in person. Where's his office?"

"I was about to go there when you showed up. I'll lead the way," I offered, swigging down the last of my drink. "Let's go."

Graham had rented a Chrysler Sebring. Although it was a convertible, he had the top up on this pleasant first evening of July. Maybe he was afraid someone was going to shoot him. I had to admit it didn't seem like an unreasonable fear.

As I headed down to Front Street, it occurred to me that I didn't know how far I could trust Graham. He might look more like Tom than the bogus Graham did, but that didn't mean he had his father's integrity. On the other hand, we were on our way to see the sheriff. I couldn't think of a safer destination.

Or a stranger one, given Curtis's presence as a confessed killer. I couldn't imagine how—other than with a sizable bribe—he figured into the Cavanaugh mix. If that were true, then the plot must have been hatched after mid-May, when I decided to bring him on after he'd graduated in early June. Shaking my head, I pulled in next to Vida's car.

I didn't see any sign of Curtis's beater. I wasn't sure what Marisa drove, so I didn't know if she'd arrived yet. Graham, who had followed me closely, parked a couple of spaces down from Vida's Buick. I waited for him on the sidewalk by the sheriff's entrance. A moment later, Tom's son was striding purposefully toward me.

"Is there anything about this Curtis I should know?" he asked, pausing with his hand on one of the double doors.

"Not really," I said. "Obviously, I don't know him very well, either."

Milo, Vida, and Doe Jameson were talking behind the counter. Curtis was nowhere to be seen.

Vida was the first to speak. "What took you so long?" she asked before staring at Graham. "Who is he?"

"Graham Cavanaugh," I responded.

Doe scowled at us; Milo seemed skeptical; Vida, however, paused, tapping her cheek. "Yes," she finally said. "I can see that. It's the way you carry yourself, Graham." Coming through the swinging gate, she held out her hand. "I'm Vida Runkel, the *Advocate*'s House & Home editor. Yes, you're definitely Tommy's son."

Graham, looking somewhat taken aback, perhaps at Vida's reference to "Tommy," shook her hand. "I think my dad mentioned your name a couple of times."

"Possibly," Vida remarked and gave Graham a dose of her toothy smile.

I leaned on the counter, closer to Milo. "Where's Curtis?"

"In my office," Milo replied. "He can't escape. No windows in there."

"Do you believe he's your perp?" I inquired.

The sheriff shrugged. "He says he is."

"Motive?"

Vida intervened before Milo could answer. "It's nonsense! Curtis insists he did it for you. I don't believe a word of it."

I turned to Doe. "What do you think?"

Doe's broad face was inscrutable. "People usually don't confess to crimes they didn't commit."

At that moment, Marisa Foxx came through the door. "I'm here to represent Curtis Mayne," she announced, all brusque business. "Where is he?"

Milo gestured at his office door. "Go ahead. I read him his rights."

Marisa marched through the gate and into Milo's office without bothering to knock. She moved so quickly that the door was closed before I could even glimpse Curtis.

"He's not suicidal, is he?" I asked.

"I doubt it. In fact, the kid seems kind of upbeat." Milo glanced at the closed door to his office. "Goddamnit, now I can't get at my own desk." He eyed Graham. "And you're here because . . . ?"

"My sister, Kelsey, has disappeared," Graham said without emotion. "I'm worried about her."

"Okay," Milo said wearily. "Come over to that desk at the end and fill out a missing person's report. Doe, you handle this one." As the deputy opened the gate for Graham, Milo turned to Vida and me. "What are you two doing here? Posting bail for your nitwit reporter?"

"You're not taking Curtis seriously, are you?" I said.

"I think he belongs in the psych ward," Milo retorted. "Why the hell did you hire him in the first place?"

"Desperation," I replied. "Qualified candidates are hard to find because the written word is an endangered species. Did Curtis come to you or did you go after him?"

"I thought maybe I'd fish Sawyer Creek for a change. I headed up the ski lodge road, but it was still kind of early, and I was hungry, so I stopped at the lodge's coffee shop to grab a bite and get coffee to take along. Your loony reporter was there talking to one of the waitresses." Milo made a face. "The next thing I knew, he cornered me before I could go up to the counter. He said we had to talk. We went into the lobby, and he told me he'd killed Volos. Before he could say anything else, I hauled his ass in here. The kid had a real jumbled story—he should be writing fiction. But he confessed, so I had no choice. If nothing else, he's a danger to himself."

I was still skeptical. "Curtis is a flake, but I've never thought of him as a nutcase."

"Whatever." Milo waved a hand at Vida and me. "Go home. There's nothing you can do here. I have to keep the little creep overnight because I can't formally charge him until morning, when the judge shows up. If that Foxx woman wants to post his bail, she's out of luck." The sheriff picked up the phone and glanced at Graham, who was filling out the missing person's form while Doe sat in silence. "I'm bringing in some extra help. If I have to, I'll ask the state patrol for some dogs to track down Kelsey—if, in fact, she's really missing. G'bye." He turned his back on us and finished dialing. "Sam," Milo said into the phone, "you're up first for extra duty. Get your ass in here ASAP."

Vida and I exchanged baleful glances. I'd expected her to argue about leaving, but she kept quiet and joined me as I started for the door.

"Now tell me about Graham," she demanded as soon as we were out on the sidewalk.

I hesitated, taking in Front Street with its scattering of vehicles passing by, a handful of pedestrians strolling along past city hall, the courthouse, the Clemans Building, the Burger Barn, and the Bank of Alpine. Some of the red, white, and blue bunting had already been hung from the power poles in preparation for the upcoming Fourth of July celebration. I smelled sawdust from the mill and diesel from a big truck that rumbled past us. Raising my head, I could see the buildings and homes that marched up the steep slope of Tonga Ridge all the way to the tree line. Church spires mingled with tin roofs, and brick with shake exteriors and aluminum siding. I managed to make out my own little log house, snug against the evergreens. The view seemed so normal, though my private world did not.

"It's crazy," I finally said to Vida. "Somebody appears to have been impersonating Graham. He was in New York until this morning. I don't know what to think or believe anymore. I've lost my bearings."

"Temporarily derailed," Vida asserted.

"I hope so." I smiled ruefully. "Do you want to come back to my place and have dinner?"

Vida pondered the renewed offer. "No, I think not." She gazed at the iron post clock by the bank. "It's almost seven-thirty. I'll fix something at home. Thank you just the same. I'll phone you later, and you can finish filling me in. I must confess, I don't know what to think about all this, either. Most mystifying."

I didn't coax. Frankly, I needed some peace and quiet in order to sort out the most recent unsettling events. Five minutes later, I was standing in the kitchen, wondering if I really felt like cooking any of the meal I'd planned for two. I'd been shortchanged all day on food, but I had no appetite. An apple would hold me until I got hungry again.

By nine o'clock I still didn't feel like eating. I checked my e-mail, but there was no word from Adam or Ben, only the usual messages soliciting my business for everything from floral arrangements to horoscope forecasts. What I really needed was a swami who could figure out what was going on with the so-called Cavanaughs.

Vida still hadn't called, though I figured that she was catching up with some of her other fruitful sources. I refrained from contacting Milo, assuming—maybe incorrectly—that he'd let me know if there were any new developments, such as Curtis claiming to have been reincarnated after his career as Jack the Ripper.

Just as twilight was turning to dusk, I heard an odd sound that seemed to come from outside. I looked through the front window but saw nothing except for an elderly man from down the street walking his collie. I heard the noise again a couple of minutes later and went to the kitchen. All was calm when I gazed from the window facing my backyard. Cautiously, I opened the door to the carport at the side of the house. Nothing.

Maybe I was starting to imagine things, I thought. Reality

beckoned in the form of my full garbage container under the sink. I collected the plastic bag and went out the back way to the trash can beyond the woodpile.

The lid lay on the carport floor, and some of the contents were strewn haphazardly on the ground. It wasn't an unusual occurrence, especially in the colder months, when wildlife was forced to seek food below the snow line. Deer, cougars, bears, wolves, and other animals were often sighted in town. With their habitat dwindling from relentless human encroachment, they were even seen occasionally in big cities, such as Seattle. I picked up the debris and put it back in the can.

I was about to go inside when I saw something move in the shadows near a big Douglas fir. It wasn't an animal but a man. I froze, aware that I had more to fear from another human than from the forest creatures. Curtis's confession aside, I was sure that a killer still lurked in Alpine. I might be next on the hit list.

Paralyzed, I watched the man walk slowly toward me. Then I gasped in relief. The long gray hair and beard were familiar. It was Craig Laurentis, the reclusive artist whose painting hung in my living room. I hadn't seen him in almost a year. Surprised, I waited in the carport, watching him approach with his peculiar, unhurried grace.

"Emma Lord," he said when he came within ten feet of me.

"Craig Laurentis," I responded, smiling at him as he stopped at the edge of the carport. I could've sworn that he wore the same ragged tank top and pants he'd had on when he rescued me after a nasty fall the previous August. "I never tire of looking at your painting *Sky Autumn*."

"Good." He regarded me with his intense green eyes. "The cubs came calling."

"What? Oh!" I looked at my garbage can. "Of course. I didn't think of that. Where are they?"

He made a slight gesture with his hand. "Somewhere by those cedar trees, probably the one that was damaged by lightning last February." His voice was rather hoarse, a quality I'd noticed on our first meeting, when I had guessed that he seldom spoke to other humans.

"Are you going to raise them?"

He shrugged. "If they stay. That's up to them."

"Can I get you something?" I asked.

Craig shook his head. "I don't need anything. But I have something for you."

I was puzzled. His hands were empty. "What is it?"

"A girl," Craig replied. "She says her name is Kelsey. She wants to see you. Shall I call to her?"

I was nonplussed. "Well . . . yes, of course."

Craig whistled, long and low. I stared across the sloping expanse of my backyard, but daylight was fading fast. I couldn't see Kelsey or the bear cubs. After what seemed like a long time but was probably less than a minute, a hunched figure emerged from behind a fallen log just a few feet beyond my property line. Kelsey moved uncertainly, slowly, and, it seemed to me, fearfully, as she approached the carport.

I turned to Craig to ask if she was okay. But he'd vanished like a wraith, moving noiselessly across the grass on bare feet while I focused on Kelsey.

She faltered a few feet from where I was standing. "Ms. Lord?"

I hurried to meet her. "Yes, of course. How are you?" I asked, putting an arm around her.

"Scared. Tired." She leaned against me as I led her inside.

While I settled her on the sofa, I noticed that her short-sleeved linen blouse and matching cropped pants were dirty. Feathery maple seedpods, green fir needles, and clusters of small cedar cones clung to her clothes and even to her hair. "Can I get you something to drink? Or eat?"

Kelsey shook her head. "I just want to rest. I'm so tired."

I sat down in the armchair by the hearth. *Give her time,* I admonished myself, sensing that she was in a very vulnerable state. Kelsey huddled at the end of the sofa, staring at the floor.

"That painting behind you was done by Craig Laurentis," I said after a long pause.

She lifted her chin but didn't turn around. "Who?"

"The man who brought you here," I replied. "He's an artist."

"Oh." She seemed unimpressed.

"How did you run into him?" I asked.

Kelsey frowned, as if she couldn't quite remember. "Ah . . ." She hesitated, running her fingers through her blond hair and dislodging a couple of maple pods. "I was in the woods," she finally said, closing her eyes as if she had to visualize where she'd been and what she'd done. "I ran away from the lodge." Opening her eyes, she looked at me in puzzlement. "I was scared, really scared."

"What scared you?" I inquired in a matter-of-fact voice.

"I heard Dylan and Sophia talking in the other room," she replied slowly. "They didn't know I was there. They thought I'd gone to lunch in the coffee shop, but I hadn't because I'd forgotten my key card to the suite, so I had to find it in the bedroom. Then I hid until they left."

"What did Dylan and Sophia say to upset you?"

Kelsey's face crumpled. She was on the verge of tears. "They were going to send me . . . somewhere. It was called . . . Resthaven. It's a place for . . . crazy people."

"I don't think they can do that unless you want to go there," I pointed out.

Agitated, Kelsey shook her head. "Sophia told Dylan I'd do anything he wanted me to. I always have." She leaned her head back against the sofa. "It's true. I love him very much."

"But you wouldn't let them do that, would you?"

"Well . . ." She rubbed at her nose. "My mother used to go there sometimes. But she always came back home. After the last time she went, she took too many pills and . . ." Kelsey's voice trailed off, and she frowned. "It was awful."

"I know," I said quietly and waited for her to go on. But she didn't. Instead, Kelsey continued to frown and stare at the carpet.

"I'm going to call your brother," I finally said, getting up to fetch the phone from the side table. "He's been looking for you."

Kelsey's blue eyes grew wide. "Graham's here? Oh, I'm so glad!"

Holding the receiver, I looked down at her. "Who is the man calling himself Graham?"

Kelsey grimaced. "He's Sophia's brother Nick. I never saw him before in my life until he came to the ski lodge."

I was stunned. "You mean . . . this Nick is also the brother of the man who was killed at the motel?"

Kelsey nodded. "I guess so. But I didn't know he had a brother. Or what his real name was. He always called himself Thor."

I stared at Kelsey. "Thor?"

She nodded. "One of the deputies told me his full name was Maxim Roth Volos. I guess he turned his middle name around because it sounded more artistic."

Thor. Roth. Josh Roth, the man who was staying at the motel, the man who'd been killed, the man who was . . . ?

"Did he father your baby?" I asked with reluctance.

Kelsey nodded again. "He wanted me to get an abortion, but my father wouldn't stand for it. I think he paid Thor to go back to New York. That's how Graham met Sophia. To make sure Thor really left San Francisco after we'd come back there, my father sent Graham back East with Thor. Then Graham married Sophia a while later, but it didn't work out. I never realized Sophia was Thor's sister. They were married at somebody's house on Long Island."

"Did Thor ever meet your son?"

"No. I never saw Thor again." She sighed. "I missed him, but later . . . well, he sort of faded from my mind, especially after I met Dylan. Then I saw Thor's picture in your paper, and at first I wasn't sure it was him. He'd shaved his beard and cut his hair. I was afraid to ask Sophia. She scares me. I felt trapped. I had to pretend that Nick was Graham or they would've . . . you know."

I could guess. "Do you know who killed Thor?"

Kelsey turned away from me. "I don't want to know. I just want to be with Graham. Thor never loved me, and now Dylan doesn't love me, either. He never did. Like Thor, he only cares about my money. I just realized that these last few days." She pressed a hand to her temple. "I think you can only trust family. Without Graham, I'm all alone."

What if I told her she wasn't alone, she had me? But she didn't. I was a stranger. And yet she'd come here, apparently of her own volition. For the moment, all I could do was dial the sheriff's office.

Doe Jameson answered the phone. "Is Dodge there?" I asked.

"No," she replied. "He went home about half an hour ago."

"Where's Graham Cavanaugh?"

"I don't know," Doe said. "He left, too. Do you want his cell number?"

I told her I did and scribbled the information on a notepad I kept by the phone.

"Is Graham coming?" Kelsey asked plaintively before I could dial his number.

"I'm calling him now," I said, entering the numbers and waiting for her brother to pick up.

He answered on the second ring. I told him that Kelsey was at my house. Graham expressed his relief and said he'd come right away. He'd been sitting in the ski lodge parking lot, hoping that she might show up.

Kelsey let out a deep sigh when I relayed the message. "Now everything will be okay," she said.

I sat back down in the armchair. "Tell me how you met up with Craig."

"Craig?" She seemed mystified.

"The artist who lives in the forest."

"Oh." Kelsey cleared her throat, sat up straight, and folded her hands in her lap, looking like a pupil reciting in class. "I went into the woods and found a trail. I followed it, and after a while it sort of disappeared. I was afraid to go back down in case they were looking for me, so I sat on a log for a long, long time. It was so peaceful there and I could hear water, so I finally got up because I was thirsty and followed the sound. The creek was really pretty, with ferns and moss and even some little white flowers in bloom. I got a drink from it. I've never tasted water so wonderful. But I wasn't sure how to find the trail again. I didn't know what to do. I hadn't taken anything with me, not even my cell phone. Then I saw those little bears. At first, I was scared. But they didn't seem to notice me and went farther on to get their own drink from the creek. That was when I saw the man coming close to them. He didn't see me at first. He looked like one of those homeless people you see in San Francisco. I wondered if I should be afraid of him, so I didn't move. And then he saw me and walked down the hill to ask if I was lost. I told him I was. The little bears had gone off by then. The man—you said his name is Craig?"

I nodded. "Craig Laurentis. He has a home in the forest."

Kelsey nodded. "He asked me where I wanted to go. I told him I was afraid to go back down the trail because . . . I couldn't say why. He asked if I had any friends around here. I said I didn't, and then I thought of you, so I told him. He knew where you lived, and that's where we went. So did the bears."

"You were lucky he came along," I said. "He's very kind."

The doorbell rang. Kelsey gave a start. I checked first through the peephole to make sure it was Graham. He looked impatient, shifting from one foot to the other.

"Come in," I said after opening the door.

Kelsey had gotten to her feet. "Graham!" she cried and flew into his arms. He held her close for a long time as she said his name over and over again.

Tom's children. His immortality, tangible evidence that he had lived. Clinging to each other in my little log house. It was almost as if Tom was standing beside me.

I began to cry.

Graham and Kelsey finally eased out of their embrace, but he kept an arm around her as they moved to the sofa. I went into the kitchen so they couldn't see my tears. It took me a couple of minutes to regain my composure. I wiped my eyes with a piece of paper towel and returned to the living room.

Graham spoke first. "I'm appalled," he declared. "Kelsey's telling her side of this ghastly story. Can't your sheriff arrest all these creeps on enough charges to put them in prison? Fraud, conspiracy, identity theft. Even if that reporter confessed to the murder, these people are criminals."

In light of Milo's rigid adherence to following procedure, I hesitated. "If you two brought charges against them for Nick Volos's impersonation of you, Graham, then the sheriff could bring him in for questioning." I looked at Kelsey, still in the circle of her brother's protective arm. "Did Dylan or anyone else threaten you with bodily harm?"

"No." She closed her eyes and shook her head.

I sat down again in the armchair. "Do any of them own a gun?"

"I don't know," Kelsey said in a rueful voice.

Graham frowned. "If they declared it was in their luggage and they'd bought it legally, it's possible."

"It might have been acquired illegally," I murmured as a thought occurred to me. "I'm going to call Milo. The sheriff," I clarified, getting up to reach the phone. "I've never heard if he checked the flights these people arrived on. Sophia and Maxim were here first as far as I know. But this Nick came later, after you got into town, Kelsey."

I dialed Milo's cell. He picked up just before the call went over to his voice mail. "What now?" he demanded.

"Call off the dogs," I said. "Kelsey's here with me."

"You found her?" Milo asked, sounding surprised.

"She found me. I'll explain later," I said and then posed my query about the suspects' arrivals. "Anybody who came before Volos was killed?"

"Frigging red tape," Milo grumbled. "We didn't hear back until late this afternoon. I'd left by then. What's wrong with these idiot airlines?"

"And?" I coaxed.

"The phoney Josh and Ginger Roth arrived at Sea-Tac late Tuesday from New York. Fake IDs from California, but nobody caught that. Graham Cavanaugh, a.k.a. Nick Volos, was on a flight out of JFK the next morning. We haven't had a chance to check on Graham the Second."

"Never mind," I said, glancing at Graham. "I believe him. I believe Kelsey, too. But what about the real Dylan Platte?"

"He took a flight out of San Francisco just after Kelsey left to come here. That means he's out of the loop as the killer."

"Yes, it does." I paused. "Hang on. I've got a question for Kelsey. She and Graham are here at my house."

Kelsey suddenly looked on her guard. "What?" she asked.

"Where was Dylan before you flew into Sea-Tac?"

"Here," she said and gasped. "Oh! No, of course not! But he told me he was coming to Alpine to see about the house and look into the newspaper purchase. Dylan left San Francisco Tuesday. I thought he must still be here. I never saw him again until he came to the ski lodge."

I'd been holding the phone out in front of Kelsey so Milo could hear. "Did you get that?" I asked him.

"Hell, yes. So what name did he use? Humpty Dumpty?"

"That's up to you to find out," I retorted. "It sounds as if he tried to cover his tracks by taking two flights, the second one under his real name. He must have holed up in between somewhere in the Bay Area."

"Shit. This thing's the biggest mess I've—" Milo stopped himself. "Never mind. I'm going back to work."

"Good," I said. "Why don't you arrest somebody?"

"Maybe I will, goddamnit." He hung up.

I put the phone back in its cradle. "You both must be hungry," I said to the Cavanaugh siblings. "Let me fix you something. I've got a dinner for two almost ready to go."

Kelsey looked at Graham. "Should we?"

He hesitated before responding. "Well . . . if Ms. Lord doesn't mind."

"No. Of course I don't," I assured him. "My own dinner was interrupted. It'll take only a few minutes. I'll boil the potatoes instead of baking them. Would you like something to drink while you wait?"

Graham nudged his sister. "A little wine, maybe?"

"Oh . . . no," she said. "We can't stay at the ski lodge tonight, so I need my things. Everything's there. Can we get them while Ms. Lord makes dinner? Please?"

Graham shook his head. "I don't think that's a good idea. Maybe somebody can bring your belongings here."

Kelsey, however, was surprisingly stubborn. "I know where everything is and what I brought. Please, let's go. If you're with me, it'll be fine."

Graham looked like a man arguing with himself. "Maybe," he said, turning in my direction, "we should ask somebody from the sheriff's office to go with us."

"The sheriff may be on his way there now," I said. "Call his office." I recited the number. "Go ahead, use my phone."

I went to the kitchen to start the meal I'd intended for Vida and me. My mind was preoccupied with sorting through the information Milo had given me. I still couldn't believe Curtis had murdered Maxim Volos or shot Leo. It simply didn't make sense. But neither did much of the case that surrounded the conspirators.

I'd just turned on the broiler when I heard Graham and Kelsey leave through the front door. I didn't know what they'd been told by whoever had answered the phone at the sheriff's office, but I presumed they'd been assured of their safety.

As I waited for the potato water to boil, I was suddenly overwhelmed by fatigue. It had been a long, eventful day, as turbulent as any I could remember in the last few years. The Cavanaughs had a knack for disrupting my life. But this time there was a bright side. I was finally getting to know Tom's children, and that meant more to me than I'd ever dreamed it would.

Yet there was a lingering fear that Graham and Kelsey might also be my worst nightmare.

TWENTY

A T TWENTY-FIVE MINUTES AFTER ELEVEN THAT NIGHT, THE
lamb steaks were drying out, the potatoes were turning to
mush, and I'd yet to put on the corn for its three-minute boil.
Graham and Kelsey had been gone for over half an hour. I
waited by the window for five more minutes and then called
the ski lodge.

Carlos, the night desk clerk, answered. He hadn't seen
Kelsey Platte. "I'm sorry," he said wearily. "I don't know what
this other guy looks like. I thought Graham Cavanaugh was already staying here."

"That's not his real name," I pointed out, not wanting to
explain the convoluted situation. "I'll bet Sophia Cavanaugh
registered for both of them."

"Do you want me to check?" Carlos asked.

"No, not now. Has the sheriff or one of his deputies come
in during the last hour?"

"Yes," Carlos replied. "Dodge got here a while ago, but I
don't know where he went. He had that lady deputy with him."

"What about Dylan Platte and the Cavanaughs? Have you
seen them lately?"

"Not since they came back from dinner," Carlos answered. "That was about nine or a little later. Do you want me to ring them?"

I considered his offer. "No," I finally replied. If they were in, Milo might be with them. I didn't want to interrupt the sheriff's investigation. "But if you see Kelsey Platte, could you please call me back?"

"Sure," Carlos said. "I go off duty at one a.m."

"I understand," I said and rang off.

I'd remained standing by the front window while I talked to Carlos. Only two vehicles had passed by, neither of them the Chrysler Sebring rented by the real Graham Cavanaugh. I thought about calling the sheriff's office, but instead, I phoned Vida. She usually didn't go to bed until after eleven, and then she often read for a bit before turning out the light.

Vida, however, sounded drowsy when she answered the phone on the fourth ring. I apologized for bothering her, but as soon as I launched into my story about Kelsey and Graham, she became alert.

"I'm so glad that Kelsey is safe," she declared when I finished. "Or is she?"

"I don't know," I admitted. "They've been gone for at least forty-five minutes."

"Perhaps Milo ran into them at the ski lodge," Vida speculated. "They may be with him if they planned to file charges."

"That's possible," I allowed. "Still, I'm worried. I can't seem to track down any of these people."

Vida offered to come to my house. "It won't take long for me to dress," she insisted.

"No, please don't," I told her. "I'll call you as soon as I hear anything." A faint ringing caught my attention. I realized it was my cell phone, which was in my purse at the end of the sofa. "I've got to go," I said. "I'll keep you posted."

I'd already hurried over to my purse to retrieve my cell. I clicked it on just as Vida hung up.

"Emma," Milo said, his voice unusually brisk. "Your other line was busy. Are those Cavanaugh kids at your place?"

"No," I replied. "Where are you?"

"In the ski lodge parking lot," the sheriff answered. "The rest of that bunch isn't here. Doe and I looked all over. It looks like they've cleared out. Their rooms are empty."

"Damn!" I cried. "Did anyone see them leave?"

"No. I've got an APB out on both rental cars. The lodge had the license plate numbers. But they could be all the way to Sea-Tac by now. Or even up to the Canadian border."

"What about Graham and Kelsey?" I asked. "Have you tried to call him on his cell phone?"

"No answer," Milo replied. "Doe tried it twice."

"Damn," I said softly. "Graham was driving a Chrysler Sebring."

"He was?" The sheriff turned away from the phone. I heard him tell Doe to check out the parking lot. I had a feeling that she wouldn't find the car. "You don't know the plate number, do you?" Milo asked me.

"No. I wish I did. But I imagine he rented it this afternoon at the airport."

"Okay. I'll have Sam Heppner check the rental agencies." The sheriff clicked off.

Feeling antsy, I double-checked to make sure I'd turned off everything in the kitchen. Then I went back into the living room, staring outside. Few lights were on this late. The street was deserted. A breeze had picked up, blowing down from Tonga Ridge, ruffling my shrubs and the Japanese cherry tree I'd planted a few years ago in the corner of my front yard.

I finally turned away, drawn as ever to Craig's *Sky Autumn*. I wondered about him, a not infrequent musing. The two times I'd seen him up close he'd played the part of rescuer. According to Donna Wickstrom, who owned the art gallery that sold Craig's paintings, she rarely saw Craig in person. His forays into town once or twice a year were always furtive and usually after dark. Yet it dawned on me that he knew more about Alpine than we knew about him. Otherwise, he wouldn't have known where I lived. A strange, almost comforting feeling came over me as I considered how Craig might often be watching the rest of us from the forest, keeping back in the shadows, observing the comings and goings of our so-called normal world.

The phone rang again. I rushed to answer it.

"I was sure you'd still be up," Marisa Foxx said, sounding irritable. "Your reporter didn't kill anyone."

I uttered a strange little laugh. "I honestly didn't think he did. Why did he confess? Or should I guess the reason?"

"If you guessed he thought the experience of being considered a murderer would win him a Pulitzer Prize, you'd be right," Marisa said. "Curtis had some odd notion that if he went through the ordeal a real killer would endure, he could bring a personal perspective to his story, thus making it more 'real,' as he put it. I don't approve of such a stunt, but I won't charge him for my time. It'd only end up costing you money."

"I appreciate that," I said. "Besides, I'll probably fire him. Did he say why he was at the motel the day Maxim Volos was killed?"

"Yes," Marisa replied. "He was calling on some girl named

Cammie who'd come to Alpine to break up with her boyfriend. Curtis told me he wanted to console her. I'll bet he did."

Cammie, short for Camille. I should've guessed. She'd been with Curtis at Mugs Ahoy when I'd tried to track him down to find out what progress he'd been making with the homicide story. "Dare I ask how Milo reacted to all this?"

"Angry at wasting his time," Marisa replied. "He's keeping Curtis in jail for the weekend, hoping it'll cure him of doing anything so foolish ever again. How on earth are you going to handle this in the paper?"

I sighed. "I'll worry about that when the time comes. I've got enough on my plate right now to stew over."

"Of course. I'll let you go, but I wish you better luck with Curtis's replacement."

"I'll need it," I said bleakly. "Thanks again."

I immediately dialed Vida's number. As I'd expected, she exploded. "Such a ninny! I thought so from the get-go. I hope Milo charges him with obstruction or whatever he deems fit for Curtis's outrageous behavior."

I agreed, then brought her up to date with my few scraps of new information.

"Worrisome," she murmured. "I don't like it. What can we do?"

I admitted I didn't know. "I'm truly frustrated," I confessed.

"Of course. Well, keep me posted, even if you have to wake me up."

I promised that I would and rang off. Lucky for Curtis that he was in a jail cell or I would have wrung his neck. Now I was without a real advertising manager *and* a reporter. I didn't want to think about what the next few days at the *Advocate* would be like.

Midnight. I should've gone to bed but realized I wouldn't

sleep. I felt helpless. It suddenly occured to me that I'd forgotten to call Rolf. In fact, I hadn't given him a thought since speaking with him earlier. It was too late to call now. Maybe, I thought wistfully, it was too late for us in every sense. Not knowing what else to do, I checked my e-mail again. It was mostly advertising and come-ons that I quickly deleted, wondering why it didn't all get sent to the junk mail file along with the rest of the ten or more messages that had automatically been dumped into the computer's trash bin. There was no word from Adam, which annoyed me, but Ben had posted a message earlier in the day.

> Had some time to catch my breath this afternoon so took a walk along Whiskey Island Drive by Lake Erie. It's not far from St. Helena's, and the weather's warm but not unbearable. Got an e-mail from Adam yesterday, saying they've got nineteen hours of daylight this time of year. Hope you're not still peeved at him. He's doing his best, under the circumstances. Here comes trouble in the form of a parishioner who wants me to perform an exorcism to rid his house of his mother-in-law's evil spirit. Since she's still alive, I don't know what he expects me to do, even if I were willing to do it. Maybe I'll give him a copy of the classified ads so he can find her a new place to live. Until later. Go with God.

I was glad to hear from Ben but couldn't help feeling that Adam had found time to write to his uncle but not his mother. At present, my son's "circumstances," as Ben put it, couldn't be any more wrenching than my own. I doubted that Adam was fretting over the possibility of a killer on the loose in St. Mary's Igloo.

My phone rang again. I snatched it up at once and heard the

sheriff's voice at the other end. "The Chrysler Sebring is parked just off the Icicle Creek Road where it forks into First Hill. We didn't find it, but Gus Lindquist, of all people, spotted it about a hundred yards from his place by Disappointment Avenue. He was out prowling around because he hasn't been able to sleep since he shot that mama bear."

"What about the cars belonging to Sophia and Dylan?" I asked.

"No sign of them here or anywhere else so far," Milo replied. "By the way, next time try hiring somebody who isn't a nut job."

"You don't need to remind me," I snapped. "Have you still got those dogs from the state patrol?"

"No, but I called them back in," Milo said. "I don't see what good it'll do. This is one hell of a mess."

"Don't tell me something I already know." I paused. "Weird—out of habit I just thought of sending Curtis to take some pictures. I guess I'll have to do it myself."

"Forget it," Milo ordered in his most severe voice. "Stay put. I don't want to have to go looking for you."

I didn't argue. The warning didn't faze me. My mind was already made up. "We'll talk later," I said and was about to disconnect when the sheriff spoke again.

"There's another car not far from the one Graham Cavanaugh rented," he said. "It doesn't belong to the other Cavanaughs, but it looks like a rental. A Ford Focus, real clean, 'no smoking' sticker, only six thousand miles on it."

"You could get into it?"

"No. I used a flashlight to check out the interior," Milo said. "I wanted to make sure there wasn't a body in the backseat. Maybe I should've busted open the trunk."

"Not funny," I remarked.

"Sure as hell isn't," he agreed and hung up.

I considered asking Vida to come along and bring a camera. If there were any pictures to be taken, she could handle that duty much better, since I was an utter dunce when it came to photography. I called her on my cell just before going out to the car. "I can pick you up," I said. "I'm leaving now."

"I'll get dressed," she said. "Don't honk. You might wake the neighbors."

Sure enough, four minutes later Vida appeared on her porch as I drove up to her house.

"What did you do?" I asked as she fastened her seat belt. "Throw your clothes up in the air and run under them?"

"Virtually," she replied. "Is Milo still up on First Hill?"

"I don't know," I admitted. "I'm not sure of anything except that I couldn't sit still and do nothing."

"Quite so," she agreed. "Have you contacted Graham or Kelsey?"

"Doe Jameson tried twice," I said as we drove past the cemetery. I hoped it wasn't an omen. "No luck. You want to see if he picks up now? My cell's in my purse."

Vida dug it out. "What's the number?"

Fortunately, I'd memorized it. But Vida shook her head after placing the call and waiting a few moments. "Nothing. Oh, dear."

I took a right at First Hill Road, passing the high school and the Dithers sisters' horse farm. The rocky area on the other side of the road was the first of two hills where several old mine shafts still existed under cover of wild blackberry vines, moss, and ferns. When I'd moved to Alpine, there were only a handful of houses among the trees, but in recent years a dozen or more homes had been built to take advantage of the view.

As we approached the turnoff to Disappointment Avenue,

there was no sign of Milo and his deputy. "Now what?" I asksed, slowing down.

"I see a parked car," Vida said, gesturing up ahead. "Is that the one Graham was driving?"

"Let's look." I pulled over onto the verge and approached even more slowly. "Yes," I said, recognizing the Chrysler symbol on the rear end. "That might be the Ford Focus across the road from the Dithers sisters' gate."

We got out of the car, stopping first to check Graham's rental. The car was locked. Vida had a small flashlight attached to her key chain. She clicked the light on and looked inside. "Nothing except maps, a pair of sunglasses, and bottled water."

We trudged up the hill and across the road to the Ford. It was parked by an old railroad spur that had been used to carry logs down the steep incline to the millpond. Much of the century-old wooden portion of track had rotted away or disappeared under grass and weeds. A ramshackle Great Northern caboose sat nearby, a relic from the distant past. The stumps of giant evergreens stood like monuments to the heyday of logging. I gazed down the hill, where only a handful of lights glowed in the darkness. The wind had grown stronger, blowing through the alder and maple trees that had sprung up after the last clear-cut, in the seventies. Looking up, I saw only a few stars. The old moon had faded into a pale sliver as clouds rolled in from the south.

Using her small flashlight, Vida had been inspecting the Ford's interior. "Milo was right," she said. "There's nothing of interest."

"Where did Kelsey and Graham go?" I asked in a helpless voice. "Why didn't they come back to my house?"

Vida didn't respond but shook her head and bit her lip. We

went back to the car. My cell phone rang before I could turn on the ignition.

"We nailed 'em," Milo announced in triumph. "The state patrol stopped both cars just north of the King-Snohomish county line."

"Them being . . . who?" I asked as Vida leaned close to me in an attempt to hear what was being said at the other end of the line.

"Platte, Sophia Cavanaugh, and the phony Graham, the other Volos," the sheriff answered.

I was torn between relief and worry. "What about Kelsey and the real Graham?"

"No sign of them," Milo said. "I'm heading to Everett, where this bunch will be booked. I'll argue jurisdiction later. I'm beat."

"But I want to know where—" I stopped as Milo ended the call. "Damn!" I breathed, turning to Vida. "Did you hear that?"

"Yes." She frowned. "I must admit, I don't understand what's going on. Is Milo charging all three of them with murder?"

"For all I know, they've been arrested for shoplifting." I drummed my nails on the steering wheel. "We might as well go home. Kelsey and Graham can't be in danger if the rest of them are under arrest."

"You don't believe that," Vida said.

"No." I stared through the windshield. "I'm still worried. If they had car trouble and left the rental here, I could understand that. But it's that other car that bothers me. Who could it belong to? Were Kelsey and Graham meeting someone?"

Before Vida could respond, I dialed the ski lodge. It wasn't quite one o'clock. Carlos was probably still on duty.

He picked up on the first ring. "Have you seen Kelsey Platte and her brother since we talked?" I asked.

"No," Carlos answered. "Everything here's quiet."

"Could you do me a favor? Would you see if Kelsey's belongings are still in the suite?"

"Well . . . okay. I'll send somebody up to look and call you back," Carlos said.

"No," I replied. "I'll stay on the line. I have to know now."

"I'll put you on hold," he said.

Vida frowned at me. "You're assuming Kelsey didn't get her belongings from the lodge?"

"I think she intended to, but something scared her away," I said. "Carlos never saw her or Graham. Of course, he might have been busy and missed them, but somebody would've noticed. Kelsey didn't have her key card, so she'd have had to ask to be let in because she wouldn't risk running into the rest of that crew."

"True." Vida adjusted her raffia fedora, which had slipped down over her right eye. "Where were those other wretched people going?"

"The airport?" I suggested as a click on the line indicated Carlos had taken me off of hold.

"Jerry—one of our bellboys—just called from the Queen Margrethe Suite to say that there were some things still there, mostly women's clothes," Carlos said. "No purse, though, nothing of importance, such as airline tickets or valuables."

"That figures. Thanks, Carlos. I'm sorry to be a pest."

"No problem. I hope everything turns out okay."

"So do I." I rang off.

I relayed what Carlos had just told me. Vida made a face. "The others must have taken anything useful, perhaps to impersonate Kelsey. They seem very good at being other people."

I turned the ignition key. "I surrender. Let's go home. To-morrow is another day."

"It's already tomorrow," Vida reminded me.

"So it is." I started the car and drove a few yards up the narrow road to find a place where I could turn around. The verge widened close to the old railroad spur, so I angled the Honda onto a patch of gravel and was about to reverse when something caught my eye.

"Did you see that?" I asked Vida. "Some kind of flash?"

"Lightning?" she replied. "I don't hear any thunder."

"No, it was more like a . . . a light that went on and off." I hesitated, peering into the darkness. "It seemed to come from that old caboose."

"Teenagers," Vida said in disapproval. "I'm told they party there. It's a wonder they haven't burned it to the ground."

We sat in silence for at least a minute but saw nothing except the outline of the caboose and the trees that lined the old track. "Whatever it was, it's gone," I said, putting the car into reverse and keeping my eyes on the rearview mirror.

"A reflection from your headlights, perhaps," Vida said. "It's a good thing there's no traffic on this road, especially so late at—" She stopped. "I see someone by the caboose."

I braked and looked straight ahead. A lone figure was moving purposefully toward us. "Who is it? Gus Lundquist?"

"No," Vida said, peering through the windshield. "Too tall. Gus is short and stocky. There's someone with him, I think."

Vida was right. I saw two more figures behind the man who was heading our way. I held my breath as he moved within thirty-odd feet of my car. The tall man was walking faster with a familiar gait. He waved. I gasped in shock. "Tom!"

Vida gave a start. "What?"

I felt light-headed, as if I were in a dream. I closed my eyes, wondering if I might be losing my mind. Then I heard a voice call out: "Mom! It's me, Adam."

I *was* dreaming. I had to be. I started to shake from head to toe. Vida put a firm hand on my arm. "Stop. Open your door."

I couldn't. I was frozen, utterly helpless. The door wasn't locked. Adam opened it for me.

"Mom," he said, bending down to look at me, "are you okay?"

I must have been holding my breath because I let out a huge sigh that was accompanied by a little wail of release from my shocked state. "Oh, Adam!" I gasped. "I don't believe it!"

"Didn't you get my e-mail?" he asked.

I was beginning to focus, just like a real person. "E-mail? No."

"I sent it from Sea-Tac after we landed around nine o'clock," he said. "I didn't bring my laptop, so I had to use a computer at the airport." He paused. "You look pale. Are you sick?"

"No. No." I shook my head several times. "Just . . . shocked." I finally looked beyond him to the two other figures. Kelsey and Graham seemed uneasy, standing awkwardly while they observed the unexpected family reunion. "I'm utterly flabbergasted," I said. "Is that Ford over there your rental?"

"Right." Adam grinned at Vida. "Hi, Mrs. Runkel. I like your hat."

Even Vida was speechless.

"Come to the house," I said to Adam. "You can explain everything there, and for God's sake, bring Kelsey and Graham with you. I'm so rattled I don't know if I can drive."

"You don't always drive so well when you're not rattled," Adam said and straightened up before turning to his half brother and half sister. "Let's go, guys. Maybe we can cadge some food from Mom."

I waited until Adam got into the Ford and the two Cavanaughs reached the Chrysler. "I'll let them lead the way," I
told Vida. "I need a minute or two for collecting my wits."

"Yes." Vida still seemed nonplussed. "My, my."

"Should I drop you off at your place?" I asked as Adam
drove off.

"Don't you dare," she retorted. "My, my."

Neither of us spoke again during the short drive back to my
house. After I pulled into the carport, I had enough presence of
mind to call Milo before I went inside. He didn't pick up, presumably because he was busy with the perps in Everett. I left a
message about finding Kelsey and Graham, then dialed his office, where Sam Heppner answered.

"Kids these days" was all he said when I relayed the news.

My son and the Cavanaughs were on the front porch. "I
can't find my key," Adam said, a backpack slung over his
shoulder. "I could've sworn I still had it with me."

"You've probably lost it—as usual," I said, opening the
front door.

As soon as we were inside, I grabbed Adam and hugged him
tight. "You've got some explaining to do. Start now."

"We're hungry," he said after I released him. "We'll forage
first."

Kelsey and Graham, who hadn't said a word, followed
Adam into the kitchen like a couple of lost lambs. *Babes in the
woods,* I thought, *poor babes in the woods.*

"I'll make tea," Vida said. "You sit. You're still very
washed out."

I didn't argue. I needed a few minutes alone. As soon as she
went into the kitchen, I opened my laptop to see how I could've
missed Adam's e-mail. A new message appeared on the screen:
"Postmaster—delayed delivery." It happened sometimes, for

reasons known only to God and Bill Gates, though not necessarily in that order. Sure enough, Adam's message appeared.

Arrived at Sea-Tac, coming to Alpine tonight, will give you details when I see you. Love and prayers, Adam, The Wandering Priest.

Vida came back from the kitchen. "Kelsey and Graham seem like decent children," she murmured. "Polite. Respectful. Though Kelsey's a bit vague, don't you think?"

"I already mentioned that," I said in a low voice and tapped my temple. "She's got some problems, but she's not stupid."

Vida sat down next to me on the sofa. "How on earth did Adam get involved? Had you any idea he was coming to Alpine?"

I turned the laptop so that Vida could read my son's message. "This would've been the first I knew about it—*if* it had come through immediately. Maybe there was a snag because Adam had to send it from a computer at the airport. I'd checked my e-mail around midnight. The only personal note came from Ben." I stared at the screen after Vida finished reading what my son had sent. "Ben mentioned something about Adam 'under the circumstances.' I thought he meant the usual trials and tribulations of being a priest in a remote mission parish. Maybe Ben knew more than he let on."

"Ask Adam," Vida said as my son came into the living room carrying a sandwich and a peach.

He sat down in the armchair by the hearth. "Kelsey and Graham are eating in the kitchen. They feel like intruders."

"They're not," I said. "They're family."

Adam chuckled. "That concept is eluding them. Anyway,

they're going to stay at the ski lodge. Graham checked with the sheriff's office and found out about the arrests."

"Fine." I couldn't cope with anything other than Adam's presence. "Please, tell me why you came here. I'm not quite over the shock."

Adam sighed. "You may not like it."

"There isn't much I've liked for the past week," I said. "What's one more horror story?"

My son swallowed a bite of sandwich. "It's not exactly a horror, but it might upset you. I'll cut to the chase. My dad wanted to leave me his newspaper empire."

I almost bolted off the sofa. "*What?*"

"My goodness!" Vida exclaimed softly as the teakettle sang in the kitchen. "Excuse me. I must take care of that. Can you speak louder, Adam? Or do I call you 'Father'?"

He shrugged. "Take your pick."

Vida hurried out of the living room. Adam kept his voice down, despite her request. "While I was still in the seminary, Dad came to visit me in St. Paul. You may remember that. He was making a new will before you two got married. He'd leave all his real estate to Kelsey and Graham, along with a hefty trust fund for each of them. To make up for being an absent father during my first twenty years, he intended to bequeath the newspaper chain to me. But he wanted to make sure I'd be okay with my inheritance. He worried that if I learned I was potentially rich, I might chuck the priesthood. Frankly, I wasn't thrilled at the prospect of eventually being rich, but that seemed far into the future, so I told him if that was what he wanted, I wouldn't stop him. If nothing else, I could sell it off and use the money for charity. I did ask why he wasn't leaving it all to you. Dad said he'd thought about that but felt you wouldn't want the responsibility." Adam paused to take a bite of peach.

"I'm stunned," I said as Vida came out of the kitchen with two mugs of tea.

She scowled at Adam. "I only heard snatches of what you told your mother. How can your congregation hear your sermons if you don't speak up?"

"The churches where I say Mass are only slightly bigger than a phone booth," Adam replied. "In fact, some of them aren't even churches. And believe me, Mrs. Runkel, my homilies are usually cures for insomnia."

"Dear me," Vida said, sitting back down, "I'm glad Pastor Purebeck at First Presbyterian is livelier. Though when he talks about sin, I'd appreciate it if he named names. How does one know whom to avoid? After all, sex offenders must register. Why not other kinds of sinners?"

"Uh . . ." Adam was obviously trying to figure out if Vida was serious. "Love the sinner, hate the sin," he finally said. "I'm telling Mom about Dad's intentions in the new will he was making."

"Yes, yes," Vida said impatiently. "I heard some of that. By the way," she added, turning to me, "the Cavanaugh children just left through the back door. They're exhausted."

"Who isn't?" I muttered, though I seemed to have acquired a shot of adrenaline since Adam's arrival. "I'd hoped they'd stay here," I added, despite realizing it wouldn't be practical in my little log house. I turned back to my son. "So what happened to the new will?"

His expression was ironic. "It was made but disappeared. The secretary at the San Francisco law firm remembered drawing it up for Dad to sign, but there's no record that he ever did. Then, a month or so after Dad died, his lawyer was murdered."

"Mr. Vitani," I said. "I wondered about that. So the old will was the one submitted to probate?"

"That was all they could do," Adam replied. "To be honest, I didn't follow through. I was getting ready to be ordained, and all my mental processes were focused on that. When I finally thought about the will, a few months after I became a priest, I figured there were legal hoops to jump through. By the time I got around to calling the law office, I found out that Dad's estate had been wrapped up and his other two kids had inherited everything. They also told me that Mr. Vitani was deceased. The way they said it made me suspicious, so I checked the San Francisco newspapers and learned he'd been shot. A random killing, apparently, so I didn't try to connect the dots. I figured Dad had changed his mind, which was why I didn't mention it to you."

"I can guess why Vitani was shot," I said. "When I heard he'd been killed, I wondered if your dad might have left *me* the newspapers. It never crossed my mind that he'd leave them to you, but I'm glad he did." I smiled fondly at my son. "So you decided to rescue your mother?"

Adam nodded. "Sort of. When you told me about the Cavanaughs trying to buy you out, I wondered if the new will had been found, and if they were making an end run to see how much you knew. I had a wedding and a baptism, so I couldn't leave until today. I didn't want to explain all this in an e-mail." He grinned ruefully. "I knew you'd be upset. Face-to-face is much better. Dad would never have wanted to cause you any grief. I figured I owed it to you both to see if I could help."

"So considerate," Vida murmured. "Just like my grandson, Roger."

I didn't dare look at Vida but kept my gaze fixed on Adam, who continued with his account. "I got Kelsey's and Graham's phone numbers from the law office and called them when I got into town around eleven o'clock. Kelsey didn't answer, but

Graham did. He told me he and his sister were heading for the ski lodge. I asked them to wait for me outside the lodge—I'd stopped by Old Mill Park on my way to see you, but Graham said they were coming back to your place after collecting Kelsey's belongings. I said I'd meet them first, because I wanted to make sure they really were Kelsey and Graham. I knew I'd recognize them from Dad's funeral."

Regretfully, I shook my head. "I hardly remembered seeing them."

Adam smiled slightly. "You were out of it. No wonder. Anyway, when I got to the parking lot, Kelsey and Graham weren't there. I'd given Graham my cell number. He called while I was trying to figure out what to do and said they'd run into Sophia and Dylan outside the lodge. Sophia had insisted on meeting them in a secluded spot off the Icicle Creek Road so she could explain to Graham about why she'd left him. Graham suspected a trap, so he veered off onto First Hill and told me to come there. We talked for a few minutes before we heard a car coming. Thinking it was Sophia and Dylan, we hid in that old caboose. It turned out to be the sheriff, but Kelsey had become hysterical by then and refused to budge. Anyway, the sheriff left just as I recognized his Grand Cherokee out on the road. Kelsey calmed down, and we were about to take our chances when you came along." He shrugged again. "End of story."

I felt limp just from listening to my son's adventures. "I still can't believe it," I said. "You're here." I wanted to say how proud I was of him, how stupid I felt for doubting his loyalty to me, how satisfying it was to see him not just as my only child but as a man capable of great courage and compassion. Adam had seemed so young when he was ordained. It wasn't that he'd visibly aged very much but he'd matured into a genuine human being. I could see that in his eyes. Something new was there, a steady, calm gaze that seemed to come not from his brain but from his soul. "Your father would be so proud of you," I said softly.

"Yes," Vida agreed, standing up. "Tommy would approve."

I thought Adam might wince, but he didn't. Instead, he smiled. "Thanks, Mrs. Runkel."

"You're welcome," she said. "I'm going home now. It's very late."

"Your car's not here," I pointed out. "I'll drive you."

Adam also stood up. "I'll do it." He looked at me and shook his head. "You're a train wreck, Mom. Go to bed. Come on, Mrs. Runkel. It's too bad nobody's out and about. I'd like people to see me driving with a lady who wears such dashing hats."

Vida actually simpered.

They headed for the front door, but I stopped them. "Key," I said. "You need my key." I reached into my purse and tossed the key ring to Adam, who caught it neatly. "You're still losing things, it seems."

He smiled at me. "Not everything. Not what matters."

"No," I whispered. "No."

I didn't arrive at the office until ten o'clock the next morning, and even then, I felt foggy. Vida had gotten in a little after eight. Amazingly, she looked none the worse for her late-night adventures. Ed, however, was in a tizzy.

"Now what'll I do?" he demanded as I was pouring my first mug of coffee. "The house deal's collapsed. Snorty called this morning to tell me the buyer had been arrested. Why do these things always happen to me? We're out the down payment on our new place."

"Where *is* your new place?" I inquired.

"Ah . . ." Ed's round face turned red. "It's actually not here yet."

I didn't think I'd heard him correctly. "What?"

He turned away, ostensibly studying some papers on Leo's desk. "Well . . . it's a double-wide mobile home, and it's at an RV lot in Monroe."

"I'm sure you'll find another buyer," I said as kindly as I could manage. "Now we've all got to pull together to get out next week's paper. In case you haven't noticed, we're a bit shorthanded."

Ed mumbled something I couldn't hear. Vida had been on the phone, but she hung up before I could retreat to my cubbyhole. "Leo's doing much better this morning. I just spoke to Doc Dewey who told me he's awake and alert. I'll go see Leo at lunchtime."

"I'll go with you. Adam was heading to the hospital as soon as he finished breakfast," I said as Milo loped into the newsroom.

"I saw you pull into your parking place," he said. "I knew you'd want the latest news. Fleetwood's already got it, but that can't be helped. It's a matter of record."

"Sit," I said, noting that Milo looked as worn out as I felt. "You might as well let all of us hear what's happened to the crooks."

The sheriff poured himself some coffee and snatched up a bear claw. "The rats have ratted on each other," he announced, sitting at Curtis's desk. "Typical Californians. They like to make deals."

"Sophia's from New York," I pointed out. "So's her brother."

Milo looked vaguely interested. "More slick flash and dash. Anyway, they spent last night squealing like the Three Little Pigs."

"And?" I prodded, aware that Vida's nostrils were flaring like those of a racehorse impatient to leave the starting gate.

"I'll make this quick," Milo said after a big swig of coffee. "There were four of them in on it at the start, Sophia and her two brothers and Dylan Platte. Maxim Volos and Sophia were your original impostors, coming here to size you up. Dylan had come a few days earlier, too, checking out the town—and Ed's house."

"Why did they get my hopes up?" Ed asked in a pitiful voice. "That's so wrong."

Milo regarded him with an indulgent expression. "They intended to buy your place. Dylan wanted to get out of California, where he was up to his neck in all sorts of illegal deal making. According to Sophia, Kelsey was going to have some kind of accident or get institutionalized. Dylan was either giving her the wrong kind of medication or withholding the right kind, to treat her emotional problems."

I nodded. "I figure she can't cope with reality, so she withdraws and becomes very vague. The world's a scary—"

"Hey," Ed broke in, "do you think Kelsey might want to buy our house anyway?"

Vida shot him a withering glance. "Please, Ed, be quiet."

"Go on," I said to the sheriff.

"The rest is simple enough," Milo continued. "Thieves fall out. Once Maxim was on his own, he decided to double-cross his brother and his sister—Dylan, too—and somehow take all the action for himself. It wasn't just about buying the *Advocate*—that seems to have been a cover for the real reason behind this whole mess. Sophia had fallen madly in love with Dylan, and she wanted the two of them to get together and run the show, somehow squeezing out both Cavanaughs. Nick Volos was probably a marked man as soon as he'd finished pulling off his impersonation of Graham. And Maxim was already dead." Milo paused to take a bite of bear claw. "If I stay on this job for another thirty years, I'll never run into a criminal plan this weird."

I agreed. "Convoluted, incredible—and yet it must have made sense to the perps. Let's keep it simple for us small town folks. Who killed Maxim and shot Leo?"

"Good question," the sheriff answered after a pause. "A .38 Smith and Wesson was found in Dylan's rental car. It's not registered, and the serial number's filed off. Nick says Dylan was the shooter. Dylan says it was Nick. I'm not buying either of their stories. My money's on Sophia."

Vida frowned. "Who did Sophia say did it?"

"She didn't say anything," Milo replied, "except to put the blame on her brother Maxim for sending you the bracelet that Tom supposedly gave his wife. The bracelet belonged to Sophia, and she wants it back. She's a real piece of work and the only one who lawyered up. As far as I'm concerned, that makes her the shooter."

I remembered an odd scrap of information from Minnie Harris about the used-up notepad in the victim's motel room. "I'll bet Maxim Volos practiced Tom's handwriting on it and forged the note that came with the bracelet. Tom had terrible penmanship, which would make it easy for a crook to copy."

Milo shrugged. "Maybe. I'm just glad this wacky case is over."

"We all are," Vida said. "Though you still have to deal with the San Francisco police about Mr. Vitani's murder."

Milo stared at Vida. "Who?"

I spoke before she could respond. "Never mind that now. Milo's tired." I moved to where he was sitting and put a hand on his shoulder. "We'll talk about that later, when our brains are working better."

"Tonight?" Milo said hopefully.

"Sure," I said. "You'll get a chance to see Adam."

The sheriff looked disappointed. "Oh. That's right, I forgot he was in town. I'll get back to you later." He took another drink of coffee. "Got to go."

"What about Curtis?" I asked. "When will you release him?"

"Sometime today," he said. "I'm sick of his whining. You want him back here?"

I grimaced. "Not really. But he'll have to collect his belongings."

"Good luck with that," Milo said and loped out of the newsroom.

After he'd gone, I called the ski lodge and asked to be connected to Kelsey. Henry Bardeen came on the line.

"Mrs. Platte and her brother checked out about a half-hour ago," he said. "They were going to get a flight back to California."

I was surprised—and disappointed. "Did they leave any messages?"

"No," Henry answered and then added with a note of regret, "I'm sorry, Emma. I got the impression they were in a big rush."

"I understand," I said.

It was the truth. *It's an odd thing about motherhood,* I thought. No matter how neglectful, how difficult, or even how crazy, most children still loved the woman who had given them life. It was a natural bond that was hard to break, and no one could ever substitute for the real thing.

I was still pondering that fact of life when my phone rang.

"I forgot to tell you something," Milo said. "That Laurentis guy got permission to look after those cub bears until they're ready to go off on their own."

"That's good." I sounded bleak.

"I don't think so," Milo said. "The cubs will get used to being fed and taken care of. How the hell will they ever be able to live on their own? It's unnatural."

"You're right," I said. "But you can't blame Laurentis for trying."

Milo paused. "Maybe not," he conceded.

"At least he means well," I said. "Doesn't that count?"

Again the sheriff didn't answer immediately. "Yes," he finally said, "I guess it does. I never blame anybody for giving it their best shot. So to speak."

I smiled into the phone. Milo had spoken enough.

ABOUT THE AUTHOR

MARY DAHEIM is a Seattle native who started spinning stories before she could spell. Daheim has been a journalist, an editor, a public relations consultant, and a freelance writer, but fiction was always her medium of choice, and in 1982 she launched a career that is now distinguished by more than forty novels. In 2000, she won the Literary Achievement Award from the Pacific Northwest Writers Association. Daheim lives in Seattle with her husband, David, a retired professor of cinema, English, and literature. The Daheims have three daughters: Barbara, Katherine, and Magdalen.

ABOUT THE TYPE

This book was set in Sabon, a typeface designed by the well-known German typographer Jan Tschichold (1902–74). Sabon's design is based upon the original letter forms of Claude Garamond and was created specifically to be used for three sources: foundry type for hand composition, Linotype, and Monotype. Tschichold named his typeface for the famous Frankfurt typefounder Jacques Sabon, who died in 1580.